HIGH PRAISE FOR BRIAN LYSAGHT'S
EYE OF THE BEHOLDER

D0047197

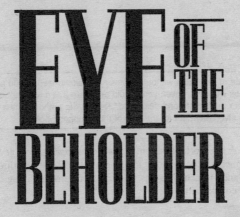

EYE OF THE BEHOLDER

BRIAN LYSAGHT

POCKET BOOKS

New York London Toronto Sydney Tokyo Singapore

This book is a work of fiction. Names, characters, places and incidents
are products of the author's imagination or are used fictitiously. Any
resemblance to actual events or locales or persons, living or dead, is
entirely coincidental.

POCKET BOOKS, a division of Simon & Schuster Inc.
1230 Avenue of the Americas, New York, NY 10020

Copyright © 1995 by Brian Lysaght

ISBN: 0-671-00115-9

First Pocket Books printing August 1997

10 9 8 7 6 5 4 3 2 1

POCKET and colophon are registered trademarks of
Simon & Schuster Inc.

Printed in the U.S.A.

Revenge is a dish best eaten cold.

—*Sicilian Proverb*

1

ROBERT VARGO PAUSED AT THE EXIT OF THE HOTEL Havana Riviera and looked north and south along the Malecón seafront. He was a short, squat man of fifty, graying at the temples and sweating profusely in the Caribbean heat. His gestures were quick and muscular, his head turning out of habit born of four years on the run. Seeing only bicycles and rusting American cars, he walked out.

It was near dusk and what coolness there was drifted lazily in from the sea. He checked his watch and found there was still time for a quiet walk along the seafront wall connecting Old Havana with the sparkling Vedado, the area now jokingly called the commercial district. He knew the walk would not quench the fear now eating at him like a large dog. In one hour a boring, beat-up car, undoubtedly Russian, would arrive to take him to one of the indistinguishable government buildings spread throughout the Plaza de la Revolución. There, after endless recriminations, and endless threats, he *might* be given one last chance to plead for his life.

The car arrived for him and it was as he expected, a Soviet-made Moskovitch. The driver smiled a gold-toothed grin and spoke in broken English. Vargo grunted a short reply. He knew the man was a spy just as he knew everyone the Cubans put near him these days was a spy, right down to the pretty cabin boy on his jet. That was once fine with Vargo, even useful if he had some disinformation to pass on. But now he had no stomach for anything but gnawing fear.

The car drifted silently into the developing twilight. There was still enough light to make out the three or four identical political billboards filling every block. The first inevitably announced, "Imperialist Aggressors Will Never Make Us Afraid." The second, a hundred feet beyond, always proclaimed a sentiment for "Peace, Life, And Against Imperialist Aggression." The face of the leader of the Cuban revolution was on every poster, looking a great deal younger and slimmer than Vargo had ever seen him. It was all of a piece in Vargo's mind. Bring back the mob.

The Moskovitch turned north and hugged the coast. Suddenly, the car lurched to a crawl and the driver pointed grinning toward the moonlit beach. A magnificent black woman in an orange head scarf danced on the sand before a group of fifty chanting comrades. Her flowing dress twirled easily as she turned. The white dress ballooned at the shoulders and was held tight with elastic bands, then swooped at the waist to form a full skirt. The pale light of the moon showed hand-sewn orange-and-purple birds and flowers set in erratic patterns, all held in a flock by a wide orange-and-black fabric belt. From the belt hung a squadron of multicolored silk kerchiefs: bright green, purple, lavender, tangerine, yellow. As the woman spun, her dress followed her movements with disciplined ease. Her deep black features remained serene and unmoving as she worked hard through the dance. The crowd, excited, moved aggressively with her, shouting as her movements lifted their voices. Nearby drums beat a heavy repetitive rhythm for her.

"Rumba," the driver explained, turning and grinning with his gold tooth. "You heard of rumba?"

"Yes, certainly." Vargo knew rumba as a bad dance old people did at bad hotels. The rumba he knew had nothing to do with what this magnificent woman was doing on the moonlit beach. This exhibition was a part of Cuba he had yet to figure out: an overt African culture deeper than colonialism, deeper than rusting 1950s-era American Chevrolets, and certainly deeper than his partners' promises. This woman was reenacting a tribal dance fresh from the bonfires of the African plains, a secret decadence which emphasized Cuba's deep African subculture. The light skins of the minority-ruling Castilians proved that the Spanish had made their mark. The rumba on the beach proved that their decaying state sat tottering atop the much deeper culture of imported African slaves.

The Moskovitch left the beach and seemed to cruise aimlessly around Havana. There was still enough light for Vargo to make out an enormous bust of Lenin in Lenin Park. The bust was white granite, a monochromatic, unsmiling face with none of the colors of the rumba dancer. Underneath the granite face was an inscription in Spanish hailing Lenin's revolutionary accomplishments. Beneath that was the single word "Fidel." When that man dies, then we will find out the fate of the rumba dancer, Vargo thought. Until that day Cuban socialism was as permanent as a monarch's eccentricities.

It was dark when they reached the ministry. The concrete square in front of the building was black and unlit. High above them a single row of lights was the only illumination in an otherwise brooding concrete-slab building. The conference room, Vargo knew. He got out of the car, gathered up his briefcase, and waited.

Suddenly from the darkness behind he felt a pair of arms grasp him. He half-turned in anger only to be doubled over with the shock of a rifle butt driven deep into his stomach. He fell to his knees and would have fallen further but the strong arms of the soldiers held him up. He gasped for air and choked. His eyes filled and he felt blood rise in his throat.

He looked up in mute protest and saw the driver in front of him standing with legs parted. The driver grinned his gold-toothed grin.

"Are you ready to die, *señor?*"

Vargo hunted for the breath to answer but found nothing. He struggled ineffectually against the soldier's grasp and was rewarded with a backhanded slap that split his lip. The blood from his lip joined the blood gurgling from his throat and formed twin tributaries of pain that flowed down the front of his shirt. He stopped struggling and looked up at his tormentor.

The man smiled again. His eyes had no compassion. "Do it," he said, nodding at the soldiers.

Vargo panicked. He finally got a breath and tried to fight. The soldier on his left yanked at his hair and pulled his head back. Vargo's white, puffy neck was exposed. A steel bayonet flashed in the soldier's hand, lit by highlights from far-off windows in the plaza.

Vargo stiffened for the pain of death. The blade flashed again and this time stopped, caressing the exposed neck. The razor-sharp blade touched the skin and opened a thin line of red. The driver came forward.

"Not here," he said. The soldier looked up. "At the post."

Vargo's eyes filled with tears. The post was one of a series of posts three meters apart in a concrete quadrangle in the hidden rear of the Plaza de la Revolución. The posts had been used often since 1959 and always with great effect. The leader of the Cuban revolution had not held power for thirty years by civic virtue alone.

The soldier on his left produced a black hood and the world turned dark. They hauled him to his feet and dragged him along the thin, rock-strewn walkway to his place of death. Once there he heard the quiet laughter of a cadre of young soldiers, guns undoubtedly slung casually over their shoulders, cigarettes burning in their fingers as they stood at ease and watched his panic. He was fastened by metal restraints to the scarred and blood-stained block of wood. He screamed at them to take off the stifling hood and heard more laughter. He screamed again with loud and useless rage as he heard the cadre called to order and the metal scraping of a half-dozen rifles yanked off the ground and readied on young, calm shoulders. The laughing stopped. He screamed a final time for mercy and a chance to explain. Then his hearing blurred and he only faintly heard the order to fire. He did hear the explosion, which surprised him, and then consciousness left him.

He woke slowly, groggily, and without comprehension. He sagged against the metal restraints. The hood was still in place. He coughed at the closed air and smell of blood. He heard a voice.

"He's awake."

"Take off his hood."

An unseen hand pulled the hood off. At first it was all he could do to gulp the clear night air, cold and clean, more beautiful than any experience he could remember. Then the horror came back and he opened his eyes. He fought through the blur and focused. The driver was standing before him, staring, grinning.

"How do you feel?"

Vargo didn't answer. The driver gestured and a soldier with a key removed the restraints. Vargo slumped to the ground, dazed and in shock. The driver stepped forward.

"It is time for your meeting."

Vargo looked up, uncomprehending.

"The meeting, *señor*. You remember, I drove you to the meeting."

"But . . ." Vargo coughed again and tried unsuccessfully for a semblance of dignity. "I don't understand. Why . . . why did you . . . did you bring me here?"

"Here? Why, to be a witness, of course."

"A witness? To what?"

"To an execution of a traitor." The man gestured.

Vargo turned and the sight froze him. Three meters away a naked figure hung limply from the adjacent post. His chest was a mass of red pulp, the result of the explosion Vargo had heard and thought was meant for him. The man's head was gray and empty, the dead eyes open and staring sightlessly at his killers, now lounging and smoking, their guns leaning quietly against the far-off wall. Vargo said nothing. The ashen dead face was too familiar. A wrong word and he would join him.

"Do you recognize this man?" the driver asked.

Not in that form, Vargo thought. The last time he had

seen General Suarez the man had been clothed in Cuban military splendor. He had his hand out, to be sure, and Vargo had been putting a Cayman Islands bank draft in it. But Suarez *always* had his hand out.

"I asked you a question," the driver said gently.

"I know him," Vargo said. He got to his feet and brushed himself off. Suarez was a thief and now was no longer available for Vargo's purposes. The good news was that Vargo was alive and likely to remain so. This was an elaborate demonstration. No one, not even the Cubans, went to this much trouble for someone they intended to kill.

He turned away from Suarez to the driver. He reached into the driver's pocket for a cigarette. The driver nodded as Vargo lit it with calm hands, acknowledging either courage or insight. Vargo blew out the smoke and flicked the spent match toward Suarez's spent form.

"I'm ready to go now."

2

THE ROOM WAS FULL WHEN HE ARRIVED. ELEVEN Anglo men huddled in a tight group, dressed in the olive green of the Cuban military, crisp, pressed, short-sleeved uniform shirts crested by red stars on the shoulder epaulets. Ten other men were more spread out and dressed in a polyglot of military garb: three island nations, the Hondurans, the Guatemalans. The Colombians and Peruvians were fat men with short-sleeved white shirts which hung over black pants. Their importance went much deeper than empty military plumage.

Vargo was led by the arm to the head of the table. The room quieted and the men took seats around a large, colonial conference table. "Good evening," he said in Spanish. There was no response. He unlocked his briefcase and saw that his hands had begun to shake again. The room was rock still with anticipation.

He decided on the spot to start with the operational reports, which he hoped would spark the least controversy. He pulled down a large map of the Caribbean basin. The West Indies chain, with Cuba at its center, dominated the map. Red lines in intersecting arcs sliced through the Caribbean Sea and the Gulf of Mexico. The lines started from the northern coast of Colombia and Venezuela, then passed southwest of Cuba. Half of the red lines terminated on the Mexican mainland or the U.S. coastline in southeast Texas or New Orleans; half terminated on the west coast of Florida and Miami.

"In the past, our main distribution channels—chutes, we call them—flowed through the Yucatán Channel," Vargo began. "The jump-off points have always been Santa Marta, Barranquilla and Cartagena. The product was transported by freighter and aircraft through the Caribbean Sea to Belize, Guatemala, and Isle of Pines."

"Isle of Youth," a Cuban interrupted.

Vargo squinted at the map. "Isla de la Juventud," the man had said. What was he babbling about?

"Island of Youth," the man said again. "The name was changed from the Island of Pines in 1979. Before that, it was called Devil's Island. And maybe before that, Treasure Island. When you are dead, we may call it Treasure Island again."

The room roared with laughter. Vargo felt the surge of fear and fought unsuccessfully against it. His hand still shook slightly as he raised the pointer again.

"Cuba has over four thousand small islands and keys scattered on its southern boundaries," he continued. "I can assure you none of the events in Panama or Los Angeles will affect these operations. We can still use these islands interchangeably, so that the American forces—"

"Imperialist forces," the same Cuban said.

Vargo suppressed a sigh. "The imperialist forces at Guantánamo do not detect our activities. The vessels and aircraft operate under our protection until they leave the Cuban and Guatemalan bases. After that thirty percent of our shipments end up on the Mexican mainland near Tampico"—he tapped the map—"twenty-six percent unload at New Orleans, Brownsville, Corpus Christi, and Galveston, and the remainder at Fort Myers, Sarasota, and of course, Miami.''

The pointer shifted again. ''Three years ago, as a result of U.S. interdiction, we began to shift our main U.S. reception point. Instead of Miami, which is crawling with DEA agents, we now funnel the majority of our product through Los Angeles, which has always been our main customer base anyway. There are multiple advantages to this change. Even in decline the size of the southern California economy dwarfs that of southern Florida. This creates many more opportunities for recovery of currency.'' That was Vargo's favorite euphemism for ''laundering.''

The group was paying close attention now, nodding soberly. Then the Cuban heckler approached the map, and Vargo knew what was coming.

''It is a magnificent arrangement,'' the Cuban said. ''We are injecting poison into the veins of the imperialists. And they pay us millions for the privilege.''

''A couple of billion actually,'' Vargo said.

''Yes.'' The Cuban ran his finger over the red lines. ''These lines are the lines of death for the imperialists, the veins into which we inject our poison. What do you call them, 'chutes'?''

''Yes.''

The Cuban smiled and Vargo felt the fear come back. It was the smile of an enemy. The man wheeled to the group.

''When will you tell us about our Panamanian funds, Mr. Vargo?''

''That was unavoidable,'' Vargo said quickly and he hoped confidently. ''No one could anticipate an American invasion.''

''And your jewelry operation in Los Angeles? With the Armenians? Was that also unavoidable? And the twenty-one tons of product at the warehouse in Sylmar, near Los Angeles. Unavoidable? And our cash rotting in attics. Unavoidable?''

There it was, all on the table, and there was little he could do to deny it. The jewelry mart in Los Angeles had been his most effective laundering operation. For two years a mighty river of rumpled tens and twenties had flowed through the mart, $40 million in cash a month, counted and separated by high-speed machines, packaged with phony invoices and deposited in friendly banks to be flash-wired overnight to accounts all over the world. The bust had come in the middle of the night, with the counting machines whirring and the phony jewelry invoices spread throughout the five-story structure like confetti. One hundred thirty arrests. Tens of millions in seized cash and frozen accounts. And the worst of it was the disruption of the money flow, a flow that fed the needs of the men at the table just as surely as their cocaine fed the crack addict in the street. There was talk of pallets of cash rotting in moist attics. These men were not interested in Vargo's excuses.

"We have contingency plans," Vargo said lamely.

"When will we receive payment?" the Honduran whined. "We have made promises to our soldiers."

"Relax," the Cuban said. "He has 'contingency plans.' You can pay your soldiers with that."

Vargo heard Spanish curses. He had one hope. The Colombians hadn't spoken yet and until they did, the decision to kill him was not final.

"What do you propose?" The question came from a Colombian and was directed to the Cubans.

The Cuban shrugged. "It is the same as General Suarez."

The words chilled Vargo. He again saw in his mind the blood-splattered concrete wall and the man's head lolling against a lifeless chest. He turned quickly to the Colombian for reassurance.

"Suarez was a thief," the Colombian said. "He deserved to die."

"And this Vargo is not a thief?" the Cuban howled. "Don't you remember how he came to us?"

"True," the Colombian said. "But he was a thief only in his own country. With us, he has been honorable."

"Honorable? How do you know what he has done? How can you know this jewelry business and this warehouse business was not intentional? To cover up his thievery."

9

The room murmured again. The Cuban turned to the Honduran. "Besides, won't it be easier to placate your soldiers if you show them the head of a thieving American?"

Easier for everyone, Vargo knew. But the Honduran was not important, only the Colombians. He turned to their leader, a fat man in a short-sleeved shirt. "The Cubans despise me because I support you. You and the Peruvians control production and refining. They are simply a pipeline to deliver the product, no more important than our other chutes."

The Colombian smiled. "You are overstating matters, Mr. Vargo."

"Perhaps. They are important. But not so important as the producers." The Colombian nodded. So did the Peruvian.

"And what about him?" shouted the Cuban. "The Panamanian accounts are frozen. The American accounts are frozen. This man has produced nothing. He should be eliminated."

"Nothing?" the Colombian said. "Before he arrived, we shipped our product to the United States in the bowels of mules. He has established an organization. He has made a fortune for your country."

The Cuban could not disagree. But he could complain. "And the funds he has now lost us. Will you make those up? Will you pay the Honduran soldiers?"

"No," the Colombian said. He turned to Vargo. "That is a problem that will be solved, true?"

"Of course."

"How?"

"We will set up new lines, new chutes," Vargo said.

"When?"

"Immediately."

"There you have it," the Colombian said. "Mr. Vargo will return to the United States immediately to make new arrangements."

Vargo blanched. "Return to the United States? That is impossible."

The Cuban smiled. "Impossible? Is that your solution?"

The men at the table laughed loudly. The Colombian flushed with anger.

"You are joking, Mr. Vargo. Correct?"

"No," Vargo said. "It is not possible for me to return. I am a wanted man in the United States. There is a man in prison for fifteen years because of National Diversified. There are also very dangerous people with whom I have had . . . unfortunate business disagreements. If I were ever to go back—"

The Colombian's face was now purple with rage. He screamed, "I said you were joking. Do you understand?"

"Yes, sir," Vargo said quickly.

The Cuban pressed his advantage. "When? When will he return and resolve this?"

"Immediately," the Colombian said. "Correct?"

"Yes, sir," Vargo said quickly. He saw out of the corner of his eye men in white shirts and dark pants moving toward the exits. He knew a Colombian killer when he saw one.

"Excellent." The Colombian turned to the Cuban. "Any more problems?"

"How long?" the Cuban said.

"Thirty days. Mr. Vargo will be on a plane by Thursday. If he does not resolve this to our satisfaction in exactly thirty days," he hesitated, "you may provide him a necktie."

The room laughed uproariously. Big joke, Vargo thought. A Cuban necktie was now a favored means of execution. A slit throat from ear to ear with the tongue pulled through the opening. It was supposedly in great favor among the Cuban killers in L.A.

"If I am arrested at the border, I will be of no use to anyone," Vargo said.

"True." The Colombian turned to the Cuban. "Can you make arrangements?"

"Yes."

"Then it's settled." The Colombian rose and the rest of the room did likewise. "Thursday, then, you will leave."

"Yes," Vargo said.

"Excellent," the Colombian said. He gestured and the other fat, short-sleeved men followed him to the exit.

When the Colombians left, the Cuban heckler came close to Vargo, then took him by the head and kissed him flush on the lips. "It is the first of June. You have thirty days, *amigo.*"

The La Tropicana cabaret is as out of place in Cuba as Guantánamo. Notwithstanding the revolution, dark black beauties covered only by skimpy net stockings, spangled bikinis, and elaborate headdresses still dance wildly in high-heeled shoes for the pleasure of men. The cabaret, opened in 1931 by the Mob, remains the most exotic bar in the West Indies. Some say the lure of La Tropicana's forbidden pleasures was once the great cement which held Cuba securely allied with the Warsaw Pact. There haven't ever been many such cabarets in Moscow. And there's never been any in Sofia.

Guatemalan General Alejo Fuentes found the pleasures of La Tropicana as irresistible as any Bulgarian. He particularly enjoyed the attentions of a dancer who called herself Irena. The relationship had worked well for years: Irena had a more or less steady source of income whenever the general was in Havana, and General Fuentes a source of very exotic sex. Irena was a star and therefore got to share her dressing room with only three other dancers. That worked out well too.

The confrontation with Vargo broke up about 1 A.M., and General Fuentes was driven immediately to his favorite table at La Tropicana. Irena danced near the end of the show, a brazen number with a thin black man dressed in white satin and spangled pumps. The two dancers performed a decadent rumba that left little to the imagination. The act would have fit in nicely on a Vegas stage.

After the show, General Fuentes walked backstage with studied casualness, nodding with slight embarrassment at the door manager who tried not to stare at the florid medals which covered his peacock uniform. The dancers crowded into a communal dressing room which separated the sexes only by a thin partition. Irena's private room, the size of a large closet, was considered a great privilege reflective of her star status.

12

The general knocked softly, three times as always. Irena heard the knock, checked to see she was alone, then pressed a button hidden under her wooden dressing table. The beep which answered her touch told her the system was armed and rolling.

General Fuentes entered the room and embraced her. He loved it when he found her still flush from her performance. He gently helped her off with her enormous headdress; she was otherwise naked and the streaks of sweat glistened in the glare of the dressing room lights. She moved against him easily, stretching her arms wide. He grabbed her by the buttocks and pulled her close, reveling in the feel and smell of her, groaning immediately. She led him to an armless chair, then straddled him, grinding her groin into his. His hands moved over her flesh, sliding over the wetness of her. His mouth fastened on her left breast and he sucked noisily.

"You were late this evening," she complained, feigning passion and gazing at the clock on the table.

"I am sorry, Irena. I almost missed your show. There was a very important meeting." He sat back with a self-satisfied smile. She poured him some rum. He was already drunk.

"A meeting so important you were late for me? What was it, more discussion of tractors?"

The general smiled. "No tractors tonight, my dear. A full meeting of the Council. To hear an American beg for his life."

Irena smelled a bonus. She made her eyes grow wide. "Really?"

General Fuentes nodded. "And you'll never, ever guess what the American has agreed to do." He drank his rum and laughed, now digging his fat fingers into her flesh.

She could now taste her bonus. She immediately refilled his glass then knelt at his feet. He groaned as she made a show of licking her finger, smiling, and reaching for him.

"Will you tell me?"

3

FORTY-EIGHT HOURS AFTER GENERAL FUENTES HAD HIS soul sucked from him at La Tropicana, Assistant United States Attorney Juliana Kai Beck buckled herself nervously into the coach seat of a 747 at LAX. She gripped her armrest tightly and shut her eyes as the plane accelerated down the runway. Seconds later, the nose of the plane rose and she felt herself pressed against the seatback as the engines roared at full power, thrusting the giant plane vertically over the Pacific Ocean. This was the part she hated, the first fifteen minutes, when she was convinced that all the technology in the world would not keep this million-ton hunk of metal in the air. What if the engines suddenly quit? A vapor lock, maybe? The thing would drop like a stone, probably backward. The ordinary bumps and grinds of an aircraft rising to cruising altitude always convinced her, although she had heard the same sounds a thousand times before, that the inevitable had happened and she was beginning the ride to a fiery death below.

The irrational fear was the product of too much logic and too little science. Julie Beck was a lawyer. And to her lawyer's mind, it made absolutely no sense that one of these iron giants actually flew.

As always, the plane eventually reached cruising altitude and she started slowly to relax. She immediately ordered a drink and sat back, shutting her eyes while the vodka coursed through her, dulling the sharp edge of her fear. Her weakness infuriated her and she cursed silently. She never noticed the well-dressed man sitting next to her until he noisily cleared his throat.

"Well, five hours to Dulles."

What a line. She opened her eyes and reached for her briefing book. "Yes."

The man ordered a bourbon on the rocks. "Another for you?"

"No, thank you."

The man sipped while he mentally hunted for an angle like he was rooting through a sock drawer. "Business or pleasure?"

"Pardon?"

"Washington. Business or pleasure?"

"Business. Although to me, that's pleasure." She mentally kicked herself. The drowning man would now go for the straw.

"Really? What business are you in that causes you so much pleasure?" The man said it like it was a hilarious off-color joke.

"I'm a prosecutor. With the Justice Department." She knew exactly what was coming next.

"Is that right? I can't believe anybody that looks like you is a prosecutor."

"Thank you."

"Yes." The man edged closer. "I mean someone who looks like you, I can't believe . . . you would really enjoy putting a guy in prison. Do you? Enjoy it, I mean?"

Julie Beck never looked up. "Immensely," she said flatly.

The man pretty much shut up after that. What irritated her most about these daily confrontations was the reminder that she was losing a lifelong battle. For as long as she could remember, she had been rated first on her looks and maybe, rarely, if she was lucky, sometime later on her skills. She knew with precise clarity that women who looked like her were never taken seriously; they were always the subjects of crude jokes and superficial jobs, whatever the training, whatever the talent. That unshakable opinion made her committed to one goal: whatever it took, however long it took, that life would never be her life.

She had been delighted to turn thirty the year before and even happier as she imagined her body's clock ticking on. She had never feared advancing age; she welcomed it, convinced that age was an ally assuring that her days of fighting off misperceptions and unwanted approaches would soon be behind her. She was wrong. Although she had taken pains to crop her white-blond hair boyishly short the perverse result was that it just made her Eurasian olive-tinged face even more striking. What she couldn't hide by a refusal to wear cosmetics and an insistence on black, boring suits was a pair of intense green eyes and a long athlete's body which the years had not destroyed but only nicely rounded. Nor could she hide a naturally husky voice, low and hoarse, softened by whatever stew was caused by the mix of her German father and Taiwanese mother. A bedroom voice, they said in the courtroom, and what a face. Every time she heard herself on tape, she wanted to rip out her vocal cords.

Well, at least this guy had been easier to get rid of than most. She pressed the button to let her seat slide back, and shut her eyes for the flight.

The ride to Washington bumped along on the crest of a June storm and she was exhausted when she landed in Dulles. It was almost midnight by the time she tipped the doorman and leaped into an ice-cold shower.

Although she wanted desperately to sleep, she wouldn't permit it, instead calling for coffee and propping up in a straight-backed chair with fat briefing books from the Baker trial. The Attorney General's pup had said the meetings the next morning would include people at the highest levels. To Julie, that meant at least the Associate A.G., the number-two man in the Justice Department, and maybe Manion himself. There was also a hint of an interdepartmental task force, maybe with NSC. That the FBI would be there was a given. This was not a meeting she intended to screw up.

She skimmed the court clip from the trial four years before, remembering the satisfaction she had felt when the clerk read the verdict form. Baker's face had flinched with pain and his lawyer had pounded the table with a fist. Julie had stared straight ahead, the ice queen, neither smiling nor exulting. Of all the people in that tumultuous courtroom, she and Baker were outwardly the calmest.

Her victory had never been complete, however, some might even say Pyrrhic, and had. Vargo by that time was long gone, leaving behind only dead bodies and out-of-luck investors. Four years later, his escape still ate at her.

Now, against all odds, she might have a chance to remedy what she regarded as the great failure of her life. When Manion got her on the line the day before he told her the Vargo case was being reopened. They knew where the man was. "Cuba," Manion had said casually.

"Cuba?" Julie had forgotten every delicate, political skill she had so painstakingly perfected. The question had come out of her mouth involuntarily, as if she were in shock.

"That's right, Cuba," the Attorney General said. "It's this island nation just south of Florida. We have a Navy base there. Guantánamo."

She recovered fast. "Yes, sir. I know. It's just that Vargo and Cuba . . . it just doesn't make a lot of sense. Vargo is one of the great financial criminals of all time. I don't understand what he and—"

"Might have in common? Maybe they're both baseball fans."

Manion was definitely an asshole, Julie concluded, just like everybody said, albeit an asshole that was Attorney General of the United States. "What do we know, sir?"

"Ever since Vargo escaped, he's been working with drug rings in the Caribbean basin. The cartels, as you probably know, are working hand-in-hand with the official military. With drug money, Cuba may survive the loss of Warsaw Pact money."

Julie was stunned. "You think he and Vargo are partners? In the drug trade?"

"Ms. Beck," the Attorney General said sarcastically, "you were recommended to me because you are supposed to be knowledgeable. On Friday I expect *you* to be telling *me* what's going on."

"Of course. I'll get the file out of storage immediately."

"That would be nice," Arthur Manion had said.

After a time, she moved to an armchair to get more comfortable. She curled her long bare legs under her and yanked the oversized T-shirt so it covered her to her knees. At 2 A.M., still staring at the briefing books, she fell asleep in the chair.

* * *

She left the Lafayette Hotel at 5:30 A.M. dressed in a blue pullover sweatshirt and matching cotton sweatpants. She began a slow, measured run along the sidewalk, angling with the sun toward mall walkways sunken with uncaptured debris. She ran by her watch, ignoring the morning chill, knowing the stiffness from hours in the chair would ease and loosen after five minutes. The lack of sleep did not bother her; she rarely needed more than four hours in any event. When she reached the Capitol end of Madison Drive, the walkway became thick with runners. Through the mist, she could make out the distinctive outlines of the Smithsonian and the famous obelisk rising above the western end of the mall.

She loved Washington, and her affection for the city had never been dulled by the scores of business trips she now routinely made into Main Justice. She still made sure she saved free time to listen to empty legislative sessions in the Capitol and oral argument at the Supreme Court. Only occasionally would she venture to Wisconsin Avenue or M Street for some Georgetown nightlife, but she always tempered it, so that the next day she could tour again, once spending an entire Sunday going from one grandiose church to another—the National Cathedral, the National Shrine of the Immaculate Conception, the Altar of the Most Holy Trinity, St. John's, even the Mormon Tabernacle. She loved power and monuments to power. And she wanted to be part of it.

As she ran past the five-mile marker, the stiffness left her and her pace quickened. She felt satisfied, as she always did running. She had overcome a lot to get where she was, mostly the view, shared by men and women alike, that a woman is either beautiful or competent, one or the other, no exceptions. For years, they saddled her with mindless bank robberies. "Ladies and gentlemen of the jury. There is the defendant in that chair. You have seen the videotape of the defendant pushing a gun up the teller's nose. We ask that you convict." There was even a joke around the U.S. Attorney's Office that Julie Beck's idea of a heavy document case was a bank hit with a note.

Then Vargo came along and she watched the case

grow, nurturing it like a flower. When they realized how big it was, they tried to pull it from her, but she protected it like her firstborn. In the end, when Vargo escaped, she settled for Robert E. Lee Baker and loved every minute of it for reasons she had stopped thinking about years before. She got her verdict and rode the glory like a fine horse. And never looked back.

4

IT HAD ALWAYS SEEMED TO HER THAT THE ONLY OFFICE in Main Justice that wasn't windowless and hermetically sealed was the Attorney General's. The rest of the offices were blank cages, little better than the cages of federal inmates, resting, contemplating their wrongdoing, in the prisons selected for them by the men and women in this anonymous structure.

She walked down a half-mile corridor, avoiding messengers skating along the slick tile, to the first of three security checks leading to the great man's antechamber. A secretary with green hair pointed to a conference room. The six men sitting around the government-issue conference table rose correctly to greet her. Manion looked up and she watched his demeanor change. A man like all the others, she realized with great disappointment.

"Ms. Beck, I'm Arthur Manion. Delighted you could make it."

"Thank you, sir."

"Let me introduce you around. This is Stuart Eisenberg, from Treasury. He's responsible for Caribbean loans. Next to him is Gilbert Ray from State. Then, Ken Barlow of NSC."

Barlow barely nodded. He had a thin unpleasant face and his eyes were bloodshot. His suit was expensive but ill-fitting.

"You know David Brennan, of course." Brennan was

head of Major Frauds at Main Justice and Julie nodded to him.

"Nicholas Miller is the FBI liaison we've brought in." Miller was a lot better dressed than the agents in L.A. The tie, for example, actually matched the suit, and he wasn't wearing Hush Puppies. Julie Beck dealt with agents every day and she gave him a grin.

"And next to him is Christopher Tarr. Tarr is from Langley."

"From where?" She knew the question was a mistake as soon as it came out.

Tarr held out his hand. "The CIA, Ms. Beck." His grip was cool. His eyes were cool. He looked even stranger than the guy from NSC.

She sat next to Brennan from Justice, her only kindred soul. Manion walked to the head of the table and began the meeting.

"We're not going to have this meeting transcribed because I don't want to read the minutes in the *Post*. Instead, Eisenberg can take notes." The man from Treasury nodded. "Since all he's interested in is money, I figure he's the kind of man we can trust."

The room gave a polite laugh.

Julie Beck studied Manion. She had never heard much good about him, and seeing him in the flesh did not alter that view. He was a jowly, red-faced man who seemed to have spent his life faking it. His tailoring was expensive, but the body underneath was ill-formed. He had the nose and eyes of a constant drinker. His mannerisms were all bluster, clear defenses for an empty suit. Julie figured he'd get hammered if he ever tried this act before a jury.

"This is an unusual meeting," Manion continued. "It's interdisciplinary, or interdepartmental, or whatever the hell we're supposed to call it. The only reason I'm here is because I've been ordered by His Excellency to make a report to the NSC on the fourteenth of this month."

Miller of the FBI had the bad luck to ask the first question. "If you'll excuse me, Mr. Attorney General, I was advised by your office to come here today but we were not advised of the agenda."

Manion stared at him. "No shit. That's because I

haven't told you yet." The color drained from Miller's face. "Yes, sir."

Christopher Tarr of Langley mumbled to himself. "Thank God for independent agencies."

Manion heard the remark. "CIA. Glad you're here. You got any more of those exploding cigars?"

Tarr apparently had a sense of humor. He chuckled briefly at the reference.

Manion gestured to Gilbert Ray from State, who to Julie's eyes seemed the only one who knew what he was doing. Ray pressed a button midway up a blank wall and a wide map rolled down. He pressed another and bright floodlights shone on the map; the lights in the room simultaneously dimmed. The map was a blowup of a small portion of Central America. The top of the map cut off at the southern Florida border; the western portion, in the middle of Mexico; the southern portion, in Colombia; the eastern portion, in the Atlantic Ocean east of the West Indies. Although not clearly marked, Julie could make out the Gulf of Mexico, the Caribbean Sea, and the islands of Puerto Rico and Haiti. In the middle of the map, dominating all around it, was the island chain of Cuba.

"On June 17, 1988," Ray began, "a seven-hundred-million-dollar entity by the name of North American Diversified Securities was declared insolvent at the request of a Los Angeles bankruptcy trustee. Its cash on hand was found to total four million. Its remaining assets were worth perhaps eleven million."

About half that, Julie told herself. She had once pored over those figures for months.

"North American Diversified was owned and operated by a man named Robert Vargo, a ruthless criminal who we now know had a history of bank frauds in his past. Vargo became a fugitive from justice in 1987, with an active grand jury under way, leaving three homicides in his wake. As best we can tell, he fled south, spending the last four years in Central America."

She leaned forward. They not only knew where Vargo was, they knew where he'd been!

Ray tapped the map with his pointer. "In the beginning, Vargo stayed on the South American mainland, mostly in Colombia. For a year, he was in Barranquilla. Then, we have him down for about seven months in a town called Ríohacha, about halfway down the Guajira Peninsula. After that he seemed to divide his time between Santa Marta and Cartagena.

"About eighteen months ago," Ray continued, "Vargo began construction of a private fortress on a small island in the lesser Antilles, due north of Caracas. The island is about seven miles wide and four miles long and this map is not big enough to pick it up. It is due east of St. Vincent and Barbados and due south of Puerto Rico, about two hundred miles west of Curaçao."

Ray put down the pointer and turned to the group. "Vargo's activities during this period would not ordinarily be of interest to us. However, we now believe that in the last four years Robert Vargo, on behalf of his partners, has parlayed that initial pot he funneled out of National Diversified into something approaching"— he paused for effect—"two billion dollars."

The room stirred. Two billion dollars was nothing to the government of the United States. But, for one criminal to have amassed that sort of a fortune was incomprehensible. Also, not very likely.

"I know you're thinking that's an impossible number," Ray said. "But understand what we believe Mr. Vargo has accomplished in four years. He has made himself indispensable to the Central American cartel, acting as an intermediary between drug distribution channels in the United States and production points in Peru. Because he walked in with money, he was trusted. To this day, he remains more or less trusted."

More or less trusted. She listened closely. The man from State had a lawyerlike quality about him. There were *facts* to be learned here.

Now Ray's pointer moved northwest, toward the Cuban mainland, but stopped short of Cuba at a small dot in the Caribbean between Jamaica and the Island of Pines. "This is where we believe the money from North American Diversified went. It's Grand Cayman Island in the Cayman chain. Technically, it's a U.K. possession, but as a practical matter it operates on its own. Its national goal is to become the Switzerland of the Caribbean; in other words, total bank secrecy.''

Christopher Tarr of Langley yawned. ''Would I be out of line if I requested that we cut to the chase?''

Ray turned to him with the contempt of a professional staring at a pretender. ''I see. A two-billion-dollar drug empire does not interest the CIA, Mr. Tarr?''

Tarr shrugged. ''Not overly much, Mr. Ray.''

''Well, let's get to something that might.'' Ray pressed another button and the map changed. Now the Cuban mainland took up the entire wall. ''Where is Vargo today?'' Ray turned to the group.

Even though she knew it was coming, she still didn't believe it.

Miller of the FBI said it without thinking. ''Bullshit!''

''No,'' said Gilbert Ray.

''When?'' Manion barked.

''Six months ago, almost exactly,'' Ray said. ''We've now received confirmation through intelligence channels that Robert Vargo is in Havana for quote 'medical treatment' unquote.''

''Why?'' Miller asked. He had apparently recovered from Manion's previous attack.

''Why? Let me show you.'' Ray pressed another button and the map jumped back to the wider view again. ''Here is the northwest coast of Colombia,'' Ray said, tapping the screen again. ''Through these coast cities— Santa Marta, Barranquilla, and Cartagena—come over ninety percent of the cocaine sold in the United States, which by our estimates amounts to annual revenues of over seven billion dollars retail, which makes it an industry larger than steel. If you look at this map closely, you may see what the Secretary and I believe is the cause of the Havana friendship.''

She strained to see. There were a number of island chains between Colombia and Miami. Cuba was directly in the way; also Jamaica, Haiti, and the Dominican Republic. There was only a thin channel of water to Miami between the Dominican Republic and Puerto Rico. East of that channel were the resort islands of the Virgin Islands and the Lesser Antilles. It was really astounding.

When you looked at a map blown up like this it was evident that there was mostly land between Colombia and Miami.

David Brennan of Justice spoke for most of the group. "I don't get it."

"Look again," Ray told him. His pointer traced a path through the blue of the Caribbean Sea. There was no question about it. The only sensible sea route from Colombia to Miami tucked in closely to the southern coast of Cuba, then through the Yucatán Channel between the western coast of Cuba and the eastern coast of Mexico, finally up into the Gulf of Mexico and around to the Atlantic Ocean to Miami. "That's the only way to get there," Ray said. "It's also impossible to fly in a straight line from Colombia to Miami without going over Cuba."

The room was quiet. Everybody was making calculations, and there weren't any stupid people in the room. Well, maybe one. Manion asked in a complaining voice, "What the hell does it mean?"

She spoke for the first time. "There's no doubt in my mind they'd be wonderful partners. It makes perfect sense if you know Vargo."

The room turned to her. Gilbert Ray recognized another professional and yielded the floor. "For those of you who do not know Ms. Beck, she was the prosecuting attorney in the North American Diversified case. What was left of it, that is. Vargo was by that time long gone. His three principal assistants were murdered. There was one fellow—Williams or something—left alive. He was convicted."

She snapped at that. "Baker. Robert E. Lee Baker. He's in prison."

"How very Confederate," Gilbert Ray said, sitting down.

"There's a lot Vargo can do for the Cubans," Julie Beck said. "He's a magician with money. And with the Caymans sitting right there off their coast . . ."

Stuart Eisenberg from Treasury now woke up because the subject was money. "What about the South American loans? Has anybody thought about those loans?"

Christopher Tarr laughed impolitely. "Isn't it a little

late for that? Aren't your banks out about four hundred billion by now?''

Eisenberg snapped back. "It was the CIA that wanted to recycle petrodollars. It wasn't the banks' fault.''

Manion held his head in pain. Julie Beck wanted to join him. What did this have to do with Vargo?

"Let's get back to the point," Manion barked. "Ms. Beck, you've been invited here to give a report. What can you tell us about this Vargo?''

"Just about everything." She leaned forward. "We investigated Vargo's operations in the grand jury for two years before we indicted. We covered everything, every check, every phone call, every investor. We had Vargo's phones tapped and his mistress under twenty-four-hour surveillance.''

Christopher Tarr yawned again. "I suppose that's why he's in jail now.''

Her eyes flashed. "Vargo fled the country two days before we indicted, after being tipped off by an accomplice who we . . . trusted. The accounts had been stripped.''

"And the murders?" Christopher Tarr asked gently.

"They were brutal. Executioner-style. The victims were the three people closest to him, except for the man we convicted. All shot in the offices of North American Diversified. Kneeling down. One bullet in the back of the brain.''

"And the man you convicted? This Williams?''

"Baker. He's been in Boron for over three years. With a lot left to go.''

The room got quiet again. Everybody had the same thought. Nick Miller of the FBI said it out loud. "There's nobody left except Baker, right?''

"Right," she said without thinking. "This was an intimate operation and the three people closest to Vargo are dead. Maybe Baker was supposed to go too.''

"What's he like?" Miller asked.

For the first time she became oddly disconcerted. Her voice wavered but the bitterness bit through. "He's . . . he's complicated. He was a practicing lawyer before this happened, a former AUSA. He was also a minor athlete, a football player I believe, although he never followed through on that. He's never followed through on anything in his life. His parents were from Tennessee, crackers some would say. His father was actually shot and killed by a police officer during a robbery. He's smart enough in a general street sense, and tough, although he was always far too disrespectful for his own good. People thought he was a man of integrity, although he usually betrayed whatever confidence was given him. He's still young—about thirty or thirty-five—and the word is he hates Vargo.''

''Hates him enough to help us?'' Manion asked.

''Probably, if the price was right.''

''And that's all we got? This Baker guy?''

''Just him and one other person.''

''Who?''

''A young woman named Angela Moore. She was a prostitute on Vargo's payroll and, well, business partner as well. Vargo used her to bait the major investors. She profited handsomely as a result.''

''Where is she now?''

Julie shrugged. ''No one knows. She wasn't one of the three bodies. She was last seen the same day Vargo disappeared. Maybe she left with him.''

Christopher Tarr leaned forward and sighed. ''It doesn't matter. If he's all we got, he's all we got.''

Julie was confused. ''What does that mean? Baker will be in federal prison for years yet.''

''I doubt it,'' Christopher Tarr said, rising. He looked at Julie Beck with undisguised contempt. Julie decided right there he was gay; no man looked at her like that unless they regarded her as competition.

''I can assure you he won't be spending any more time in jail,'' Tarr said to her, the dead-fish smile still playing across his lips. ''Are we agreed?''

''Like hell we are,'' she said.

The rest of the heads around the government-issue table nodded in agreement with Tarr. Nobody paid any attention to her at all.

5

HIS NINETEEN-YEAR-OLD CRACKER FATHER NAMED HIM Robert E. Lee Baker, out of respect for the South, and he was once the fastest and some said only white wide receiver in the history of Carson High. They called him "Smoke" back then, and designed and called plays for him with names like "Smoke-36-flash-right." When they weren't calling him "Smoke" he became just "Bobby" or more often "Bobby Lee," or sometimes, if it was all slung together, "Bubbly," like a soft drink.

The highlight of Bobby Lee's football career, and maybe his life, came early on, in high school, in the waning seconds of the 1974 California Interscholastic Federation Championship game against undefeated Inglewood. He had just staggered back to the huddle choking and coughing blood after getting squashed taking one across the middle which advanced the ball from the Carson twenty to the Inglewood thirty-six. Carson called its last time out and Bobby Lee knelt on the ground to try to get his breathing right. His face was puffy, his nose was bleeding, and his right eye was closed. The dirty-blond hair that was always too long and always in his face fell down over his blue-green eyes when he took off his helmet. With his good left eye he saw a sea of white teeth and black faces grinning at him. His quarterback, De'Andre Lewis, pounded him once on the back of the head.

"Ouch. Shit, De'Andre."

"I can't believe you caught that motherfucker, Smoke."

"I can't believe how hard that fucker hits." He looked across the line. Number 55 in the Inglewood blue was staring at him, 220 pounds of undiluted black fury still pissed that Bobby Lee had held on to the ball. He shuddered and looked away from the linebacker toward the top of the stadium arching toward a purple-and-green smog-driven sunset. The night lights were swollen by the red light of an LAPD squad car still circling the grounds hunting aimlessly for a first-quarter Inglewood sniper. The towels carried by a skinny white guy named Max arrived and Montel grabbed Max by his red curly hair. He rubbed his head hard and then everybody else did the same, because Max was lucky and was always kept close, and if you rubbed his red head good things happened, guaranteed. Then the refs walked back on to the field, chased Max away, and the team booed. The whole thing was taking place in slow motion in his seventeen-year-old mind. De'Andre smacked him in the head again.

"Hey, Smoke! Wake up!"

Bobby Lee turned to him in a daze. "Hey, De'Andre, you know what?"

"What?"

"Except for Max with the lucky hair, I got the only white face in this fucking stadium."

De'Andre was still laughing as he knelt in the huddle. "Okay, children, listen up. We're down four and we got one play to get thirty-six yards. Montel, you keep those fucks away from me."

The 280-pound all-everything left tackle grunted.

"Okay. Let's do it. Smoke, get your pale butt ready to fly. Smoke, right flash post thirty-six go red. On hup."

The huddle broke and Bobby Lee lined up at wideout in a slot east of Montel's wide ass. The crowd let out a high-pitched scream that had the players glancing involuntarily toward the stands. On De'Andre's bellowed but only faintly heard "Red" he took one step back and broke parallel to the line of scrimmage at full speed, smacking De'Andre lightly as he passed behind him. On "Hup" the ball snapped and Bobby Lee planted his right foot and flashed down the right sideline. He heard Montel's scream as the big tackle laid into three rushing defenders. The corner came up and Bobby Lee blew by him like he was standing still, then faked looking over his left shoulder for the ball. De'Andre was seven yards deep, set in the pocket, and pumped once. The safety bit, saw the corner beat and panicked, leaving his position to rush to cover. Bobby Lee dropped his head, planted again, and broke left, firing past the flailing safety toward the now wide-open post. He knew De'Andre had the ball in the air just as surely as he knew 55 was coming hard from the other side. It all came together at the five—Bobby Lee turned, jumped, and De'Andre's spiral hit him dead in the chest. The linebacker simultaneously crushed him and they all landed together, Bobby Lee still on his feet stumbling in the wrong direction to the ten, careening sideways like his drunken father after the cops shot him. His hearing was gone and he never heard the gun explode. His feeling above the waist was gone and he never felt or even remembered the safety bang him to the seven or the corner bang him to the four or Montel and 55 hit him together with almost five hundred pounds of full-speed beef so that he spun high and soft through the air like a lazy leaf into Carson history.

He did remember Montel ripping off his helmet, crying, and smacking his blond head into the cold ground. He always remembered the party till dawn with the team and the pretty black girls and Max, his head rubbed raw by the celebrants. And he never forgot the four of them at dawn—Bobby Lee, De'Andre, Montel, and Max—sitting on a mountaintop above the Pacific, watching the sun escape the eastern smog and light up the drunks on the sand far below. They drank beer, hugged, and made a pledge: they'd all go to USC together and win a national championship, just like they won the CIF.

Even Max, who was a smart little fuck and who cared if he couldn't play football, said he'd go to SC too, and they'd all stay together. And whoever didn't go to the pros, Max'd figure out something for him to do, become a businessman or lawyer or whatever.

And then they drank the beer to seal the deal and Bobby Lee laughed out loud and hugged everybody again. It was dawn and they were CIF champs and he was seventeen years old, good-looking and fast. He'd either be in the pros or let Max figure something out.

What could ever go wrong?

Robert E. Lee Baker, Federal ID number 6874-B, woke up on the morning of his thirty-third birthday in the same room he had slept in for three solid years. At first, he struggled to get his bearings, squinting against the line of light that sliced through the crusted window high above him. Then his confusion vanished with the desert night when the fat naked man on the bunk five feet away coughed and stirred. Baker closed his eyes at the sound and leaned back on his institutional pillow, waiting with dread for the 7 A.M. siren to sing its song trumpeting the beginning of a bright new day in the California high desert.

The wait gave him time to think, time to set up the psychic roadblocks against the gloom now hurtling toward him like a runaway truck. Christmas and birthdays were the worst, the old-timers said, and Bobby Lee figured that was only half-right, no more. Christmas was bad, with all the phony cheer, pressed turkey, and tinsel in the rooms, but at 80 degrees in the desert it was there and gone before you knew it. Birthdays were different. Birthdays were the destroyers of rationalizations, silent, crystal-clear, ice-cold laser beams of reality blasting away the carefully constructed walls of denial and hope. A birthday was perceived fearfully and dimly six months before it arrived and loomed larger and ever more dangerous as it approached, like a train roaring through the fog. A birthday meant only one thing: one more year of my life wasted; one more year in prison.

Bobby Lee waited for the gloom, felt it and knew right away there would be no good way to deal with it. He rose stiffly and faced the window, stretching to see through the lowest slit, feeling a strange disorientation as he watched a purple, shaded sun crest the hills. The desert was an ocean of sand and brush to the east. To the west was the town of Boron, God's dual revenge on the crackers who lived there and the once mighty who lived behind the chain-link fence. As he watched, the black of the desert floor paled. The weak promise of light seemed to trip a wire. An alarm sounded and a switch set by a timer threw a blanket of glare throughout the prison. A deep recorded voice announced the time through a hundred speakers: "It is now 0700 hours. It is now 0700 hours." The naked fat man on the mat groaned and twisted in an ugly, futile attempt to evade the light and sound. Bobby Lee Baker watched him with disgust. Good morning, Boron. Good morning, thirty-third birthday.

There were worse places to do federal time: Marion, Leavenworth, Terminal Island—"T.I.," it was called, right on the beach outside San Pedro where the white surf met the white-collar federal defendants. T.I. was a holding tank with a nice view but it was no good place to do years. Then there was Lompoc—not bad on the farm but the shadow of the maximum facility on the same grounds spoiled everything. And McNeil Island in Washington State, where you'd be a cold man to send your wife even after the divorce.

No, given the alternatives Boron was the Palm Springs of federal prisons. Nice desert location: balmy in the winter and 110 in July. Dormitories instead of cells. Minimum security: just walk away if you like, but when we find your worthless ass we'll stick it in Marion to amuse the Cubans. Even a tennis court with a metal net. Club Fed, they jokingly called it, but after three years Bobby Lee Baker wasn't laughing anymore.

He left his window and lit a cigarette, a nasty new habit picked up in prison, then threw on some clothes while the fat banker farted his way to consciousness. If he played it right, he'd have almost an hour to wander the grounds, shower, and still never have to say a word to the piece of shit sneak thief who shared his room. He caught a glimpse of himself in the mirror as he dressed and was surprised. Superficially he still looked good: a little over 6'2", 180 tight pounds, with sun-lightened dirty-blond hair, still a little too long and unruly. But the lines in his face had aged him as they deepened in the desert sun and multiplied in the quiet of his early morning rages. The mirror also didn't show the fire in his belly and the coughed-up blood at three in the morning when he thought of the injustice of it all and raged again. The mirror showed a fit, healthy man, still youthful and vigorous. And lied.

Baker crept out the door and into the desert air. It would be hot later, no doubt about it. A few of the coed guards were already wandering around the periphery staring at the sky and pointing like medicine men looking to make a change. He eased past them, lighting another cigarette. They gave him some shit out of habit, asking him how he and the fat fuck in his room were getting along. Baker ignored them out of habit. He had long since abandoned banter with the armed guards who smiled amiably during the day and then locked him tightly in his room each night.

An hour later, the sun was a third of the way up the horizon and the temperature had swelled to 85. He settled against a hillside and looked up with closed eyes, letting the dry sun dance off his face, wondering what the day would bring. Maybe a visitor on his birthday. Max was a possibility. It hadn't been the thrill of his life, the conviction of his partner and publicity and all, but Max was nothing if not loyal. He had represented Baker like a lion throughout the trial and never doubted the innocence of his partner. That twelve people in the box came out the other way hadn't changed his mind at all.

Who else? Montel? No, Montel had his ancient all-Pro body down in the Raiders' training camp in Thousand Oaks. Montel came when he could but it was painful. They never talked about much and never, ever mentioned the old days. Who else? Maybe his former client, the world-famous Robert Vargo, the one man responsible for it all. Baker laughed and rolled on the hill at that one. Wouldn't that be nice. To grab Vargo by the throat and squeeze, watch the eyes bulge before the fucker died. Maybe stop squeezing for a while and let him catch his breath. Then start again. Over and over. Sweetly ending it for the great man. Yeah, maybe he'd visit. For the thirty-third.

After breakfast, Baker again walked out alone toward the broad, parched hillside. Around him, the bald bankers and stock manipulators, stripped of toupees, were rolling joints from home-grown cultivated on the sunny side of dope slope. As always he ignored the background noise of talk about appeals, real estate deals, money, and fallen dreams. Money dominated all conversations among the once proud. Tomorrow they all would get out.

And when they did there was this penny stock deal in Dallas that was just sitting there. Whoever was smart enough to put together a group could . . .

The irritating buzz of voices was broken by a shadow across his face and the sensation of wood tapping against the ball of his foot. He squinted into the light and saw Suzie Hernandez, Boron's weak excuse for glamour. She intentionally wore her olive green prison-guard uniform at least two sizes too small. The black gun belt and truncheon were her fashion accessories. She tapped his foot again.

He kicked at the wooden stick. "Suzie, you do that again, I'm gonna take that stick and use it on you."

"Yeah? What are you gonna do with it, Bobby Lee?"

"Probably the same thing you been doin' with it. Why don't you try a man, Suzie?"

She smirked. " 'Cause the only men I know are like you, Baker. Fucked up and in jail."

Touché. He stripped his shirt off and rolled over. The lean muscles danced in his upper back. "C'mon, Suzie. I gotta get a tan."

"Forget the tan, sweetie. They say come get you. Bring you back by the nards, if I got to."

He sat up. "Who?"

"Nivens, baby." She gestured to the gray administration building where the warden stayed hidden from the dangerous fat bankers.

"Why?"

"Yeah, they tell me everything, sweetie. C'mon."

6

BOBBY LEE BAKER WAS PUSHED HALF-ASLEEP DOWN A gray hallway into a concrete-and-steel anteroom to Warden Arthur Nivens' office. Suzie had his hands clipped behind him and he bumped cursing into the warden's door. Suzie wasn't giving him a hard time—she even smiled as she clipped the bracelets on, then patted him on the ass to get him started—it was just procedure at Boron. Nivens had spent his career in the state system, mostly San Quentin, where once an inmate had killed a guard from solitary with a sharpened plastic spoon. As a result Nivens addressed inmates only from a P.A. system or closed-circuit TV monitor. It was a big event when one of the dangerous bankers was actually brought into his presence, an event always attended by the highest security.

Baker had never been in Nivens' office in the two years the man had been in charge. He found it a depressing place, barely more hospitable than a cell and probably with more bars around it. The furniture was federal gun-metal gray. The one door in was a double door with multi-ple, visible sliding bolt locks. The single window, barred, looked out on a concrete walkway leading to a guard station. Nivens looked pretty safe from whatever invest-ment advisor might be out to get him.

The warden sat behind his gray desk flanked on one side by a uniformed guard and the other by a man in a dark suit and burgundy tie. Suzie took the clips off and motioned Baker to a chair.

He rubbed his wrists. "Thanks," he told Nivens.

"For what?"

"My thirty-third." Bobby Lee looked around. "Where's the cake?"

Nivens turned to the suit. "See what I mean?"

The stranger held out his hand. "Mr. Baker, I'm Spe-cial Agent Gary Truman of the Internal Revenue Ser-vice." He handed Bobby Lee a card.

Baker looked at it and handed it back. "Any relation to Harry?"

The man gave a fake smile. "Do you know why I'm here?"

"It's about my returns, right? You see, my income's been down for the last few years."

Nivens scowled at the impertinence. "It's all through his file. It's a fuckin' mess I got here. Last week—"

Truman dismissed Nivens with a small wave of his hand.

"For the record, Mr. Baker, failure to file is a misdemeanor. Even for inmates."

"And a parole violation, too," Nivens added hopefully.

"Nivens, I'm not on parole. I'm in fucking prison."

"*Warden* Nivens," the man barked. "And when—"

"Please, please," Truman begged. Nivens sank into his chair, mumbling. Truman leaned toward Baker. "Listen, Robert, may I call you Robert?"

"I'd prefer you called me Arthur. Arthur Bandini."

"No problem. Arthur, I'm not here to ask about your tax returns. I'm here to ask for your help."

Bobby Lee had to decide whether to laugh or leave. He couldn't leave so he began to laugh, first quietly then louder. At the end, he was wiping his eyes. "Sorry, Special Agent," he said finally.

"That's all right, Arthur." The man sat on the edge of Warden Nivens' metal desk. Baker knew what was coming: the tender approach. Use the guy's first name a lot. Touch him. Sympathize.

"Arthur," Truman said, patting Bobby Lee's knee, "we know you're bitter. You've had a lot to think about these past years. After all, you're the only one in prison. Robert Vargo's not in prison, is he, Arthur?"

"No, sir, he's not."

"And never has been, right, Arthur?"

"Christ, stop calling him that!" Nivens screamed.

Special Agent Truman waved him off. "I'm not interested in formality, Warden." Nivens rolled his eyes. "Now Arthur," Truman began again. "If you had a chance to help us find Robert Vargo or his mistress, wouldn't you jump at that? Make them suffer like you've suffered?"

Baker shrugged. "Vargo's long gone. As for Angela—his mistress, as you say—I've got nothing against her. I hope she was smart enough to get away."

"Quite so," Truman said smiling. "But if it were possible for you to help us, would you do so?"

"No."

"Why?"

"That's my question. Why?"

"To help your country."

"My country put me here," Bobby Lee said. "My country—actually AUSA Julie Beck—told a federal judge that fifteen wasn't long enough. She made us beg for the fifteen."

"I know," Truman said soothingly. "But Julie's a hard ass, you know that."

"Julie's a c—"

"Stop it," Nivens screamed. "Look, this ain't gettin' you nowhere. Give him what you got to give and let's move."

"Fair enough. Arthur, what would you say to a reduction in term for cooperation?"

Bobby Lee tried to be casual, tried to smile. He felt the corners of his mouth twitch. "Like what? Maybe I ought to talk to my lawyer."

"What for? You're a lawyer, aren't you?"

"Not anymore."

"Well, so we'll talk to your lawyer. Max Rafferty, right?"

"Right."

"But first, how about helping me out a little? Just a couple of questions, you know?"

"What kind of reduction we talkin' about?"

"We'll work that out with Max, okay?"

"Go ahead."

Truman smiled like a car dealer. He took out a legal pad and flipped some pages.

"Now as I understand it, you started representing National Diversified in late '86, early 1987, right?"

"Max and I did. Rafferty and Baker."

"But you worked with Vargo?"

"For a while. Then Max took over. I had a . . . uh, conflict, I guess you'd say."

"What kind of conflict?"

"It's not important. Ask Ms. Beck."

"All right. But you—well, your firm—did go to work for Vargo about nine months before the end?"

"That's right."

"And your job, if I may say so, was to assist Vargo in getting out of the country with investor funds, right?"

"Wrong." Baker felt his face flush an angry red, but there was little to say.

Truman consulted his file. "I thought that's what they got you for. Conspiracy under 18 U.S.C. Section 1952 to aid in a racketeering enterprise using interstate—"

Baker held up his hand like a traffic cop. "That's what they got me for."

"Right, I understand. We don't have to rehash the past. Just a little background, you know?"

"Go on."

"You tipped Vargo that the indictment was coming. He killed three people and fled with all the investor funds. Ever see him after that?"

"No. I didn't tip . . . never mind. I last saw Vargo on a Tuesday night. It was the next afternoon that the—"

"Bodies were found?"

"Yes."

"And Ms. Moore? Angela?"

"Same thing. She was with Vargo that night."

Truman took his notes and leaned back. "Let me ask you something. During the time you knew Vargo, did he have contact with any . . . well, agent of a foreign power?"

"You mean like Russians?"

"Not particularly. How about Cubans, Nicaraguans, Mexicans? Anybody you can think of?"

Baker shrugged. "A lot of the banks he dealt with were Chinese-run. Cubans and the rest, I don't know."

"I see. And narcotics. Do you know anything about that?"

"Just what Warden lets us smoke on the hill."

"That's an outrageous lie," Nivens bellowed. "Why, during my adminis—"

"Never mind that," Truman snapped. He turned to Bobby Lee, this time the smile gone. "Look, we've been chasing our tail on Vargo for four years now. We know you helped him get out, and we know he got out with everything National Diversified had. Now we think he's coming back. You probably know more about this guy than anybody, and we're ready to make a deal. Now, will you or will you not help us?"

Truman's tirade had given away his hand, just like so many had in the old days. Baker remembered staring in the eyes of prosecutors who used to threaten his clients. He had a rule in those days: the larger the puff the larger the bluff. Nobody who holds the cards has to talk about them. Truman's face was flushed with exertion and need. There was somebody he'd have to report to and Truman was afraid of that someone. Bobby Lee stood up and held his hands back for Suzie's cute bracelets. "Talk to Max," he said amiably.

7

NOT THAT IT REALLY MATTERED, SHE THOUGHT, BUT IF they wanted to release the fucking guy, why did they make her try the fucking case to begin with? When that thought grabbed her, she was watching a yellow tennis ball rise toward her off the tan clay surface of a court in the back of her parents' Pacific Palisades home. The man who hit it, Jack something or other, was a pro dressed in a polyester sweatsuit. On his chest was the green diamond logo of the Riviera Country Club. She had been hammering balls at him for almost two hours now. Before that, she had run four miles along Sunset and cooled off afterward by doing laps for twenty-five minutes in the pool. She thought it might help; now she knew it wouldn't matter. Orders were orders.

Jack what's his name on the other end actually had a name, Jack Wagner, and he was the assistant pro at Riviera. He almost crashed up the hilly roads when he heard Julie Beck wanted a game. He had seen her around the club since she was a long-legged teenager in short white dresses, her muscled legs dancing as she turned to hit the ball. She was a loner back then, sometimes hitting with a pro, sometimes playing with a pro, more often just meeting her rich father for lunch or a drink. All that money and that lean, white-blond look were enough to set any pro dreaming. They said she was a princess but he thought he could handle that.

At the beginning he left his sweats on, figuring he'd stay in the middle, work her right to left, get her panting a little. After five minutes, he found himself moving side to side as her returns got sharper. After ten minutes, he was slicing backhands to keep in the game; he wasn't quite ready to hit a defensive lob but he wasn't ruling it out either. Finally, she was at the net. He hit hard shots right at her and watched her skip to the side and volley with precision. Finally, he tried to pass her. She saw it coming, moved quickly down the line, and crunched a cross-court backhand winner.

He expected her to be happy. He was wrong.

"Hey, Jack, if you don't want to play, maybe you won't get paid. Understand?"

Bitch, Jack thought. She needed to be put in a closet with the Raiders for about an hour and a half. Just the linemen. After they had drunk about a case of Coors.

"Sure, Julie. Don't worry. You just made a good shot."

She picked up the balls on her side of the net. There was no use snapping at Jack what's his name. It wasn't his fault and the man couldn't help. Sooner or later, she was going to have to make the call she dreaded. She turned and waved at the pro. "That's all, Jack. Good game."

Sooner or later, she had to make the call. She went into her father's study and stared at the phone, then picked it up and twirled the cord. She waited for a miracle and none came. Nobody from Washington called to change her orders and no great ideas entered her mind. Finally, she grabbed the phone and dialed. Max Rafferty came on the phone immediately, leading with the same Mick bullshit that had once made him and his partner famous.

"Don't tell me. I got indicted. You weren't satisfied with Bobby Lee?"

"Knock it off, Max."

"Incidentally, Julie, I got a quick question. What do you think about the two of us now? I mean, now that we aren't adversaries, you think it'd be unethical if we kind of—"

"Max, shut up. I called for a reason."

"That I figured, Julie."

"It's about Baker."

"What, did he break out?"

Keep it simple. No jokes. They were like two divorced people. Better not pick at any scabs.

"No, he's not out, Max. But something has come up. Something important."

"People tell me that, I start feeling for my wallet. Just to make sure it's there, you understand."

"We'd like his cooperation."

"No shit. In what? Vargo pick up another case?"

Not yet. "I can't talk about it right now because it's still confidential. I need to meet with him. I can't do that without your approval."

"The answer's no."

She cursed silently. Max already smelled she had something to sell. "What will it take for a private meeting with him?"

"A deal."

"I can't do a deal until I know what he's got to say." Max started whistling. "What kind of deal?" she said finally.

"Out. That's spelled O-U-T. Out now. Like the old Vietnam War chant. You can talk to him in the fresh, open air of Santa Monica. I've got his old bungalow in back of the office waiting for him."

"That's out of the question."

"So's his cooperation."

"You're being way too hard, Max. We've got other places we can go." Julie said it out of habit. Rafferty was going to ram that one right back at her like Jack what's his name from the club.

"Julie, can I get back to you? I got a call coming in."

Julie gave the bluff one more try. "Okay."

"Fine, tomorrow. Okay?"

"Asshole."

Rafferty was laughing. "Come on, I deserve it."

"When can I see him?"

"The deal is you talk to him and if you like what you hear, he's out."

"The question was 'when,' Max?"

"Whenever. He's not going anyplace."

She hung up the phone and immediately called her office. Her superior, James P. Price, a man, of course, came on the line.

"Well?" he said.

"I did it."

"Good. How did he take it?"

"Like we expected. I hoped he'd give us something for nothing, but Max is too smart for that. He wants Baker out with no questions asked."

"So how do we know he'll cooperate?"

"That's just it, we don't. We've got to rely on Baker's hatred of Vargo. We could get screwed."

"I don't like it." The man paused and the line clicked while he thought it over. "But I guess there's nothing we can do."

"Bullshit," she said.

"Julie, give it a rest. We've got orders."

"The orders said get him to cooperate, whatever the cost. They didn't tell us what deal to make."

"So?"

"So I say we bluff. Wait until the end, until he can taste getting out. Then back off, tell him we changed our mind. He takes our deal or he goes back to Boron."

She could almost hear the man shudder on the end of the line. "Julie, you are one cold lady."

"Yeah, yeah, I know. What do you say?"

"I say get the deal done, like Washington says."

"My way?"

"Any way."

"That sounds like permission to me."

"Only if it works, Julie."

What a courageous guy. "I understand."

"I've got to do a memo to you today. Put it all on the record."

"Right."

"And if you fuck it up, it's your own cute ass. I won't protect you."

"Don't worry," she said. Her voice became absent and slightly faint. "I know him. I guarantee he'll fold."

8

ROBERT VARGO LEFT HAVANA ON JUNE 8, 1991, ON A dawn Interflot flight to Lima which bounced off the potholed runway and slid into the sky pitching and bucking like a reluctant rodeo animal. Vargo was too obsessed to pay any attention to the wild ride. The purposeful foot-dragging by the Cubans had already cost him seven precious days. In addition, two Cubans known to him only as Manuel and Hector had met him in the passenger terminal and now sat on his right and left in the forward section of the plane. Manuel was squat and stupid and had a killer's quiet concentration. Hector was his boss, an officer as these things went. Hector's job was to make sure Vargo performed. Manuel's job was to act, when it was time.

At the Lima airport, Hector and Manuel led him by the arm to a car, which whisked him to a private hangar two miles south of the commercial terminals. A twin Cessna was waiting, its engines humming quietly. The wash from the props blew against him as he was led like a condemned man up the steps to the seats in back of the cockpit.

The plane barely seated four, with a bit more room in back of the seats for storage. Hector sat up front with the pilot. Manuel buckled in next to Vargo in the rear seats, then searched with his free hand among the baggage, finally yanking out a black satchel. He opened it and began expertly snapping together a small arsenal of weapons, starting with a MAC-10 automatic assault rifle.

When they were off the ground, Hector turned to him, shouting over the din.

"Give me your passport."

Vargo didn't object. The passport was a crude forgery given him in Havana. It worked fine at the Lima airport but would never stand a chance at LAX. Hector glanced at it briefly, then pitched it toward the carpet of jungle below. Vargo watched it drop with an odd sensation; instead of his photograph, that could be him fluttering helplessly toward a jungle death.

The Cessna twin leveled off at one thousand feet, skimming for two hours like a hovercraft over the green jungle sea. The airstrip appeared magically, sliced from the dense forest as if by a knife. The plane tipped its wings twice at an unseen MAC-10–loaded sentry, then banked to land. The pilot never touched his radio.

They were met on the ground by a small Japanese jeep and driven farther into the jungle. Vargo knew where they were heading, to a Sendero Luminoso guerrilla base. The base had originally been used to receive and distribute arms from Havana; now, like all Peruvian paramilitary bases, it was given over largely to the manufacture of coca base for transshipment to Colombia for refining into powder. Vargo relaxed a little; this was his business.

When the road gave out the jeep left them off. They marched for an hour under a canopy of squawking jungle green. Even at this early hour the heat sent shafts of sweat and soot down the faces of the marchers, soon joined by tiny green and yellow bugs. This was the Peruvian Amazon basin, an uncharted area bigger than Idaho, occasionally severed by brown dirt landing strips and controlled by no government except the gunmen of the Sendero Luminoso. Vargo was now completely relaxed. The mayor of the district of Uchiza, one hundred miles east, had long been on his payroll. The reach of the Cubans would soon be severed.

They began to smell the encampment an hour before they arrived. When they were three miles away they had to cover their faces with red kerchiefs to block the stench of boiling pots of coca mash coupled with the bad hygiene of hundreds of workers. The latrines were little more than shallow trenches scraped from the soft jungle floor. He gagged as they got closer and breathed slowly, trying to become accustomed to the rank air. They were all coughing in their kerchiefs when the camp came into view.

He was led to a large jungle hut separated from the

rest of the base. Shining Path guards with the ubiquitous MAC-10s at the ready flanked the entrance. He nodded briefly as he passed. Immediately they moved behind him, expertly intercepting Hector and Manuel. There was a loud argument in Spanish behind him. Vargo knew the two Cubans were now expendable. He turned to watch them die but was disappointed. Manuel had expertly brought his assault rifle to his hip, staring down the Peruvian guards. The guards froze and not a shot was fired. There was no doubt about it, Manuel was good. In twenty-one days, Vargo realized, he might find out just how good.

The hut was much larger than it first appeared. The anteroom was really a small kitchen where three young serving girls chattered in Spanish over a boiling pot. The smell of the food mercifully blocked the smell of the camp. Vargo's eyes acclimated to the dark and he stopped.

"Juanita," he said. "Is that you?" He spoke in Spanish.

A slight, dark-eyed girl looked up. "Yes, sir. Juanita."

"Is the American here?"

"Yes, sir. Inside."

Vargo walked quickly toward the inner rooms of the hut. A man sat quietly in the semidarkness smoking crack out of a crude pipe. He held the pipe in his right hand; in his left he held a small glass of clear liquid. He didn't rise when Vargo entered.

"Covington Barrows. Does your government know where you are?"

The man didn't move. He inspected the burning bowl of his pipe. "I am here on assignment."

"Right. You've been assigned to diddle a young Spanish girl in a jungle encampment. And at the same time collect your coca profits. American policy has changed since I left."

Barrows sighed. "I told them it was a mistake to send me. They insisted."

"The Americans?"

Barrows smiled slightly. "Not the Americans."

"No shit." Vargo poured himself a shot of Barrows' tequila. "How did you get here?"

"A military transport. We left from a Honduran base before dawn and I hooked up with a small plane in Lima. I'm supposed to be making a cash deal for arms."

"A regular Oliver North."

"Sort of. I charge more than he did."

"Are you sure about that?"

"Quite sure. His cut came from our share. We resented it at the time."

Juanita came in then to clear away Barrows' plates. She attended him like a slave, removing his glass and setting a new one before him, refilling his pipe, pouring another tequila. Since the day was hot, she also brought Barrows a crisp, white shirt and waited while he stripped a sweat-soaked one off. Even though Vargo had been speaking to Barrows in English, he remained quiet till the girl left.

"And then, there's Juanita," Vargo said unnecessarily.

"Who is not alone out there," Barrows said equally unnecessarily.

Barrows was getting progressively drunk, held aloft only by the piercing smoke from the crack pipe. Nevertheless, even drunk, the man was more than dangerous. Barrows was long and lean, with ice blue eyes set off by a deep tan and full white hair. His nose was so patrician it could have served as the prow of the *Mayflower*. Those looks, a searing intelligence, frightening ruthlessness, and an elegant if now poverty-stricken patrimony had swept him through Yale and into the highest levels of the DEA, in charge of the agency's money laundering and interdiction efforts in the Peruvian theater. He had managed the traitor part on his own.

"Tell me, Barrows, how long have we known each other?"

"Too long, in my judgment."

"Let's say three years. You've made a fortune since I've been involved, true?"

"Your point?"

"Well, I've always wondered. Why?"

"Why what?"

"Why you do it? You're still a high-ranking DEA official, with a full career in front of you. So why? Just money? Or the little Spanish pussy down here waiting? Or maybe because here they treat you like the king you think you are? Is that it?"

Barrows stared at him with unforgiving eyes. "I've never liked you, Vargo, and I hope the Cubans slice you like the piece of discarded meat you are. You're a thief and a multiple murderer. And a liar. And a pederast. Do you still like boys, Vargo?"

"Especially little Cuban ones. About the same age as Juanita."

"And money?"

"I like it as much as you do."

Barrows smiled. "Then we understand each other. Let's talk business."

They drank and talked until dark. Juanita and her companions kept their glasses full and their plates clean. The girls tried to work on Vargo but he ignored them, convinced they were spies. At 4 P.M., the Peruvians finally got it, and the girls were replaced by two fourteen-year-old boys, adorable brown berries who jabbered at him in Spanish, grinning the whole time. Vargo hated to be regarded as stupid. He rudely ordered them away.

The light was just starting to fade in the jungle west when they stopped talking. Barrows rose and stretched.

"Let's see if I've got this. You are pouring millions' worth of product into the U.S. But the cash is not coming out?"

"Correct. The Panamanian general was our best outlet of funds. Now that he's been removed, the dollars are backing up at an alarming rate. Also, I've had some problems in Los Angeles."

"I've heard."

Vargo pounded the table for emphasis. "Each day millions of dollars are being pushed into one end of the pipeline. And the other end now has a cap on it."

"So what are you going to do about it? The Panamanian, the jewelry operation, the warehouse, the bank, all of it was your creation. The Cubans trusted you."

Vargo snorted. "The Cubans are dogs." He hesitated. He didn't know how much the traitor from DEA knew. "Anyway, I'm going to work around it. Create a cut-out.

A chute, I call it. A tributary from the main river. A bypass. You get the idea."

"Tell me about it."

"Forget it."

Barrows smiled. "I'll learn about it sooner or later."

"You'll learn what I need to tell you. Other than that I'll be the only one who knows."

"I'm supposed to help you, at least that's what they told me. I can't do that if I don't know your orders."

Vargo smirked at that. "My orders are to correct the problem in thirty days or get a new tie." He checked his watch. It was now dawn on June 9. "I have until June thirtieth."

"All right. How can I help?"

"I'll need a passport."

"Of course. Under what name?"

"James Ashley. British businessman." He handed Barrows a photograph showing Vargo with a close-cropped black beard and an elegant dark suit. "I'll fly into Los Angeles from London. The passport should show frequent travel as any international businessman might."

"What cities?"

"Non-controversial ones. Sydney. Rio. Cairo. Nothing to do with . . ."

"I understand. What assistance do you need in the United States?"

"Money and a contact. The money should be wired to an account at the Asian Interbank Trust in Monterey Park, California, just outside of Los Angeles. About one million will do. The account is in the name of Charter Properties, Ltd."

"An offshore entity?"

"Gibraltar registration. It's a shelf corporation I've used from time to time. It's been dormant for years."

"And the contact?"

"One in Los Angeles and one in Hong Kong. Charter Properties will appear to be a real estate investment firm seeking to place Chinese dollars in U.S. property before the Hong Kong takeover in 'ninety-seven. There's billions of Hong Kong flight money flowing into southern California, and Charter will never be noticed. But for safety's sake, I need an office in Hong Kong with someone intelligent on the other end. That's also how I'll get information and instructions to you."

"By phone?"

"By fax. Anyone can tap a phone. No one can tap a fax."

"Excellent. And the contact in Los Angeles?"

"Again, someone smart. I'll need access to legal and financial services. Plus security. You know, a driver with . . . with ability."

"As to the first, you'll need a lawyer."

"But someone good. The last thing I need is a drug lawyer."

"Understood. You had a lawyer once before, true?"

"Yes, for the criminal investigation they had going. He's in prison now. And I'd like him to remain there during this operation."

"Why?"

"He knows me and he's . . . well, potentially dangerous."

Barrows made a note. "Anything else?"

"Two things. First, don't fuck this up. I promise I'll take you down with me."

"I'm terrified. What else?"

Vargo poured more tequila into his glass. He was now thoroughly drunk and the last of the day's light was sliding weakly through the jungle foliage into the room. He had no stomach for work anymore. "Those little boys. Tell Juanita to bring them back."

9

ROBERT E. LEE BAKER WAS OFFICIALLY RELEASED TO the free world on June 10, 1991, four days after he was brought down to Los Angeles from Boron. For those four brutal days he was housed at the Metropolitan Detention Center in downtown L.A., or MDC as it's known in the trade. The MDC is a brand-new, forty-story, windowless concrete slab designed to prevent what had become a rash of escapes by pretrial detainees from Terminal Island. From the front steps, it looks pretty much like a bad Hilton, ringed on the first floor by glass doors and pleasant ferns with a normal-looking reception desk right inside. However, just past the receptionist is a thick steel door and armed guards behind windows tightly covered with wire. Once past that door the guest has pretty much seen the last of light and air for a while.

If Julie Beck's goal was to soften Baker up, a few days at the MDC was just the ticket. He was strip-searched three times a day, an indignity no other inmate suffered. His only allowed recreation was an alert walk along the corridor outside his cell. At night, a siren blared and thousands of dead bolts clanged shut simultaneously. Every two hours in the midst of fitful sleep, a guard came by and flashed a high-powered light into his face.

On the afternoon of the fourth day, brown-uniformed Boron guards arrived to deliver him across the street to the custody of the FBI. This exercise was another ridiculous excess, designed only to intimidate and embarrass. For the two-block ride, he was dressed in a vomit-green Boron jumpsuit, cuffed and chained at the ankles and wrists, and flung in the back of the square Bureau of Prisons van.

He relaxed only when the van turned onto Spring Street and made a left turn into the subterranean parking lot underneath the federal courthouse. In a way, he was now home, back in the building where he had once made his living, where he was always a winner, at least till the end. There was a time he knew everyone in this building, from the lawyers, judges, and clerks to the marshals and secretaries, to the probation officers and social workers, to the little old lady selling coffee on the fourth floor. He had also been convicted in this building, which certainly ended his winning streak, but that was another story.

He relaxed even more when he saw the FBI agents who came to take him from the Boron guards, hard-looking men but men who knew him, who knew the respect that was once due him. He sat back against the yellow plastic seatback of the government van, shifting slightly to ease the mild cramp caused by the cuffs. José Medina, a short, rotund Hispanic with baggy pants, was the agent who got there first. He yanked open the back door of the van.

"Okay, we'll take it from here." He didn't say "please."

The prison grunts didn't yet know they were in over their heads. The driver flashed his badge. "Crenshaw. Bureau of Prisons."

"Congratulations." Medina leaned through the back door and offered Baker his hand. "Okay, Bobby Lee, you're home." He helped him to his feet. "Christ, they got him clipped for the ride of two blocks. Get these off," he ordered.

Crenshaw bristled. "Are you now taking control of the prisoner?"

"Yeah," Medina told him. "We'll make sure he doesn't hurt you. Now, how about taking these fucking things off like I just told you?"

The man moved fast. Baker was soon rubbing the irritation and swelling from his wrists.

"Where's my documentation?" Crenshaw whined.

Medina snorted. "Fuck off."

They took him into the marshal's lockup first, not to book or process him, but to talk. The agents shifted in in clumps to listen and hang around. Then they brought Max in and gave him some coffee and doughnuts; Max wanted to get it over with but Medina told him to shut up and eat his fucking donuts. They tried not to ask about prison at first but eventually Medina broke down.

"So, what's it like, Bobby Lee? Bad as they say?"

Baker shook his head from side to side. "Not at all, it's actually a piece of cake. No women to give you shit. No booze to give you a hangover. No bosses around, just guards telling you when to eat, sleep, shit, whatever. All paid for by the government so you don't have to worry about bills and taxes and all." He stretched and rubbed his face, now weary from the tension of the last four days. "Just a real piece of cake."

The room got quiet. Max looked up at Medina, who

was studying his hands. He figured this was his chance and moved fast, grabbing Baker roughly by the arm. "Let's go, Bobby. They're waiting for us."

They all went to an empty magistrate's courtroom on the tenth floor, a sort of poor cousin to the ornate red-draped and marble district courtrooms on the second floor. Baker knew these courtrooms well; it was in a magistrate's courtroom, maybe even this one, that he had been arraigned four years before. Then, for all its modesty in comparison to the real courtrooms downstairs, it had seemed an imposing place, presided over by a court functionary with the power to free him or jail him, to set bail at something he could make or leave him to rot out in T.I. with the illegal aliens, the ten-plus club, and everyone in between. It was then he had first seen her in action on his case, standing with ice-blond coolness and telling a seventy-five-year-old magistrate of Vargo's flight, and the government's concern about the flight of his co-conspirator, Robert E. Lee Baker. Baker was page one by that time, and the old man was not about to make a mistake. She asked for a million bond and got it, Rafferty's screams bouncing harmlessly off the walls like the misplaced shots they were. Later, after the conviction, they had to beg her to get credit for the pretrial time served at T.I. First she had to "think about it."

Now he saw her again, leaning in a fixed way against a wooden railing, staring at him with those same intense eyes while he limped in cuffed at the wrists and ankles, with chain link connecting the two cuffs. She wore a black, funereal suit set off by a crisp white shirt. The white-blond hair was now cropped short and fell in a tousled, natural way. Baker searched for the lines in her face the three years should have brought, the same as the ones now etched around his eyes, but didn't find any. Yet although unlined, her face was not carefree; if anything it had taken on a leaner, harder look, like a runner's face after the softness is burned away. Her body was like that too, beyond slim, taut as a guy wire.

She was not alone. A half-dozen men in dark suits milled about, broken into clumps looking like medieval judges. She was the chief judge, his accuser and sentencer, her white-gold skullcap distancing her from the others.

Medina led him through a wooden gate and sat him at an aging brown counsel table, then unlocked him. Baker leaned toward him and gestured.

"Who?"

Medina whispered under his breath. "From D.C. All sorts of different agencies. The two near her are from Main Justice."

"She's looking good, Medina."

The agent laughed and said "shit" under his breath, then moved behind Baker, standing properly in a protective posture. Max sat down next to him.

"What the hell's all this about?"

"This is where we finalize the deal."

"What 'finalize'? I thought we already had a deal."

"Yeah, maybe." Max grabbed a yellow pad and made some columns on it, doodling as much as anything. "She's been stalling, and to tell you the truth I don't know what the fuck she wants anymore. Let's just shut up and find out what she wants to buy. Then we'll sell it to her, whatever it is."

A moment later, a court reporter appeared. The man set up next to Baker, flipping open his machine and unspooling a white ribbon of paper. Baker stared at him wordlessly, remembering with eerie clarity the last time he had seen this man in this courtroom. When he was ready, the man nodded to Julie and she stepped forward.

"Hello, Robert." The court reporter noiselessly pounded his keys. Baker was stunned at the sound of her voice, how it brought it all back. He tried to say something flip but found himself just nodding wordlessly. Cowed, like a fucking kid. Robert, for Christ's sake.

"Do you know why we're here?" she asked softly.

He cleared his throat. "Not really."

"They didn't tell you at Boron?" She gestured. "Max didn't tell you?"

"He said I'm going to get out. That's all I heard."

"I see." She moved and sat on the edge of the other counsel table, the prosecutor's side. She crossed her legs and put a pencil to the side of her lip, crinkling her brow as though concentrating hard on how to explain something difficult to a child, maybe a mental defective.

"Let me try to make this very clear for you," she said finally. "Just so there's no misunderstanding." She held out a hand and one of the faceless suits put a folder in it. "This is the written agreement we'll all read, understand, and sign today, then put on the record." She tossed it on their table, the loser's table. "Read it," she ordered. The reporter pounded noiselessly in the background.

Rafferty opened the folder and scanned the document inside, then made a face. "This doesn't make any sense. I thought he was getting out."

"I don't care what you thought. This is the deal and it's the only deal I'm offering. We need it in writing and we need it on the record today."

Rafferty threw the folder in disgust to Baker. "This doesn't give us shit. We might as well finish the term."

Bobby Lee didn't like the sound of that at all but was sensible enough to keep his mouth shut. He loved Max's choice of words: "We" might as well finish the term. Goddamn Max wouldn't have to finish shit. Nevertheless he shut up and pretended to study the document.

"I'm sorry you feel that way, Max. I think you're making a mistake. Nevertheless . . ." She managed a resigned, theatrical sigh and gathered her papers, preparing to leave. She extended her hand toward Bobby Lee, requesting the return of the folder, letting the skirt inch up insolently on her thigh as she did so. He couldn't help it, he squeezed the folder tighter and turned away, staring at her like a dog with a bone. He almost growled.

Rafferty saw it all and interceded. "Just give us a moment."

"Sure."

Rafferty grabbed Baker by the arm and walked him fast into a corner. He still clutched the folder with white fingers.

"I hope you're not playing poker in Boron, Bobby. I thought you were going to drop to your knees there. Maybe start begging."

"What's that 'we' shit, Max? Why don't I sit there and be cool, and you go back to Boron if the deal goes sideways?"

Rafferty laughed. "Fair comment. Have you read this?"

"This is shit. She's giving us nothing."

"That's right. She's got you on a leash that would choke a dog. You get released to the custody of the Department of Justice, which means you got an agent with you twenty-four hours a day. They put you in a safe house to quote 'assist the Department in an ongoing criminal investigation' end quote. That means you help them get Vargo. If all goes well, they will quote 'consider such assistance in making further recommendations to the Court regarding sentencing' end quote. That means they can fuck you at the end for any reason or no reason. If they don't get Vargo, they remand you for the full term. No questions asked."

"So what are we buying?"

"Not much."

"Is it negotiable?"

"It might have been before they saw you slavering."

Baker thought about it, doodling on the back of Julie Beck's tan folder. There wasn't much of a choice. She'd let him out and dress him up and use him to try to get Vargo. He'd do that for free anyway. At the end, if they got Vargo, she might let him go or she might not. If Vargo slipped through, which was likely, she'd throw him back where he was, and never look back.

"Tell her she's got a deal."

10

AFTER THE PAPERS WERE SIGNED, THEY ALL FOLLOWED Julie downstairs to the real courtrooms and trotted out United States District Judge John Francis O'Donnell to put the deal on the record. The sight of O'Donnell resurrected all the memories of three months of hell, day after day of O'Donnell's alcoholic rages from the bench, face distorted and purple veins sticking out in his neck.

O'Donnell was an early Meese-vetted Reagan appointee who believed the entire trial process was a useless impediment to the government's right to put people in jail as it saw fit. On any question that required a ruling from O'Donnell the U.S. Attorney's Office was undefeated, and had been since the day O'Donnell was confirmed. Nothing that happened in Baker's trial broke that string.

O'Donnell took the bench by banging noisily through a set of double doors, slumping into his chair, and grinning idiotically at three cowed law clerks sitting in the jury box. As usual he was flush from a flock of Wild Turkeys bagged over lunch which caused him to rage incoherently. He screamed about politics in Washington, judicial salaries, and the incompetence of federal prosecutors when compared to his day. When he was through, he rubbed his face with both hands to clear the fog and asked what the hell everyone was doing there. Beck gently told him the purpose of the hearing.

"I thought I already sentenced him. If I didn't, I'll do it now. What's the max on this?"

"The court is quite right," Julie Beck said soothingly. "The sentencing was three years ago."

"And now he wants a reduction? Forget it. Let him write his congressman. When they give me a raise, I'll think about it."

The courtroom erupted with sycophantic laughter from everybody but Rafferty and Baker.

"No, it's not quite that, Your Honor," Julie said when the hilarity died down. "Let me explain." Baker listened to her quiet competence and wasn't surprised. In the last three years, her courtroom act had gotten even better and it was plenty good enough back then. She spoke slowly and simply, recognizing without saying it that this time she really was speaking to a defective. O'Donnell's head moved in rhythm to her words; the only thing missing was a ring in his nose, one that wouldn't get in the way of the shot glasses.

When she was done, O'Donnell did what he was told, signing the order with a shaky hand, then shuffled off the bench for his emergency afternoon snort. Julie turned to Rafferty.

"You're all through, now."

"I know."

Rafferty shook Baker's hand. "If they let you, call me. I'll be waiting."

"Thanks."

Medina led him alone to a windowless room on the tenth floor, then unlocked the cuffs, patted him on the back, and left, shutting the door behind him. Baker listened to the door slam and waited out of habit for the snap of a lock engaging. When it didn't happen, he felt confused, then anxious, finally faintly exhilarated, the first small, tentative rush of freedom.

The feeling didn't last very long. Ten minutes later, the door opened again and she walked in alone. She shut the door behind her and leaned against it, staring him down. Her eyes didn't blink and her face was a formless mask. Baker hunted for some human emotion in the perfect oval eyes and found none, not hate, not bitterness, not vengefulness. Nothing.

At the sight of her his embryonic exhilaration immediately faded, replaced in a blink by a mixture of emotions too novel and disparate to identify. She walked away from the door and sat on the edge of the table and stared some more, roiling the soup. This time she wasn't as careful as in the courtroom; her skirt rose even higher when she sat and her bare legs meanly revealed themselves to him. Baker literally backed away into a corner. When his shirt pressed against the wall, it felt clammy.

"Hi, Bobby," she said. No "Robert" now. Her voice was soft and dangerous, still husky, the bedroom voice she could switch on and off like the computer oddly balanced on her bedroom nightstand. His jury had loved that voice; all her juries loved that voice.

"Hello."

"Why don't you sit down?"

"I'm okay."

"Are you? You sound a little hoarse. You also look a little pale."

No doubt. "I'm fine."

"Good."

56

Baker shifted, not really knowing what she wanted him to do. She might sit there with that blank look forever, content to show him her tailored suit and white hair and white unattainable legs and enjoy watching the rivulet of sweat drift trickling down his cheek. It was really no contest. He gave in early.

"Okay," he said finally. He walked to a chair.

"Thank you," she said. She gave him a smile that was all white, even teeth. Not for him. Not the smile, not the legs. Not any of her.

"Pardon me for not smiling back."

"No problem. You hate me. I understand that."

"I don't hate you." He breathed deeply, fighting against the lie. "It's just that none of it was necessary. You did it out of . . . out of . . ."

She nodded with the false empathy of a paid-by-the-hour shrink. "I understand how you feel. Every criminal feels the prosecutor has a vendetta against him or her. It's perfectly natural."

Every criminal.

"Anyway," she continued, "that's the problem we're here to solve. Can you work with me or are your feelings so deep that that would be impossible?"

Baker wasn't yet so scared that he couldn't see the easy ones. Yes, he stayed out. No, he got stuffed back into Boron with the fat naked guy who shared his room.

"Of course I can work with you."

"You'll have to do better than that, Bobby. You know I can't take any more chances with you."

"I said I could work with you. What more do you want?"

She laughed merrily. "Oh, lots more. If I don't believe you, Bobby, I'm not going to take any chances. I'm never going to take any more chances with you. You know that, don't you?"

"What the hell does that mean? O'Donnell signed an order. I'm supposed to get out."

"And you will if I believe in you. At least for a while."

"And if you don't?"

"Then you won't. I'll go right back downstairs, ask for a hearing, O'Donnell will rescind his order, and you'll be back in the MDC for dinner. Do you doubt that?"

He was past fighting with her. "No."

"Excellent. Then let's get to the only thing that's important to me now. Why should I trust you? Why should I ever believe that you'll put it all behind you and work with me? Talk to me, Bobby."

"I just . . . just think there won't be a problem."

"Why not?"

"Well, we've had our problems, true. But I suppose you were just doing your job. As you saw it, I mean."

"Is that how you feel?"

"Yes."

"Bullshit." The word was spit out and not even the fake smile followed. "You don't lie well, Bobby. Not here. Not on the stand, either. Once you lied well, but not anymore."

He tried unsuccessfully to swallow the rising anger. He walked away from the wall until he was face-to-face with her. Their noses were inches apart. "Why are you doing this to me?"

This time she did smile. "To find out the truth. Your release was not my idea. I'm hoping you'll give me a basis for changing some minds."

He was incredulous. "You want me back in?"

The smile faded and her face hardened. It was now slate smooth, without contour, without a hint of compassion. "Yes," she said. "For the full term."

He was stunned. "I can work with you," he said quickly. "No problem. Just give me a chance. Please."

"And the reasons?"

He said what he knew she wanted to hear, even if it was a lie. "To get out and stay out. Prison is horrible."

"Better," she said, like a proud teacher. "Anything else?"

"To get Vargo."

"Of course. He got out with the money and left you holding the bag."

"That's right."

Her voice tightened. "You must have felt very stupid."

"Yes."

"Taken advantage of, maybe. Made the fool." Now

she was off the desk, in his face, the veins prominent in her otherwise white, smooth neck.

"That's right."

"How did that make you feel, Bobby, to trust somebody like that? You opened up to him, maybe told him things about yourself that nobody else knew, things that he could hurt you with if he wanted. And then, after you felt how good it was to share your thoughts with a partner, even if it was a partner in crime, he betrayed you. Did that demean you, Bobby?"

"Yes."

"I bet it did. And Angela did the same thing to you, betrayed you, didn't she?"

He knew how she wanted it to go. "Her too."

"That's right, her too." Now her face was flushed, the warmth rising through the tense features. "Were you sleeping with her, Bobby?"

"No."

"Don't lie to me."

"She was Vargo's mistress."

"That wasn't my question, Bobby. Answer me. At the time we . . . at the time this was all happening, were you sleeping with her?"

"Okay, yes."

"That's better." She sat back and relaxed, the prominent veins receded as her opinions were confirmed. Now the smile had some warmth in it. "We need to get her, Bobby."

"Okay."

"And you need to get her to get even, right? The way anybody would when a lover commits an act of betrayal."

She really didn't know Angela, Baker realized. If she did she would understand. But right now his only problem was to convince her of what she already believed in her shoes.

"That's right," he said.

She stared some more, this time with confidence, looking for some secret hint of betrayal. Whatever she saw calmed her.

"That works," she said finally.

11

THE FIRST TIME ANGELA MOORE DID IT FOR MONEY WAS long before she ever met Robert Vargo. It was in 1981, in the winter, in the cold after her mother's 1971 Ford pickup coughed and spit and died on the way to Reno. They were really up against it that time. The latest man in an endless string of men who passed for Angela's stepfather was long gone and the two of them were heading off for a "new start." That meant Reno, because her mom read an article that said the casinos were dying for help because the kids wanted to work in Tahoe, so they could go skiing, or in Vegas, where they could get whatever they wanted.

"Everybody hates Reno," her mom told her. "So that's where we're going."

Angela Moore was known as Sandra back in those days, Sandra Blodgett. Her mother—Muriel Blodgett—hated the name as much as her daughter did, but was sort of proud of the man who gave it to her.

"He was a smart man, your dad was. I heard he went on and became an engineer. You don't know it, but they don't let just anybody be an engineer. You have to be smart."

Sandra had no idea what an engineer was, what it took to be an engineer, nor anything else about what Muriel called the "educational amenities." Muriel heard the phrase once tending bar and never forgot it.

"The man who told me that was a teacher, and he said the most important thing for kids nowadays is the educational amenities. That's somethin' I never had. But there ain't no reason you can't."

Sandra didn't go along with that at all. She thought there were lots of reasons she shouldn't have the educational amenities. For one, she was never in a town long enough to learn the names of her classmates, much less

60

whatever amenities went on in class. For another, the only thing she was certain of about school was its hopeless, remorseless tedium. Ever since she was a small child the only activity she engaged in at school was sitting with statuelike boredom from the opening bell to the end of the day, watching with circling eyes as the second hand went around on the classroom clock. Years later, she could close her eyes for four or five minutes and tell within a second or two how much time had passed. She liked to entertain Vargo's clients with the trick as a sort of last treat, while they lay in bed, in the early morning glow.

Yet even if she wasn't the smartest kid in her classes she was easily the most popular, at least with the boys. By the sixth grade she was 5'9" and sprouting, with a shock of bright red hair that fell in uncontrollable waves around a milk white face. She was as lean as a deer, except where it counted, and in that department she was borrowing her mother's bras by the age of twelve. She also loved boys, like some little girls like dolls or horses, without restriction or limit, the handsome ones, the dumb ones, the brains, the nerds, it didn't matter. In one Arkansas school she seduced six members of the seventh grade before they threw her out, including a speckled preacher's son who was so besotted with her that he ran into the barn crying whenever she came to visit with her mother. Sandra recognized the signs and one day followed him into the barn while her mother occupied the preacher. She stripped the boy in the hay and fell on him like a hungry predator. She sucked him dry and then made him do it again and again until her mother and the preacher began beating a shovel against the locked barn door. Later they said the lad was never the same, eventually breaking from the preacher and impregnating a local farm girl at the age of seventeen. Angela was the maid of honor at the hurried ceremony and the boy never took his eyes off her, even during the vows.

But no amount of seduction of preacher's sons and expulsions would stop Muriel from extolling the virtues of education or stop Sandra from cutting school whenever she was forced to go.

"You didn't get any educational amenities, Mom," she always protested, when her back was to the wall. "It never hurt you none."

Which dubious wisdom was probably true, to some extent, but ultimately and inevitably led to the side of a road on Route 80 just outside of Deckom, Nevada, about 120 miles east of Reno. They had started out from Salt Lake City that morning, and from Indianapolis the morning before, but Deckom was as close to Reno as they got. The pickup lurched before its final death throes, aggressively coughing puffs of smoke from under the rust-scarred hood as it expired. Muriel panicked and hit the brakes and the bald tires skidded wildly across the grooved highway. Sandra shouted "Mom!" once and Muriel calmed down. She directed the truck, now completely silent, over to the cold shoulder of the highway.

There is nothing more desolate than a Nevada highway on a winter night. Muriel lifted the hood for the Highway Patrol to see and come help, but Sandra laughed at that, figuring the chances of that happening in this lifetime were nil. Why should a cop get out in the cold if he could just blow on by like he didn't see them? Even then, she had a pretty good handle on the tendencies of most men she would meet.

They might have frozen on that Deckom highway if nature hadn't forced Sandra out of the truck to a narrow ravine off the gravel shoulder. The next trucker who rumbled by almost jackknifed when he spotted Sandra yanking down her jeans in the dim light left by the failing day. He took both of them to Deckom, no problem, even called for a tow truck from the radio in the cab.

Sandra sat in the middle and the trucker got to play with her puss in the dark with the dirty fingers of his right hand while her mom cursed out the window. Sandra didn't mind and Muriel wasn't watching so she figured what the fuck, it's not hurting anybody, I'm warm, he's happy, and I'm getting a ride to a town. When they got to the wooden Deckom sign the trucker suddenly squeezed and stiffened, his eyes glazing. Sandra watched him with interest, even reaching down to caress his hand under her short dress in the dark of the truck. Then his eyes opened and he smiled at her.

"This okay?" he asked as he pulled over.

"Just fine, sir," Sandra told him.

They waited for almost an hour by the dirt road next to the Deckom sign. Eventually, Muriel and Sandra watched an aged, red tow truck pull up with the pickup hung like a dead fish on the back. For whatever reason Muriel made her sit by the window this time.

There was only one guy working the station that night, a man named Amos Dean. The Nevada desert was black and cold around him. Amos Dean was a cowboy, fifty-five or sixty years old, skinny, grease-stained, and powerful. He sat quietly, watching the tow truck haul in the dead pickup. When he rose, put aside his cold coffee, and started to work, he did so wordlessly, sucking on soiled, unfiltered cigarettes. Finally, he gave Muriel the bad news: about five hundred dollars in parts and labor. Muriel screamed that the goddamn truck wasn't worth that much. Amos Dean shrugged—he didn't disagree.

Sandra knew what would happen next. Muriel had already sprung for an eight-dollar motel room with a black-and-white TV next to the gas station. Now Muriel raced to the flatbed of the truck for her "valise" and "personal things." Her Seagram's and pills, Sandra knew.

Sandra walked to the edge of town and watched the dark desert for an hour. It was quiet and she liked that. Then she went back to check on her mother. Muriel was lying on a white pillow, her face ashen, discolored lines etched under her eyes. Her mouth hung open and she half-snored with a gurgling sound. The Seagram's bottle was three-quarters empty and the water glass from the bathroom was in Muriel's hand, its contents spilled down the front of her dress. A half-filled prescription bottle was on the table. Sandra had a lot of experience with this. She got her mother undressed, hung the dress from the shower rod, and had Muriel tucked in and comatose in twenty minutes.

Then she shut out the lights and went back to Amos Dean.

The station was almost black by the time she got back. It was a quarter-mile down the dirt road to the next building, a hardware store, and that was shut up too. The winter wind was blowing flat and harsh over the Nevada desert. It seemed the only light in town was a naked bulb in Amos Dean's office.

She walked in and was blinded by the harsh light. Amos Dean sat behind a desk doing his figures, his gnarled hands streaked with the remnants of oil that had settled into the broken lines around his fingers. His face was as cracked as his fingers. He looked up when he saw her, and didn't look surprised at all.

"Where's your mama, girl?"

"She's asleep, sir."

"She start drinking? Your mama drink a lot?"

"A bit, sir, yes."

Amos nodded. "She ain't gonna have the money to pay for this, is she?"

"No, sir, I don't suspect she will."

"Yeah, I figured that." He had his own money problems and broke the pencil in half, then stared at it.

Sandra should have been scared, but never was. She waited quietly in the bleak doorway looking at him with interest, letting him decide. Nothing she did was the least bit provocative, not a word, not a gesture. As the cold swept through her she pulled her mother's bulky parka tight around her. It didn't matter. Amos had seen all he needed to earlier.

"Five hundred dollars. That's a lot of money. Of course, a lot of it's labor." Amos seemed to be debating the issue internally. "But it's cold and . . . what the fuck?" He looked up. "You willing to help out your mama, girl?"

"Yes, sir, I sure am."

"Then come on over here."

Years later Vargo loved the way she told this part of it, the slow walk in the cold dark garage to the waiting man. Back then, she was fascinated at the way grown men looked at her. She had always wondered what it would be like to be alone with one of those men in her mother's bar, the ones who drank shots with beer chasers, and stared at her with angry, disappointed looks.

Now she would find out. Amos Dean took her hand and pulled her toward him. His hands were cold, the skin broken by hard work; hers were white and smooth as cream, a young girl's hands.

"This your first time, girl?"

"Yes, sir," she lied. Well, in a way it was. The first time getting paid, except for maybe the truck driver on the way in.

She always told Vargo she could never understand, then or ever, why men paid money for her when she so readily gave it away for free if they were nice. If they asked. She watched with detached curiosity as the man slowly became aroused. She took off her jacket and held up her arms. "You want to take 'em off or me, sir?"

His voice was cracked. "Me."

His hardened hands fumbled over her. His eyes were fixed and flat as he pulled her to him. She could feel the rough stubble of his face against her now bare chest. His voice sounded as angry as the men in the bar had looked.

"If you're teasing me, girl, I'm going to take the skin off you."

"No sir, you won't have to do that. 'Less you want to."

"Jesus," Amos Dean moaned.

Sandra made sure Amos Dean got his five hundred dollars' worth that night. She sat on his lap and kissed his oil-stained face. She knelt before him and took him in her mouth, experimenting with the sensation, wondering how close she could bring him before backing off. She sat astride him, moving cautiously, keeping Amos in the game, going to school on a man's reaction to her. He finally took her bent over the desk, howling like a wolf as he charged down the stretch. The whole thing had taken a full hour from the moment Amos first laid hands on her. He lay back panting, his face red and running with sweat, oblivious to the cold.

"Lord, honey, you got to go easy on me. I'm an old man."

"I'm sorry, sir."

"Sorry?" Amos Dean coughed and spit out a thick, brown liquid. "Sir? I tell you, child, if you was around here ever day I'd be broke and dead in thirty days. Shit, who cares?"

Then Sandra made a small mistake which Angela Moore never made. She asked to get paid. "You gonna help my mama?" she asked.

Amos Dean's eyes flattened and lost their dazed look. "Don't worry, honey, you'll get paid."

Sandra recovered fast. "It's my mama, you know. That's the only reason I asked."

"I said I'll take care of your mama."

She rushed to him, knelt next to him and put her head in his lap.

"I got an idea, sir."

"Yeah?"

"It's when you're done with the car?"

"I'm listening."

"After that, how about doing me again? Just for fun, you know."

Amos Dean's grin looked like it would crack his face into small pieces. "Girl, you are too much for an old man. Lemme ask you something?"

"Sure."

"How old are you, anyway? Am I going to get in trouble here?"

"No, sir, you're not going to get in no trouble. No way I'd let that happen."

"Good."

"I'm thirteen."

Muriel never knew what went on that night in Amos Dean's garage. She just knew that when she woke up there was a complimentary breakfast at the coffee shop next to the motel, courtesy of Mr. Dean, and a Ford pickup that ran like it was straight out of the showroom. She also didn't know about the fifty-dollar bill Dean slipped into the back of Sandra's jeans on the way out, giving her a little pat good-bye as he did so. Sandra decided correctly there was no real good way to explain that.

It would be another year after Amos Dean before Sandra Blodgett became Angela Moore, and a year after that before her face was splashed luridly on the cover of millions of videocassettes in chain stores across America.

Muriel hadn't wanted her to be that kind of a star. She wanted her daughter to be a serious actress in films you could take a family to, that or marry an engineer, one of the two. But after Reno bombed they were back in L.A. and the only job Sandra could get in show business was making coffee for the cast in the kitchen of the rundown apartment in West Hollywood where they did the shooting. That's where she got lucky, like Lana in the drugstore.

Her break came on the third film she worked on, a pirate film called *Long John Watson*. Long John was a legend in the business, a man who never needed to be fluffed, and the actresses who worked with him were but a foil for his considerable talent. John and Sandra first spotted each other while Long John was expertly servicing his costar on camera during a scene in which the pirates invade the castle and ravage the queen. For a castle, they used the living room of the West Hollywood apartment with a backdrop and dim lights. The queen was bent over the throne with her royal robes hoisted to her shoulders. Long John stood in back of her working hard for the camera. That's when Sandra moved into Long John's line of vision and made sure he understood that beneath her short blue-jean skirt was nothing but opportunity.

After twenty minutes of ravaging, the director shouted cut, more for the queen's sake than Long John's, and the crew broke for coffee. Long John, still long, walked past the throne to the kitchen, grabbed Sandra by the arm, bent her face down over the kitchen table and proceeded to demonstrate again why he was a star. Sandra's wails, only partly feigned, got the attention of the crew, who began filming the event. Never had the director seen Long John so long.

The former queen became a lady-in-waiting and a new queen was born. The film, *A Pirate's Revenge*, sold two million cassettes domestically and more in the Asian market than the accountants could count.

Neither the producer nor Long John cared that Sandra was only fifteen at the time. They told her to find some ID to prove she was eighteen and gave her some helpful hints as to how to do that. It all sounded too complicated to Sandra, who eventually just stole a driver's license from a black girl's locker at Van Nuys High School.

"Doesn't look much like you," the director suggested gently, examining the black girl's picture on the license.

"Come on, man. This is the best I could do. This or nothing. I lost weight," Sandra suggested helpfully.

"I don't know," the man said, but not for long.

Angela Moore. The queen had a stage name.

Robert Vargo met Angela Moore three years later, when she was eighteen years old and legal. He was referred to her by one of his "assistants," in effect pimps, responsible for stocking his parties with elaborate women. He tracked her to the pool at the Bel Air Hotel, where Angela was resting after a weekend of fucking the lead singer of a heavy metal band called White Trash. After five minutes of conversation, Vargo booked the next five-thousand-dollar weekend, just to sample the goods. By Sunday, he knew he had found what he needed.

"I want to talk to you," he told her on Sunday morning. He sipped the coffee she served him. "A special kind of conversation."

She grinned. "I *love* that. Would you like me to undress first?"

Vargo shook his head. "I want to talk to you about a job."

Angela Moore ran into this problem every Sunday morning. "I'll have to look at my calendar. I may be booked . . ."

"I don't mean that. I mean a permanent job."

They all loved her on Sunday morning. "Mr. Adams—"

"Ralph."

"Okay, Ralph. I can't stay with any one guy. Even though in your case it's something I'd really like to—"

"How would three hundred grand a year sound to you?"

Angela Moore tried to be cool but didn't make it. "I'm sorry?"

"Three hundred grand a year. Exactly what you'd make if you worked every weekend. Fifty in advance, all cash. And nobody to take a cut, particularly not the IRS."

North American Diversified at that time was pushing a net worth of $300 million. One tenth of one percent to Angela would not hurt the bottom line.

"I don't understand . . . ," she began.

"It's simple," Vargo said. "I am the owner of a very wealthy organization. In my business, I do a lot of entertaining. Sometimes it's necessary for me to convince people—say a banker, a seller, maybe a councilman—to see things my way. I need someone like you to . . ."

"You mean you want me to . . . entertain?"

"Yes, Angela, that's exactly what I want."

"But my career," she began.

"That's over. It's all over. You'll work exclusively for me. At six thousand cash per week."

It all sounded very pretty but she was used to pretty stories that never went anywhere. She smiled gently at him. "I'm really sorry, Ralph. I just can't."

Vargo looked crestfallen. "I just don't understand. Oh, well . . ." He stood up. "Go take your bath. I've got to make a phone call."

"I'm sorry, Ralph."

She luxuriated in the warm tub wondering if she had made a mistake. It certainly sounded like a lot of money, but who knew with these guys? Guys were always promising her things: money, jewelry, cars. When they got what they wanted it was all over. No, she was happy with her choice. She leaned back and closed her eyes. At least with the acting she got paid in good old cash.

She was almost asleep when the door exploded with a splintering crash. She screamed and sat up, the warm soap running down her bare breasts. Two huge black men stood in the door, their muscles stretching against tight T-shirts. Dazed, she watched them walk to her. They each held one handle of a massive laundry basket covered by a beige blanket. They hesitated when they got to her, examining her with cold eyes. Then the one on the left yanked off the blanket and tossed it in the corner.

They held the basket high over her head for a moment, then turned it upside down. A torrent of green paper fell over her, into the water, sticking to her, falling leadenly and water-soaked to the bottom.

The black men left and Vargo walked in.

"Do we have a deal?"

Angela didn't say anything. Then Vargo leaned over and kissed her hand. The green bills were stuck to the soap on her breasts and the shampoo in her hair. The bills in the water were piled up so high that some of the twenties toppled over the lip of the tub and began tacking toward her. She picked up a soapy hundred from her breast and examined it.

Well, if Grace Kelly could leave show business, she supposed.

12

ANGELA MOORE BEGAN OFFICIALLY WORKING FOR Vargo on a musty, blue-sky April afternoon in 1986 at a gig at a yacht club in Newport Beach. It was a semiformal affair, a kind of dressy cocktail party, and Vargo had her in something white and sleeveless with thin straps. He picked out all her clothes in those days and had them tailored to exact written specifications. The white dress was snug and revealing at the top and loose and thin at the bottom so that the stiff ocean breezes off the Pacific in the early evening would whirl the skirt around and provide a good view of tanned legs. One of her best features, Vargo said, and she had to agree with him there. Now at nineteen she had blossomed and sprouted to a lean six feet, all legs, smothered by a mane of red curls which all but hid her face and cascaded down to the middle of her back. The white dress was chosen to set off her tan, which, as it turns out, is a big deal at yacht clubs with guys in their fifties.

Angela paid off like a slot machine for Vargo from day

one. Her first day on the job, at the Newport Beach yacht party, he handed her off to a white-haired suit named Jules Graham, the owner of a small, moderately crooked Orange County S&L Vargo had his eye on. Graham got sloppy drunk within an hour, babbling to Angela first about his wife, then of his conversion to Jesus, and then back to his wife. Vargo told her to play it like a good girl and she did, smoothing her dress over her knees and gently discouraging his hand as it rested ever higher on her brown thigh. She eventually agreed to be driven home and watched with amused detachment when he came at her like a pagan in the back of the limo. Being a good girl, she continued to gently attempt to resist. Angela had played this scene lots of times in the porn flicks; everyone said she was like Bernhardt.

The reluctant consent came and went with startling quickness on Graham's white leather couch under a picture of Oral Roberts. Afterward, huddled in his arms, her pretty white dress rumpled at her feet, she listened first to a thick glaze of drunken guilt and then pay dirt. After the wife and the conversion came the bank. He had been drinking much too much. The bank was in trouble. FSLIC—the federal regulatory agency which changed the locks in those days—was at his door. He needed to sell immediately. He needed peace.

Vargo got the information that night. Within thirty days he acquired Graham's S&L in a reverse triangular merger into a shell public company he picked up for $5,000. He paid Graham $50,000 in cash and $200 million in notes due in two years. Over those two years, he siphoned $56 million out of Graham's bank into the Caymans, then defaulted on the notes. The S&L collapsed on the day of Vargo's belated indictment, three days after he disembarked in Barranquilla. Graham himself was indicted six weeks later and eventually hung himself from a shower rod at the Beverly Wilshire on the morning of jury selection. His suicide note said he loved his wife and Jesus but his lawyer was incompetent.

The Graham caper validated everything Vargo believed about Angela and drew her to him and fixed her there, a critical appendage. For her part Angela thrived on the injection of Vargo's frenetic energy, learning his business with a fury and precision that would have made Muriel proud. They were a perfect if incongruous match. Vargo was a dreamer, the ideas flowing through him unfiltered, his mind a mere switching station for an obsessive flow of options and schemes. For execution, he had three Filipino accountants and Angela, fed by daily meetings which lasted until midnight in Vargo's penthouse condominium on the water. Vargo would pace and drink and talk while Angela and the Filipinos would pace after him, writing furiously, the next day trying to put at least a fraction of the more rational ideas into action. The explosion in real estate prices that shook southern California in the early 1980s was a booster rocket for Vargo's company, North American Diversified, and in one wild six-month spree in 1986 its net worth exploded from $5 million to $100 million. Vargo immediately stole $25 million and shifted it to the Caymans and still had pretty enough financials to drag in the thousands of investors begging to give him their money.

But the real estate deals were mere prologue for the S&Ls. It all began with that troubled S&L from the religious Mr. Graham and the wolf at his door and ended in a moment of pure inspiration. For most of its career, North American Diversified was broke, hustling lenders and begging banks for extensions on old money, for new money to pay off old debt. Suddenly, in the midst of one of his midnight ramblings, Vargo realized that now that he was the bank, all his begging days were over.

Angela Moore didn't really understand the plan when North American Diversified Savings and Loan opened up its shiny new offices in Newport Beach, California. Surrounded by some of the most expensive real estate in the world, Angela just assumed the S&L would cash in on the local deals. And even her new job did not raise her suspicions: traveling around the country fucking brokers with clients' money to lend. "Brokered deposits," it was called. Minimum deposit of at least one hundred thousand dollars, worth one hour with Angela, all secured by the federal government, and all paying jumbo rates of interest.

Angela only asked once how Vargo was going to raise the money to pay off all that jumbo interest. Vargo told her not to worry, that her job was to make the brokers horny, leave the rest to him. Back in Newport Beach, Vargo was lending all those jumbo deposits to himself and his offshore corporations for every development deal he could slice a piece of. Angela was also regularly fucking the accountant, who was completely in love with her, so the books showed North American Diversified climbing from a tiny, $20 million local S&L to a billion-dollar financial giant in a period of thirteen months. That's when Vargo discovered the Chinese.

It was almost a year after Vargo began dealing with the Chinese banks in Monterey Park that Angela realized what he was doing. At first, she didn't get it at all. Monterey Park? A little nothing off the freeway with a few good Szechuan restaurants and a lot of strange, one-story concrete buildings with small Chinese letters on the outside. When she said that to Vargo during one of their midnight meetings, he laughed.

"Is that what you think it is, Angel, kind of a Chinese laundry? With a few restaurants?"

Angela shrugged. "I don't know. It's not Newport Beach. What's it got?"

"What if I told you that the population of Monterey Park was about sixty thousand?"

"So what?"

"How many banks you think a town with sixty thousand people might need?"

"I don't know. A couple."

"You know how many banks are in Monterey Park?"

"No."

Vargo threw back a full scotch before speaking. "Eighty-seven." He laughed again. "A Chinese laundry? Maybe you're right."

Even later Angela remembered getting a confused, sinking feeling when she heard Vargo laugh that night.

That was one of only two times he ever discussed the Chinese banks with her. The second and last time, at another midnight session, Vargo showed her a check. It was a crumpled-up, tissue-thin piece of paper in the face amount of $100,000. It was dated about six months before and was smudged and all but undecipherable. On the back of the check was a series of endorsements that extended from the top of the check to the bottom. There must have been thirty of them. At the bottom was stapled a white piece of paper about six inches long with thirty more endorsements on it. Two more white slips, equal in size, equal in the number of endorsements, were stapled to the bottom of the first white slip.

All the endorsements were in Chinese.

"Can you figure out where that check's been?" Vargo had asked.

Angela stared at it and then shook her head.

Vargo was hopelessly drunk and laughed louder than Angela had ever heard him before. "Neither can anybody else!"

13

IT WASN'T THAT ANGELA DIDN'T HAVE A LIFE APART from Vargo during those two years; she did. It was just limited by her ever increasing duties. But sometimes she managed to get away.

The 26th of September, 1986, was one of those days. It was 90 degrees and smoggy, the white-brown haze sitting like a blanket on the hidden mountains in a ring around the city. The visibility downtown was about a block and a half. The Asians with cameras kept wiping their eyes and sneezing, wondering what demon had possessed them to leave Osaka for this hellhole. Then the air-conditioning broke in the fifty-story tower Vargo was calling home, and Angela stormed into his office.

"I've gotta get out of here. I'm dying."

Vargo's shirt was off and sweat was pouring down the gray hairs of his bare chest. He was hunched over a computer typing furiously. The filtered sun blasted in chunks through the dust-splattered window.

"Robert, did you hear me!"

He looked up and blinked. "What?"

"I said I'm dying. The air-conditioning's broke."

"Oh yeah." Vargo gestured to a chair holding his jacket, tie, and shirt. "Next the pants go. Wanna help?"

"I want to go. Do you have anything for me or can I get out of here?"

"How much did we get in today?"

"Lots." She gestured to the screen. "The deposits are all in there."

Vargo nodded and wiped his brow. "I got to get it moving. They're after me, you know."

She did know. The grand jury was subpoenaing everybody they did business with now. The noose was starting to squeeze. It was all they ever talked about.

"I know." She sighed. "But I can't work in this heat."

He turned back to his computer. "Be back by six."

"You got it."

She was on the beach in Santa Monica forty minutes later, stretching like a cat on a small towel. She wore something tiny and orange that had been the undoing of a broker at Shearson with inside dope on a merger earlier that summer. She had walked a mile up the beach north of the pier, separating herself from the crush of other refugees from the city's heat. Now, more or less alone, she sat back on her elbows, spread her knees wide, and tilted her face into the ozone-crusted sun.

Bobby Lee Baker, running easily along the beach with Montel, took one look, tripped on some driftwood, and fell sideways into yellow and black effluent flowing from a drainage channel into the dark brown ocean.

Montel stopped and laughed, leaning forward on the tree trunks he called legs to catch his breath. He was in the shape of his life, his massive dark black body chiseled by weights and buffed out by the steroids that fixed his knee and put thirty pounds of muscle into his thighs and shoulders. He hadn't lasted long at USC once the doctors got to him, just about long enough to realize a rehab program and a shot at the pros was a hell of a lot easier than any alternatives out there. By December of his senior year the daily, secret shots enabled him to work the leg machines twice a day, seven days a week. By spring he passed a six-hour physical at a Hilton in Chicago, then ran a 4.8 forty at a camp in Arizona. The Raiders, drooling, got him in the first round.

That left Baker and Max back in law school, or at least as close to law school as SC ever got. Baker gave a lot of thought to taking secret shots like Montel but by the spring of his senior year he gave it up, about the time he realized his knee clicked like a metronome when he walked upstairs and he could no longer beat Montel in the forty. The pros have little use for wideouts that can't run faster than offensive tackles, even a superhuman specimen like Montel.

Three years later, to everybody's shock, Baker graduated and passed the bar. They threw a huge party for him and Max about four blocks from the Coliseum and everyone from Carson came, De'Andre and Montel, the girls from Carson with three kids apiece, even the guys from SC. The party was nice and then they all left. Bobby Lee was glad he didn't have a gun because he might have stuck it in his mouth and ended it right there. Montel caught his depressed look and sat next to him. He handed him a beer.

"C'mon, Smoke, smile."

Baker smirked. "What for?"

"What for? You and Max got it made."

"Got it made? Is that what you think?"

"Absolutely. These fuckin' lawyers get to steal with both hands. Believe me, you got nothing to be sad about."

"That's not the way I see it."

"And why's that?"

Bobby Lee didn't answer, just gestured toward the window. The Coliseum loomed outside, a huge fake Roman granite structure flanked by two dark brass Olympians. A sign proclaimed the upcoming Raiders-Packers contest. Bobby Lee had played for SC in that Coliseum, and now Montel would be playing there for the Raiders. Across the parking lot the Sports Arena crowd ambled in for a preseason Clippers game. All around him, there was either vast urban devastation or professional sports. And instead, he was going to be a lawyer.

Montel got it. He looked intently at his friend.

"Hey, Smoke, you know what?"

"What?"

"You would've never made it."

Baker flushed. "What are you talking about?"

Montel leaned over and smacked Bobby Lee's bad knee with the full beer bottle. The shock took a second to register and when it did Baker howled with pain.

"What the fuck are you doing?"

"Trying to tell you something."

"What?"

Montel reached over with the bottle again and Baker flinched, retreating. "What's the matter, Smoke, afraid of getting hurt?"

"You're goddamn right."

"So what do you think it would feel like if somebody like me went after that knee for real? Somebody who gets paid maybe a couple million to send fast wideouts with soft hands to the hospital. With his livelihood on the line. What would that feel like, Smoke?"

Bobby Lee didn't answer. The very thought of Montel or anyone like him going after his knee put bumps on his arms and a clamp on his mouth. Even the beer bottle had made him scream.

"So you know what that means?"

"What?"

Montel grabbed him by the back of his hair and pulled him close. His friend's breath was beery. Bobby Lee tried to pull away but his head felt like it was nailed to a tree.

"Stay with Max. Do what he says. Chase pussy like you always done, which is all you do good anyway. Drink beer and be happy it's not worse. And one more thing."

"What?"

"Stop being a fucking baby."

Baker hadn't finished first at SC and hadn't finished last, "somewhere in between" he always told people when asked, but he finished. He didn't have a clue what job to try for so he turned to Max, who took him to visit the Republican U.S. Attorney for the Central District of

California, a man's man and an SC alum. Bobby Lee sized the guy up as a jerk after thirty seconds, a typical chip off the old block of drunken boosters who were forever smacking him on the back and talking about O.J. and student body right. Get a life, he always wanted to say, at least until Max got him programmed.

"Hi, I'm Del Crandall," the man boomed, pounding Baker in the same spot all the alums did. "This here's my chief assistant, David Shank."

Shank held out a weak fish of a hand. "Hello. I clerked for Blackmun."

"What?"

"Ignore him," Crandall bellowed. "So you're a goddamn Trojan, right?"

No more. "Yes, sir. Through my junior year."

Crandall nodded soberly. "I heard about that. A terrible thing to catch a knee." He said it like Baker had lung cancer.

"Thank you, sir."

Shank intervened. "Who have you clerked for? We need to find out who you clerked for." His tiny voice had an edge of panic in it.

"Oh Christ, shut up," Crandall barked. "I don't give a fuck about that. Goddamn, Bobby Lee Baker. Shit, you had soft hands. That game against Michigan, in the Rose Bowl, corner of the end zone? They slammed you out of bounds right up that cheerleader's dress and you still held on. You remember that?"

He vaguely remembered the catch; he vividly remembered the cheerleader. "Yes, sir, like it was yesterday." He wished it was yesterday.

"Shank, this son of a bitch led the Pac-10 in receptions his sophomore year. And man, could you take a hit. What game did you catch that knee?"

It was actually spring practice his junior year but Max had trained him well. "Up in Palo Alto, sir. Against the Cardinal."

"Stanford. Bunch of fucking pansies."

Shank looked shocked. "I went to Stanford," he whined.

"Jesus." Crandall shook his head. "They make us hire

these fucks. Anyway, Bobby Lee, you and Max want a job here, it's yours."

"We want it, sir," Max said quickly.

"But there's no clerkship," Shank screeched.

Shank insisted on being designated his instructor, to show him the ropes, guide him through rookie row, and teach him how to try cases. "A trial is the culmination of the federal criminal justice process," Shank intoned on Baker's first day. "And it is critical that the jury understand the solemnity and majesty of that process. There should be no levity, no frivolity in a trial. Our dignity is what separates federal prosecutors from the defense lawyers."

"Our dignity?" Baker asked.

"Yes, dignity." Then Shank began drawing his ideas on a blackboard and didn't stop for three weeks. At the end of those torturous days Shank told Baker he had a surprise for him.

"Yeah, what? More drawing on the blackboard?"

"No, we're done with the academics. It's time to do a trial. I've talked to Crandall and he's agreed to let you second-chair my next trial. It will be a real doozy."

Second-chair. Doozy. "Shank, what are you talking about?"

Shank walked around the room and waved his arms. "It'll be huge. A group of executives at a major defense contractor were submitting phony invoices and ripping off the government on fighter jet parts. Counterfeit ball bearings, too, if our informant is to be believed. We indicted seven of them, plus the company. We've got them on millions in overcharges. They'll fight like pigs with the best talent in the city on their side."

Baker thought about that, then smiled and put his arm around Shank's shoulders. "David, I underestimated you. Let's go."

It took six months for the case to come to trial and as the great day approached it became crystal clear, even to a rookie like Baker, that the government's case was a complete disaster. The defendants had seven sharp downtown firms with gray hair and dark suits. The government had Shank, his brains, and his paper, Baker second-chairing his first trial, and a couple of agents who sort of understood how an F-18 was put together. The government was as outgunned as the British at Dunkirk, and had much less chance of getting the troops off the beach. More importantly, Shank was gagging. With three days to go, there was no doubt in Baker's mind that Shank was stiff with fear.

"Shank, let me ask you a question," Bobby Lee said finally, when he couldn't take it anymore. It was 1 A.M. on Saturday. The jury was to be impaneled on Monday.

"What?" Shank screamed. His face was ashen. The more scared he got the more memos he wrote. The only problem was no one could understand his memos.

"The jury will be just regular people, right?"

"That's right, postal workers, secretaries, regular people. Where's our trial brief? I lost the trial brief."

"Forget the trial brief. I got a question that's more important."

"What?"

"Now don't take this the wrong way. You're a smart guy and all, and I've been listening to you for six months tell me how to try a case, and how you'll try this case, and all that stuff."

"So? Your point?"

"My point is I still don't know what you're talking about. And if I don't get it after six months of listening to you, and it's my job to listen to you, how do you figure the postal worker's gonna get it hearing it once?"

They said later that Shank's breakdown either occurred immediately after Baker's precise observation or a few hours later. Whatever, by 9 A.M. Shank was at Cedar Sinai with an I.V. in his arm rehydrating him and a team of physicians trying to find out how he had lost so much blood.

"He ulcerated something, that's all we can say," the G.I. guy told Crandall. "We'll know more in about seventy-two hours."

Crandall turned to Baker. "Seventy-two hours? The fucking trial starts Monday! What are we gonna do?"

Baker didn't see the problem. "Try the son of a bitch, I guess."

"Bobby Lee, the man's in there bleeding through his gut."

"I'm not surprised."

Crandall nodded. "Me neither. He begged me for a big one. I should have left him shuffling papers. Shit!"

"I still don't see the problem, sir," Baker said softly.

Crandall looked at him. "You mean you think you're ready to do it alone?"

"That's right."

"With a small army on the other side?"

"Same army as yesterday."

"But at least yesterday you had him." Crandall jerked a thumb toward the groaning figure in the next room.

"That's right, too. And today I don't."

Crandall laughed a little. "You mean things may actually have improved in the last few hours?"

Baker shrugged. He didn't need to bury Shank. Crandall knew. The U.S. Attorney walked over to the window and stared out. After a full minute he spoke.

"You'll need somebody. Who?"

"Give me Max."

Crandall snorted. "Another rookie."

"Max is as smart as they come. And tough too. It's up to you but we can do it."

Crandall considered it. "We could get you an extension. You want that?"

"No, sir, I don't. I don't want an extension, no grace, not anything. I want to go on Monday, just like it's scheduled, with Max."

Crandall grinned. "You got balls, Bobby Lee. I'll give you that."

Baker shrugged.

"You got brains, too? And judgment?"

"Some, I guess."

Crandall laughed heartily. "Go for it, son."

It was mobbed in Courtroom 10 at 9:30 A.M. Monday. The seven defendants sat in a row, each with a lawyer at his side. The lawyers and the defendants were indistinguishable, a picket fence of dark suits, white shirts, and striped ties. In the first three rows of the gallery the defense had an army of support—cute little paralegals, earnest, young associate lawyers, high-paid jury consultants, investigators, and palookas to schlep the documents and briefcases back and forth. The next three rows were filled with journalists from the financial and regular press reporting on the scandal and the start of the trial. Everyone on the east side of the courtroom was prosperous and well-groomed, the national elite.

Not so the west side. Filling all the spectator seats on the west side were the men and women of the jury pool, an ocean of retired postal clerks, housewives, and unemployed defense workers. On the east side of the courtroom the dress code ran heavily to Armani and Brooks Brothers. On the west side there wasn't a tie to be seen.

At the almost empty prosecution table Max and Baker sat stoically, a scared agent next to them fumbling through mostly irrelevant papers. Max was exhausted from almost forty-eight consecutive hours of immersion in the sins of the defendants. Now he could recite every document in the case by heart. Baker was exhausted too but for a different reason. Before Crandall would finally agree to the switch he made Baker sit and listen to Shank tell how he would try the case if only he hadn't gotten ulcers. That two-hour talk would be enough to exhaust anyone.

"Remember," Shank began, wincing with pain, "the opening statement is critical. You must immediately tell the jury that you are Assistant United States Attorney Baker representing the government in these proceedings. Retain your dignity. Don't argue in the opening statement or you might draw an objection. It's terrible when they object because the judge may admonish you in front of the jury. Be reserved and polite at all times. The jury will respect you."

After two hours of Shank's wisdom Baker had a screaming headache and a pretty fair idea how *not* to try cases. He cured most of the headache with Excedrin, coffee, and a snort of early morning Black Bush to send him out the door and by showtime he was ready. When he stood with the rest of the courtroom as the judge took the bench Baker got the first pure rush of adrenaline he could remember since he was returning kickoffs against Arizona. Max was pale with beads of sweat around his eyes. Baker grinned and poked him.

"What?"

"Man, isn't this fun!"

Max stared until the pounding of the gavel brought the room to attention.

Judge Arkanian was a no-nonsense Armenian who had no respect for bullshitters, downtown pomposity, or most of the people he had met in his life. He had more money than anybody in the room, including the first dollar bill he ever saw. He ran his trials from nine in the morning till seven at night, and if the pace was too much for you, no problem, plead or dismiss.

An hour after the judge took the bench the twelve peers and two alternates had been chosen, placed in the box, and sworn. Arkanian turned to Baker.

"Mr. Baker, you may open for the government. And all counsel should remember the opening statement is not for argument. Understand?"

"Yes, Your Honor," Mr. Hogart said. Bradford Hogart was from Jenkins & Dorman, and a pillar of the community. He sat with a satisfied air and rocked back in his chair.

Baker walked up to the podium and immediately started grinning. He couldn't help it. Here he was starting his first trial with the seven brides and seven brothers staring sullenly at him from the defendants' table and the twelve peers in their seats and the court reporter with her fingers poised above the keys and Max in back of him sick as a dog and his agent losing the exhibits and Arkanian rocking back with his fingers in a little steeple. Baker got to the podium and just grinned. Two of the jurors, one a grandmother with blue hair, grinned back. He wiped his still too long dirty-blond hair out of his blue-green eyes and grabbed the mike.

"Hi, my name's Bobby Lee Baker and I'm here for the United States of America." His hand swept toward the large flag above Arkanian's head. Everybody, including the defendants and their lawyers, looked toward the flag. When the heads of the jurors looked back two more had small smiles.

"And my job here today," Bobby Lee continued, "is to tell you what happened back in 1984. It's not a pretty tale, I gotta tell you that right up front. Matter of fact it's downright ugly. But facts are facts and when you hear these facts your flesh will crawl all over the ground, I promise you. 'Cause the plain fact is that these folks"— his hand now swept the defense table—"stole enough money from every one of us in one year to kill a pig."

Hogart launched from his seat like an Atlas rocket from a pad in Canaveral. His feet actually left the ground and when he landed again there was a thump. The smug grin was gone and in its place was pure purple rage.

"Your Honor," he screamed, "he is arguing! This is improper!"

Arkanian seemed vaguely amused. "Well, maybe the 'kill the pig' part, Mr. Baker."

"Okay," Bobby Lee said, turning back to the jury, "to choke a pig."

"Your Honor," Hogart bellowed.

"Sustained," Arkanian said with a larger smile now. Three members of the jury were now openly giggling. The rest looked happy, satisfied, like patrons at a movie waiting to be entertained.

"So let's get to the facts," Baker went on. His voice had suddenly and magically recaptured a far-away Southern laziness picked up either from a long dead ancestor or hanging around Montel and De'Andre too many years. Either way it worked. His slow voice, easy grin, and the mop of hair that fell involuntarily across his face when he got excited had the grandmother adopting him as her firstborn and the thirty-five-year-old twice-divorced receptionist forgetting about the trial, and instead wondering what it might be like to haul this handsome young man home for the evening, just the two of them, maybe really muss up that hair. Even the men relaxed when Bobby Lee spoke, the anxiety raised by the unfamiliar, ornate room and the pomposity of the stern suits melting in the warm cadence of Baker's simple presentation.

He spoke for only fifteen minutes that day and when he was done every juror on the panel wanted to take a bullet for him.

The jury went through the formality of listening to the suits talk but it wasn't the same. Hogart was first and took an hour and a half and then the other six did the same. By the time the third of them got through the entire jury panel was staring stone-faced with their arms folded across their chests. Then came the fidgeting and yawns, all ignored by speakers infatuated with the sound of their own voices. At the end Baker turned to Max.

"We got this locked."

Max's eyes were wide. "You are nuts. Certifiable."

"Take my word for it. These guys are toast."

Bobby Lee proved even more naturally adept as the witnesses came on. He had an innate way of keeping things simple without patronizing the jury, and they loved him for it. The downtown suits, blinded by their ability to master complex facts, showed off at every opportunity. At one point Hogart, explaining a technical point, led with his chin. "This may be difficult for a layman, but we professionals in the legal community refer to this as a . . ." The jury wanted to shoot him.

Six weeks later it was over. The final arguments were made—Bobby Lee's took thirty minutes; the defense took six hours. The jury instructions were given by an obviously delighted Judge Arkanian, and the jury retired. When the marshal closed the ornate door behind the last of them Arkanian turned to the lawyers.

"Well, that's that. You can go but not too far. You're all on thirty minutes call. Any problems?"

"Just one, Your Honor," Hogart droned. He walked officiously to the podium. "I'm due to deliver an important address in San Francisco in four days' time. Will the court indulge my schedule and permit me to participate in these proceedings by conference call?"

"That won't be any problem, Mr. Hogart."

"Thank you, Your Honor."

"No way is this jury going to take four days."

It didn't even take four hours. Max and Baker left the courtroom, stored the thousands of pages of binders and documents, and then went immediately to Max's office to break out the Black Bush. Baker raised his glass.

"To the Irish and their whiskey."

"I never saw anybody who toasted more than you," Max said, nevertheless tipping his glass. "Don't you know it interferes with the rhythm of drinking?"

"Max, we are done, fucking done. Do you get that?"

"That I'll drink to." They clicked glasses.

"Me, too," Crandall boomed. He came in and grabbed the bottle.

"Sir," Max began apologetically. "We really don't do this very often. It's just . . ."

"I'm fucking shocked," Crandall said. He poured a half water glass of the Bush, left out the ice, and drank half of it down. He shuddered as it did its job. "Nothing like wrapping your lips around a cute little Black Bush on a Friday afternoon. Speaking of the whiskey of course."

"Of course," Max said.

Crandall turned to Baker. "How do you feel?"

"Me? Like I just won the lottery. I'm done."

"That's all?"

"What else?"

Crandall drank again. He seemed to need the burn. "Yeah, one more thing. Bobby Lee, let me tell you something. I got over a hundred Assistant U.S. Attorneys in this office. I've been a lawyer for twenty-two years. I've watched hundreds of jury trials and tried a hundred myself."

"Yes, sir."

Crandall walked over close. His breath smelled of the whiskey he was drinking. "There is nobody, you hear me, nobody, that is any better than you. You got rough spots, everybody does their first time, but it don't matter. That jury *loved* you, that's what matters. One time you were fumbling up there and the old lady with the blue hair almost cried. That's nothing I can teach, Bobby Lee."

"Thank you, sir." He guessed it was a compliment. Either that or he was being told he was dumb and cute.

"All I can tell you, Bobby Lee, is you'll be doing this for a long time." Well, who knew. They clicked glasses and drank a little more fire. Baker was spared more hosannas by a banging at the door.

"What?" Crandall barked.

The door opened tentatively and a pasty face crept in. It was Shank, freshly back from his ulcers.

"Sorry to disturb you, sir, but it's important. They're back. They got a verdict."

14

ANGELA HAD SPOTTED THE TWO YOUNG MEN RUNNING toward her long before they got close. The runners intrigued her and she rose on her elbows to watch. The big black was awesome. He ran with a light effortless gait that belied his size. His pale companion was lean and muscled. The sun had lightly tanned his otherwise fair skin and even more than the big black he seemed to glide over the ground, his feet lightly pushing off the hard sand at the water's edge, the high speed easy for him to maintain. Both were cruising hard and fast over the dark sand. Both were athletes, she had no doubt about it.

Either one, Angela thought as they got closer. Either or both, preferably both.

She thought they'd just pass her by until Bobby Lee caught her smile and tripped. Montel's laugh was long and deep, and she was stunned by the sheer size of him up close. She had never seen anybody like him, and she found herself staring at the three hundred plus pounds of steroid-and-barbell–pumped muscle, all jammed into a six-foot-six frame. One could only imagine what it might be like to . . . She suspended her speculations to inspect Bobby Lee.

He got up wet, sandy, and embarrassed. He was shirtless and smooth, with none of the daunting mass of the black. Angela laughed easily at the sight of his sand-caked running shoes. Cute, she thought, and after all, this is why I came here. He took his shoes off and held them up.

"This is your fault, you know."

Angela had no doubt. "I do know."

"So what are you going to do about it?"

"What should I do about it?"

What a beautiful day, Baker thought. "Have dinner with me for starts?"

"I'd love to," Angela said.

In retrospect, from the perspective of a quiet evening watching sitcoms in the Boron playroom, it was not such a beautiful day, but back then who knew. They all stayed around on the beach and chatted for a while until Montel announced he had to get back to work. The Jets were teeing it up against the Raiders the next afternoon, and Montel had to go get taped up or anesthetized or whatever three-hundred-pound offensive tackles did the day before a game. That left Bobby Lee to hang around, which he did. Max and Bobby Lee were on their own by now, practicing out of a converted California bungalow high on the Ocean Avenue bluffs overlooking the beach. There were actually three small Craftsman bungalows on the property, one they used as an office, the other two they lived in. It was the sort of operation that didn't really require either of them to go to work unless they wanted to. Right now Baker definitely did not want to.

They talked on the beach until the sun started to slip away and it got cold, then agreed to meet for dinner at seven-thirty. Rafferty had a client with a restaurant on Pacific Coast Highway who owed them money. The deadbeat restaurateur arranged the full show: table outside on the bluffs, champagne on ice as they arrived, lots of expensive appetizers, a solicitous waiter. The client came by at the beginning and assured them it was all on the house. Since the guy owed them about twenty thousand in back fees, he wasn't being all that much of a sport with the free meal. Nevertheless, Angela said she was impressed.

There were a few million times in Boron when Baker remembered this evening, and inevitably wondered how it might have all turned out if only he had been a little more cautious. Then again, the way Angela looked . . . She arrived wearing something sleeveless, short and floral, a dash of summer flash set off by a daze of red-and-green costume jewelry and a gorgeous smile. She was all tan legs and brown bare shoulders wrapped in light silk.

"Versace," she explained, "a gift from a friend."

Baker nodded, barely hearing the words, never asking about the friend.

The evening slid easily past sunset and into darkness. The deadbeat owner kept the champagne flowing past the crash of the sun as it slipped into the pocket of the horizon. Baker found himself wrapped in a warm blanket of wine, food, and the sight of Angela's shock of red hair and grass green eyes. She spoke and laughed easily, listening hungrily, opening him wide like a fresh clam. It was expert, almost as though she did it for a living.

By the end of the second bottle of champagne, she had covered his playing days at Carson, friendship with Montel, time at SC, and lack of religion. Then she turned to business.

"You know we've been here all this time and I don't even know what you do."

"I'm a lawyer."

"Really?"

He gestured. "Me and Max have an office down the coast in Santa Monica. Max is the brains."

"What kind of work do you do?"

"All trial work. We're both ex–Assistant U.S. Attorneys and that's what we did there, try cases. Now all kinds of people come to us, particularly business crooks."

Business crooks. Angela leaned forward. "What kind of business crooks?"

"All kinds. Bankers, stockbrokers, lawyers, engineers, doctors, nuns, priests, you name it, they're scamming. You'd be surprised how many little games are working out there."

She didn't look that surprised. "Are they all guilty?"

Baker shrugged. "Some yes, some no. Sometimes a guy will just have a bad attitude. The regulators will hound him to his grave. Other times . . ." He spread his hands. It was the question everyone wanted answered. How do you represent someone you believe in your heart is guilty? The answer—that you never believe it in your heart because you never ask the question; that it doesn't matter anyway to a professional because he has a job to do, like a plumber; that the question has no meaning—not only is not satisfactory to the average person but tends to infuriate instead of explain. Given that inevitable reaction, most defense lawyers will mumble something about constitutional rights.

But Angela didn't ask that question. She asked another. "So, if you've got, say . . . suspicions about your client, what do you do?"

"Depends. If we're just giving the guy advice, we move him back to the middle, try to keep him from getting indicted. If he's already been indicted—"

"Then it doesn't matter whether he's guilty or not, you just do your job, try his case, and try to win?"

"Right. An innocent guy is too much pressure anyway."

Angela poured some more champagne. The waiter came over but she waved him away.

She probed for the next hour and decided halfway through she had found what they had been so desperately looking for, a straightforward, no bullshit trial lawyer who knew his way around federal court. Vargo had by that time been attracting the feds like a dog attracts flies: bank regulators, securities regulators, a grand jury investigation, and at least three search warrants that they knew about. An AUSA named Beck had subpoenaed their best investors and had the FBI swarming over their records. Yet when they went storming into the offices of their white-shoe downtown lawyers—the same stiffs who made millions putting together the deals to start with—they were greeted not with immediate action but horrified stares. Angela got it right away. Their traditional lawyers had as much interest in helping them as the passing cops had on that cold Nevada highway so long ago. She needed somebody different, somebody with balls and brains. A simple enough requirement, but thus far an impossible combination to find.

There was finally a pause while she sorted it all out. Baker broke into her reverie. "How about you?"

"Me?" she said absently. "I'm a businesswoman, I guess you'd say."

"Really? What kind?"

She ignored the question. "Listen, I'd like you to meet somebody."

"Who?"

"A . . . friend of mine. He's in trouble and I think you can help him."

"Sure."

"I'll just be a second." She got up and walked out as the entire restaurant stared wistfully after her. Vargo was out but she left a message that she would meet him at his office at midnight. Important. Then she went back to Baker.

Bobby Lee was depressed. With the help of his dead-beat client he had arranged a night that would melt this woman's heart and maybe even lift her pretty silk dress. But instead of romance it turned out she was a business lady, interested in the product he had to sell. Okay, he'd listen, then turn it over to Rafferty. Rafferty had the business head, and Baker smelled that's what her friend's problem was.

Angela sat down. Her face was animated. "My friend's not there. Is there any way we could meet tomorrow? At your office?"

"Sure. I'll tell Max to come by."

"No."

"Pardon?"

"I said, 'no.' You've got to be there."

"That's flattering but . . ."

She grinned and leaned over; the sea breeze caught her light dress and pressed it against her. "I really am good about sizing up people right away. And I need *you* there, not your partner."

"Thanks, but I'm in trial now. Anyway, if it's some complicated business deal, I got to tell you that Max is the one who understands that stuff. I'm good in front of a jury maybe, but—"

She put a finger to his lips. He shut up right away. "Listen, I know we're asking a lot. Maybe . . . well maybe you should charge my friend a premium."

"A premium?"

"And maybe," Angela said smiling, "you can charge me a premium too."

"Yeah?"

"Yeah."

Bobby Lee Baker met Robert Vargo for the first time at eight the next morning. They were in Rafferty's office watching the pelicans feast on sewer-engorged fish skimmed from the top layer of scum on Santa Monica Bay. Vargo came with Angela, the two of them dressed identically in dark business suits. Vargo carried a briefcase that he kept by his side, locked with some sort of high-tech combination lock.

Physically, Vargo appeared to Baker a gnome, short and squat, muscular, with oily skin and a dark, full mustache. He was constantly in motion, constantly talking, impatient at any hint of failure to satisfy his whims. He paced incessantly, stared sightlessly out the window, spoke into walls or the floor, lectured rather than conversed. His hands never stopped moving, adjusting his tie, smoothing his hair, gesturing. In the first thirty minutes, he took off his jacket and put it back on three times by Baker's count.

To call him high-strung would be a crude but true assessment. He bellowed out a harangue, sometimes coherent, of the failures of his previous lawyers. They were cowardly and stupid, fit only to kill trees with reams of unintelligible paper and charge large fees. Now that he needed them, now that matters were tense, the pussies were nowhere to be found. He needed a change.

Baker got bored with Vargo's act fairly quickly and let his mind wander to the question of what sort of premium Angela might have in mind. It seemed that since he left the U.S. Attorney's office, now six months behind him, these kinds of thoughts were more and more ruling his life. Midlife crisis, he supposed. When that thought struck him, Angela turned, caught his gaze and meaning, and smiled an assurance. That was pretty much the end of Bobby Lee's judgment on the intake of Vargo as a client.

Rafferty was more hardheaded, maybe because he hadn't heard about the second premium. Even so, this was his kind of case and he wanted in. He let Vargo's ravings wash over him, politely ignored all of them, then asked the tough questions.

"Let me get this straight. Is there or is there not a grand jury investigation? Just start there."

Angela interjected. "Yes." She turned to Vargo. "Robert, we must move this along if you want them to help us."

Vargo sat down. "Yes," he said. "They got a grand jury."

"Who's running it? Bobby Lee and I used to work down there. We ought to know the assistant assigned to it."

"Hell, I don't know," Vargo sputtered. "It's a lot of bullshit. Let me tell you about this one deal they're looking at. It's clean, I tell you, clean. They got nothing on—"

"Beck," Angela interrupted gently. "Julie Beck is the Assistant U.S. Attorney." She handed Rafferty a copy of a subpoena with Beck's name on it.

Rafferty looked at Baker and shrugged. Whoever this Beck was, she was new.

"Never heard of her, which can cut both ways," Rafferty said. "She's not someone we know, so it may be harder to deal with her. On the other hand, maybe she hasn't been around long enough to really know what she's doing."

"She knows enough to fuck up my life, I can tell you that," Vargo barked.

"What exactly is she looking into?"

"North American Diversified and everything it owns. That grand jury has subpoenaed my S and L, my off-shore corporate records, my accountants, and my real estate partners. She's got everybody I've ever dealt with scared shitless. I can't do business like that."

"What do your lawyers say?"

Vargo laughed. "My lawyers send me thirty-page memos I need to hire a lawyer to translate. My lawyers are worthless pieces of shit."

"Did they tell you how long?"

"Six months. They found out that much. Six months to indictment."

"We've got to move fast, then." Rafferty hesitated. "It will be expensive." Baker smiled inwardly. Rafferty wanted in but not enough to commit suicide.

"How much?"

"We'll charge you by the hour with a substantial retainer."

"You didn't answer my question, but that's all right. Let's cut through it." Vargo held out his hand and Angela put a checkbook in it. He wrote hurriedly, ripped a check out, and gave it to Rafferty. "And he has to work on it, too." He jerked a thumb toward Baker. "I don't know why but she wants it. To me, the guy hasn't opened his mouth."

Baker came alive at that. He didn't like Vargo and didn't want to work on his lousy case. "Max, I'm in trial," he pleaded. "Besides, with all these numbers and documents, this is really up your alley. Anyway . . ."

Rafferty handed the check to Baker. It was for $100,000, marked "Retainer."

"I figure that'll get you started," Vargo said. "When that gets low, we'll throw you another bean."

Bean. What an interesting way to refer to $100,000. How many more beans might there be before the case was over?

"So it's settled, then," Angela said. "You'll work on it?"

For the beans. And the premium. And the love of the law. His current trial wouldn't take forever.

"Sure," Bobby Lee said.

15

SO THEY WEREN'T SAINTS. BUT THE WORLD ISN'T MADE up of saints. By and large.

At the beginning it didn't matter because Baker was pretty much out of it. He'd come around and show his face from time to time, just to keep the peace, but nobody really expected him to do anything. Max was the only one who could understand an elaborate scheme like Vargo's, and Baker figured when the time was right Max would tell him what he had to know.

That time came a lot sooner than Baker wanted, on a Friday night three weeks after Vargo entered their lives. The two partners were sitting on the front porch with their feet up, watching the traffic congest on Ocean Avenue. The twilight was thick with sea breeze and in an hour the sun would sink, orange and tainted with the reflected poisons of the city, into the injured blue waves. There was a green park across from their bungalow office which hovered on a bluff above the Pacific Coast Highway. The human refuse from the city used it as a dormitory. The blankets and shopping carts were already being assembled in the choice spots in preparation for the weekend.

Baker had been sitting with his feet on the railing contemplating the universe by the time Max joined him. Max held a bottle of Black Bush, a bucket of ice, and two small glasses.

"To our first bean?" Max offered.

"I don't know. Does that mean I'm drinking to Vargo?"

"Nope. Just his money. You can even call him an asshole while you're drinking."

"Fair enough." Baker allowed Max to pour him a drink, then held the glass up in tribute. "To Robert Vargo, our esteemed client, an asshole." Baker drank that burning toast and winced. "And believe me, I appreciate you keeping him out of my face."

That much was true. For the past three weeks Max and Vargo had been inseparable, and Baker was sure that Max now knew everything there was to know about Vargo's sleazy empire. Max even carried around a thick black binder filled with notes and graphs about Vargo's deals. Baker leaned over and grabbed the binder, opening to a page at random. The page was a chart filled with odd names and intersecting arrows.

"I hope to God I never have to understand this," Baker prayed.

That deserved another toast, which cheered him. Things could be a lot worse. Here they were out by the beach, far from the stiffs downtown, sipping good Black Bush bought with a bean from a guy who needed them like a man with a brain tumor needs a surgeon. Now, all Max had to do was figure out how to do the work, then spoon-feed it to Baker to work the Mick magic.

Yet, maybe it wasn't as bad as it looked. Baker picked up Max's incomprehensible chart and squinted at it.

"If I ask you to explain this, can you do it in two minutes?"

"Sure," Rafferty said, pouring another for the journey. "You'll have to learn it sooner or later. Pick a company."

"Montana Corp."

"Good choice. Montana Corporation owns an office building in Century City. About five hundred thousand square feet. Montana is owned one hundred percent by Brighton Corporation, a Nevada corporation." Max pointed to the arrows on the chart.

"Yeah?"

"Now Brighton in turn is owned one hundred percent by Achilles Limited. That's a Cayman Islands limited liability company."

"Yeah? So who owns Achilles?"

Max's finger traced along the page. "Right here. A Liechtenstein *anstalt* named Euclid Management, S.A. And before you ask, Euclid is nominally owned by a Liechtenstein lawyer in Vaduz named Dr. Argot. On paper he owns thousands of corporations, or *anstalts* as they're called. Under Liechtenstein law, he is forbidden from disclosing the identity of the beneficial owners."

"Convenient."

"Quite."

"So what's the point?"

"Well, remember where we started, with the building in Century City?"

"Yeah."

"Well, the building on paper cost ninety million to construct."

"You mean maybe it didn't?"

Rafferty shrugged his shoulders.

"It's now rented out to commercial tenants and the rents are paid into accounts in the U.S., then wired out to Dr. Argot in Vaduz."

"And what does Dr. whatever do?"

"He pays the bank loan down. Of course with a ninety-million-dollar loan to work down there's no profit on paper and no taxes to pay. But at least the bank makes money."

"What bank?"

"An S and L."

"Which?"

Rafferty tapped a pencil at the chart. At the source of one of the rivers of names was Liberty Home S&L, pouring money down the various streams. Montana Corp. wasn't close to the top.

"Vargo's S and L?"

"Vargo owns nothing. North American Diversified owns one hundred percent of Liberty."

"But cut through the bullshit. He's loaning to himself. If the deal works, he gets rich. If not, the taxpayer eats it."

Rafferty smiled. "That's close enough." He poured for his partner. "Drink up, Bobby, you'll need it. Someday you'll have to explain all this to a jury.'

Once they figured out that Baker couldn't even read the charts, much less understand them, they decided to play to his strengths.

"He'll never get this," Vargo screamed at Rafferty. "I left a box of documents in his office to review, but . . ."

"I saw that," Angela agreed. "He turned pale."

"So, what's he good for?" Vargo stormed.

"Lots," Angela said.

"She's right," Rafferty said. "Bobby Lee's the kind of guy people believe."

"So what? I repeat, what's he good for?"

"To try the case, for one thing," Rafferty said. "Nobody's better in front of a jury than Bobby Lee Baker. That was true in the U.S. Attorney's office and it's true now."

Vargo snorted.

"Just put a few women on it," Angela said. "He'll do fine."

"You people are crazy. I don't want a jury. I don't even want to get indicted. What can he do for us now?"

"Something very important," Rafferty said. "Right now we need to get somebody to get inside Julie Beck's head, find out what she's thinking. When is she going to indict? What counts? What deals is she making with cooperating witnesses? What documents does she have access to? What informants? Who's going to testify at trial?"

Vargo turned to Angela. "I can't believe this. He thinks she'll just open up to Baker."

"He's the best. He won't get it all, but he'll get something."

"If it was me—" Angela began.

"Yeah, yeah, we know," Vargo interrupted. "But with all due respect, that doesn't eliminate many people."

Angela smiled. "Respect acknowledged."

"So I say, let's send him," Rafferty said.

Angela had no doubt. "I'd send him anyplace."

Vargo snorted again. "A fuckin' waste of time."

It wasn't until a month later, in January of 1987, that he finally went. It was the best day of a bad year, a twisted, perverse omen in retrospect. The fake mountains surrounding the real federal courthouse downtown were visible for the first time in months, bright and snow-capped from a recent storm, ringing the city inside a dark blue setting of sky. The faithless air was so pure it gave everyone a headache because the carbon monoxide was gone. Baker figured things could be a lot worse: the air was clear, Vargo had thrown Max another bean, and Angela had let Bobby Lee know she hadn't forgotten. And now a no-brainer at the U.S. Attorney's office, a little schmoozing, a little old-time Irish bullshit, and see what he could walk away with.

What could go wrong?

The U.S. Attorney's office in Los Angeles is downtown, hard against the wheels of rebellion, safe against sin on the twelfth floor of the federal courthouse. The elevator opens on to a secure anteroom dominated by portraits of the U.S. Attorney and the ongoing President of the United States, whatever the respect due either. Along a wall is an alphabetical list of the one hundred twelve AUSAs and their specialties. AUSA Julie Beck was in criminal, Major Frauds, third from the bottom.

Baker left the list and walked over to the bulletproof glass–encased receptionist. A microphone faced him from the wire-glass grate.

"How's tricks?"

The receptionist looked up in shock.

"Well, look what the cat drug in."

"Nice talk, Marcia. I was just about to comment on your weight loss."

"Shit, Baker." Marcia was about two hundred forty pounds in her stocking feet; she used to be two hundred ninety when Bobby Lee was an assistant.

"It's true. You been dieting, right?"

"Off and on. You really think so?" She squirmed a little in her seat.

"Absolutely." He stuck a hand around the frosted glass enclosure and let her slap it.

"Anyway, Baker, who you here to see?"

He sidled up close to the microphone in front of the glass booth. There was nobody in the anteroom.

"Somebody new. What do you know about somebody named Julie Beck?"

Marcia rolled her eyes. "Forget it, Bobby Lee. She ain't your type."

"Why not?"

"A little cold, you know what I mean?"

"I'm not here to ask her out. I got a client."

"Who the hell hired you?"

"Nice talk, Marcia. Now that I look closer, maybe you kept it on after all."

Marcia's many folds rolled with her laughter. "Too late, Baker. You already told me the truth."

"Come on. Time is money."

"She's gonna chew you up, sweet stuff."

"Yeah?"

"That's the word. Heart like a rock. Smart, too."

Shit. "Who's she been working with?"

"Mostly herself. Nobody wants any part of her."

"That bad?"

"Supposed to be rich as shit too, Baker. So maybe she is your type, the way you like to work."

"C'mon, Marcia, think. There's got to be somebody."

"Let me see." She fiddled with a pencil for a while. "Frederickson," she said finally.

"Jesus Christ." Nobody worked with Frederickson. The guy was the only assistant who actually managed to lose every now and again.

"I'm sure. They tried a tax case last year."

Two outcasts. "Is he in?"

She consulted her list. "Yup."

"Marcia, beam me in."

Marcia buzzed and the lock disengaged. Alumni status had its privileges. He wandered around unescorted, nodding amiably at the familiar agents who passed him in the hall. The fourth door down was Al Frederickson's.

Baker had forgotten just how depressingly gun-metal gray the U.S. Attorney's office was. In hundreds of tiny indistinct offices crammed with paper, young lawyers toiled away at their three-year commitments. For the best of them, it was a staging area for the money and prestige private practice would bring at the big downtown firms. In the meantime, the top assistants got headline-grabbing trials, and everyone, the good and bad alike, got to lead federal judges around like show ponies. And for all the publicity it was really a pressure-free job because it took a significant effort to actually lose anything as an AUSA.

Al Frederickson was equal to the challenge. Scrawny, bald, ill-tempered, and fifty, Frederickson had been losing cases at the U.S. Attorney's office for as long as anyone could remember. He had a whiny, nasal voice combined with a terror of public speaking. His initial appointment had been a favor to a one-term congressman from the Valley; now, absent an act of treason, he had a lifetime job. Frederickson was not one of the sparkling assistants the downtown money was lining up to seduce.

"Al, how's the boy?" Baker roared as he came in the door. He pounded Frederickson's back and shook his hand. Al looked stunned, not clearly remembering when anybody had ever done that before.

"Bobby, nice to see you," he said, looking right and left.

"Hell, yeah, it's good to get back, see everybody, you know?" Baker kicked the door shut. Frederickson reacted as if he'd been shot. Baker sat on the edge of his desk. "So what'ya been up to? Any interesting stuff?"

"Oh, yes," Frederickson whined, his eyes darting. "It's always exciting."

"I heard about that bank robbery acquittal. Too bad. Couldn't get the videotape in, huh?"

"Oh, no, we had good photos. They had a defense, you know, that it was an evil twin. Everybody supposedly has a twin someplace."

God. "Hey, those cases are tough." He patted Al sympathetically. "How about office scuttlebutt? Who's screwin' who these days? How about Judge Harrigan and that court reporter?"

"Well, I usually don't hear too much about that, Bobby. You know that."

"The hell you say. I been hearin' about you, Al. It's always the quiet ones."

"I . . . don't understand."

"Right. How about six months ago? Tax case? You and a certain new assistant. I heard you showed her more than the ropes."

Frederickson squinted. "Julie? Is that who you mean?"

"Julie. Yeah, that's her. What's she like, Al? From the inside."

"If you think I . . ." All of a sudden Al Frederickson began laughing. It was the first time Baker had ever heard him do that. It was a weird, choking sound which was maybe why he kept it hidden.

"If I think what, Al?"

"Oh, goodness." Frederickson wiped his eyes. His voice was firm. "No way, Bobby."

"Not a beauty, huh?"

Frederickson again laughed so hard he got the hiccups. "You never met her, Bobby," he said when he finally caught his breath. "I know that now."

"C'mon, Al, give."

"She's gorgeous."

"Yeah?"

Al closed his eyes. Baker felt like he was watching a guy at a peep show. "Ice-blond, almost white hair. Cut real short, like a boy's, you know?" He began using his hands. "And just an unbelievable body. Tight and round and—"

"Okay, Al, I get it. So why'd you laugh? You should be all over that like a cheap suit."

Al shook his head. "She don't like boys."

"Bullshit."

"I'm telling you I tried. No luck."

"That don't mean she don't like boys, Al."

"Dyke city, Bobby Lee. No heart, either."

"What does that mean?"

He leaned over. "You know that tax case?"

"Yeah?"

"The guy was a first offender. No record. He's out on bail the whole time. Just beggin' us to make a deal, you know how they get. Me, I said 'okay.' She says, 'yeah, we'll make a deal, plead to five counts. No lids, take your chances.' Shit, we only indicted him on six counts."

"No deals."

"Right. Then at the end, she makes a pitch to the jury that just fries this guy. Jury's back in two hours. The guy's wife and two kids are watching from the cheap seats. Boy, ten, girl, six."

"Let me guess."

"You got it. Elliott's the judge and he lets the jury go. It's just us, the defense, the wife and kids. I'm listening to them cry in the back. I figure, what the fuck, set bail, let him appeal, put his life in order. I never got the chance."

"Jesus."

"She got up and told Elliott she wants an immediate remand, no bail pending appeal. She even had a brief already written. The guy's wife and kids are bawling and the defense is screaming. I'm hiding my face. It don't matter."

"Elliott never ruled against the government in his life."

"Didn't this time, either. Told the guy to stay put and walked off the bench. Two minutes later, the marshal comes in and cuffs him. Right in front of—"

"I get it."

Baker got a little unnerved by the story. This was a true believer, the worst kind. Ruthless, smart, and good in front of a jury if she won a case with Al on it. He was concentrating so hard he never heard the door open. Al brought him back to earth.

"Bobby?"

"Yeah?"

"I'd like you to meet someone."

Baker turned and saw her standing there. Her arms were filled with accordion folders and there was a pencil in her mouth. She did have a magnificent body.

"Bobby Lee Baker, say hello to Julie Beck."

16

"I'VE HEARD OF YOU," SHE SAID, SITTING BACK AND studying him. She shook her head and the white-blond hair swept from her eyes. The eyes were worn, sliced with lines. They were also emerald green, oval, and beautiful.

She had led him down the hall to her bleak office four doors south of Frederickson, then pointed to the straight-backed wooden chair. Case files were piled on every horizontal surface, including a fabric couch and two metal cabinets. Three carts from the library were cluttered with books; many more were lying open on the floor, littered with yellow tags. The walls were bare and depressingly functional: no diplomas, no posters, no newspaper clippings, no artists' renditions of Julie on the job, no pictures, not of her, not of anybody. There was a bland government calendar tacked next to her. It was crowded with entries and more yellow stickers.

"I can explain," Baker began.

"Two guns, the stories go. Bobby Lee Baker and his pal, Rafferty. They'd try anything and never lost. A regular legend around here."

"Like you and Frederickson."

"Right." She chuckled faintly.

"Anyway," he said, "it's not too hard to win here. Anybody who's got the flag and the judge is off to a pretty good start. They ought to make these judges employees of the office and cut down on paperwork."

"Some guys lose. Take Frederickson, for instance."

"No thanks. From what I hear, he's yours, darling."

"Darling?" She glanced at the ceiling considering the phrase. "How quaint." When she looked down at him again her jaw was set. "And now you need to see me," she said stiffly.

"I got a client. Me and Max."

"Congratulations."

"His name is Robert Vargo."

"I see." Her eyes glistened with interest and she leaned forward. "I'm listening."

Baker had to promote her to the "A" team right away. The only imperative in this type of meeting was to get information and avoid giving information. Flattery, guile, flirtations, bullshit about SC football, all were permissible if they led to that single goal. The cardinal rule was a simple one: whoever talked lost; whoever listened won. Trading information was permissible, sometimes mandatory, as long as the net information received was greater in quality, not necessarily quantity, than that given. When in doubt, look to that same north star: whoever was talking was losing; whoever listening winning.

Baker decided to fill the room with meaningless noise, create the illusion of talking, tell her a lot but nothing she didn't know.

"He's a new client," he began. "We don't even understand his business yet. I figure rather than get confused, maybe interfere with your investigation, I'd come down and just talk to you. Who knows, maybe we can make a deal.''

She never flinched.

"Who knows," she said.

Jesus, Baker thought. He grabbed a pad. "So what's he done?"

"Violated a wide variety of federal laws."

"That I knew. C'mon, what's he done?"

She waved the question away. "Let's start at the beginning." Now she grabbed a pad. "What's he told you about this case so far?"

This was starting to look like a long rally at Forest Hills. "How much he's going to pay us."

"How much?"

"Right."

"Better be careful. It's probably stolen."

"Bird in the hand and all that." He smiled at her.

Now Julie Beck shifted a little too. She was usually in charge at these meetings, quickly watching a defense lawyer's arrogance crumble before her until he begged for a deal. She could kick Baker out at any time but didn't want to. Part of it was the case, and what they might get, part was to see how the great legend handled himself. Besides, she had to admit, he didn't look so bad sitting there across from her, with his hair falling boyishly across his face. Nice lean hard body too, she noticed. She decided to take a chance, invest a little information, see what happened.

"Okay," she said finally. "We're six months to indictment."

"For what?"

"Securities fraud. Tax evasion. S and L fraud. That's for starters."

Baker wrote it all down then held up his hands like a movie director framing a shot. "I think I got it now. I see about a six-month trial with the jury asleep for five of them. I put on no case. Then in closing I tell the jury, 'Maybe she understands what just went on, but I don't and I don't guess you do either. Anyway, if you do, go ahead, convict. If not, let's all go home.' "

Julie actually smiled at that one. She dropped her pad on the desk.

"Where did that Tennessee twang come from?"

"It's in the family. Juries bring it out."

"So I heard. What are you gonna do next? Push the hair back? Bat the baby blues?"

"Always."

She laughed and tried not to remember that she didn't laugh much. This was fun and her cases weren't often fun.

"C'mon," Baker said softly. "Tell me what you got. Make it easy on us."

"I don't know yet."

"You're playing games."

"No, really, I don't. Not specifically anyway."

"What generally?"

"Some transactions we know are fraudulent. His S and L is a joke. There's other deals we have suspicions on but we're not sure."

"Like what?"

She hesitated. "Ask him about the Chinese banks."

"In China? Who the fuck deals with Chinese banks?"

"That's sweet. Profanity designed to intimidate." She raised her index finger and wagged it back and forth.

"What's that?"

"That's a guy wagging. Guys come in here all the time and wag at me just to show me they've got one. That's my signal back. You got one, Bobby Lee?"

Baker found himself flushing with quick anger. He leaned over her desk. His face was close to hers. "I got one. I promise you," he said softly.

"Okay," she said abruptly. Her smirk was gone.

"You know something else?" His voice was still soft and his face was still close.

"What?"

"You're fucking gorgeous. There, I said it again."

She tried to be cool. "Thank you."

"You're welcome. Now let me ask you something else."

"What?" She tried not to imagine what someone might think who walked in the door. Their faces were inches apart.

"Have dinner with me. The hell with Vargo, let Max take him. I hate the son of a bitch anyway."

106

"I can't."

"Why?"

"You know," she said, now barely audibly.

"I do know. Frederickson told me."

Her head snapped. "Frederickson? What did that worthless . . . What did he say?"

"You're a homosexual. Everyone knows it. Bull-dyke city."

She lost it then, burying her face in her hands. When she raised her head, she had a grin. "I'm going to castrate him."

"Watch your language. People might think you have one."

"Anyway, forget it."

"Why?"

"I told you."

"Not now?"

"Right."

"You didn't say not ever."

She nodded, then rose to her feet. She walked around the desk and sat on it facing him. She crossed her legs and her skirt rose. The smiles had now left both their faces and had been replaced by concentration. When she spoke her voice had gotten husky, what he would soon learn was her own special jury voice. "No, Bobby Lee Baker, I didn't say never."

When Baker got back to his office, the night was black, an eerie blackness because the windows opened only onto a moonless ocean, unbroken until a line of coast lights flickered in the distance twenty miles north in Malibu. He turned on the lights, heard a sound, and wheeled toward Rafferty's office. The door was closed.

He listened for voices and heard none. The door was locked. He took his passkey and opened the door.

Robert Vargo was sitting behind Rafferty's desk, carefully going through Rafferty's drawers.

Baker had opened the door so softly that Vargo still didn't see him. Vargo was intently examining what appeared to be a financial file. Occasionally he made notes on a green, flat pad.

"Don't move," Baker said softly.

Vargo looked up and blinked. Just blinked. Baker could almost hear the man's brain shifting into high gear, trying to come up with an explanation like he was sifting soft sand hunting for a lost diamond. Bobby Lee's intense dislike for the man now beautifully matured into hatred.

"How did your meeting go?" Vargo said finally, stalling for time. "Can we make a deal?"

"What?"

"I said, can we make a deal? Your meeting today was critical. I need to know every detail."

"You've got to be kidding."

"No. Please begin."

Baker walked over to him. "How about if I begin by ripping you out of that chair by the hair?"

More blinks.

"Get up."

Vargo glared at him, then complied. He kept the folder in his hands.

"What's in there?"

"Personal papers. Max kindly allowed me to use his office after our meeting this evening."

"Did he kindly allow you to go through his drawers?"

"I put some papers in his drawer during our meeting. I was retrieving them."

"Right. So let's call Max and check it out."

"Please do. He's in the back office."

Rafferty answered on the third ring. "Max, this is Baker. Okay, how you doin'? Listen, I'm in the office. Did you authorize Vargo to stay? . . . Okay, what about papers in your desk? . . . Okay, it's your call."

Baker hung up the phone. "You're covered."

"As I told you." He started to walk away but Baker grabbed his arm. "Let me go."

Baker ignored him and grabbed the folder from the man's hands. He leafed through the pages. They appeared to be Vargo's financial documents, yet of a curious sort. On the left-hand side were addresses: a jewelry operation in downtown L.A.; a warehouse in the Valley; a bank in Century City. The middle column contained names: Carlos, Andre, Jeremy, Pablo. The right-hand column contained numbers and symbols: 127X; 1323YLX; 8727Z4X; and similar undecipherable codes. Various entries were checked; some had asterisks; some nothing. Whatever it was, it had nothing to do with the firm of Rafferty & Baker.

Baker flipped the folder back to Vargo. As he did so he felt his deep distaste of Vargo rise in his throat. It was all he could do to be moderately civil and that ability was fading. He breathed deeply.

"I don't have all night," Vargo said finally. "What is your assessment? Is a deal possible?"

"I don't think so," Baker told him flatly. "Not now, anyway."

As he talked he felt rather than heard a stirring and turned. Angela was standing in the doorway watching him. The whole world had a key to his office.

"Repeat that for her," Vargo said. "Immediately."

"Yes, please," Angela said. She sat in a chair cross-legged and tried to be prim. It didn't work that well.

"I said no deal for now. She's looking at an indictment in six months."

"Can you promise us that we have that long?"

"No way. She told me six months but that means nothing. Could be six days."

"Why won't she make a deal?" Angela asked.

"We don't have anything to sell. He's the target."

"I doubt that's it," Vargo said. "I suspect the approach was just incompetently handled." Baker felt his brain sizzle. Vargo got up to walk past him and decided to poke Bobby Lee in the chest to get him out of the way.

That did it. Forget Rafferty and his premium. He'd throw this fat fuck down the elevator shaft and get Angela a good lawyer. She'd flip on the prick and that would be that.

"Bobby, stop!"

He was reaching for Vargo's throat and had his hand on the man's coat. He looked up to see Max staring at him.

"What?"

"Cool it, Bobby." Rafferty looked at Vargo. "What's all this about?"

"Your partner. He appears to be unbalanced as well as incompetent."

"He's neither," Rafferty said.

"I don't think so either," Angela said.

Vargo looked up at Baker. "You haven't said anything. Maybe you agree with me."

"I do," Bobby Lee said. He grabbed Vargo by the lapels and lifted him bodily off the ground, then hurled him across the room in an unsuccessful attempt to hit the opposite wall without a bounce. He didn't make it. Vargo landed heavily halfway across, crashing into a glass coffee table, spreading Rafferty's bric-a-brac to the four corners. Rafferty froze. A small smile crossed Angela's face.

"Nice toss," she said.

Vargo got up, purple with rage. "You're a dead man," he screamed.

Great, a death threat. "I'm terrified," Baker said. Then he decided a better response was simply to throw the greasy fuck into the ocean. There was an open window down the hall. He stepped forward.

"Stop it!" Rafferty screamed.

Everybody froze. Vargo and Baker stared at each other, breathing heavily. Angela chuckled softly in the background.

"I want this guy gone, Max," Baker said. "He's nothing but problems."

"Relax," Rafferty said. He walked over to Vargo. "You all right?"

"I refuse to work with this man."

"Don't worry about it," Baker told him. "You've already been fired."

"Shut up," Rafferty barked. He turned back to Vargo. "What do you want to do? It's up to you."

"We want you to continue to represent us," Angela said.

"Bullshit," Vargo and Baker said simultaneously.

"Robert, shut up." Angela walked to Baker and straightened his tie. "We still want you," she said.

Max turned to Vargo. "That right?"

Vargo was breathing easier now. "Whatever she says."

"Fine." Rafferty sat on the desk next to Bobby Lee. "Listen, buddy, I got no doubt you're right. But I still want this case."

"Take it then. Just keep this asshole away from me."

"Done," Rafferty said. "We'll keep you two apart, like we had a Chinese wall."

"A what?" Vargo asked.

"Chinese wall. Like the great wall of China. You don't talk to Bobby Lee and vice versa. You never have to deal with him."

"Agreed," Vargo said quickly.

"Agreed," Baker said.

"Pity," Angela said.

17

BAKER BEGAN THINKING IN EARNEST ABOUT JULIE BECK ten days after Rafferty erected his Chinese wall. At the beginning he was simply relieved to be free of Vargo and wondered how Julie would fare against Rafferty, who for all his brains was not the world's best trial lawyer when he had to do it all alone. Then he began feeling guilty as he imagined Julie crushing Max, with Vargo led off in cuffs by the marshals after the jury verdict. That led to fantasies about what Julie would be like in a courtroom: taut, unruffled, in command. Max would have a hard time shaking her—they were too much alike—but Baker thought he could get to her. Could he make her laugh? Throw her off her game? Would she be less effective against a casual, insolent opponent who was not intimidated? From those musings it was a short trip to other fantasies, other imaginings about Bobby Lee and Julie outside the courtroom. Maybe inviting her out for a conference at the bungalow, yap at each other for a while while the green sun splashed into the brown waves. She'd be surprised at the two houses in back. "Yeah, I live there," he'd say. "Would you like to see it?"

On the fourteenth day, he couldn't take it anymore and called her.

"Mr. Baker, what an honor. Twice in one month."

"Don't be smart. I've got news."

"Yeah? What?"

"I'm off the case."

"What case?"

"Vargo. I got fired."

There was a pause. "Too bad," she said finally. "Why did you get fired?"

"Insubordination. Rafferty's gonna try it now. We've got a Chinese wall."

"You only need a wall if there's a conflict."

"Right. We got one."

"What's that?"

"Well, not yet. But we're going to have one."

"I'm listening."

"Well, Rafferty will be representing the defendant."

"Right."

"And I'll be seeing the prosecutor."

Silence.

"I see," Julie said finally. "If that ever happened that would be a conflict."

It took him four tries and a lot more sweet Southern bullshit to get her to agree to meet him for lunch. They met at the Biltmore at 2 P.M. on a Friday afternoon. The chairs were overstuffed, the food French, the waiters in tuxes, and the room dark. It was late and half the lunch crowd was gone when she arrived. She was dressed in a tight, white suit. The skirt was as high as the court would permit. The close-cropped hair was tamed and quiet makeup brought out the stark arresting features of her face. The legs which fled from her short skirt were lean and athletically muscled.

Bobby Lee was wearing what Max called "the suit." It was a dark blue Armani that was trotted out once per trial, for the closing argument to the jury. It was set off by a crisp white shirt, gleaming black Ferragamo loafers, and a multiphased burgundy Hermès tie. The "suit" had never let him down.

He rose as she approached the booth and took her hand.

"Now I know why you win so much."

She smiled. "People in glass houses, Mr. Baker . . ."

They left that salvo a draw and took up stations in the booth, close enough to be interesting, far enough away to maintain the illusion of propriety. Julie was intrigued by this far too cocky young man and just as determined not to show it. Nevertheless she found herself imagining her fingers running through his unkempt hair, maybe grabbing it hard sometimes, and getting him out of that pretty blue suit he was so proud of. She'd also wipe that smirk off his face, of that she had no doubt. It may have been a while but she still knew how to cause a man to squirm, particularly such an obvious specimen as Mr. Baker.

For his part Bobby Lee had no chance. She was even more beautiful than he remembered and he knew he'd do anything she wanted.

He asked her if she wanted wine and she said yes, before thinking. The waiter brought something buttery and cold, a Napa chardonnay that was going to set Baker back about fifty bucks. The waiter put the remains in a bright silver bucket.

"Trying to get me drunk?" she asked.

"Would it help?"

"I don't think so." Her face was bright. "Anyway I've got hearings this afternoon."

"Liar." This was Friday. You could machine-gun every chambers in the building and not hit a judge.

She grinned at that. "I keep forgetting. You've been there."

"True, but never on Friday afternoon." He sipped the soft wine and stared at her. She held his gaze steadily. "Anyway, tell me the truth. Do you have to get back?"

"Why?"

"Do you always answer a question with a question?"

"Do you?"

He dropped his head in surrender. "I think this will be a difficult romance," he said. The ice-cold prescience of that remark was lost in the swoon of a late Friday afternoon hooky getaway with a beautiful woman. And white soft wine. And no clues.

They ate and drank till six and the maître d' shooed them out to make room for the dinner crowd. He asked if he could take her to the beach and she agreed. They stood on the bluffs on Ocean Avenue and watched the turquoise sun dance offstage into the sewer-blackened waves. It got cold then and he gave her his jacket, just like in the movies. Then they walked along the bluffs for two blocks to the bungalow offices.

"Nice," she said, standing back and looking. The green bungalow was dark in the dying light. A small sign said, "Rafferty & Baker, Lawyers" and that was it.

"Thanks."

"And you live in the back?"

"Right. There's two small guest houses, one for me, one for Max." He hesitated. "Would you like to see?"

She didn't hesitate. "Sure."

He held out his hand and she took it, just like in the fantasy. Who knew?

18

ROBERT VARGO REENTERED AMERICA ON JUNE 14, 1991, landing at LAX on a Virgin Atlantic flight nonstop from London. He was fresh-eyed and relaxed after a drug-induced thirteen-hour sleep in which he occupied both front row seats of the first-class section of the plane, known as "upper-class" on Virgin. Immediately after touchdown, Virgin stewards hustled the upper-class passengers through passport control and customs and he cleared within forty minutes, narrowly missing an admixture with a fully loaded Aero Mexico flight from Guadalajara. Once through customs, Vargo, now known as James Ashley, British importer, melted easily into the L.A. night.

It had been a circuitous route for Vargo. His first phony passport took him from Lima to Rio and from Rio on a direct flight to Rome. In Rome, that personage, a

Brazilian named Saeta, vanished forever and James Ashley was born. Ashley then traveled by train from Rome to Calais and across the Channel by hydrofoil. There followed a harried two days in London and its surroundings, during which Ashley ate British, dressed British, and even played eighteen holes on the old course at Sunningdale. Then it was a quiet nondescript car to Gatwick and the Virgin nonstop into LAX.

Vargo's reentry into the United States was so smooth he would be battling overconfidence were it not for the ever-ticking Cuban clock. To combat complacency he focused relentlessly on details. After customs he went immediately to the Virgin VIP lounge and groomed himself, putting the finishing touches on a gently bearded look which was crowned by cropped gray-dyed hair, a businessman's quiet dark suit, and red polka dot tie. At the baggage area, he faded into the background and let a porter stand with his tickets at the carousel. When the bags were off he put down his paper, dutifully tipped the man, and followed him to the outside curb. The car that sat waiting was a late-model tan American sedan. He crawled into the backseat.

The driver was Hispanic and kept his eyes forward. Vargo said nothing and the man pulled easily into the airport traffic flow. He eased the sedan into the escaping traffic on Sepulveda and from there to the San Diego Freeway. The rush hour was in full bloom and the sedan quickly became simply one of ten thousand others meandering slowly northward. Next the driver took the Santa Monica Freeway heading east and the traffic lightened. He exited at Robertson and again headed north, passing the sign welcoming Vargo to Beverly Hills. At Wilshire he turned to the west, chasing the setting sun. He pulled into the ornate valet-cluttered parking area of the Beverly Wilshire Hotel. Neither Vargo nor the driver had spoken.

Vargo exited the car quickly and melted into the hotel, leaving the man to handle the car, tip, and bags. At the front desk he was pleased to learn that arrangements had been made efficiently and well. He was told his room was, as requested, a moderate suite, quiet and separated from the main portion of the hotel. The check-in process then proceeded as smoothly as customs. Because of the substantial advance payment arrangements, there was no need for credit cards or any other formality. He flashed his phony passport and was shown to his suite.

His meeting with Barrows' emissary was scheduled for seven-thirty that evening. He stripped and showered and settled back for a fitful nap. With only sixteen days to go, there would be very little time for anything but naps. He thought of the hurdles that might await him. After the three murders, there remained very few people who knew him or his operation. Baker was one of them. I wonder how Baker is enjoying prison, Vargo mused before falling asleep.

Bobby Lee Baker was led shackled into a one-bedroom apartment in Oakwood, a high-crime ghetto in Venice. Although the government apartment was only a few blocks from the beach, it was the opposite of luxurious. Even in the midst of the devastation around it this building stood out, a fifty-year-old, graffiti-scarred stucco relic with an auto body repair shop in the rear. On either side of the broken and largely windowless structure were rival hot dog stands, each of which competed only for the biker and gang trade. The open doorway to the downstairs hall was a magnet for the city's homeless. Baker had to step over a few on the way into the dank hallway. Once in the hallway, the stench of stale urine permeated the peeling walls.

"Nice place," Baker told Medina.

Medina wiped his hands against the wall. "Christ, you could get diseases here." He nudged Baker. "Let's go. Number fifteen."

Number fifteen was a unit fit only for Boron inmates on thirty-day leave being punished by a vengeful AUSA. The white-painted metal door was a security replacement for a wooden door that had been kicked in during a drug bust. There were no bars on the door, but plenty on the single, tiny window. The only furniture was four card table chairs and a matching table folded in the corner.

"There's supposed to be a bed in the other room, but we got to find some sheets." Medina flipped a switch and nothing happened. "Got to get some electricity too."

Baker was in shock. "Christ, Medina. I had it better in Boron."

"Well, Robert, you can always go back," a female voice said sweetly from the other room.

After his nap, Vargo shaved and changed into a tan Valentino suit, custom-made white shirt, and brightly patterned silk tie. His six-hundred-dollar Italian loafers had been burnished to a high shine by the hotel staff. As he dressed, he sipped on twenty-five-year-old single malt scotch from the bar in his room. The room swam in a fragrance of fresh cut flowers left by a grateful manager to welcome him.

At seven-thirty sharp, there was a soft knock at his door. He opened it to find an efficient-looking Asian woman of about forty years old in a rose business suit. She came with a companion, a slight, dark, soft-skinned man of about twenty-two. He was dressed in a dark sportcoat and matching turtle-neck sweater. His head swiveled as he inspected the room.

"Hello, I'm Amanda Wong. This is my assistant, Vicente. Or, if you prefer, Vincent."

Vargo ignored Amanda Wong's proffered hand and examined Vincent. The young man smiled at him easily. Vargo decided to save those thoughts until later.

"Come in and sit down."

The woman opened a pad and sat down with the primness of an efficient administrator. Vincent sat on the edge of a chair, still watchful. Vargo poured himself more scotch but didn't offer any.

"Okay, what do you got for me?"

Ms. Wong bowed faintly. "Mr. Ashley, it is not my place to presume. I am here to assist you in any way you need." She gestured toward the young man beside her. "I should say *we* are here to assist you."

"I have a little over two weeks. I need many things."

The woman nodded in understanding. She had her pen poised over the pad.

"First, an office here in Beverly Hills within walking distance of the hotel. Nondescript. Small conference room and reception area. Excellent location and view. Fully computerized."

"Already arranged. We have sublet furnished office space on the corner of Camden and Wilshire. It is two blocks from here and you may move in at any time."

"Fine. Next, I need clerical help available twenty-four hours a day. You will do. You have office skills?"

"Of course."

"Good. Next, a lawyer was to have been made available to me. Has he?"

Amanda Wong reached into her briefcase and produced a card. "The man's name is Charles Wendel. I believe you know him?"

"I do indeed. Has he been paid?"

"He has received a substantial retainer. You may expect excellent service."

Vargo nodded. "Next, bank accounts. Have they been arranged?"

She handed Vargo a finely embossed checkbook and credit card. "The sum of one million dollars has been deposited in the name of Charter Properties in a money market account at the Asian Interbank Trust," she said. "When you write a check, the money will automatically be debited to your account. When you use this credit card, it will also be automatically debited. Here is an example of the signature you should use."

Vargo saw that the signature was simply a series of vertical lines, easy to copy.

"The hotel. How long?"

"Charter Properties has made an advance cash payment for seventeen days' lodging. In addition, there is a ten-thousand-dollar account in Charter's name with the hotel. The balance will be returned to you upon your departure."

"A car?"

"Downstairs, a dark nondescript Lincoln. Vincent will be your driver."

"Security?"

The woman nodded to Vincent. The young man simply

opened his coat. Underneath was strapped a black shoulder harness and a blue-black .38 automatic. Vargo liked this boy a great deal.

He turned back to the woman. "Tomorrow morning, report to my office at six A.M. The working day will typically run from six A.M. till midnight."

"No problem," Amanda Wong said.

Vargo stood up and paced. Two weeks was not a lot of time, only barely enough if everything went well. "Tomorrow, I want to see the warehouse in Sylmar. They'll probably still have it cordoned off but I want to drive by anyway. In the afternoon I want an appointment with that Armenian from the jewelry operation. I don't remember his name. He's the fellow who—"

"We know his name," Amanda Wong said.

"Fine. We'll meet him at two o'clock. Then I want an appointment with the lawyer at four P.M."

"Yes, sir."

Vargo rubbed his face. Notwithstanding his long sleep sailing over the Atlantic, he was getting tired. He had done enough for one day. "Ms. Wong. Thank you for your time. Get started on those assignments right away."

She turned to the young man. "Let's go."

Vargo raised his hand. "Not him. We have matters to discuss."

Amanda Wong began to speak and then seemed to think better of it. She gathered up her notes and quickly left.

Vargo walked slowly to the back of the black walnut bar and poured another scotch. He took a long pull and enjoyed the slow burn. He looked at Vincent and the man returned his gaze without blinking. Then he beckoned. Vincent was Latin and slim, his muscles taut under the jacket. His face was smooth and young, as Vargo knew it would be. Vincent looked up quizzically, as any young killer might. His attitude was mocking. The attitude irritated Vargo.

"Would you like one?" Vargo gestured to his drink.

"Thanks," the boy said.

Vargo put the bottle on the bar and a glass next to it. When Vincent approached him, Vargo reached over and grabbed him by the lapel of his sportcoat, then pulled him close. The sneer left Vincent's face and was replaced by concentration. Not fear, concentration.

"The bedroom's over there," Vargo told him abruptly. "Take the bottle and glass with you when you go."

19

JULIE BECK'S TOUR OF BAKER'S BEACH HOUSE WASN'T supposed to take fourteen hours. It was supposed to be a quick tour, a little stroll through the office and bungalow followed by a walk on the bluffs to watch the sunset, then maybe a little dinner. They missed the sunset and missed dinner and then missed sunrise and breakfast as well. They would have missed lunch too except Julie started complaining.

"Bobby, stop, please!" She was lying naked facedown on his bed. There were fresh beads of sweat on her back and her short-cropped hair was mottled. The bedclothes were clumped in a ball at the bottom of the bed. Two bedside lamps were lying on their sides on the floor. The room looked like the site of a barroom brawl.

"Stop what?" He was kneeling next to her, also naked. Periodically he leaned over and licked some of the sweat off her back.

"That," she said. She shivered at his touch. "Bobby, I'm starving."

"Me too. That's why I thought I'd help myself to a snack." His kisses moved lower on her body and she laughed.

"Don't you ever get tired of that?"

"I wouldn't know."

She turned over, looking at him without shame. "I had a wonderful night." She thought about it. "And an even more wonderful morning. But Bobby, I'm *starving!*"

"Okay, we can go," he said. He leaned over and nuzzled his unshaven face against her bare belly. Then he kissed and nibbled and began the march south again. She stiffened and trembled.

"You're a pervert."

"And a proud one," he said. He figured he was about three inches and thirty seconds from touchdown. "So you want to go now?"

"Yes."

"Okay." He moved down for the kill. She was now rigid as a board.

"Bobby!" she screamed.

Touchdown. "Yes," he said innocently.

Her eyes grew flat and intense. She grabbed his hair and yanked his head to her. "You bastard," she whispered.

For months, they were sneaks, meeting for quiet lunches and dinners during the week, hikes in the mountains on weekends, trysts late at night at the beach cottage. Nobody knew. They sought out quiet private harbors in the frenzy of the urban jungle around them, and for all the world knew they had simply become a little more reclusive of late. Since they were both known to be loners anyway, it was easy to pull off.

What wasn't so easy was the lying to Rafferty. They convinced themselves they hadn't planned to do that, didn't even want to do that, but the truth was they derived perverse pleasure from the secretive tension. They fed the danger of it with looks and touches when others were around. They claimed they couldn't wait for all the lying to end and that was a lie too.

It was not until five months later, in the late spring of 1987, that Rafferty and Vargo got suspicious. The tip-off happened just before a banquet. A new U.S. Attorney was being inducted, a downtown tight-ass with a wire to the reigning Republican senator. The old U.S. Attorney was on his way to the academic stud farm. A black-tie affair had been arranged by the downtown rabbis to honor federal prosecutors old and new. Rafferty and Baker were on the alumni list; Julie was on the active list.

Baker was home dressing when he got a call from Rafferty.

"I need to see you."

"Why?"

"I'll tell you later. Some place quiet. How about Father's Office?"

"Max, I'm wearing a tux!"

"So what, you'll spruce up the place."

"Okay, thirty minutes."

Father's Office is a beat-up Santa Monica hole-in-the-wall a mile from the ocean. It has successfully resisted the gentrification that has made Montana Avenue the Rodeo Drive of the far Westside; its only concession to the glittering boutiques flanking it is a new specialty in microbrewery draft beer from the Pacific Northwest. A grotesque fat man in a dirty apron pours the beer, shuffling painfully through the sawdust to pull down the drafts housed in sixteen adjacent gleaming receptacles.

"Try the spring ale," Rafferty told him as he sat down. "It's only here for thirty days."

Baker signaled the fat man and he soon had a tall, light Oregon ale in front of him. The fat man gawked at the tux but didn't say anything. Baker sipped the amber ale while he waited for Rafferty to get around to it.

"Who do you think will be there tonight?" Rafferty began innocently.

Baker shrugged. "All the same faces."

"Harrigan? Do you think Harrigan?"

"Maybe."

"Yeah, what about Wilson?"

"You never know."

"I guess you're right. How about Jennings?"

Baker looked over at his friend. "Did you invite me here to go down the entire list?"

"Jesus, you're in a shitty mood."

Baker shook his head. "I'm in a great mood. But I know when you've got something on your mind. Just say it."

Rafferty played with his glass for a while. "You want another?"

"Sure." The fat man poured some more and stared some more at the tux. Baker sighed, sipped, and finally got exasperated. "Max, how many of these I gotta drink before you tell me what's bothering you?"

122

"You're making a mistake, Bobby."

"How's that?"

"Beck," he said simply.

Baker froze. "Come again?"

"You heard me."

"What are you, my mother?"

"Bobby, Vargo is freaking. He thinks everything we say is going straight to her."

"How the hell does he know anything about this?"

Rafferty looked uncomfortable. "She called tonight. Vargo took the call."

Bobby Lee exploded. "Are you nuts? Shit, Max. Why don't you just give him some keys?"

"He's got keys."

"What!" Baker screamed. The fat man looked over quizzically.

Rafferty waved the concern away. "Don't worry, I'm being careful. But what about you and her? It just doesn't make sense."

"What did she want when she called?"

"Something about meeting you tonight." Rafferty took out a crumpled phone message and handed it over. Baker recognized Vargo's scrawl. The message asked whether Bobby Lee might be available to attend a dinner Julie's father was giving after the reception. It was a code; there was no dinner, just Julie inviting Baker to spend the night. Next to the note Vargo had written five exclamation points and underlined them. "Yeah, I'd say he's freaking," Baker agreed.

"So what are you gonna do about it, Bobby? You gonna help me out on this?"

"Sure, Max." Baker slapped his partner on the back and gestured to the fat man. "Give this man another spring ale."

Baker drove to the U.S. Attorney's reception in a fog. This woman with the husky voice and the cropped, white hair was becoming an obsession. And now it was out. Rafferty was right. Under normal circumstances, he should walk away from this before it blew up in his face. But these weren't normal circumstances.

The reception was held at the Riviera Country Club in Pacific Palisades, in a seventy-five-year-old white Spanish clubhouse overlooking the golf course and what was once some of the most expensive real estate in the world. He walked in through the stucco portico and was given a name tag to pin to his lapel. He got a drink and looked around for her.

She was easy to find. She came to him from across the room, a grin lighting her face. At the sound of her husky voice, his mouth went dry.

"Did you get my message?"

"Vargo did. He passed it along."

Julie blanched. "Vargo! That was Vargo I talked to?"

"The one and only."

"God, that was stupid." She grabbed Bobby Lee's lapels. "What did he say? C'mon, give."

"What about the attorney-client privilege?"

She gave him a fake smile and talked in a fake little girl voice. "If somebody doesn't start talking guess what somebody is not going to be allowed to do tonight."

The woman had no morals. "He thinks I've gone over to the enemy."

"The *words*, Baker. What *words* did he use?"

"I understand the actual quote was 'fucking Baker and that gash ought to be shot.' "

She looked puzzled. "Gash?"

"That's you. I'm 'fucking Baker.' "

She shrugged. "Me too." Then she brightened. "Incidentally, I forgot to ask you. My dad's party? Can you come?"

"Your dad's party?"

"Well, our party."

"Absolutely."

She grabbed him by the arm, excited as a girl. "This'll be great. You've never been to my house. It's just across the course." She pointed toward the darkened golf course outside the clubhouse door.

He followed her gesture and saw a large white ultramodern structure ringed with party lights. It sat high above the now blackened course like a castle over the peasants' fields.

"You live there?"

"In the guest house, just like you. Can you handle it?"

"I don't know. What does Dad think about dowries?"

"For the right man, not a problem."

They left it at that and mingled a bit. Baker tried to make the best of it, schmoozing with the assistants he had cases with and passing out cards to the alumni. He pretty much stayed away from the judges on principle. About an hour into it, the room was called to order and the guest of honor made a cookie-cutter speech that must have been made by every new U.S. Attorney since nationhood. The new appointee—a balding politico from a Republican bastion in the Valley—announced that crime was not a public good; that gangs in particular were dangerous; and that he would do all in his power to combat both. He then turned the floor over to his rabbi, who made an eight-minute speech and announced there would be ten speakers to follow.

Baker was pretty sure he and Rafferty were not among the ten. He inched toward the back of the room where a bar was set up on a small veranda overlooking the golf course. Halfway there, an arm touched his.

"Where you going?"

The voice was croaked and husky. He grabbed her hand. "Follow me and you'll find out."

They squeezed along the back wall and then out to the veranda. The night around them was black except for the sprinkling of light from the reception inside. He looked over the edge of the wall. There was about a four-foot drop to a cart path. She was laughing. "Baker, you're nuts."

He grabbed her hand again. "Let's go."

They tumbled laughing to the ground, then ran across the darkened golf course like escapees from school, glancing back only to see if the adults would catch them. They cut across a fairway fifty yards wide and into some trees, then back out the other side into another fairway. The trees now blocked all light from the clubhouse. They were alone on a massive, darkened sea of manicured green grass and they knew it. Julie took off her shoes and ran barefoot. They raced from tee to green and in five minutes, they were far enough from the clubhouse so that the only light came down dimly from the houses high above the course. There was no sound at all.

Julie stopped. "Hold it, Baker. I've got to rest." She threw her shoes down and stretched out on the grass, looking upward at the sky. There was a wooden marker near her head.

"This is the thirteenth hole," Bobby Lee observed. He had no idea why he made that remark. "Four hundred twelve yards." He craned his neck. "Dog leg right it looks like."

Julie sat up. "Hey, Bobby, come over here."

Baker looked over stupidly. The throaty drawl had unnerved him. "What?"

She laughed. "This is the great trial lawyer? I said come here."

He didn't need much encouragement. He took off his jacket and put it under her head. Then he bent over and kissed her hard.

She closed her eyes and let her tongue rub over her lips. "Ouch."

He kissed her again, even harder this time. Her arms came up to him and he grabbed her wrists. She stretched against him, wincing as his teeth nibbled her lower lip. With his free hand he traced the outline of her face. Where he traced, he kissed and nibbled, first gently then harder. When he reached her throat and breasts, she twisted. "Bobby, I don't know . . ."

"Shut up," he said. "Please." His free hand opened her jacket. Underneath was a white blouse. Underneath that were soft breasts already rising with the hope of meeting his hand.

"This isn't what I expected. Not here . . ."

"You mean on the thirteenth tee?"

She twisted some more. "Yeah."

"We could move to the fourteenth. Or you could save time by just saying . . ." His fingers moved to the button of the white blouse.

"Saying what?"

"Saying yes." His fingers left the button and traced the outline of her breasts.

"Yes."

"I can't hear you."

His fingers undid the first button.

"I said you're a creep."

His fingers undid the second button.

"What kind of creep?"

"A dirty creep."

He undid the fourth button and spread the blouse. Underneath was nothing but opportunity. "Somebody didn't wear her—"

"Yes." She broke her hands free and pulled him to her.

"Thank God for golf," he said.

20

FOR JULIE, BOBBY LEE BAKER REPRESENTED A SEA change in her always underutilized love life. Men had always been afraid of her, as she wanted them to be, and soft lights did little to smooth the hard edges. In the two years prior to Bobby Lee the only man in her life had been a sorry tax partner with sad eyes at a downtown firm. After three weeks of an emotion that was either sympathy, curiosity, or boredom, she permitted him to take her home. After a lot of fumbling on the couch, she found herself more or less undressed and lying beneath him, curious where it was all going and staring at a soft membrane that fear was holding captive like a prisoner of war. She tried to help by just saying candidly that the two of them were in the middle of a disaster, a tactic that had more to commend it in forthrightness than compassion. Eventually, the man mounted her like he was climbing a mountain, his face contorted with effort. Seconds later, when he finally spurted sort of between and around her legs, it was hard to tell who was the more relieved.

With Baker it was always different. Bobby Lee was neither afraid of her nor especially interested in her bright mind and fine prospects. He wanted her physically and took her physically with ruthless single-mindedness. For all Bobby Lee cared, she could have been a waitress, a social worker, a nun, it didn't matter. He wanted her with her clothes off and it brought out the harlot in her.

By the middle of that final month, the fourteenth of June to be exact, she was beyond obsession. She had a trial that month, a routine bank robbery, and it was all she could do to remember the name of the defendant. At the end of the trial the judge droned out legal instructions to the jury, and her mind left the marbled sanctuary to skip across town to the bedroom where she knew he was napping, naked and facedown on top of a thin sheet, flush from a run along the beach, maybe still with a stubble if he played hooky altogether, the same stubble that the night before had rubbed roughly against her breasts and the inside of her thighs, now even sharper and more insistent. The jury was halfway out the door before she remembered to stand up.

They weren't out long. Another conviction, another victory, another notch in the gun. She demanded that the defendant be remanded out of habit. They dragged him away in chains and she went back to her office. She jammed two briefcases with Vargo grand jury documents and ran to the parking lot, throwing the bags into the trunk of her car. She had the key in the ignition when her FBI agent put a hand through the open window onto her arm.

"What?" she said abruptly.

"Did you see this?"

He handed her a copy of a one-paragraph memo. It was from central calendaring, reminding her that the Vargo grand jury was about to expire in fourteen days.

"Shit," she muttered.

"No shit," the agent agreed.

"Do we have everything we need?"

"I think so. All three of the Filipinos have testified. You just gotta figure who to indict and on what."

That was the easy part. Vargo on everything. With Vargo's three Filipino assistants testifying for the government the trial would be a slaughter. She couldn't wait.

She grabbed the calendar and looked at it. The grand jury expired on a Friday. The best day to indict was Wednesday the twenty-fifth. She drew a big twenty-five on the memo and circled it, then showed it to her agent. "That's your date," she said.

"We'll pick him up."

Julie Beck thought some more. "We'll indict in the morning and keep it sealed. You pick him up at noon. We'll have a press conference at three."

"You sure you don't want me to let him come in by himself?"

"You gotta be kidding."

He grinned. "I was."

By the time she got back to her house, the skies had opened and an uncharacteristic rainfall was flooding the Palisades. Riviera was vacant, soggy under the wet mush. The wind blew the palms seaward, stretching them. Bobby Lee Baker's car was covered with blown moss. It had been there for a while.

She knew where to find him. The main house was empty, the course was empty, and the night was coming in with a bum's rush. He was as she expected him to be, facedown on the bed, his arms wrapped around a pillow.

She dumped the boxes in her study and put the calendaring memo on top. Caution was washed away by a more primitive urge and she ignored the tickle at the base of her brain. The memo remained faceup on top of the Vargo boxes.

She went to the bedroom and looked at him. He breathed easily, sleeping with the innocence of the dead. She let herself become slowly excited by the muscles running along the back of his legs. She sat next to him.

Without hesitation she ran her hands along the inside of his thighs, letting them finally linger on his smoothly muscled buttocks. She could not imagine ever doing anything so brazen before. She watched him wake up, startled, and was intoxicated as she felt her power over him. When he turned over she scraped her fingernails roughly across his chest and down the line of hair on his belly. He closed his eyes. She smiled and straddled him.

She watched his eyes open and grow hot. She wanted to nurture his rage and ruthlessness, tease it till it flowered. She took off her jacket and threw it aside, then she reached for her buttons.

"Shall I?" His smile was weak and phony.

"I don't know," she said with a false innocence she knew would irritate him.

The smile left his face and he sat up. He grabbed her blouse with both hands.

"Hey, watch it." He pulled his hands apart and the material ripped, exposing her from neck to waist. She pushed him back and kissed him hard. All she wanted to do was finish it. Soon her skirt was at her waist, her pants were also ripped, and she was astride him with her face intent and contorted. There was no doubt about it. Bobby Lee Baker was not the tax partner.

Later on, she lay naked beside him, her head on his chest. His arm was folded across his eyes. She kissed his taut stomach, biting some of the hairs and pulling gently on them. He opened his eyes and looked at her quizzically.

"Sorry, that wasn't fair. I have to work now."

"Bring it in here."

She laughed. "I don't think that would be a good idea."

"Why? I'll help. What do you got, the closing on the bank robbery?"

Back then she never edited her thoughts. "No, that jury came in today. This is your friend. It's D day."

"Who?"

"You know."

His eyes had widened. "No shit?"

She walked away, giving him a little wiggle to remember her by. "That's right, no shit."

She went into the other room and thought about security, then thought about Bobby Lee and decided what the hell. She lugged the boxes back to the bedroom and spread the papers over the bed. "I've got two weeks," she explained, "so I have to move. If I don't indict by the twenty-fifth, it's a new grand jury. Then I have to start from scratch." She flashed him a look at the memo with the big twenty-five in a circle.

Baker never moved. "You got all the witnesses in?"

She nodded. "We've got him by the balls. We've got three of his people who made deals and already testified. They just laid him out."

Bobby Lee still never moved. "Who?"

She grinned and leaned over him. She thought maybe this time she wouldn't stop at his chest. "Forget it, sweets. Try to guess."

When she leaned over him again, he stopped asking questions.

21

VARGO'S THREE FILIPINO ASSISTANTS—A MAN OF forty-five, his cousin Ariella, thirty-seven, and his niece, Inez, twenty-four, all of whom had been granted immunity by Julie Beck, all of whom had testified extensively before the grand jury but of course not yet at trial—were murdered together at approximately 2:40 P.M. on June 22, 1987. They were found two days later, twenty-four hours before the grand jury expired, exactly as they had been left.

The murders were committed gangland style in Vargo's office. The three victims were found with their hands tied behind their backs with chicken wire. Each one had been shot in the back of the head and fell facedown on a very expensive Oriental rug. By the time they were discovered, $363 million of investor funds had been wire-transferred from thirty-seven North American Diversified accounts in eleven banks in Monterey Park, California, to a blizzard of accounts in the Cayman Islands and Panama. From there the Cayman bankers, acting on written instructions from Cayman lawyers, immediately transferred the funds to innumerable and completely unknown accounts worldwide. Vargo himself was on a plane from

LAX to Costa Rica and from there, with a new identity, to the Dominican Republic awaiting passage to a long planned if temporary hideaway off the Colombian coast.

Julie Beck learned of the murders from her agent. She was sitting in her office going through a summary of the grand jury testimony when the phone rang. Her agent's voice was stiff and choked.

"Julie, I'm at Vargo's office."

That didn't make sense. She didn't want her agent out there until the next day when the indictments were returned. "You're where?"

"Julie," the man said, "they're dead. All dead."

Julie had never heard an agent speak like this. The man seemed close to tears. "What? Who's dead?"

"They were shot in the head. There's blood everyplace."

Julie felt a cold chill grip her. It couldn't be what she thought. "Goddamn it. Who are you talking about?"

"All three of them, Julie." The man's voice was now hoarse and broken. "Even the girl. All three of them."

She didn't need to ask more questions. Later, thinking back on it, she remembered feeling the blood drain from her face.

"Julie . . . Julie . . . you still there?"

She didn't answer. The thoughts and suspicions clicked in her mind like tumblers, one by one. Her three Filipino witnesses were dead twenty-four hours before indictment. If they were facedown in Vargo's office, then Vargo was long gone. Somebody talked. Her mind raced down a list of all the people in her office who knew about the indictment date. Nothing. Then she thought of outsiders and her stomach flipped. It couldn't be.

Her agent was still talking. "I tried them at home like you told me. I been trying for two days. Nothing. Then I got nervous and came over here. Julie," he screamed, "it's such a fucking mess!"

She stared at the wall, the anger rising within her like a storm. "Don't move," she said finally. "I'm coming out."

As she drove to Vargo's office, the black night settled in around her to match her mood. She remembered that

Baker was waiting for her at the guest house. She thought about driving there and confronting him and then replaced the idea; before she met him, she wanted to see the bodies, to fuel the pain and anger. She pointed her car toward Vargo's office. The local police had the building blocked off but she ignored the roadblocks. Her agent was waiting and quickly escorted her through the maze of blue uniforms.

Every office of National Diversified was empty. The secretarial bays were cleaned out, devoid of all the pictures and personal effects a working office would have. The files were strewn around the floor, as though someone had carefully selected out the important documents and trashed the rest. She flipped an electric switch. Nothing happened. "Why is the electricity shut off?"

Her agent shrugged. "There was no electricity anyplace. We got it restored to some of the wings."

Julie thought about that and her jaw set. "He turned off the power," she said finally. "The cheap son of a bitch had so much advance notice, he told the electric company to shut off the power."

Her agent shrugged again. "He had enough."

Vargo's office was a swarm of suits and blue uniforms. She showed her identification and walked into the death room. A homicide detective identified himself as lieutenant something or other and started to ask her questions. Julie ignored him. She approached the bodies, three lumps under white sheets, still huddled in their death spasms.

"Let me see them," she said.

The tone of her voice convinced the lieutenant not to argue. He nodded at a blue uniform and the man pulled back the white sheets. Julie felt rather than saw the horror of the murders. The gunshots to the head had obliterated the features of the victims. If it weren't for the clothes, she couldn't tell the man from the two women. The skin was part alabaster, part gray, drained of blood. Whatever blood once was inside was now collected in grotesque coagulating brown pools around the deep maroon-and-blue rug. She felt no nausea at the sight.

"How old were they, Jack?"

The agent pointed. "She was twenty-four, he was in his forties, and her, I don't know, thirty-five or so."

"Twenty-four." She spun on her heel. "I'll see you tomorrow, Jack."

By the time she got home it was almost midnight. The main house was dark. Bobby Lee's car was parked in front of the guest house. She walked in to find him over the stove, mixing up what looked to be a large pot of bouillabaisse. He was whistling. A bottle of red wine was on the counter near two glasses. He came over to kiss her. She allowed herself to be kissed and smiled at him.

"Baby, I missed you."

She kept the smile on. "I missed you, too."

He poured the wine. They clinked glasses and sipped. "Come see what I'm making."

"Sure." She breathed deeply from the pot. It sickened her. "Smells delicious."

He looked at her pale face with concern. "You okay?"

"Dandy." She took another sip of the wine and fought to keep it down. Then she decided the hell with it and drained the glass. She held her glass out for another. Baker looked at her in an odd way but obliged.

"So what'd you do today?" she asked.

He shrugged. "I had a quick hearing this morning and then I kind of played hooky. I tried to find Max but he's working like a dog."

"On our friend?"

"What else?"

She nodded. "Rafferty's a hard worker. If I know him, he'll be working twenty-four hours a day on this case."

"He has to, Vargo's in his face."

"I believe it. Where is the great man these days, anyway?"

Baker grinned. "Aren't we getting out of bounds?"

The fixed smile was starting to cramp and she let it slip away. "Maybe a little. I was just curious."

He shrugged. "He's in and out, you know. Other than that, I don't see him."

"When was the last time you saw him?"

Now his eyes narrowed to slits. "What?"

"I asked when was the last time you saw him."

Her smile was now long gone and not likely to return. There was a clock in the room that must have been ticking all along. Now the tick seemed thunderous.

"Let me try that again," he said softly. "What?"

"It's a simple enough question. When did you last see him?"

"Okay, I'll play along." He thought about it. "Maybe last week, maybe yesterday. I don't remember."

"Really? You saw him yesterday?"

"I think so. Hell, I'm around the office, he's around the office. I don't keep track. Maybe Tuesday night, him and Angela."

"But at least on that you'd be sure. The yesterday part, I mean."

"I don't know. I guess so."

She forced the smile back. "Don't be nervous. It's nothing important."

"I'm not nervous," he lied.

"How about Max? He must see him all the time."

"He better, he's Vargo's lawyer."

"How about today? Is Max seeing him today? Just in case I have to get some information to him."

"I guess so, he sees him every day."

"And you're sort of sure about that, too, right? I mean about Max seeing him today."

He held up his hands in exasperation. Anything to stop the bleeding. "Absolutely, one hundred percent sure. He sees Vargo *every* day."

"And that's not something you'd lie to me about, right?"

His eyes were now narrow slits. "There's nothing in this world I'd lie to you about."

This time her smile looked genuine. "How very sweet. And *so* romantic."

"Thank you. Now will you tell me what this is about?"

"Sure." She took a deep breath. "Let me try it all in one sentence. Okay?"

"Fine."

"You see, that way I don't have to spend any extra time talking to you, understand?"

His eyes stayed fixed on her and didn't twitch.

"So here goes. I was supposed to indict tomorrow like I told you but all three of my key witnesses were murdered two days ago and Vargo has left the country with about three hundred million dollars and I don't know where the hell Max is and you just lied to me three times and I know you tipped them off to the whole thing and I want you to get out of here now or I'll call some agents to throw you out."

Then she paused to catch her breath. That done, she took a small sip out of her full wineglass and threw the rest in Baker's face. He still didn't flinch. The red liquid cascaded down his shirt like newly flowing blood. Then she took a step closer to him and swung with a closed fist with every ounce of strength she had. Her fist hit flush against the side of his head. She felt something crack in her hand and she knew she probably broke it. His head snapped and returned and other than that didn't move.

Between the pain in her hand and the flood of her anger, she was close to tears she'd never let him see. "Get the fuck out," she screamed.

22

THEY SAY THERE'S ALWAYS A SILVER LINING AND IN THE case of the Oakwood monstrosity Bobby Lee was now calling home, that lining was gold. The smelly unit was a dump, but a dump that was actually a highly effective vaccine against a virulent virus named Beck, who seemed to hate the place even more than Baker. After about an hour or so of abuse for the sake of abuse, she left, leaving him more or less permanently to the care of Medina.

"Okay, sport, it's up to us," Medina said when she finally left. "What do you want to do?"

"Fucking shoot her."

"Outside of that."

"I don't know, I haven't thought past that for three years."

"So here's your chance. Think."

He did. "What are the rules?"

"Hell, we can do anything long as it don't cost money."

"Do we have to stay here?"

"Hell no, I don't want to stay here. I got a car."

"Really?"

"Absolutely. FBI Ford." He grabbed the newspaper. "The town's ours. We can go see a movie, long as it's got some skin in it. The Dodgers are in town, if you like to watch triple-A. UCLA against Arizona in college baseball. Sunday the Raiders start summer workouts out in Thousand Oaks."

The Raiders. That meant Montel was in town. His friend would be so proud.

Medina flipped the page. "Then there's about four plays about guys with AIDS. Maybe that'd help you at Boron."

"Nice talk, Medina." He didn't have time to go to the movies, or even see Montel for that matter. He grabbed Medina's arm. "Let's go."

In the old days, when everything was great, it was known as Rafferty & Baker. Now Rafferty had some new partners and the big green bungalow had a new sign: "Rafferty, Bernson, Faldo & Finch, A Professional Corporation, Attorneys at Law." Baker had no idea who the hell Bernson, Faldo, and Finch were.

Rosie the receptionist screeched when Baker walked in the door. Medina looked on with amusement as a crowd of secretaries and clerks came over shaking Bobby Lee's hand and pounding him on the back. One man emerged from an office to see what the excitement was about. He was coatless and wore suspenders and a bow tie over a short-sleeved white shirt with a calculator stuck in the pocket. He watched with cold detachment.

When the crowd quieted he came forward and held out his hand. "Hello, I'm Ray Faldo."

"Bobby Lee Baker."

"I know." He gestured to the group. "You're a legend around here. Of sorts."

"Of sorts?"

"Yes." Faldo cleared his throat. "So what brings you back. I had understood you were . . ."

"Incarcerated?"

"Well, yes. I'm sorry, but that's what I was told. Incarcerated for a number of years yet."

"We made a deal. Talk to Rafferty about it." Bobby Lee gestured to Medina. "Incidentally, this is José Medina. Medina, this is one of Rafferty's new partners."

"Glad to meet you." Faldo shook his hand. "Are you a friend of Mr. Baker's?"

"I'm an FBI agent."

Faldo blanched. "I see."

"Don't worry about it," Baker assured him. "While he's here the typewriters are safe."

"How fortunate," Faldo said, and seemed to mean it. He cleared his throat again. "Anyway, Max isn't here. Is there any way I can help?"

"Yes. I need all the files from the trial. And an office to work."

Faldo's eyes became desperate as he hunted around for an excuse. "The files. They're extensive, I believe."

"You believe right."

"And they're in storage now."

"I assume so, it's been over three years."

"Extensive files in storage." The man could really put it together. Where did Rafferty get him? "And an office, too? I just don't know."

Baker was about to go for his throat but Medina intervened. "It's really a request of the U.S. government, Mr. Faldo."

"Well, in that case . . ."

"Hey, Faldo," Baker said.

"Yes?"

"Get the fucking files."

It took two hours to bring them up. In the meantime Bobby Lee and Medina sat in a back conference room and played gin. It was the sort of thing one got good at in prison, and pretty soon Medina was down two hundred on the pad.

"This sucks," Medina complained. "If you keep pissing me off I'm going to leave you cuffed to a chair in that rat hole with the black-and-white T.V."

That was a credible threat. "Don't worry about it," Baker said quickly. "I'm going to let you work it off."

They brought the files in taped boxes piled on carts. Bobby Lee threw Medina a yellow legal pad. "Here. Make yourself useful."

"Sure. What are we looking for?"

"The 302s." The 302s—Form 302, to be exact—are filled out by the FBI every time an agent takes a witness statement. Medina knew all about 302s. The government is obligated to give the 302s of its trial witnesses to the defense, and in a complex criminal case, they are always provided months before trial, as a matter of simple fairness. Ms. Fucking Beck, with the same warmth and cooperation she exhibited throughout the trial, had dumped the 302s on Rafferty's desk the morning of trial.

The 302s were bound and indexed in a red accordion file. During the trial, Baker had mostly skimmed the statements, hunting for strands of favorable testimony the FBI had forgotten to delete and concentrating only on the witnesses who would actually testify for the government. Now he had a slightly different agenda.

"How many are there?" Medina asked. He was already nervous about this commitment.

Baker checked the index. "About fifty. The cops who found the bodies. Vargo's outside accountants. Some outside lawyers. People in the building. Nobody knew shit by and large."

"How about his organization?"

"What organization? There were only three or four people real close to him. Three he killed. One got away. Outside of that just a few puppets."

"Who?"

"Who what?"

"Who got away?"

"A girl who worked with him. His—I don't know what —partner, assistant, or whatever."

"They never found her?"

"They tried. She went underground big time after those murders."

"So she's important."

"Real important. She knows more about Vargo than anybody."

Medina nodded, flipping through the 302s. "Hey, here's one with your name on it. Rachel Strange. Receptionist. Says maybe she saw you talking to Vargo the last day."

"By the time of trial there was no maybe."

"Here's another. Mildred Woosman. Says she saw you and Vargo in the parking lot after hours. He had his trunk up and you were handing him some documents."

"At a distance of one hundred fifty feet in the dark without her glasses."

"She says she's sure you were handing him grand jury material. She could see the caption."

"Right."

"Then there's Andrea Watson, computer programmer. Thirty-six years old."

"And never been kissed."

"It don't say that. She says she saw you and Vargo leave together the last day. She remembers you wearing a leather jacket and glasses."

"They turned my house upside down to find that."

"Right, and then she ID'd the jacket they found." Medina looked up. "You sure you didn't do this?"

"You know how many leather jackets there are in the world? Besides, Medina, what did they tell you in FBI school about ID testimony?"

"It don't stand up."

"Why?"

"It's unreliable. Five minutes after they see something people don't know what the hell they saw. Besides, juries don't believe ID testimony."

Baker had to smile at that. "This one did."

It was after six before Medina and Baker tired of hacking through the Vargo files. They hadn't found anything except old, bad memories and a lot of frustration. Faldo, who still suspected a rat, couldn't bring himself to leave, even after Max had called in and approved the whole thing. Finally Baker stretched and bellowed.

"Hey, Faldo."

The man was there in an instant, the result of hovering near the door.

"Are you ready to leave?" Faldo asked hopefully.

"Almost. You got the key to Max's office?"

"Yes."

"Great. There's usually some Bushmill's or Black Bush, bottom right drawer. Maybe get some ice too."

Faldo stared. "You want to start drinking whiskey now?"

It really was a staggering partnership choice. He'd have to talk to Max about it. "Only if you can find the key," Baker said gently.

"The ice, too," Medina suggested.

Faldo did a reasonable job getting the Bush and then tried to leave, but they made him stay and drink. After two pops, he mellowed.

"You know," he said, "you guys aren't so bad. I didn't mean to give you a hard time. It's just—"

"I know," Bobby Lee told him. "Listen, how long you been with Max?"

"Almost two years."

"What do you do?"

"Real estate and tax. Sometimes some corporate."

"No trials?"

"God, no, I've never even seen a trial."

Baker and Medina smirked. The guy wasn't even a real lawyer. Nevertheless Bobby Lee decided to mine for a little low-grade ore.

"You ever have anything to do with Vargo?"

"Sure, lots."

"What?"

"Well, when Vargo became a, what do they call it—"

"Fugitive?" Medina offered.

"Yes, fugitive. After that, all his companies went into bankruptcy. I was asked to organize everything."

"Like what?"

"Everything. Bank statements, insurance policies, stock holdings, you name it, I organized it."

"For who?"

"Originally, for the bankruptcy trustee. But once the"

trustee realized there was no money left, he also realized . . .''

"He wouldn't get paid."

"Right. So he lost interest."

"So what happened to all your pretty organizing of the files?"

"Nobody's ever asked for it," Faldo said, a little hurt. "But, it's all there. In the Green Bible."

Bobby Lee let a beat go by. "In the what?"

"I'll go get it."

Faldo left and Medina chuckled. "See what happens when you're nice?"

Faldo came back with a thick green binder. "It's all in here."

"Show me."

"Look." He proudly displayed the index. "Behind one of these tabs is a Vargo company. And there's a fundamental order to his mind, I found. You know the old line 'all roads lead to Rome'? Well, in his case, all roads only *start* in Italy, Tuscany to be exact. And *end* in Monterey Park, California."

"What the hell does that mean?"

"I'll show you. All of Vargo's shell corporations are named after an Italian town in Tuscany. Look at the index: Chianti Corporation. Montelcino Corporation. Siena Corporation. And at the end of the day, once you cut through it all, all his corporations are owned by a single holding company. Firenze Holdings, S.A."

"What's that, some sort of Swiss deal?"

"Liechtenstein *anstalt*. Same thing."

Baker stared at the index and had a sense of déjà vu. He remembered being in this same Ocean Avenue bungalow four years before, staring with bored eyes at the same obtuse, indecipherable organization of Vargo companies. Back then Max had tried to explain it all to him and he had brushed his partner off, too lazy or indifferent to pay attention. He had the same urge now, to cut and run. Then he remembered what the last bout of laziness had bought him and he jabbed at the chart.

"I want to understand this exactly. Where did his money go? Just flying offshore?"

"Exactly. Every quarter was transferred from thirty-seven Firenze Corporation bank accounts three days before the end."

"Transferred where? And how?"

"Wire transfer. First to the Caymans, Panama, and Gibraltar, then to Vaduz. After that, who knows? There's total bank secrecy in Liechtenstein."

The urge to bail swept over him again and he again resisted. "Once again," he said slowly. "Thirty-seven U.S. accounts wire out hundreds of millions three days before the end." He wrote it down as he said it. "Is that it?"

"Almost. The thirty-seven accounts fed like tributaries into a single U.S. account, kind of a mother ship account I uncovered. Then the mother blasted all the little babies to Gibraltar and the rest."

"One big mother of a mother account?"

"Exactly."

Now Baker knew the question to ask. "Where? Which one?"

Faldo flipped some pages. "Account number 427893-VH maintained in the name of Firenze Holdings S.A. at the Asian Interbank Trust." He looked up. "Location, Monterey Park, California."

"Asian Interbank Trust." Baker wrote it down. "Japanese?"

"Chinese."

Bobby Lee pointed to the whiskey. "Guys, drink up. We got more work to do."

23

ON THE SEVENTEENTH DAY OF THE VARGO CHASE, JULIE Beck was secretly panicking. Part of her anxiety was due to simple loss of sleep. For the past three weeks she had either been in an airplane, a hotel room, or her office. She had slept in the office in her clothes for the last two days and had returned home only to shower and change. She ate only at her desk, the leftovers from hurried sandwiches now blending into the brown stains from a hundred styrofoam coffee cups. Her desk was a mass of paper and faxes and telephone slips; her eyes were slit at the edges and ringed with the red of burst capillaries. Her head was throbbing and blurred from the pain of a four-day uninterrupted migraine.

It all would be worth it to her if they were actually making progress. Yet for all her agents on the ground, at LAX, at the bus stations, at Amtrak, and sprinkled at a hundred useless locations around L.A., she had nothing to show for it except memos and stupid meetings and sleepless nights. Not a hint, not a sniff that the great man was in town and hunting.

And now this: a memo from the Attorney General's pup to her. Julie was the most political of animals and knew a setup when she saw it. The memo was innocuous enough on the surface, a simple congratulations on her appointment as head of the Vargo task force and a quiet reminder of the importance of "apprehending the subject" within the next fourteen days. "Thank you very fucking much" Julie had scribbled on her copy before she crushed and trashed it.

But it was the final paragraph that completely toasted her few remaining calm brain cells. In order to "assist in an orderly completion of the project," the memo said, "the Drug Enforcement Administration" had requested that one of its "senior officers" be permitted to act as a "liaison with Justice." And because of the importance of "early interagency cooperation" Main Justice had delivered Julie's head on a plate, assuring the DEA and its "senior officer" that "all appropriate resources" would be provided by the "field attorney assigned to the matter."

"Field attorney!" Julie Beck figured that was Manion's euphemism for "field hand." So now, in the middle of everything, with only fourteen days to go, she had to babysit some flunky from Washington. From DEA no less. What the hell could DEA do except screw things up?

But, orders were orders. She smoothed her skirt, tried unsuccessfully to rub the red out of her eyes, and politely rose when the "senior officer" entered. She even managed a smile.

"Good afternoon, I'm Julie Beck."

"It's a great privilege to meet you and I mean that sincerely," the man from DEA said, holding out his hand. His voice was soft, deep, and self-assured, patrician even, and his firm grip was confidence-inspiring. He looked to be in his late forties, tall and slim, with a shock of silver hair encircling ghostly pale blue eyes. His suit was gray and expensive, conservative yet oh so elegant. His shirt was white and the pale Italian tie appropriate for the occasion. The man's every gesture screamed that he was trustworthy and powerful.

"I'm Covington Barrows," the man said.

Julie let a beat go by, blinded slightly by the smile. She felt something ancient and primordial at the back of her mind twitching the nerve endings, the sort of sensation that in prehistory advised our simian forebears of the approach of a carnivore. Now she shook her head to scratch the itch. The remnants of lost sleep, she supposed.

"Pleased to meet you, Mr. Barrows," she said, correctly shaking the offered hand. "They said you might arrive today."

"Did they? How kind of them." The smile again. "Ms. Beck . . ."

"You can use my first name."

"Of course. Julie. May I sit?"

"Whatever you like. Let me move those papers."

"No, stay there." Barrows cleared away a chair and successfully avoided making a face at the disarray surrounding him. He sat, then leaned forward. "Before I begin I must make two observations."

"Observations?"

"Yes." More forward leaning. "First, I know you must be offended by my presence. I have spent many years in government and know there is nothing more important than turf. And rightly so, I might add. We all have chosen public service because we believe we have important contributions to make. We therefore regard as critical the opportunity to make those contributions without improper interference."

What a pretty bureaucratic speech. Julie knew she was being stroked but didn't mind. At least the guy was making the effort. And besides he sounded good when he talked.

"I'm not offended," she said simply.

He smiled indulgently. "Please, you can be honest. It is never comfortable to have another . . . another . . ."

"Cook?"

"Yes, cook. You're probably an excellent one." The smile again.

"Not really. I don't have the time."

"You should make the time. I do. Italian is my specialty."

All those pretty smiles and good pasta, too.

"Anyway," she said flatly, "I'm not offended."

"That's fortunate because I think we can help each other."

"I know. I got the memo."

"Ms. Beck . . . Julie . . . I'm not talking about the memo."

"No? What then?"

Barrows paused. "My views on Mr. Baker are the same as yours."

Interesting. She sat back and studied him. "And those are?"

"I think . . . no, not think, *know* . . . that it was a monumental mistake to release him."

She smiled. "We do have the same view on that."

"And my opinions are quite firm. I have great admiration for you, for what you accomplished. You worked hard to convict and sentence a dangerous criminal. Now, because of bureaucratic incompetence and a misguided strategy concerning Mr. Vargo, that criminal has been released."

She pointed a finger at him. "Right."

"And it goes much deeper than that. This is neither a minor crime nor a minor criminal. Mr. Baker is the man responsible in large part for Vargo's successful escape.

Not to mention the fortune that was stolen. Not to mention . . ."

"Three gruesome deaths?"

"Exactly."

"So what do we do about it? I want him back in Boron. You want him back in Boron. How do we get him back in Boron?"

Barrows stood and paced, seemingly lost in thought. "Where is Baker now?"

"I've got him stashed at an FBI apartment in Venice. I picked the crummiest one I could find. The building is all drug dealers and bums. We forfeited it last year when we busted the owner for dealing."

"He's guarded?"

"An agent's with him at all times. José Medina."

"Good man?"

Julie shrugged. "Sure."

"All right, what are your plans now to have him . . . uh, participate in the project? Do you think a man like him can ever really be trusted?"

"I doubt it. I had a long conversation with him when he was first brought down from MDC. He's in the same state of arrogant denial as before. As far as I'm concerned, he can just rot in that apartment for the next few weeks and then rot in Boron for the next not so few years." She spit out the words.

"Your instincts are exactly right. Now what about Vargo? What do we know so far?"

"I know he's in, he's got to be. Where and when, what name he's using, what he looks like now, who he'll try to contact, we don't know." She pulled out a thick folder. "Here's what we got so far."

"May I?"

"Of course."

Barrows went through the documents quickly, occasionally reading one with concentration, otherwise flipping through casually. He made notes on a yellow pad. "May I get a copy of this file?"

"No problem." She buzzed for a secretary and gave the instructions. "It'll take a few hours. This is the government, you know."

"I do know. I'll read the file in my hotel this evening." He paused. "You receive reports daily?"

"Yes."

"Would I be out of place to request copies as they come in?"

"Not at all."

"Thank you. I'm very grateful. Now, what about meetings? Live briefings? How do you convey to the agents their marching orders?"

"Every other day all hands in the P.M. Breakfast with the Bureau."

"How civilized." The white smile again.

"It's coffee and doughnuts."

"Even so." Barrows considered this schedule for a moment. "I'd like to assist you, Ms. Beck . . . Julie, in a way that does not interfere with your work in the slightest. I guarantee I will do all in my power to assure that *both* our goals are satisfied." She knew what he was talking about and there was no need to respond. "I've never tried to hide my admiration for your efforts. Personally, I think you're doing an outstanding job and I've conveyed that to Arthur Manion."

"Thank you."

"At the same time I have my own orders. My superiors will expect to be kept informed."

"I understand."

"I must report to them frequently and appear . . . well, somewhat knowledgeable, I suppose you'd say."

Julie nodded, wondering where this was all going.

"All of that leads me to one conclusion. I'd like to make a deal with you."

"A deal?"

"Yes. We have very few days left. I propose that you continue exactly what you're doing without interruption or interference. I ask only that you copy me on the incoming agent reports and briefly consult with me once a day on your progress. I may suggest techniques from time to time but the final decision will always be yours. Other than that I will confine my activities to making your life easier and using my connections to accomplish our *common* and I emphasize *common* goals."

It was the second time in two minutes he had alluded to Baker. Julie felt a small red light go off but again couldn't identify the source. The offer was fine, the presentation elegant, the man serious and purposeful. Why the red light?

"And I never have to take instructions from you?"

Barrows laughed politely, the sort of small laugh that must have wowed them back at Washington cocktail parties. What a foolish question, the laugh said. " 'Instructions' is certainly not a word I would use," he said. The laugh again, sharing a joke.

Julie didn't smile back.

"What word would you use?"

"Consult. I'm here to consult."

"I see."

"Each day, briefly, we consult. For example, are you meeting your agents tonight?"

"Yes, six o'clock."

"Can you report to me at seven o'clock? We could have drinks."

"I'm not a drinker, especially when I'm working."

"I understand. Dinner, then."

She considered it. She had a lot to do but she had to eat. Besides, she needed him to be on her side.

"Where?"

"I'm staying downtown. At Checkers. I could make reservations for eight o'clock."

"I have to work tomorrow. Tonight also."

"Make it seven then, right after you meet with your agents."

"All right. Seven's fine."

"Excellent." He got up and gave her his grin and hand. It was a manicured, formal hand, with strength and texture.

"I ought to say good-bye to Jim Price on the way out," he threw in as he walked to the door.

James P. Price. *The* United States Attorney for the Central District of California. Her boss. And if they got Vargo, maybe with help from people like Covington Barrows, her predecessor.

"Well, tell Jim we'll give you all the support you need," she said.

The look, the serious, purposeful glance, the package of absolute trust. Who could deny him anything?

"Be assured that my conversations with Jim Price and others will be of great benefit to you."

"Seven, then."

24

MEDINA SIPPED THE BUSH AND SMILED, TOASTING THE falling sun slipping quietly down the window to the west. "Now this is great booze. You give me enough of this, I don't mind working."

"Thank the Irish," Baker told him. "You want great tequila, go Mexican. People should do what they do best."

Medina nodded in agreement, then dumped a pile of unsorted paper onto the conference room table. He flipped through it casually, trying not to think of how boring it would be to actually read through this garbage. He was about to complain to Baker when an eight-by-ten glossy caught his eye. He held it up, took a gigantic sip of the Bush, and began choking.

"*Madre de dios,*" he whispered when he finally caught his breath.

Baker looked over. "I don't think so. She's not the maternal type."

Medina was now mumbling incoherently in Spanish, holding the photo tightly with both hands.

"It's gonna be disgusting if you start licking that."

"Who is it?" Medina finally gasped.

"That's the girl I told you about, the one that got away. Her name's Angela." Baker grabbed for the photo but Medina held tight. "Don't be a goddamn baby," Baker said and ripped the picture away. It was a still from one of her hit pictures, *An Amazon's Revenge*. Angela was naked and tied to the branch of a tree with her arms stretched high. A group of half-naked women with spears gazed lustfully at her.

"She's a paleontologist in this one," Baker explained. "An evil professor brings her to the jungle to steal artifacts from a remote Amazon tribe. They kill him and introduce her to the ways of Amazon love. At the end she becomes their queen. She always became the queen in the end. It was like a trademark."

Medina stared in disbelief.

"I'm telling you it was good. Admittedly the motivations were not fully developed, but the relationship between Angela and the young novice Amazon was terrific."

Medina coughed. "You're fucking sick." He grabbed the photo back. "Is the video here?"

"Maybe." Baker flipped through the pile of papers. "Anyway, here's one with her clothes on."

Medina reluctantly gave up Angela the Amazon in return for Angela dressed, sort of. She was standing in front of a bar on Sunset Boulevard with a bouncer near her left elbow. The bouncer came up to her shoulder. She was dressed in a sprayed-on gold-sequined shift that could not possibly have had anything on underneath. Behind her, in gold plate, were the words CAMDEN CLUB. The wide, natural grin and the cascading red hair almost obliterated the sign. Medina held the photo close to his eyes, then grunted.

"Like it?"

Medina ignored the question. He reached in his pocket and extracted a faux Swiss army knife with a magnifying glass attached. He popped the glass out and focused it on the picture.

"I heard Jack Nicholson does that from a distance of thirty feet when the Laker girls take the floor."

Medina put down the glass. "Andy Achille."

"Pardon?"

"The guy next to her. Andy Achille. He cuts people for Dominick Romano."

"Who's that?"

"The guy that used to own Camden Club. He's in charge of the greaseball trade out here."

"Pardon?"

"Sorry. The *Italians*. You like that better?"

"Actually, yes."

"Well, he's the one. There's not a lot of them in L.A. but what there is is nasty."

" 'Are' you mean."

"What?"

" 'Are' nasty, not 'is.' The Italians, I mean."

"Blow me," Medina said amiably and picked up Angela the Amazon again. "Jesus, I'd give up everything. God, country, whatever."

Medina's panting focused Baker on a very important issue. Angela had *always* been joined to Vargo at the hip. If they could possibly find her . . .

"What did you say the name of that place was?"

"Shut up," Medina said. "You know, licking this is a possibility."

"Here, do it to this one." Baker gently took Angela the bar decoration and handed over Angela the Amazon. "Now come on, Medina, where is this place and who is Romano?"

"I really don't know."

"Come on, goddamn it, give."

He sighed. "Camden Club was Romano's headquarters till about three years ago. OCID busted it and Romano moved on."

OCID was Organized Crime Investigative Division, an LAPD operation. It had nothing to do with the FBI. But Medina had everything to do with OCID.

"OCID?" Bobby Lee laughed heartily. "Medina, you dog."

"Blow me, Baker."

"Patsy Mulligan. May the saints preserve us."

"Baker, you want to go back to butt-fucking some embezzler in Boron?"

"Don't be so sensitive. I thought you two were, you know . . ." He held two fingers together and separated them.

"We are."

"Too bad. Patsy is the hottest cop to strap on a . . . well . . ."

"Right, it could be anything. Plus she's got the worst temper and foulest mouth in the LAPD."

That might be true. Patsy was the daughter of a cop and the granddaughter of a cop and probably the great-granddaughter of an IRA hit man. She was the youngest of eleven children: ten boys and Patsy. The boys were LAPD, DEA, IRS investigators, anything with initials. Patsy grew up with a family that never noticed she was a girl. But Medina noticed.

"She may have a bad temper but she's also got a tightly organized little—"

"I know," Medina said, "believe me I know." He sighed at the thought. "Anyway, it's over."

"When?"

He shrugged. "I don't know."

"Liar. When? This was like a five-year deal you guys had."

He coughed. "Tuesday."

Baker laughed uproariously. "Tuesday! Hell, there's plenty of time for a reconciliation." He grabbed the phone. "What's the number?"

"For the third time, bite me, Baker."

"Sorry, buddy, this is too important." He got the number from information on the first try.

"Hello, Patsy, hi, search your memory. This is Bobby Lee Baker. . . . Doin' good, how you doin'? . . . Really? Well, hey, don't give up on him yet. . . . Me, yeah, I'm out, sort of on parole. . . . Thanks, you're right, I didn't do it. . . . Actually, I'm calling for a favor. . . . Well, thanks, I'd help you out too anytime I could. . . ." He winked at Medina and watched his face darken.

"Yeah, it's about a girl I need to find who hung out at a place called Camden Club. . . . Right, I know you closed it. I'm thinking maybe the guy who owned it re-opened. . . . He did, great!" Baker put his hand over the mouthpiece. "Romano's got a new place," he whispered.

"I'm thrilled," Medina growled.

"Anyway," Baker said, "this is about my case and I'm wondering if maybe you could help me out. . . . Sure I got a picture of her. . . . Tonight? Yeah, I could drop it off." Medina's face turned purple. "Right away's great, see you then."

He hung up the phone and started whistling. "It's like riding a bike, you know?"

"They're all the same," Medina muttered. "I still got my shoes over there and she's already bending over the desk. And for a goddamn criminal!"

Baker grabbed the photos, then grabbed Medina. "She knows I'm innocent. Besides, cons have a special attraction."

Medina mumbled to himself in Spanish as Faldo walked in, confused, still hoping it would all go away.

"Bring him too," Baker shouted as he headed to the door. "First Patsy's, then some Chinese food."

25

ROBERT VARGO PLACED HIS WAKE-UP CALL FOR 4:30 A.M. The young killer in the bed with him groaned as the phone rang. Vargo let it ring until the punk stirred.

"Don't let that happen again," Vargo snapped.

Vincent stared at him dumbly.

"Now!" Vargo barked.

Vincent leaped out of bed and answered the phone. Vargo took time to admire the man's naked body. A young David, Vargo concluded. The body of a boy and the strength of a man. Smooth, Hispanic, hairless, with a taut musculature that was the natural inheritance of the young. Vargo admired, as he had the night before, the cruel scar extending down the middle of the man's back. At first he had traced it tenderly with a finger. Then, when the young man had laughed derisively, he had demonstrated with venom that there existed a cruelty equal to his own.

"Now call for breakfast," Vargo ordered.

Vargo showered and dressed while Vincent arranged his breakfast. Barrows had chosen well with this young man; he was not only handsome but clearly a professional. Last night Vargo had questioned Vincent closely about the men and women he had killed. Vincent had been forthright. At thirteen he was doing drive-bys in the barrio south of Jefferson off Alvarado. By fifteen, to avenge an insult, he and his friends had sprayed automatic weapons into a bridal party celebrating in the front yard of a home in La Habra. Nine people died in that one, including the bride, the groom, and a fourteen-month-old baby in the arms of a dead grandmother. By sixteen he was in a penal youth camp in the Tehachapies, sleeping in a cabin, chopping wood during the day and getting strong. He was released on his seventeenth birthday and welcomed back to the barrio with a party and a new MAC-10. Six months later he and his friend Alphonso Lopez took out a buyer with what they thought was a suitcase full of cash. He escaped with the suitcase never realizing that the buyer was a DEA undercover agent whose death was carried live on a transmitter strapped to what had once been the man's chest. The feds hunted him like a dog for three weeks while he rotted in a basement. Then Miranda—his leader, his patron, his life— smuggled him out of town and gave up two mules named Meza and Gutierrez. The feds were happy and he was back in L.A. from Guadalajara six months later.

Upon his return Vincent became a celebrity within the L.A. Latin drug community. Miranda kept him under wraps and used him only as a threat—merely a reference to Vincent and he got what he wanted. When Barrows demanded the best for this project Miranda didn't hesitate.

Vargo had no illusions about Vincent's loyalties. The boy would report everything back to Barrows or Miranda immediately. But Vargo was used to that from his days in Cuba. He was now an expert in using such spies to his advantage.

At 6 A.M., they left the hotel. Vincent took the wheel for the drive to Sylmar. Vargo sat in the back surrounded with documents. Vargo had little recollection of the area and was appalled when he saw it, as he had been with most of the L.A. environs since his return. Sylmar was nothing more than a warehouse city ringed by ground zero undeveloped lots, scrub grass, and motels. The busted warehouse which had almost cost Vargo his life was a nondescript corrugated steel building a hundred yards from a rail line. It was one of thirteen identical metal buildings standing shoulder to shoulder parallel to the line. The famous warehouse, ultimately and inevitably dubbed the "Powder Room" by the L.A. press, was number six in the tawdry line.

In its heyday, the Powder Room was regarded in Havana as Vargo's first demonstration of pure genius. The cartel had never been able to store large amounts of cocaine indefinitely, a problem which led to the unsatisfactory requirement of selling in bulk to distributors—and at a deep discount—in such outlets as Tampico or Guadalajara. The distributors then gladly took the risk, and the enormous extra profit, of transshipment from Mexico to L.A.—the new Miami. For ten years the cartel chafed at the lost profit.

Warehouses like the Powder Room changed all that. With reliable L.A. storage facilities Vargo could smuggle in bulk and intermingle the square brown packages with ordinary commercial containers. He could then download the product by delivering the wrappers to the blacks and Mexicans in exchange for cash. By 1989, he had tested the system with a few hundred pounds, moving up to a ton by early '90. By 1991, when the bust occurred, he had recklessly allowed twenty tons of product to be sitting unprotected in a single warehouse. Street value—his life.

Vincent circled the warehouse slowly, the Lincoln slicing grudgingly through the heat and smog. Even at this early hour, the sun fought only faintly through the whiteout of summer haze and ozone. Here, miles from the beach, an offshore breeze was just a rumor.

The warehouse was surrounded by a makeshift chainlink fence and a sign warning of guard dogs. When the Lincoln stopped, a black shepherd sprinted for the fence, leaping and snarling. Vincent turned to Vargo, who was casually examining documents in the backseat.

"I'd like to look inside, Vincent," Vargo said without looking up.

Vincent got out of the car and shut the door behind him. He left the engine running and the air conditioner on. He took a steel bar from the trunk and walked to the fence. The dog's ears flattened and a low guttural sound started in his throat. Vincent and the shepherd eyed each other with a certain professional respect. Then Vincent raised the bar and banged it loudly and repeatedly against the fence.

The shepherd lost it, leaping and grabbing for the steel bar with saliva-dripping jaws. Vincent jabbed the bar through the fence and let the dog grab it. He tugged back once and the dog held on. Satisfied, Vincent pulled a .38 from his waistband and put it in the dog's mouth, substituting the gun for the steel bar. The sound was barely more than a faint pop. The shepherd's head exploded. Vincent pulled the stained steel bar back and broke the padlock with it. He opened the fence, returned to the car, and straightened his hair in the mirror.

"Not bad," Vargo told him. "Now pull around back, then go clean up the mess. Let me know when you find a way in." His head went back to his documents.

Fifteen minutes later, Vincent had the dog cleaned up, a window jimmied, and the back door to the warehouse open. He shut off the engine and opened the door for Vargo. Then he led him inside.

The warehouse was empty and dark, what light there was fighting weakly through mud-encrusted high windows from the searing white-hot day outside. Vargo tried a few switches until he satisfied himself that all the power was cut. That explained the absence of an alarm. It also meant they were safe from surveillance cameras.

They walked around through what was now a bombed-out war zone. The floor was braced with rows of bare metal frames, once bursting with wooden pallets, now empty except for the remnants abandoned by the police.

The manager's office was a frosted-glass cubicle at the far end of the building. The man had been selected by the Cubans and Vargo had never had any real control over him. After the bust, he had disappeared. Vargo pointed.

"Check out that office. Find out where the manager lives."

When Vincent left Vargo inspected some more. The cocaine had been intermingled with everything from dead files from law firms and insurance companies to potatoes for a local supermarket chain. Vargo's last shipment was inside used furniture from second-hand stores, shipped from Mexico for resale in L.A. It was as safe as Sunday until somebody tipped the DEA.

Vincent interrupted his reverie. "I found something."

He came out with a brown box filled with folders. "I think these are time cards."

He was right. The cards went back years, long before he had set the Powder Room up. "Look for 1990. I want the manager."

Vincent rummaged through the files until he found 1990. He flipped through those. "There were six guys working here then. How do I know who's the manager?"

"Check the hourly rates. Whoever's the highest, that's him."

Vincent hunted some more, arranging the cards in neat piles. "This is him," he said finally. "Gilbert Martinez. Ten seventy-five an hour."

"You got an address?"

Vincent tapped the card. "Right at the top."

"Good. Go visit him."

"Yeah?"

"Yeah. After you drop me off. I want to know everything by tonight."

"What if he don't want to tell me?"

Vargo laughed without humor and Vincent felt a sudden chill. "You better pray you can be persuasive, Vincent."

26

THEY LEFT PATSY'S APARTMENT AT 8 P.M. AS THE SUN was dipping into the Pacific. Baker stopped to watch it before he got in the car. Because of the smog, the sun was luminescent as it neared the horizon. The night sky formed a pencil-thin line along the blue water and the orange disk slipped cleanly into it. In thirty seconds, it was gone, leaving behind a pyrotechnical light show as the ozone and pollutants, unimpeded by the competition of the bright sun, seemed to explode into an orgy of color. And they say no good comes from smog.

Baker climbed into the car next to Medina, who was still cowering in the back hoping Patsy wouldn't see him. Faldo was driving. Medina was in a foul mood.

"Where now?" he barked.

Baker studied Faldo's Green Bible and focused on the great switching station for all Vargo funds, the Asian Interbank Trust. "You like Chinese food?"

"I guess."

"Then that's first. Monterey Park."

"What's second?" he asked, clearly worried.

Baker started humming the wedding march. Medina stared disgustedly out the window.

Baker already knew a fair amount about Monterey Park from his days in the U.S. Attorney's office. He remembered the city as a hole-in-the-wall just off the San Bernardino Freeway about five minutes east of downtown. Until the Chinese money hit, the town was a forgotten Latino barrio. However, in the mid-1970s, for reasons no one understands, the city became Hong Kong by the Pacific, attracting over a hundred thousand upper- and middle-class Chinese fleeing from Taiwan and Hong Kong, displacing the Latinos who preceded them, establishing an affluent enclave distinct from the impoverished Chinese in the downtown Chinatown district. Every street sign in Monterey Park now sported Chinese characters as well as English. All of the local services from the police to fire to the schools had staffs of Mandarin-speaking community representatives. The restaurants stood ten to a block. And then there were the banks.

Baker remembered endless grand jury investigations of those banks, investigations which took years, subpoenaed thousands of documents, and inevitably went nowhere. In the 1970s, the banks were nothing more than safe houses for money fleeing currency restrictions in Taiwan and the approach of the communist hordes in Hong Kong. By the 1980s, however, those first few banks had buckled under the flow. New banks sprang up like weeds, fueled by the money out of Southeast Asia and headed by managers who promised and delivered complete anonymity. And where Taiwan money went, so too went the Bamboo Gang.

The United Bamboo Gang out of Taipei is the world's largest and most successful criminal organization. It was originally a paramilitary operation for the protection of mainland warlords, but since 1949 has evolved into much more. Internationally it has a virtual monopoly on the poppy trade that flows from the East Asian Golden Triangle. In Taiwan it functions as a semiofficial shadow security force in tandem with the Kuomintang, the official Taiwanese military. The relationship between the government of Taiwan and the United Bamboo Gang is one of beautiful symmetry based on common goals. The gang ensures that all Chinese expatriates are loyal to the Taiwanese leadership. The government permits and encourages the gang's successful operation of an international heroin cartel. Both parties benefit.

The proliferation of Chinese banks in the 1980s was a direct result of the increased wealth and success of the Bamboo Gang. No longer content to simply be wholesalers offshore, Bamboo agents were now directly selling product and laundering funds in the United States. A successful laundering operation requires pliant banks. No better banks could be imagined for this purpose than the sleepy, naturally developing Chinese banks of Monterey Park.

The Asian Interbank Trust was the opposite of the imposing structure it appeared from a reading of Faldo's Green Bible. The building was little more than a small cinder-block structure taking up about fifteen thousand square feet of land. The upper of the two stories had no windows. The lower story had three windows facing the street and slits along the side. The windows were barred and blackened. The small sign with the bank's name was plastic, nondescript, and covered with soot. Next door was a restaurant with the name "Golden Dragon" emblazoned in cheap neon.

Baker tried to peer in the barred windows. "I can't see anything," he said. "Let's go around back."

Medina chuckled. Faldo was appalled. "We'd be trespassing!"

"He's right," Medina said.

"Yeah, I guess he is." Baker pointed to the garishly lit restaurant next door. The light from the Golden Dragon flooded the street, casting a pale, eerie glow over Medina and Faldo. "Why don't you two guys see if we can eat in there?" he suggested.

Medina grabbed Faldo by the arm. "Good idea. Now don't go trespassing," he shouted over his shoulder. Then they were gone.

Baker was alone. He looked both ways. There was plenty of activity in front of the Golden Dragon but none where he was standing. He quickly slipped into the far alleyway between the Asian Interbank Trust and something which looked to be a poultry slaughterhouse next door.

The space between the two buildings was tight and he had to turn sideways to get through. As he left the garish lights of the Golden Dragon, the alley darkened. By the time he was halfway down, the light had completely disappeared. The alley also got narrower and he tried not to panic. Just your imagination, he told himself.

Three-quarters of the way down, an air duct appeared at eye level. He could hear a small ventilation fan deep inside the bank. The fan blew a thin breeze into his face redolent with the smells of the Golden Dragon. He had too much trouble squeezing through the alley to wonder why a bank smelled like cashew chicken.

The back of the bank was as black as a nun's dress. He wormed his way through the opening into a small courtyard. Surrounding the courtyard was a two-story cinder-block wall and above that a moonless sky. Baker had to feel his way around the wall to gauge the size of the place. He felt like the victim in the pit trying to stay away from the pendulum.

After a lot of groping he became convinced there was only one way out, back down the skinny alley. The back wall was a wall, nothing more, no gate, no light, no nothing. It reminded him of Boron a little. The rear wall of the bank itself was almost as bleak. A knobless metal door was welded into the masonry of the building. Above it, on the second floor, two blackened and barred windows were the only break in a flat plate of gray concrete.

And that was it. Except for the fire escape.

Baker was sure that if there weren't firemen and fire regulations, there wouldn't be a fire escape hanging on the back wall. The vague federal regulations governing how a bank operates could be ignored. But when a guy in a red hat walks out the back door and points, you have to put up a ladder.

The ladder ran from the roof to the ground with a small landing outside the second-floor windows, just in case anyone wanted to break through the bars to avoid the flames. The bank employees would have the same chance of living through a fire as those girls in the shirt factory after the captains of industry nailed the fire doors shut. Baker could imagine the meeting where they discussed this: first let's build the ladder; then get it inspected; then after the guy leaves, put bars on the windows. There were worse things than losing a few employees to a fire.

Not that it mattered so much now. Maybe the bars were even good, preventing him from trying anything too suicidal like breaking into the bank. But the ladder—why not?

By the time Baker had scrambled onto the flat roof, the light from the Golden Dragon provided only faint visibility. Cast in shadows, the roof was a maelstrom of what at first looked like huge snakes, but on closer inspection turned out to be thick interconnected wires. Two satellite dishes sat sentry on the roof aiming in opposite directions. The wires and lines from the dishes ran through an elevated electronics bunker surrounded by an impenetrable steel casing. Up close, Baker could see the innards of the unit through ventilation slits in the casing. The unit was a magical combination of blinking red and green lights and digital readouts.

The blinking lights meant nothing to him so he decided to follow the thick cords, see where they led. The cords were tacked along the roof and had protective rain sheeting over them. Some left the electronics bunker and seemed to dive down through holes in the roof into the innards of the bank. Several spilled over the roof toward the alley between the bank and the Golden Dragon.

He walked to the edge of the roof and looked down. The black alley was four feet wide. Baker decided not to think; after all, in the old days he used to dive into end zones with huge animalistic linebackers hanging on his neck. He stepped back, took a deep breath, ran and jumped. The years must have taken their toll; he wound up smashing into the lip of the Golden Dragon roof, then falling face first onto the flat surface beyond. Once there he skidded, tearing a layer of skin off the right side of his face. His knee, the same one blasted in that long ago spring practice, throbbed with pain. He tried to straighten the knee and found he could only limp. And for what? Now he was on the roof of a Chinese restaurant. Not only that, how the hell was he going to get back?

He limped around until he could stretch the leg without excruciating pain. As he did so, he kept tripping over more wires in the dark. The wires from the bank building dove into the alley, climbed up the side wall of the restaurant, spilled over the lip of the roof in waves, and were connected into steel-encased bunkers. From there, the wires went down holes in the restaurant roof, just like on the roof of the bank.

Baker had no idea why a Chinese restaurant might need such fancy stuff. Maybe to order more egg rolls. If so they could probably call China directly, because the two satellite dishes on the restaurant roof were even bigger than the ones on the roof of the bank.

On the back side of the restaurant roof, there was another fire escape which worked its way to the ground. Baker again thanked the fire department for small favors and limped down the ladder. At the bottom, several of the wires from the roof converged and dove into the ground. He knelt in the soft dirt and peered into the black void. There was a small air shaft surrounding the wires. There was very little he could see, but one thing he was sure of: there was a room in the basement of the Golden Dragon that was the terminus of all this fancy electronics.

Baker hopped around to the front and casually into the

restaurant. Medina was happily chomping some mu shu pork. He waved Baker to his seat.

"They ain't quesadillas, but not bad." Then he looked up. "What happened to you?"

Bobby Lee felt his face. There was enough skin scraped off to make a new face. He felt blood on his fingers. "I fell," he explained.

"Jesus, be careful. What am I going to tell her if you get killed?"

Faldo wasn't paying attention, just intently reading the menu. "They need twenty-four hours for the Peking duck. Therefore I think we ought to go Szechuan. Do you fellows like to share?"

The waiter brought them over some Chinese beers. Medina suddenly realized he would have to mix these with the Black Bush. "I'm not supposed to drink, Baker," Medina said, a slight anxiety in his voice. "You tell anybody, I'm gonna lock you in a closet for life."

"Just be nice to me." Baker held the cold bottle against his bruised face and looked around. The restaurant was an ordinary place with ordinary tables. Most of the customers were Chinese. The help looked efficient. The kitchen off to the right was busy and large. He saw a set of stairs to the left leading down into something unknown.

"I got to go. Nature and all."

Medina shook his head. "You don't hang around too long, do you?" He waved him away.

The bathrooms were indeed near the steps, but on the ground floor, in back of the bustling kitchen. Hell, anybody can make a mistake. When he reached the stairs, he made a hard left and walked down into darkness.

At the bottom of the steps, there was a door secured by nothing more than an eye hook. Baker hunted in his pocket and found his thin, plastic ID card from MDC. He flipped the latch quickly and the door swung open. And who says prison doesn't teach useful skills.

He closed the door softly behind him and the hallway was darkened. The sounds of the restaurant above became muted. He could feel thick carpeting beneath his feet and hardwood paneling on the walls. This part didn't seem like a Chinese restaurant at all.

He inched forward feeling his way along the wood wall. Five steps along, his knee, the one already banged up by the leap across the void, collided with a large stationary ashtray. The ashtray fell with a clatter, only slightly louder than Baker's scream. That noise was immediately replaced by a high-pitched repetitive alarm. Light flooded the passageway. He could hear the thunder of footsteps on the steps behind him. Three Chinese males in dark suits sprang from behind one of the walnut doors. All of them were reaching under their lapels. They were all young and hard-looking. None looked like a waiter.

He tried the ingratiating approach. "Men's room? This way to men's room?" He grabbed his crotch and made what he hoped was the universal gesture of urinating.

One of the Chinese grabbed him by the throat and pushed his head against the walnut wall. Baker could tell right away that the wood was not a veneer. His head bounced twice. The Chinese tightened the grip on his throat.

Baker started to black out and wasn't really fighting it. A little unconsciousness and the pain in his face, his knee, and now in the back of his head would all go away. However, as quickly as the hand appeared on his throat, it was gone. In the background, through the fog of pain, Baker could see a much older man approach him. He had on a white shirt and black pants. He touched Bobby Lee kindly on the shoulder.

"You must forgive them, they do not speak English. They were concerned that you were a burglar."

"Afraid I might steal tomorrow's duck?"

The man smiled. "Occasionally, we have large cash receipts. We must take precautions."

"Of course," he said. "The bathroom?"

"Just up the stairs. You must have made a wrong turn."

Baker bowed slightly and the man bowed back. He returned to his table to find Medina and Faldo merrily munching away. Baker was rubbing the back of his head and Medina looked at him sympathetically. "Christ, Baker, you got to take care of yourself. You look worse than when you left. Here, have a beer."

"Thanks." Bobby Lee drank a long pull while Faldo filled his plate. He ignored the food. Things were moving fast and unless he stayed up he would find himself back in the high desert drawing Xs on a calendar. He quickly finished the beer and signaled for the check.

"What are you doing? You just got here."

"Sorry, but we don't have time. We got a lot to do."

"Yeah? Like what?"

"First of all back to Patsy's. I want to see if she's got anything on Angela."

Medina had forgotten that part and audibly groaned.

Baker glanced toward the stairs. The older man in the white shirt had emerged and was chatting amiably in Chinese with the headwaiter. The waiter bowed and left. Then the man in the white shirt went back downstairs, casting a quick, no doubt unimportant look in Baker's direction before he did.

27

BY 5 P.M. HER WEARINESS FROM LACK OF SLEEP WAS threatening to overwhelm her. And yet the day was not nearly finished. First a five-thirty officewide staff meeting —priorities for the fourth quarter will be major narcotics and S&L fraud, hot news—then the 6 P.M. Vargo meeting with her agents. And after that, instead of getting back to work, or maybe even grabbing a desperately needed twenty-minute nap, she had to have dinner with this guy from DEA at seven. What a mistake.

She entered the conference room for the Vargo meeting in a foul mood. She had twelve primary agents working for her now from three agencies—IRS, DEA, and the FBI—and each of them had untold subordinates on the streets. With all this horsepower you'd think they'd have the guy wrapped with ribbons in forty-eight hours. Instead there wasn't one of these mopes that had anything intelligent to tell her. The airports were all negative so maybe he hasn't come in yet, said the yutz from DEA. Right. Four million illiterate Mexicans and Guatemalans can find a way in but Vargo can't. She'd keep the airport watch on for show but that's all it was. Vargo was in.

The meeting had an unpleasant dynamic that infuriated her. All the agents were senior, and men, and there wasn't one of them that was happy to be reporting to a young female AUSA. So they patronized her, droning on in agentspeak about street surveillance and plants at the hotels and bribes of high-yield informants with all the enthusiasm of a college student telling Dad about his courses. She cursed under her breath and tried to stay cool. It didn't work that well. At six-thirty, she slammed her briefing book closed.

"Gentlemen, this is a very disappointing meeting." The men shifted in their seats. "I'll be faxing our joint status report to Washington tonight. I'll do my best to keep our team intact."

She rose and the room erupted. Suddenly the bored faces developed surprising animation. She was assured from all three agencies that progress was just around the corner. She listened carefully, heard nothing new, and turned on her heel.

"As I say, I'll do my best," she said as she left.

The door closed behind her and the room quieted. Then the agent from DEA spoke for all of them. "Fucking cunt," he said bitterly.

Checkers was only five minutes away and she had a half hour to get there. Her clothes felt clammy and the weariness now fell over her like a shroud, mixing with the anger from the agents' meeting to form a truly dangerous emotional brew. She needed to freshen up. And calm down.

She always kept a fresh blouse around for emergencies and this time she used it. She also decided for the first time in her career to use the much maligned and seldom-cleaned office shower. The shower was tucked inside a tiny cubicle in what used to be a closet. It was only used by males after lunchtime runs and reeked of sweat and used towels. She tried not to think of what she really craved, a luxurious hot bath, perhaps with some oils, in a pristine bathtub. Sometimes you had to grab what they gave you.

She entered the dark room and undressed, then showered quickly, like she was plunging into a cold pool on a hot day, just get it over with. She turned off the water and stood dripping before the grimy bathroom mirror, feeling a little better, not much. She dried herself slowly. She had very little time and was now very much alone. The smells and sights of this male-dominated locker room closed in around her and emphasized what she already knew. There was no one she could count on, not the tax partner, not her agents, not Bobby Lee Baker for sure. If only she had one ally. But there was no one.

At seven, the bar at Checkers was crowded, filled with well-dressed and prosperous escapees from nearby offices. It was a good-looking crowd. The men were youthful, the women tailored. The drinks were soft, lots of white wines and bubbled water. Nobody was ordering double shots with beer chasers these days.

Covington Barrows was standing at the bar and smiled broadly when she approached. He was as she remembered him, tall, regal, white hair perfectly in place. He had replaced the light gray Italian suit with something darker, equally Italian, equally elegant, equally tasteful. He took her hand with both of his and spoke with that same deep, smooth voice.

"I'm so delighted you could join me. I was concerned that your duties might prevent it after all."

They almost did. "I'm happy I could make it."

"Excellent. Shall we have a drink first?"

"Maybe at the table, Mr. Barrows. I have to . . ."

"Work. Of course." He signaled efficiently to the headwaiter. "We'll have you back in the office at eight o'clock. I promise."

That promise turned out to be, well, flexible, as did her iron-clad rule about not drinking while working. At the table, she reluctantly consented to a champagne before dinner, figuring she'd nurse it, no problem. She didn't, though, and the champagne relaxed her enough to permit

Covington, as he now demanded to be called, to select a wine. "Puligny-Montrachet," he told the waiter. It was ice-cold and French, thick as butter. The first glass was so good she let the waiter give her another.

Barrows—Covington—was a great conversationalist in addition to all those teeth. And Julie could tell right away he both loved women and was not afraid of them. He actually looked at her when he spoke, and when he listened, which he genuinely seemed to like to do, he was rapt, staring dead into her eyes. Julie couldn't imagine him sprawled on a couch in his boxers with a beer in his hand and a baseball game on, like some felons she could mention. It was encouraging to know there were men like Barrows around.

"You know," she said finally, "I've told you everything about me, but I don't know anything about you."

He sipped his wine and made an expansive gesture. "Please. Ask me anything you like and I will answer truthfully. Make believe it's a cross-examination."

Bad idea, Barrows, she thought. "Okay. Age?"

He laughed at that. Julie liked his laugh, too. "So soon?"

"Yes."

"Forty-seven."

At least it had a four in it. "How long have you been with DEA?"

"Ten years. And before that, twelve years with State, also in the Caribbean theater, ever since graduate school."

"Where?"

"Johns Hopkins."

"Advanced international studies."

"Very good. Yes, the Washington campus."

"Undergrad?"

"Princeton."

"Princeton, Hopkins. Very impressive. How come you're not with the CIA?"

He toasted the question. "Very good. You think everyone who goes through Princeton and Hopkins ends up in the CIA?"

"That's what I heard."

The excellent laugh again. "The truth is I was asked. The family disapproved."

The family. "Why?"

"They had a stellar history with State and a bad feeling toward the CIA."

"What history?"

"Will you hold it against me?"

"I don't know."

"Okay." A deep breath. "My great-grandfather was governor of New Hampshire. His brother was a U.S. Senator. Four of my uncles were ambassadors, one to the Court of St. James."

"And your father?"

"A drunk and a suicide. Some members of my family believe to this day that he was driven to it by enemies at the CIA."

"I'm sorry."

"Don't be. There's a black sheep in every family."

"Brothers and sisters?"

"No. Just dear Mom, now eighty-four and becoming a little, well, let's be kind, distracted."

"Hobbies?"

"Work."

"Me, too," Julie said. They both laughed nervously. "Doesn't that get you down sometimes? Like you're missing something? Sands through the hourglass and all that?"

"I rarely think about anything else."

"So what do you intend to do about it?"

He leaned back and thought about the question. "I intend to continue to work as hard as I ever have. My family taught me that public service is not a burden but a great opportunity."

He leaned forward and his voice softened. "However, I hope the day will soon come when I win the love of a beautiful woman who is as committed as I am to the concept of duty. If that day does come I will be as dedicated to that woman as any man has ever been."

His pale blues bored right into her brain as he said it. And she didn't say anything in reply.

* * *

They talked until the restaurant was empty, mostly about Vargo but not always. She looked at her watch and was startled at the time.

"Jesus, it's almost ten o'clock."

"I apologize. This is completely my fault. I know you wanted to get back to work."

Well, back then she did. Back then she was also tired, angry, and frustrated. Now she felt none of that. "No one had a gun to my head."

"No." He paused. "Well, it was not all time wasted."

No, it wasn't. "I agree."

"I now know a lot more about the excellent work you're doing. I also have some ideas how I might help."

"Really?"

"Yes. There are people in Washington who you should know, who can help you. With this and, well, other matters as well."

It was unnaturally easy to trust this man. This morning, the last thing in the world she had wanted was his help.

"I'd be grateful for anything you could do."

He thought about that. "This is the sort of thing that really shouldn't wait. I'll have to wake up someone."

"It's part of the job. It never bothers me."

"No, I don't suppose it would. The only problem is all my files are upstairs, in the suite I'm using as an office."

"So what's the problem?"

"Well, before I make the call I'll need more briefing from you. I can't very well ask you . . . ask you to . . ."

She still didn't get it. "Ask me to what?"

He sighed. "Ask you to come upstairs. There, I've said it. I'll come to your office with my files tomorrow."

She squinted. "My honor? Is that what you're worried about?"

His face stiffened and he seemed embarrassed. "In a way, yes. I don't want you to suspect in the slightest that I . . ."

She laughed merrily and for the moment at least lost the ever present edge of frustration. With one notable and hopefully soon to be forgotten exception she had never met a man whose moves lasted longer than it took to deliver an icy stare. And now this guy? It was so

171

sweet, this old-world respect. Christ, she was in more danger of getting raped by Prince Charles than Covington Barrows.

"Mr. Barrows? Covington, I mean?"

"Yes."

"We've got a lot of business to discuss. And very little time to get the job done."

"I understand."

"So let's go to your room and get started."

28

VARGO'S ROUTE TO THE GOLDEN DRAGON WAS FAR more circumspect than Bobby Lee's. It had to be because of the price on his head placed by Stewart Kwoh-Fang, the finance head of the Bamboo Gang in Los Angeles and the owner of both the Asian Interbank Trust and its next-door neighbor, the Golden Dragon. Kwoh hated Vargo as much as any man alive. Immediately after Vargo's escape Kwoh had taken a special trip to Guangdong Province in mainland China. There, at the grave of his great-grandmother, he swore by all he deemed holy that one day he would slice open Vargo's belly and feed the intestines to his dogs. Every Bamboo Gang member in Monterey Park knew of the pledge and there was not one that disbelieved it.

The cause of Kwoh's hatred was, of course, money, which was all Kwoh ever cared about. The unadorned fact was that at the same time as Vargo was sliding out of town with hundreds of millions of investor funds, he also split with the funds of several very dangerous people. Kwoh's bank handled all the last-minute wire transfers. Yet when it came time to reconcile the accounts after the final flurry, Kwoh found himself out $3.7 million and responsible to his superiors for every penny. That's when he made his trip to Guangdong Province.

Nevertheless Vargo desperately needed Kwoh and it

was time to make amends. But Vargo couldn't approach Kwoh directly or he'd never remain alive long enough to make his pitch. He needed an intermediary.

Vincent dropped Vargo in the middle of the brown steam bath called downtown Los Angeles. He exited the car quickly and walked with the lunch crowd two blocks to a garish, green-granite office building. He stopped four times on the way, doubled back once, went into a hotel restroom, and then immediately walked out again. Only when he was satisfied he wasn't being followed did he finish the journey. The offices of Charles Wendel, attorney at law, were on the twenty-seventh floor, high above the rubble of urban decay that the large downtown Los Angeles buildings have replaced with taller decay. He rode the high-speed elevator with a rush.

He emerged into an ornate waiting room encircled by glass. A blond receptionist sat behind a bank of computers. He announced himself to her using his British name.

Wendel came out immediately to greet him, showing he had been well paid by Barrows for this meeting. He was a foppish man of sixty with thinning white hair who had spent a lifetime as a quiet tax lawyer and servant. He was a creature swimming in affectations: a red carnation, loud suspenders, thin designer glasses, and a bizarre white pipe. His hand was as soft and cool as death. Wendel had only one good feature: he was the one man in the world that Stewart Kwoh-Fang trusted.

Wendel led Vargo to a windowless conference room with a circular table in the middle. A tall brunette placed gleaming cups on it. When she left, Wendel closed and locked the door.

"Help yourself to coffee if you like."

"I don't like."

"Perhaps a small scotch, then?"

"Fine."

The willowy brunette returned with a crystal ice bucket, glasses, and a very old scotch. Wendel had done well for himself. She poured drinks for them and whisked the coffee cups away. When she left, Vargo ignored Wendel and inspected the room. He ran his fingers along the wallboard and under the table. He searched diligently beneath the cabinets. He found nothing. The chairs surrounding the table were ultra-modern and black, tightly upholstered. He took out a small pocket knife and began advancing on one of them.

Wendel was aghast. "What are you doing?"

Vargo dug the knife into the back of the chair and ripped. He heard Wendel scream. Clouds of white filling puffed through the room.

"Stop that!" Wendel wailed.

"Your choice," Vargo said. "Either tell me where the bug is or I find it my way."

"Do you realize what these chairs cost? They're five grand apiece, for Christ's sake."

"All the more reason you should want to save them, I should think."

"All right, all right. Wait." Wendel reached under the round conference table and released a catch. A false panel popped to the surface housing a small and no doubt powerful tape recorder.

"See how easy that was?" Vargo advanced on Wendel with the knife, this time gently stroking the man's cheek with it. "Is there another bug?" he asked softly.

"No," Wendel said quickly.

"If there is," Vargo told him, "your face will look like that chair. Do you understand?"

Wendel understood. He had been a lawyer for Kwoh for twenty years and Kwoh had been Vargo's banker for the last four years of the life of National Diversified. He knew all about the violence that surrounded Vargo.

"Wonderful. Let's talk business. I need to meet with Stewart Kwoh-Fang."

Wendel looked at him with faint amusement. "That will not be hard, Mr. Vargo."

"Very funny. I need to see him and leave alive, to have him forget his oath to his mother."

"His great-grandmother. In Guangdong Province. To have your intestines fed to . . ."

"I understand. My question is, can you do it?"

Wendel shook his head. "I don't see how. Not with the condition that you leave . . . unharmed."

"Think again. And remember, this meeting will be profitable to both of you."

That got Wendel's interest. "How so?"

"First, Kwoh gets all his money back."

"That's three point seven million."

"Correct."

"Kwoh will take your money and then kill you."

"I know. But if Kwoh listens to my business proposition I raise it to six million. Cash up front. He doesn't have to agree to anything, just listen."

Wendel was paying close attention now. "And for me?"

"You get five hundred wired into your account tomorrow."

Wendel puffed on his white pipe. "Five hundred thousand?"

"Of course. And one other thing."

"Yes?"

"Unless I get my safe meeting with Kwoh I've got no need for your services. And right now you know where I am. That's way too dangerous for my people."

"I see," Wendel said thoughtfully. "That does change things."

"I thought it might."

Wendel made up his mind. "I'll do it."

"Good. Set up a time for me right away. I'll go to him. Tell him the owner of Firenze Corporation is available to discuss all outstanding issues. Then tell him the financial terms. Any questions?"

"Not really." The willowy brunette returned. Wendel smiled at her, relaxed now as he thought of his money.

"Another scotch perhaps?"

Wendel ordered a car and Vargo was driven back to the Beverly Wilshire as the light was drifting off and slipping into the mountains ringing the city. The early roamers were starting to physically attach themselves to the walls of the strip businesses, leaning casually against rundown liquor stores and comedy clubs, otherwise staring aimlessly at the river of flesh and cars on Sunset Boulevard. The car lights twinkled against their empty faces. Vargo hurried out of his car and into his suite.

Vincent was already there, cooling a bottle of Dom in

an ice bucket. The kid was learning, Vargo thought. He gestured and Vincent opened the champagne, pouring carefully into a fluted glass. Vargo sat and sipped. Vincent came behind him and massaged his neck muscles.

"You do that well, Vincent."

"Thanks. I been trained."

No doubt. Vincent probably learned of the anatomy of the human neck from slicing a few throats. "Well, we'll see about that later. Tell me about your day."

"I did what you wanted."

The Sylmar manager. "Martinez? You found him?"

"Yeah, at his house, him and his old lady."

"What did he tell you?"

"At first, not much. He said he didn't know shit about the bust, like it was a big surprise."

"And later?"

"Later he remembered a whole bunch."

"Can we ask him anything else now?" Vargo knew the answer.

"Not now."

Vargo found himself excited by the story. "And his wife?"

"That's when he started talking. I told him, 'Either you talk or she takes a cap to the head.' Some people just got to see things for themselves."

That happened. "Don't worry about it. Just tell me what you learned."

"He was being paid."

Yes. Vargo smelled that. "By whom?"

"Everybody. Right now the fuckin' DEA. Before that, some Cubans."

Vargo knew about the Cubans. Jesus, *he* was the Cubans, paying Martinez to run the warehouse according to instructions and keep his mouth shut. Then somebody else came along and paid Martinez to betray them all. Who?

"Vincent, somebody was paying him *after* the Cubans and *before* the DEA," Vargo barked. "That's the man who arranged the bust. Now *who* was that?"

Vincent spread his hands. "Even after his wife got it he couldn't tell me."

"Why?"

"He didn't know. He met some guy on a park bench once a month, got his envelope, and answered questions. He didn't know who the fuck the guy was."

"What kind of questions?"

"Mostly about deliveries. When a big shipment was coming in, how much, when the stuff was moved out, how much was left over, when new stuff was coming in, all that shit. He made lists and gave 'em to the guy."

"How long did this go on?"

"He said there were ten meetings, ten envelopes."

Vargo was stunned. Someone had turned Martinez and had quietly monitored his Sylmar operation for almost a year before the bust? But *who?*

"How much? How much did he get paid?"

"Ten grand in cash each time. A hundred hundreds."

"What else did he say?"

"Just that you got fucked in ways you don't even know about."

"What does that mean?"

"It means Martinez was stealing. Him and the guy on the bench."

Now it made sense. That was always the weak link in his plan, how to protect against pilferage. Just a cost of doing business he supposed.

"How much did they steal?"

"Like half."

"What!"

"That's what he said, half of what came in went to the guy on the bench."

Vargo's temples burned. Vincent was too stupid to do the math but Vargo wasn't. Ten tons of cocaine. At the distribution level at least $50 million.

"What else?"

Vincent knitted his brow. "That's about it. Once a month. Ten grand for information plus a piece of the stolen stuff. On a bench in some park." He thought some more. "I can't remember the name. Some fuckin' park."

"It doesn't matter."

"Maybe MacArthur Park. Yeah, that's it. It began with an *M*."

"Forget it, it doesn't matter."

Vincent let go of Vargo's shoulders. "No, that ain't it." He paced. "Montgomery Park. No, there's no such fuckin' thing. Wait, I wrote it down." He fumbled in his pocket and found a matchbook. "Yeah, here it is. *Monterey* Park. I knew it began with an *M*. Just give me a . . . Hey, you okay?"

All the blood had fled from Vargo's face. He aged thirty years in five seconds. "Did you say Monterey Park?"

"You got it. Once a month. Some Chink gave him his envelope."

Vargo opened his mouth and screamed. Vincent backed away.

"What the fuck's wrong, man?"

Vargo couldn't breathe. He drained the champagne in his glass, then grabbed the bottle and drank from it. The blood slowly returned to his face.

"Did Martinez tell you what the man on the bench looked like?"

"Yeah, sort of. He said he was a Chinese guy, nervous, with a bald head and wire-rimmed glasses. He looked like an accountant. And he said his left eye twitched."

Vargo held up his hand and Vincent stopped talking. It was Stewart Kwoh-Fang, no doubt about it. Now it all made sense. Kwoh had already gotten his revenge and was waiting patiently for Vargo to return, as he knew he had to, so that the vow to his ancestors might be fulfilled. Wendel was a complete setup. Kwoh had been waiting for him all along.

"Vincent, bring the car around. We're going to dinner."

29

MEDINA WAS TERRIFIED THE WHOLE WAY BACK TO Patsy's.

"Tell me again what she said when you delivered the pictures."

"Nothing. She said, 'Hi, Bobby Lee. Are these the pictures of the girl you want to find?' "

"No, I mean about me?"

"She looked and saw you and said 'Is that Joe in the car?' "

"Her exact words. Were those her exact words?"

"Exact? Not exactly."

"So give. Every word."

"You sure?"

"Yes."

Bobby Lee sighed. "She said, 'Hi, Bobby Lee, you look good for somebody's been bent over in a shower for three years. Nice pictures. Did you have these tacked up in your cell? For inspiration?' That was kind of it for the pleasantries."

That was more the Patsy Mulligan Medina knew. "And then she saw me in the car?"

"Right."

"And said?"

"Something about running you over in the street and backing up to do it again. And then some curses in Spanish that maybe you taught her."

He sighed. "She'll never help you."

"*Au contraire*. After the tirade we hugged, talked, and she said she'd have something in three hours. Her words."

"How?"

Baker shrugged. "Let's find out."

They were in front of her apartment now. Medina shut off the engine. "I can't do it."

179

Faldo woke up in the backseat and rubbed his eyes. "Where are we? This isn't home."

"And not Kansas either, Faldo." Baker opened the door. "Let's go, troops."

The three of them were waved to chairs by Patsy, who sat Indian-style on the light hardwood floor with the phone cradled against her ear. The Angela photos were on the floor in front of her. She was furiously writing on a yellow legal pad.

"Yeah, I got it. . . . Tittie bars with Ferrante down by the airport. . . . What about Romano? . . . Okay, that's called Cherokee now. . . . Right. . . . Okay, I got it."

She hung up the phone and scribbled some more. She was thirty years old, small and tight with pert breasts that pointed aggressively through her thin, white T-shirt. She was barefoot and wore jeans. Her thin shoulders rippled with muscles that curved gracefully down her back.

When she stopped writing Medina visibly stiffened.

"Well, I got some news for you, Bobby Lee. Incidentally, who're your friends?"

Baker gestured. "Medina, you know. And this is Faldo, one of Max's partners. He's helping me."

Patsy feigned amazement. "Medina! José Medina! Jesus, I didn't recognize you without your thing in your hand. Bobby Lee, in five years he didn't once come through that door and last two minutes until he had it out. For a while I thought it was on a string."

"Patsy, you're exaggerating," Baker said.

"Am I, Joe?"

"We went lots of places together," Medina said, quickly changing the subject.

"Yeah, your mother's, because she could cook. Food and his thing, that's all he cares about."

"Medina, that's terrible."

Medina's face flushed. "Just tell me what you want, goddamn it. Five years and I never looked at another woman. What the hell do you want?"

She smiled at that. "What do I want? I'll tell you. Pay attention to some part of me that isn't between my neck and my knees. Talk to me once in a while. I'll talk back.

You know a woman's mouth has more than one purpose."

Baker detected a contradiction. "Woman's mouth? That's above the neck."

"Shut up, prison punk." Baker slumped back into his chair.

"Fine," Medina said evenly. "For the fiftieth time I'll ask you straight-out. Marry me."

"What?"

"You heard me. Put up or shut up. Marry me."

"José, I told you, I don't even *like* refried beans."

"That's okay." Medina walked up and looked her dead in the eye. "Marry me and I'll talk to you till your ears hurt. I'll also do lots more."

"Oh yeah?" Patsy slung a hip off to the side, stuck a hand on it, and grinned widely. "What do you think, Bobby Lee? He had a one-track mind but it wasn't all that bad a track."

"You could do worse, Patsy."

"Maybe so." She grabbed at Medina's crotch and he jumped back a step. She laughed merrily.

"Guys, let's get to work."

They sat around Patsy's dining room table with small pads in front of them. After a time they were joined by a tall, well-dressed man in an elegant dark suit. When everyone was settled Patsy walked to the head of the table. She placed the photos in front of her.

"Okay, kids, here's how it shakes. This guy here's Detective Mike Bass, my boss at OCID. We can help with this girl but if it involves Dominick Romano, it's our tag, got it?"

"Agreed," Baker said quickly. "What do you got?"

Patsy looked to Bass, who nodded in approval. She picked up the photo of Angela in front of the Camden Club.

"Dominick Romano is a 'made' member out of Phoenix, via Las Vegas. We've been tailing him for close to six years. We know everything about him except a good way to bust him. So occasionally we bust his balls, most recently by closing down his club for health violations."

"Camden Club, you mean?"

"Right. These celebrity clubs only last a couple years anyway so I doubt we did him much damage. Two months later he was opened up again."

"What about Angela?"

Patsy picked up the photo. We know her as 'Monica, last name unknown.' She's a smart little number. Three nights a week she shills for Romano at his club. The rest of the time she's running a strip joint near the airport with a guy named Ferrante. She's made him a fortune as best we can tell."

Baker was confused. "What does 'shills' mean?"

Patsy shrugged. "Romano's clubs always have to be the hot clubs in town. That means beautiful people inside and a long line of marks on the outside. Some of the beautiful people are real, some on salary. She's on salary."

"So she knows Romano?"

"Probably not. He has tons of girls working for him."

"What's the name of the new club?"

"It's called Cherokee, on Sunset, named after an old standard Charlie Parker made famous. I guess Romano's a jazz fan. Anyway, same format: lines, rock stars, models, and dope. Lively heroin trade among the customers that we pretty much ignore, except for our archives."

"How do you know all this?"

"We got people in there three nights a week." She gestured to her boss. "That's why Mike's got such nice suits."

Baker tried not to get too excited. Angela was real close. If he could get to her, get some time with her, he knew she'd help him.

"What nights does she work there?"

Patsy consulted her notes. "Saturday, Tuesday, and Thursday."

"That means tomorrow night."

"That's right, Saturday night, date night, big night of the week."

It was time for the only question that mattered. "Can you get me in there?"

Patsy turned to Bass, who shook his head from left to right.

"I don't think so, Bobby."

"Why the hell not?"

"We just can't take a chance on a three-year intelligence operation for one girl," Bass said. "We're trusted in there, part of the crowd. If they found out there's something weird about us, we're gone."

"There's no chances to take, I promise. And it'll be worth it to you, trust me. Now please, how do we get in?"

Detective Mike considered it. "All of you?"

"I guess so."

He scratched his chin. "Whatever you get from her you share with us, right?"

"You got it."

"Go for it," he told Patsy.

She grinned. "Okay. Tomorrow night you're back here at eight sharp. Bobby Lee and Joe, wear your best get-laid suits. Joe, that means something without burrito stains."

He growled dangerously.

"This other guy, I don't care. We'll fix him up when he comes."

"I don't underst—" Baker began.

"Bobby Lee, don't worry about it."

She walked over to Medina and placed her hand under his chin. "Eight tomorrow, Medina."

"I know."

"And you better not forget what you said."

He didn't flinch. "I won't."

30

THEY RETURNED ON SCHEDULE AS THE SUN SLIPPED BEneath the stagnant canals in back of Patsy's Venice apartment. Medina was now nervous for brand-new reasons.

"I didn't sleep at all last night," he told Baker. "This is a mistake. I just got carried away."

"Look, every guy feels like that when he takes the plunge. Listen to me, Patsy's great. When you're old and fat you'll still be able to bounce quarters off that tight, little—"

Medina snorted. "Is that reason enough to marry someone?"

"That's not really the area where I'm at my deepest," Baker admitted. "So maybe look at it this way. She's also a lot smarter than you."

"I appreciate that, Bobby."

"She does seem a little coarse," Faldo said from the backseat.

"Coarse! She's goddamn foul-mouthed."

"Maybe so," Baker agreed. "But just imagine what she'll be whispering in your ear for the next thirty years."

Medina and Faldo were still chewing on that thought when they walked into her apartment. They were greeted there by Detective Mike and a tall, no-nonsense-looking woman with a tight gray bun.

"This is Pamela," Detective Mike explained. "She's a police cosmetologist."

"Where's Patsy?"

"Right here, Medina."

They turned and saw a stranger approach. She was the same size as Patsy and sounded like Patsy but there it all ended. The stranger had dark hair piled high on her head, a white open neck, a gold-sequined halter-top dress that stopped at mid-thigh, and five-inch heels that could have doubled as ice picks. Her face was heavily rouged and the thick lipstick clung to the tips of her teeth when she smiled.

"You," she said to Faldo, "sit in that chair." She pushed him toward Pamela the police cosmetologist. "And you," she said sweetly to Medina, "close your mouth before a fuckin' bug flies in."

Pamela the cosmetologist needed almost an hour to do the job. At the end Faldo was mortified.

"This is ridiculous. I'm a transactional lawyer."

Pamela handed him a mirror and Faldo stared at it in shock. He had shoulder-length black curls and his eye-

184

brows and lips sported as much makeup as Patsy's. His suede vest was rose colored. He wore no shirt and his pale bones glistened. The pants were leather with bright, gold buttons at the crotch. The motorcycle boots were white.

"This is not me," Faldo said.

Patsy walked over to check him out. "Great job, Pamela. I think this will work. Can you kind of snarl?"

"No."

"Try."

Faldo's lips curled and Bobby Lee started laughing.

Patsy put a hand on Faldo's shoulder. "Don't pay any attention to him. Just remember one thing."

"What?"

She leaned close to his ear. Her voice was soft. "Rock stars get all the pussy."

Faldo shuddered.

Even in her old life Saturday night was special for Angela, a twenty-four-hour escape from Vargo and his madness. Back then, when money was never important, she hung around bars like the Camden Club for fun. Now times were much different. She got paid to drift around Romano's club, and while the money wasn't great, the music and excitement were still tonic to her. And, from time to time, she latched onto someone to calm the ever-gnawing fear.

She left her strip joint after checking the books and jumped into a cab, melting into the night wearing what she called her red killer. The killer was a red leather outfit that was spray-painted to her body and ended eighteen inches above the knee. The "dress" itself was not much of a dress, more like thin horizontal strips of sturdy red leather separated by layers of bare skin. There was nothing underneath nor could there have been. The dress was accompanied by spikes, bare, muscled legs, and enough makeup to paint a house. She felt no embarrassment. Her dress was a uniform to her and meant about as much as a tie on an accountant.

Cherokee officially opened its doors at eight but that was just to let the help sweep up. The first customers straggled in at ten; by midnight, the place was packed. That's when Angela arrived, regally exiting her cab. A bodybuilder named Paul in a tight, black T-shirt and black jeans released the rope cord that kept the unwashed at bay, now two hundred strong stretched in a line snaking around the building. Angela ignored the sign announcing a thirty-dollar cover charge and walked briskly to a small dressing room in the back where at least ten girls were primping. The girl next to her, a Eurasian via Jamaica, spread a few lines on a mirror and inhaled hungrily through a curled-up ten-dollar bill. The girl smiled at Angela. After a moment's indecision Angela accepted the bill and bent her head over the dressing room table. The white powder bit deeply into her sinuses, burning as the chemical sliced through tender capillaries, and she coughed at the sensation. Then she did it again, through the other nostril, and her head rocked as the buzz hit her. Instantly the fear left her and her stomach became calm. She knew it would stay that way for fifteen minutes.

Angela left the dressing room and entered the raucous club. She wasn't much of a drinker but always liked to open with a couple of shooters to get her going. The first tequila burned her throat as it went down. The second made her shudder involuntarily. She closed her eyes while the alcohol numbed her. She felt a state of deep relaxation overtake her, the alcohol and cocaine joining in a brief, unholy parody of happiness. She faced the room and warmed to the look of the men upon her. On the shiny black dance floor, the music blared with a deep reverberating bass. She moved easily into the flow of the crowd.

At 1 A.M., out with the herd, Medina and Baker approached bodybuilder Paul standing with his arms crossed over his chest while he guarded his rope barrier. Between them was the legendary Slash, resplendent in his leather chaps, long black curls, and rose vest. Next to Slash, clinging to his arm, was his bitch. Patsy gazed up at Slash with reverence and adoration. Slash's vest sparkled with rhinestones. The girls in the line gasped and pointed.

"Can I help you?" Paul said.

"Yeah, move that cord. Now!" Baker snarled.

The bouncer didn't budge. Slash looked okay, but what about the geeks? "Who are you guys?"

"We're his assistants," Medina said. He moved close to the bouncer.

"Hey, back off, chump." Paul pushed against Medina's chest. As he did, he felt something hard under Medina's jacket and stiffened.

"Are you crazy? What's that?"

"Standard issue. It's given to all the agents."

"Yeah, right." The man gestured to his boss and an unsmiling suit came over.

"What's the problem?"

Faldo had been well-coached and seemed to rise to his role. "Hey man, this place sucks," he shouted. "They don't know who I am. I don't have to wait anyplace. I'm *Slash*, man, and this here is my main gash." Faldo slapped Patsy solidly on the butt, then started playing some imaginary drums. Patsy's smile froze and her eyes became murderous.

"I thought Slash played guitar," the boss said.

"Plus this guy's packing." Paul pointed to Medina.

"Yeah?" The supervisor approached Medina. "What're you guys, his bodyguards?"

"No," Medina said. "I'm an FBI agent, and this man"—he pointed to Baker—"is my prisoner. This man"—he pointed to Slash—"is a tax lawyer. She"—he pointed to the still-glowering Patsy—"is very upset at getting her butt smacked."

"Wise ass." The boss eyed Slash one more time. "Let 'em in."

31

VINCENT DROVE THE LINCOLN THROUGH DOWNTOWN Los Angeles and onto the San Bernardino Freeway heading east. Vargo sat glumly in the back, infuriated at the naked betrayal. How could they do this to him? He had trusted Stewart Kwoh-Fang, relied on him for a hundred tasks during his heyday, and rewarded the man handsomely for his efforts. Of course he had stolen from Kwoh at the end, but that was . . . well, unanticipated. Now Stewart had turned on him, bribing Martinez to tell him when the warehouse would be stuffed with white powder, knowledge that would enable him to complete his treacherous plan. Vargo had no doubt anymore who had tipped off the DEA. The feds would be indebted to Kwoh for years on this one.

The Lincoln exited five miles east of downtown Los Angeles and cruised around Monterey Park while Vargo fumed in the backseat. Restaurants and banks were elbow to elbow, jammed like subway commuters into every nondescript corner of every nondescript mini-mall along the way. All the street signs bore Chinese characters dominantly displayed over much smaller English lettering.

Vincent parked across the street from the Golden Dragon and they watched as the restaurant filled and emptied with Chinese diners. Occasionally, a well-dressed white couple, knowledgeable about the fabulous restaurants of Monterey Park, would pull in. Once, a late model car pulled up and four young Chinese men in dark suits emerged, glancing furtively in each direction before entering the restaurant.

Vincent could spot another killer when he saw one. He shifted uncomfortably in his seat.

After an hour, Vargo had made his decision. "Let's get out of here." He directed Vincent eastward through the twisting streets to a small commercial district a half-mile away. Here the banks and restaurants were fewer, the auto body shops with signs in Chinese more frequent. Vincent stopped in front of a restaurant with a green, angular, plywood depiction of a castle dominating the facade. The words "The Green Palace" were cut into the entrance of the building underneath the plywood structure.

"Can we go in now?" Vincent asked testily. He was getting a little hungry.

"Shut up and listen," Vargo barked. "I want you to go inside that restaurant and ask for someone."

"Yeah?"

"Yeah. His name is Mr. Chang. You will be directed to the kitchen. The cook will ask you your business. You will again ask for Mr. Chang."

"Right."

"You will then tell the cook that you were sent by the man from Florence and that you have a message for Mr. Chang. You must say it exactly that way, understand?"

"Yeah, Florence, got it." Vincent shifted, wanting to get moving.

"If you are lucky you will then be taken through a door in the back of the kitchen to some offices," Vargo said. "If you get to meet Mr. Chang, you will again say to him that the man from Florence wishes to speak with him concerning Mr. Kwoh and respectfully asks if he has the time to do so. Do you think you can remember that?"

"Yeah. You wanna talk to Chang."

Vargo shook his head in exasperation. He would try once more and if Vincent still didn't get it, it would become Vincent's problem in a hurry. "Listen to me and listen to me carefully. I said you are to respectfully ask whether Mr. Chang has the time to see the gentleman from Florence about Mr. Kwoh. Understand?"

"Sure."

"Okay. Do it."

Vincent got out of the car. Vargo sat in the dark and felt panic creep into his thoughts. Most of his time was now gone. Once the thirtieth day had come and gone, there would be no more talk. The Cubans had the right to act and they would.

Vargo was staring sullenly at the floor of the Lincoln when the car door suddenly jerked open. Vincent was standing there, his face ashen. There were dark splotches on his cheekbones. On either side of him stood a young Chinese man dressed completely in black. Behind them an older man with white hair bowed politely to Vargo.

Vargo gestured to Vincent. "What happened to him?"

The older Chinese man shrugged. "He was insolent." He extended a hand and either helped or pulled Vargo from the car. "Mr. Chang will see you now."

They led him around the back way. The rear door was triple-locked. The older man in the dark suit knocked in an odd sequence and received a knock in response. He replied and the tumblers fell. One of the younger Chinese was soothing a large Doberman with a silver choke collar. The dog stared at Vargo.

Once inside, they were led down a corridor to Chang's office. Vargo remembered the drill from the old days. He was thoroughly searched, although with apologies and respect, in Chang's anteroom. Vincent was pushed face first into a wall and rudely patted down.

They took two guns from Vincent. The older man shook his head sadly. "He should have told us."

"He did not know the rules," Vargo said.

"Still, it is not allowed." He gestured to one of the young Chinese. The man spun, kicking Vincent's legs out from under him. Vincent fell heavily and screamed. Three young Chinese moved toward him.

The older man gestured. "Mr. Chang awaits you."

"What about him?"

The old man said nothing. Oh well, Vargo thought. He spun on his heel and went through the open door.

Chang was sitting behind a dark, walnut desk inlaid with animal heads. He was fortyish and balding, with a boxer's physique. He smoked carefully and continually, surrounding his head with a blue aura highlighted by the few lights in the room. He studied Vargo with a flat look. Then his face broke into a contemptuous smile. He still didn't speak.

Vargo bowed respectfully. "It is a great pleasure to see you again."

Chang said nothing. He smoked quietly.

Vargo sat down. The chair was hard, rich mahogany. "I'd like to discuss some business with you," Vargo said simply. Then he was quiet.

Chang still said nothing. He looked at Vargo with undisguised disdain.

"I heard you fled."

Fled like a coward was the unspoken accusation. "I had no choice."

"You killed before you left. Three people."

"The three people had information that could have been harmful."

"But you left behind a confederate. Mr. Baker."

"Yes."

"Why did you betray him?"

"It was not a betrayal."

Chang's eyebrows rose. "No? The newspapers said he was your confederate. Are you a man who betrays his confederates?"

"No."

"But you shot three of them in the head and left the fourth to—how is it said—dangle in the wind."

That's how it was said. "There were special circumstances. Surely you often take such steps in your own business."

"Betrayal? Never. Murder of my own people? Never."

Neither of those high-minded sentiments was true but politeness demanded Vargo's silence.

"So," Chang continued, "why are you here? To betray others?"

"I'm here to make a proposition."

"A proposition?"

"Yes. A business offer."

"The betrayer and the murderer has a business offer. If I listen, am I tainted?"

Vargo almost threw up at that one. Somehow or other a cold killer like Chang would find a way around the taint issue.

Chang did. He sighed and took another long drag off the cigarette. "I will listen. If I am offended, I will ask you to stop."

"Fair enough. My proposition involves a man you know. Some say a rival."

"Who?"

"Mr. Stewart Kwoh-Fang."

Chang shrugged. "A rival? Not at all. Mr. Kwoh-Fang is a dear friend." He gestured for Vargo to begin.

Vargo spoke for twenty minutes without interruption and told Chang everything he knew about Martinez, the man on the park bench, and the diverted product. He also told Chang his guess, that there hadn't been enough time to sell it off, that somewhere, in some warehouse, probably in Monterey Park, there was $50 million of cocaine sitting in brown packages inside phony dolls or reconditioned Mexican furniture.

Chang didn't ask Vargo to repeat any of it. His face was now enveloped in blue smoke. "It was Kwoh-Fang," Chang said finally.

"Right," Vargo agreed. "He has eliminated my operation and begun his own." That Chang was not sharing in Kwoh-Fang's new operation need not be said out loud. And if Chang was not sharing then maybe Taipei was not sharing either.

"What do you propose?" Chang said finally.

"I need to rebuild my organization quickly in Los Angeles," Vargo said. "I need to get product in, to store it, to get it to distributors, to collect, and to get the money out. Also, you know, security, enforcement."

Muscle, in other words. Chang could easily supply that.

"Some of that we can help with."

"You can help with all of it and be greatly rewarded for your effort."

"I'm listening."

Vargo leaned forward. "I need to set up a new warehouse in your territory right away. You supply security. In a matter of days a major delivery will be made. You pay fifty percent on receipt. We provide introductions to the major distributors—Latins and black gangs are all they are. You then deliver to them and collect the cash, at a substantial markup. Your banks then wire the second fifty percent of the wholesale price to our accounts."

"Or hold some of it?"

"As long as profits are high and deliveries timely made, my principals will not object to a reasonable retention."

"And the competition? Mr. Kwoh-Fang? The local dealers?"

"Mr. Kwoh-Fang is your problem. Or rather your opportunity. Get rid of him and find out what happened to my stolen product."

Chang's face broke into a wide grin. He liked that. "And the blacks?"

"The blacks are irrelevant to you. They are children, teenagers in gangs. They have wars over street corners. They are retailers, nothing more. The cash they raise they give to the Hispanics for more product."

"And the Hispanics give it to us."

"Correct."

"And we . . ."

"Share."

"Yes, share."

It was a great opportunity and Chang saw that. And he also might be able to finally rid himself of the hated Kwoh-Fang. He smoked again with feigned indifference. "It is an interesting proposition, Mr. Vargo."

There was a calendar on Chang's desk. Vargo, impolitely, walked around Chang's desk and drew a circle around the thirtieth.

"Unless we complete a transaction by that date, I will be . . ."

"Eliminated?"

"Yes."

Chang understood. "We've heard the rumors. What exactly must happen by that date?"

"Money must flow from you to our foreign accounts. I must prove the new arrangement is operative."

Chang put his hand on Vargo's shoulder. "The funds are not a problem. If I obtain approval and you put product in our warehouse, the funds will flow."

"We have very little time, Mr. Chang."

Chang smoked. "If I receive the orders I expect to receive, Mr. Kwoh-Fang has even less."

32

THE INSIDE OF CHEROKEE WAS AN EYE-OPENER INTO A brave, new world. Say what you will about the Mob, Baker thought, they know how to attract the chicks. The number of mind-bending models and actresses squeezed like toothpaste into a common uniform of black spandex was beyond counting. The men were an odd mixture of what seemed to be out-of-work young actors and long-in-the-tooth businessmen. The models, mostly on salary, ignored the customers unless one of the Mob guys told them to pay attention.

Paul's black T-shirt was a theme repeated throughout the bar. The dance floor was shiny black. The bar was shiny black. The art on the walls was matte black with silver blemishes. The help were all dressed in black, the men in tight jeans and muscle shirts, the women in the standard-issue short dress. The only way to tell a waitress from a customer was whether or not she was carrying a tray.

"Jesus, would you look at that," Slash observed. "Do you realize I'm going to die and never get to experience anything remotely like that?"

"Don't be shallow," Baker said. "These girls are superficial. What about intelligence and sensitivity?"

Medina was a superficial man. "What about that *poon*," he crowed.

Patsy heard the remark. "Bobby, would you be so kind as to bring me one of the knives from that table."

"Superficial," Medina agreed quickly. "Goddamn superficial."

They wandered into a little-used area in the back with a pool table, black, with overstuffed chairs, black. They ordered some drinks. Medina, a good cop who now felt he was on duty, had a non-alcoholic beer from Germany.

Baker wanted to look around. Medina gave his permission reluctantly. "The last time you came back all bloody. I can only explain that so often."

"Don't worry. Hey, Slash, you want to come?"

Slash ignored him and started dancing inefficiently to the raunchy beat of the music. A few black dresses had already turned in his direction.

Baker left them and picked his way through the crowd to the bar, which thinned slightly near the door, then thickened again as he approached the dance floor. Suddenly, he felt a hand on his arm. He looked up and saw one of the bouncers.

"Hey, sport, you havin' a good time?"

"Sure."

"Great. How about a drink?"

"I already got one."

"So, have another." The man pointed to a table where a middle-aged, heavy-set man was sitting. "That gentleman wants you to come sit by him."

"Yeah? Who's that?"

"C'mon over and find out."

"I don't know."

The bouncer's grip tightened on his shoulder. "Sure you do, sport, you know just fine. Let's go."

His unexpected host was elegantly dressed in a tan double-breasted suit, white shirt, and powder blue tie. You could shave in the gleam off his black shoes. He looked to be about sixty years old. Baker thought he had seen him once on the cover of a magazine.

The man stood up and extended a hand as Baker approached. "Good evening. I'm Dominick Romano."

The great man himself. Baker tried to be casual. "Bobby Lee Baker."

"Pleased to meet you." The man gestured. "Have a seat. What can I get you to drink?"

"Anything. A beer's fine."

Romano gestured and a waitress ran off for the beer. Baker eased into his chair and waited.

"So you fellows enjoying yourselves?" Romano asked.

"Yeah, the place is great."

The waitress came back and gave Bobby Lee his beer. Romano looked up at her with a questioning look. "So?"

"No way," the girl said. "He doesn't even know who Skid Row is."

Romano turned back to Baker. "What she means is your friend's not quite Slash." He smiled, all white teeth. "And that girl he came in with"—he gestured vaguely in Patsy's direction—"she's OCID, I don't care how many outfits she got. So what's the play? You guys OCID too? You gonna bust me again for roaches in the kitchen?"

"No, I promise."

"No? So who are you?"

"You'd never believe it."

"Try me."

"I'm on parole out of Boron. He's a tax attorney in disguise."

Romano didn't look amused. "I love guys that pull my crank. Makes me want to yank theirs off and feed it to them."

"It's true," Baker said quickly. "We're here looking for someone."

Romano turned to a nearby bouncer. "Bring those jerks over here."

They brought Medina over looking more than uneasy. Up to now it had been fun, but he was sure there was something in the FBI manual about drinking with the Mob. Faldo was still moving enthusiastically to the music. Patsy had quickly faded into the crowd, probably trying to figure out how she would explain the whole thing to Detective Mike. Romano leaned over and pulled off Faldo's wig.

"Shit, you may *be* a tax lawyer."

"I gotta tell you," Faldo said, "I never had so many beautiful women looking at me in my life. I'm gonna wear this wig forever."

Romano turned back to Baker. "And you're the criminal? How you get out?"

"I'm cooperating."

Romano's eyes flattened. That he understood.

"But not against anybody Italian," Baker said quickly. Then he thought for a while. Who knew? Maybe Vargo was Italian. "At least I don't think he's Italian."

"What's his name?" Romano asked.

"Robert Vargo."

Romano stiffened. "Once again?"

"Robert Vargo," Bobby Lee repeated.

Romano turned quickly to Medina. "Is he tellin' the truth?"

Medina nodded. He had a quiet credible way about him that exuded truthfulness. But just to make sure he moved his coat slightly and showed Romano his weapon. Romano got it and turned to Faldo to put the icing on the cake. "How about you? Is he tellin' the truth? If you lie to me, I'll make you eat your wig and you'll never get pussy again."

"He's telling the truth."

Romano sat back and grinned. "Robert Vargo. We got some business to discuss."

Over on the dance floor, Angela Moore was driving them crazy with the red killer. She had some TV actor out there focused like a starved dog over a steak. Angela ignored him, twirling in her own world to the music.

When the music ended, the actor embraced her, running his hands over her, suggesting. She let his hands wander, a reward for the dance. Then she spun away.

"What's the matter?"

He was pretty and slim. He would have been fun to play with. Some other time.

"I'm sorry," she said. She kissed him lightly. They all had such sad eyes. What was she supposed to do? She had a job, for Christ's sake.

The actor left and Angela returned to the bar. One more shooter to keep the motor running and then back to the Odyssey Club before her "partner" got out the back door with the receipts. One burn and back to business.

She threw back the shooter and let her head slowly droop. She shuddered and again felt the rush of transient happiness. Her eyes swept the room, past Romano's table, Table One at Cherokee, then continued on. Then the fear lurched back to her stomach and she looked dead into the center of Bobby Lee Baker's eyes.

Her face broke into a cold sweat. She fell heavily against the bar.

"Hey, you okay?"

She ignored the man. Baker was staring straight at her. She smiled weakly at him. Then Baker picked up his glass in a sort of toast in her general direction. Now the sweat poured into her eyes, until the girl next to her said, "Here's to you, too!"

She watched blankly as Baker and the girl gave mock toasts to each other from opposite ends of the crowded club. Neither one was paying any attention to her. How sweet, she thought, now let me get the hell out of here!

Her eyes flashed around the room hunting for exits and right away saw she had a problem. No matter how she cut it, there was only one door out and to get there she had to walk directly past Romano's table. She needed a beard, a screen. She gestured and the actor hovering nearby came hopping over like a bunny.

"Change your mind?"

"How'd you guess?"

"Fabulous." He puffed. "My place okay?"

"Sorry. We'll take a ride, though. Don't worry."

The actor was a bit of an asshole. "Hey, honey, I ain't a teenager. I got a great place. Up by Sunset Plaza."

"I know, but I've got to go to work tonight. Tell you what. You give me a ride to work and I'll . . ." She whispered in his ear.

The actor almost fell off the stool. "You got it."

"One thing, though. There's some asshole bothering me who's sitting over at that table. Can you sneak me out?"

"No problem." The actor would have knocked a hole in the wall if she asked.

He grabbed her by the arm and hustled her to the exit, two feet from Table One, six feet from Bobby Lee Baker. Baker had his back turned anyway and was amiably chatting with Romano. Romano was laughing heartily at Baker's joke. Angela kept her head down and let the actor walk between her and the table, blocking her from view. They slipped easily into the black night.

The actor signaled the valet for his car. Angela could have stiffed him then and there but the thought never entered her mind. A lot had changed since Amos Dean, but not that.

When the car came, she slid in, letting the actor grope her as his car eased into the Strip traffic. Her breathing returned to normal. She was safe.

Inside Cherokee, Romano's hearty laugh ended the instant Angela's beautiful bottom passed through the exit.

"That her?" he said.

"That's right," Bobby Lee said.

Romano's man was listening. "Sal, you got it?"

Sal was a beefy man in his late forties dressed in a conservative dark suit. His shirt was too small for him and pinched his neck. He looked out of place among the glitz of young bouncers, as though his role were far different.

"Sure. Tell you where she goes tonight. Where she lives. Don't get made."

"Exactly," Bobby Lee Baker said.

33

JULIE BECK LEFT COVINGTON BARROWS' ROOM AT three in the morning, her honor slightly disheveled but still miraculously intact. Fortunately, at that hour the only staff left were a bored-looking tux at the reception area and some maids with vacuum cleaners. They looked at her like she was a hooker and she felt like one.

She wasn't yet sure how it would all turn out, but for once she thought she had a chance of flushing Bobby Lee Baker out of her system for good. She now understood what she really wanted, a man to take a blowtorch to her mind, searing away the Baker memory which had grabbed on like a barnacle and wouldn't let go. There was a chance Barrows might be that man; he was not only different in every way from Baker but as dedicated as she was to destroying him. "Vindicated," a great word, she decided. It must have the same root as "vindictive." She'd have to check it out in the *OED*.

When she had walked into Barrows' suite five hours earlier none of these thoughts guided her. The chilled French wine was nice, and the conversation pleasant, but the cold imperative of the Vargo chase was still uppermost in her mind. Barrows' suite was elegant and large, a series of rooms which trumpeted that he, like she, supplemented paltry government per diems with outside money. The suite had a small living area furnished with Art Deco antiques, a spacious office, and a luxurious bedroom behind French doors. Julie never even noticed the bedroom.

Barrows was always the perfect gentleman. When she entered he gestured immediately to the office portion of the suite.

"Why don't we set up over there?" he suggested. "I'll order some coffee."

"Thank you." The wine had relaxed her too much. It was now time to wake up.

There was only a small table in the office portion of the suite and they were forced to sit close to one another. Julie briefed him and he took careful notes. Two hours later he closed the briefing book she gave him and stretched. He shook his head in admiration. "You've done a remarkable job."

"Thank you. But we haven't found him yet."

"You're not that far off," he said, and his voice seemed to contain both an odd assurance and an odd anxiety. He tapped his pad. "So, what else are you planning to do? You've got the airport covered, the train stations, his former office staked out, the major hotels covered. If he tries to come in you'll get him, right?"

She shook her head. "We're looking for one very desperate man seeking to arrive in Los Angeles undetected. There's a thousand ways for him to get in which have nothing to do with airports and train stations. He could just fly into Chicago and drive to L.A. Or if he doesn't want to drive that far he can fly into San Francisco. Or Phoenix. Or San Diego, or a hundred other hubs. How can we stop that?"

"That's the Bureau's problem."

"It's mine too, and I think it's ridiculous to keep manpower on the airports and bus depots. He's either in or he's going to get in. Remember, he's down to just a few days."

"Really," he said, suddenly keenly interested. "I didn't realize your information was that detailed."

"It is. We know everything about the Havana conference where this all began. They almost killed him there."

"A pity they didn't. That would have solved two problems."

True. Vargo dead and Baker still in prison. "That's right," she said. She leaned over him to consult the black binder. She could feel him close to her. "The report of the Havana operative is under tab Q." Barrows made more notes. "According to this report," she continued, "the clock started ticking on Vargo sometime around June first. That means he's down to just a matter of days to get his act together. At most they'll give him till the fourth of July. Maybe they're patriotic."

"I don't believe so," Barrows said. He was still examining the report from Havana. There were two reports, one in Spanish—the original—and an English translation. Julie noted he was reading the original Spanish. An educated man, she concluded. He leaned back after he finished.

"What more should we be doing?"

"We should have every available agent on the streets. Forget the airports. He's in."

"The Bureau has very little experience with street crime."

"Then let's enlist local vice cops, the D.A., anybody. Let's put his picture in the paper. Let's publicize it all." Julie was getting excited. "We could let the entire city know what we're doing. It could be the greatest manhunt in the city's history."

"And if we fail?"

"Then it will be a highly publicized failure."

Barrows smiled. "You would not mind that?"

Julie shook her head firmly. "Not at all."

He laughed. "If only your superiors in Washington had your guts." He sighed, then picked up the phone and grabbed an electronic phone directory out of the pocket of his jacket. He punched in some codes. Julie saw green crystallized numerals pop up on the tiny screen. Barrows made a sympathetic sound as he dialed. "It's after four in the morning on his Virginia farm. Tough."

The phone seemed to ring a long time. When it was finally answered, Julie could only hear Barrows' side of the conversation. "Andrew, is that you? . . . Yes, Andrew, I know what time it is. . . . If it wasn't important I wouldn't be calling you at four-thirty in the morning, would I? . . . That's right, now wake up and listen to me. The AUSA who is handling this Vargo matter out here is named Beck. . . . Beck, B-E-C-K. I've just finished getting a report. I want you to call me first thing tomorrow morning and listen to what I have to say about the Vargo investigation. Then I want it followed to the letter. Understand? . . . I don't care if Michael thinks he's in charge of this. Right now he's got swarms of agents running around the airport like bees. But Vargo's in town, we all know that. It's time to move. . . . Once again, Andrew, I don't care about Michael. And after you talk to me about Ms. Beck's ideas, I want you to . . . that's right, *Ms*. Beck. Do you have a problem with that, Andrew? . . . Good. . . . And Andrew, I'd like you to spend tomorrow implementing this. Next A.M., that's day after tomorrow, I want a fax to my attention telling me how you're going to execute this new plan. . . . No, Andrew, I don't think you're going to need more than a day. In any event, I can't give you more than a day. . . . Well, cancel it, Andrew. . . . I appreciate it, Andrew, I really do." Barrows hung up the phone and turned to Julie and smiled. "Done."

Yes, it was. She would never know that there was no Andrew and that there would be no call tomorrow or ever. She would never know that he had just called his own answering machine in Washington and that the next morning he would call and erase the tape. She would never know that his only interest now was to make sure that the agents *stayed* glued to the airports and bus stations.

"I'm grateful."

"No need to be. With the effort you're putting into this

case the least I can do is get people out of your way." He looked at his watch. "Speaking of which, do you have any idea what time it is?"

"Yes, it's close to two."

"I'm going to drive you home immediately."

"It's not necessary."

"Of course it is. A woman alone at night is . . ."

"That's not it. My car's downstairs. The valet's got the key."

"Then I don't . . ."

"Understand? I meant it's not necessary because I'm not ready to leave."

Barrows didn't say anything. He stood correctly and at almost military attention. He still had his suit jacket on. She walked away from him to the window. The city below was dark; the lights reflected upward like small translucent jewels. The idea that had been once unformed was now becoming precise, and insistent. And as with all things in her life, she didn't back away from it.

"Let me ask you a question," she said, still looking out the window.

"Anything."

"What do you intend to do after this case is over?"

He still didn't move. "Do you mean as far as Vargo is concerned?"

"No."

"I didn't think so." This time he did move, to the back of the bar. He seemed to want the bar between them. He put ice in a glass and poured a small scotch over it from a decanter. There was a silver cigarette case on the bar and he took one out.

"Do you mind if I smoke?"

"Go right ahead."

"Thank you. I do this when I'm nervous." If so, his hand did not betray him. It was rock still as he snapped the lighter. "This too," he said taking a small sip of the whiskey.

She was glad he was a little nervous. She sat across the bar from him on one of the two stools and crossed her legs. He looked and then seemed to turn his head.

"You haven't answered my question."

"I think you know the answer."

"So tell me."

"All right." This time his voice was assured. "I know a great deal about you. I know, for example, even before I came, that you'd been betrayed by a man that . . . you were close to."

"We were lovers. I'll deny it if I have to but it's true."

"That's what I suspected. Therefore to answer your question, I am immensely attracted to you. I've tried to disguise that tonight but I don't think I've done a very good job."

"You've done fine."

"And I hope, when this is over, that I'll never have to hide anything from you again." He opened his hands. "I'd like to build something first based on trust and truth. After that . . ."—his hands came together with a clap— "anything is possible."

Yes. Anything. Principally the elimination of Baker from her mind. "I'd like you to do two things for me."

"Yes?"

"First, make me one of those." She pointed to the whiskey. "Second, we need to talk just a bit more."

"About Vargo, you mean?"

"No," she said, running her fingers through her hair. Her jaw was now set with complete resolve. "Not one word about Vargo."

So there it was, a decision made, and finally in the right direction. She drove home elated, and crawled into bed that way smiling at the ceiling. And it wasn't until an hour later, still awake in her own bed alone, with the birds of Riviera chirping in the early dawn, that reality swept over her with a sudden, infuriating clarity. With a closed fist, she swept the blinking clock radio off the bed table. The crash brought her fully awake, now cursing, furious with frustration. He was *everything* Baker was not. A powerful man, a man in control of his fate. Baker was an insolent convict who even before his current problems had been getting along on bullshit and that fucking hair in his eyes for longer than anybody had a right to. So what the hell was wrong with her?

She got out of bed and splashed cold water on her face,

hoping to wipe away the rage. She breathed deeply. She was right to be infuriated and right to fight the childish feelings that threatened to confuse her. Her future was only with a man like Covington Barrows, never again with the likes of one Robert E. Lee Baker.

"You know what you've got to do," she told the mirror. "Get Vargo, put Baker back, and maybe you'll stop this nonsense."

The face in the mirror almost smirked.

34

VARGO LEFT CHANG AND IMMEDIATELY ARRANGED A meeting with Barrows to take place in the backseat of the Lincoln. Vincent picked Barrows up at 4 A.M., about an hour after Julie left, and slowly cruised through the bombed-out craters of downtown Los Angeles. Four blocks from Checkers they entered skid row. He quietly pulled over to the side of the road near a dark alley. Vargo slipped from the shadows and opened the car door, climbing into the backseat.

Vincent pulled away noiselessly and took the nearest freeway exit away from downtown Los Angeles. Soon the car was cruising aimlessly over the hundreds of miles of concrete girding the city.

Vargo began without preliminaries. "I have important information for you and not a lot of time."

"Begin then."

"I've had to make some changes. The changes have all been typed up in code and telecopied to Hong Kong. I need the office in Hong Kong to make sure the information is translated into Spanish and sent to the Colombians. I need it done this morning."

"That should be no problem. I assume you gave them the instructions in your letter."

"That's right, but I need follow-up. There can't be any fuckups on this one."

"I understand. What else?"

Vargo took a deep breath. What he was now about to do was against every instinct he had. "I need to tell you about the change in plans."

Barrows smiled. "Such candor? What have I done to deserve this?"

"Look, I don't have time for your usual nonsense. I've only got, what, seven days left?"

"No."

"Okay, less. I need your help. First, I need a few more days."

Barrows' head flew back and he laughed heartily.

"What's so funny?"

"Pardon me, but that's exactly what the Cubans said you'd say."

"So what? Can you get me more time?"

Barrows shook his head. "It's impossible. The Cuban —how shall I say it—'agents' have already left Havana. They have their orders and I don't think anybody can stop them now."

"Shit," Vargo said under his breath. He was afraid of that. "Well, I still need your help. As a matter of fact it's now an emergency."

"Fine, tell me."

"I'm not going to use Kwoh-Fang after all."

"I'm not surprised. That's the man who wanted to feed you to his animals."

"He still does. That lawyer Wendel was setting us up. Plus Kwoh's working with the U.S. government."

Barrows' eyebrows rose. "He's an informant?"

"That's right. Check your contacts at the U.S. Attorney's Office. Find out who's the informant on the Sylmar warehouse."

"That has proved to be impossible so far."

"Yes, but now your job is easier. All you have to do is confirm it was Kwoh."

Barrows shrugged. "Maybe. My contacts have been . . . well, improving of late. What else?"

"Wendel is supposed to be arranging a meeting between me and Kwoh. I would have been killed at that meeting."

"It would have saved the Cubans the trouble."

"Fuck you," Vargo said bitterly. Barrows just laughed.

"Anyway," Vargo continued, "I have to use somebody else. That somebody else is a man that I've known for years. His name is Chang and he hates Stewart Kwoh-Fang."

"So?"

"So right now Chang is trying to get permission to take action against Kwoh. Kwoh betrayed us and I hope it was out of pure greed. If his masters in Taipei are unaware of his profiteering, Chang will be given permission to liquidate him."

"So what does that do for you?"

"For one thing, Kwoh dies."

"Congratulations. You'll die soon after him."

"I know that. We need to get product into Chang's hands."

"Product?"

"Yes, it's simple. The same deal we were planning with Kwoh we now do with Chang."

"You need one shipment of product in and one shipment of money out to convince everyone that you have made the proper arrangements."

"Exactly," Vargo said.

"When?"

"I need the product immediately, maybe seventy-two hours tops."

"Understood." Barrows made a brief cryptic note in a small notebook. "Anything else?"

"Just the obvious. By now you must know what the government is up to. Are they close to me?"

Barrows shook his head from side to side. "As far as I can tell they're still looking at airports. The AUSA that was after you three years ago is in charge of the investigation."

"Beck? Julie Beck?"

"That's her."

Vargo sighed with exasperation. "That bitch will just not go away."

"She's somewhat distracted now. It seems the government allowed her former lover to be released. She's more fixated on him than you."

Vargo's head rose. "Her former lover? Are you talking about Baker?"

"That's right."

Vargo was shocked. "He's released? Are you kidding me?"

"Not at all. He's in a controlled house under the supervision of the FBI. She is doing everything she can to get him reincarcerated."

Vargo was visibly shaken by this information. "Can we get him back in?"

Barrows shrugged. "We're trying. Believe me, she wants him gone."

Vargo was relieved at that. "Excellent."

35

WHEN JULIE GOT TO HER OFFICE AT 7 A.M., SHE WAS wired from lack of sleep and actually suffering the first mild hangover of her life. She decided to confront her demons head on. She called her case agent.

"Have we heard from Medina today?"

"Nope. Not yesterday either. You want him in?"

"Yes." She checked her calendar. "Nine o'clock. Have him bring Baker in."

"You got it."

The word got to Medina twenty minutes later. He woke up Baker.

"Hey, Bobby Lee, it's seven-thirty. Rise and shine."

The entourage had gotten back from Cherokee at three, about the same time Julie left Barrows' suite. Romano had kept Baker's glass filled the whole night. He didn't feel like shining. "Go away."

"You got ten minutes to get up."

"Why?"

"Because we're going downtown."

"You're kidding."

"Nine A.M. Move your ass, Baker."

She left him sitting alone in a windowless office until noon. When she appeared he was surprised at the look of her. Her jaw was set, her face pale with deep sliced lines around her eyes. The white-blond hair was rumpled, not in a carefree way but in a careworn way. He almost felt sorry for her.

"What's the matter?" he asked.

"What do you mean?"

"You look like shit. No offense."

"Another technique from charm school?"

"I'm less charming now than before."

"Yes," she agreed.

She sat down at the table heavily. She had a single pad in front of her. "This is just a standard debriefing, Bobby. I'm going to do it once a week whether I need it or not." She picked up a pen. "What have you and Medina been doing?"

"Oh, we sat around. Visited Max. Took a ride in the car. It was more fun at Boron."

"Say the word, Bobby."

She always went for the easy ones. "Anyway, we haven't bumped into Vargo."

"Have you bumped into anybody else?"

Baker bit his tongue. "No."

"What about some ideas, Bobby? What leads should we be pursuing? Where should we be looking? How about doing something useful for a change?"

"Me? Personally, I don't think you could find Vargo if he was lying under your bed."

She seemed more intrigued than insulted. "Why?"

"Because you're the people who let him stroll out of the country. What makes you think you can find him now?"

"He had some help then."

"Who? . . . Oh, I forgot. Me. Right?"

"Right. Or maybe you think he just kind of left by coincidence. Same way as he killed those three people."

Baker didn't have a snappy answer to that. In his quieter moments at Boron he often asked the same question.

"No, I've never thought it was a coincidence," he said quietly.

"Really?" She was really intrigued now. "They must be rehabilitating you in prison."

"That still doesn't mean I tipped him. It's a big world out there."

"The whole world wasn't in my bedroom." She flushed at her own words. "And the whole world didn't know about the grand jury."

"Plenty of people did."

"Who? Me? Some agents?"

"Lots of people could be guessing. The grand jury's going to expire, your whole office knows that. Maybe somebody bribed a grand juror. Maybe you've got a bad secretary. Maybe an agent went bad."

"Maybe, maybe. Or maybe Mr. Baker, Vargo's attorney, went bad."

"I can tell you one real good reason that didn't happen."

"Why?"

"Because I was in love with you," he said simply.

She laughed easily, low and long. "Yeah, I forgot that."

When Medina came to get him a half hour later, the anger in the room lit the air.

"You guys okay?"

They ignored him. "Did you ever stop to think," she shouted to Baker, "even for one minute, what your treachery meant? Did you ever get a chance to see pictures of those bodies? And how about me? How about the betrayal of me? Did that bother you at all?"

They were nose to nose and his voice was as loud as hers. "You're going to let this eat you to your grave. Whatever I say won't make any difference at all."

Medina tried again, more forcefully now. "Hey, come on. This is old news. We got to work together now."

Her voice was now taunting. "Where is he, Mr. Baker? Come on, you're working with him. Tell us. It's in your interest."

"Of course it is. If I knew, I'd tell you."

"You're protecting him. I know it."

Bobby Lee smirked. "Just like you knew I told him about the grand jury." He turned to Medina. "Hey, Medina, this is bullshit, can't you get me out of here?"

He shook his head. "Not till she says so."

"Come on, Bobby. Give me something about your buddy I can use. Give me a hint you're real and maybe I'll start believing you."

"What does that mean?"

"Tell me something," she screamed. She was right in his face now. "Tell me something I don't know. Give me a reason to trust you."

"If I'm innocent, I couldn't possibly have any information for you."

She spread her hands. "Hey, we can play that game. You're innocent as a baby. You're just real smart. You know Vargo from the old days and can make some good guesses. So you got any guesses?"

"Maybe."

"See how easy that was. What do you have?"

Baker turned to Medina, who just shrugged. "Chinese banks," he said finally.

"Pardon?"

"Chinese banks. I think you should look there first."

"Chinese banks," she said. "Where do I look? Beijing?"

Big joke. She should go on a stage someplace. "L.A. I think whatever he does, he's going to try to work Chinese banks in L.A."

Julie's lawyer's mind calmed down. "You know something about those banks I don't?"

"Maybe just something you forgot. He used them before he left. If you concentrated more on Vargo instead of trying to get even with me, you'd remember that."

She ignored the remark. "Any bank in particular?"

It wasn't time yet to show her all his cards. "No, he used a lot of them. But even if I can't tell you the right bank, I can tell you the right city."

"I'm listening."

"Monterey Park."

She knew the town and knew the banks. She made some notes to hide her rising interest. "Anything else?"

"Yeah, one more thing. There's no way he's going to look the same. Forget your old pictures."

She shrugged. "So what do we look for?"

"Put agents all over that city. Monitor every bank you've got a live CTR grand jury on. Then remember the parts of Vargo that are hard to change: a man fifty years old, height five seven, weight one hundred ninety pounds. White, fat, and oily. Anybody looks like that, and goes near one of those banks, shoot him."

She smiled. "Very good, Mr. Baker." She wrote some more notes. "Incidentally, are you sure you're not doing this just to throw us off the trail?"

"Yeah, I can't wait to get back to Boron." He turned to Medina. "Can we go now?"

"Julie?"

"Take him back to Venice." She turned to Baker. "Bobby Lee, I like your change in attitude. You can't cover for Vargo forever."

He was too weak to argue anymore and just slumped.

"And incidentally, if we go to Monterey Park?"

"Yeah?"

"I want you with me."

Then she spun on her heel and left.

36

VARGO SLEPT FITFULLY UNTIL NOON THE FOLLOWING day. He woke knowing exactly what he had to do.

"Vincent, we've got a lot to do today. First take me back to Chang's. Then tonight, after hours, I need you to visit a certain lawyer named Mr. Wendel."

"Visit?"

"Yes. Just like you visited Mr. Martinez."

Chang stood and greeted him warmly when he arrived. There was none of the game playing of the previous evening.

"If all goes well today, we will receive a call at nine this evening. The caller will introduce himself as Mr. Lee. From San Francisco."

Vargo understood. He would spend the day repeating his story to steadily increasing levels of authority in Taipei. Mr. Lee, whatever his real name, would then call at nine. He had already been identified by Chang as the most important Bamboo chieftain on the West Coast. Lee's decision would resolve whether Kwoh lived or died.

"What does Mr. Lee do, anyway?"

Chang smiled with yellow teeth behind a screen of blue smoke. "He is a journalist," he said. "He writes obituaries for the *San Francisco Chronicle*."

"How appropriate."

"Let's hope so."

The day passed quickly and the call came precisely at nine. The voice on the other end was measured and polite. It asked whether the gentleman from Florence was present and Chang answered affirmatively. It then asked whether the gentleman's journey had been pleasant.

"Actually not quite," Vargo said. "There have been disruptions."

"How unfortunate," the voice said solicitously. "What were the problems?"

"There were several," Vargo said. "First I had a long-term lease on an apartment in Sylmar. A man interfered. Now I'm forced to seek other quarters."

"That is a problem."

"It is indeed. There are others."

"Yes?"

"I had a wonderful opportunity to acquire some jewelry at a terrific price. The same man interfered."

"Again?"

"Yes. He seems determined to spoil my trip."

"Yes, it seems so. What do you suppose his reasons are? Does he dislike you?"

Vargo knew better than to lie to the famous Mr. Lee. "Yes, he does."

"Then that is his reason?"

"Only in part."

"And what is the other part?"

"He hopes that by interfering with my plans he can take the same trip himself."

"I see. With his family?"

Vargo smiled before answering. "Not a chance, Mr. Lee. He plans to travel without his family."

There was silence then. "How unfortunate for him," Mr. Lee said at last. "A man should always travel with his family."

"Yes," Vargo said simply. And then the silence dropped heavily onto the line.

"We will need verification of these travel plans," Lee said at last.

"That will not be a problem," Chang said. "We are making inquiries."

"Yes, I imagine you are," Lee said. "So are we."

"We ought to agree on a timetable," Chang said hopefully.

Lee had no problem with that. "Tonight," the well-spoken killer said. "Tonight I will decide."

"Excellent," Chang and Vargo said together.

Charles Wendel was working much later than usual. Mr. Kwoh-Fang's recent demands had been extensive. To avoid depressing the street price Kwoh had been slowly selling the cocaine stolen from the Sylmar warehouse. As a result at least $11 million in cash was casually drifting toward the Asian Interbank Trust. That meant lots of work for Wendel creating phony documents from hundreds of small businesses to justify the cash infusion.

By 11 P.M. Wendel was exhausted. Darlene—the tall brunette who served coffee to Vargo—was there as well. He paid her over one hundred thousand dollars a year to do routine corporate filings and serve his needs. She despised him.

Darlene came in promptly at eleven with a bottle of single malt scotch and a brandy snifter. Her skirt was short and her heels high, a demeaning uniform Wendel demanded of her. She was thirty-two years old and had a thirteen-year-old daughter by a long ago boyfriend long ago gone. The girl was her life and if that meant holding her nose and letting Wendel do what he wanted, so be it.

Wendel took a long drink of scotch and gave her a whiskey leer. Darlene faked a smile back and moved closer to him, letting her mind escape to a safe place. She raised her arm as Wendel lifted her skirt and groped between her legs. The man was over sixty years old and could not perform for very long. She reached for him as a matter of self-protection. She knew if she moved quickly, it would quickly be over.

This time was easier than most. Wendel was tired as well as old. He was in and out before she had the time to feel cheapened by it all.

And then, after blinking twice, she began screaming at the top of her lungs in sheer terror.

At first she thought the man in the doorway was an illusion, a black, calm shape that blended into the shadows of the nighttime lights. Then, on closer inspection, she knew he was real. He stood there quietly, still as death, dressed in a funereal black suit. He was young and dark, his features smooth. In his left hand he held a small series of picks on a round chain. In his right hand he held a gun pointing squarely at them.

Darlene's scream shocked Wendel and he fell heavily off her. He lay on the floor, his pants at his ankles, an old, white, bloated man covered with wrinkles. He got to his knees and stared at the figure in the doorway, his limp soggy penis flapping like a piece of dead skin against his leg.

"Who . . . who are you?"

The man ignored the question. Turning and checking the hallway he seemed to satisfy himself that the suite was empty. Then he shut the door and bolted it. He walked toward them.

Wendel scurried to his feet. "Who are you? What are you doing here?"

Darlene knew better than to challenge the stranger. She shut up and sat up, trying unsuccessfully to look prim.

Wendel advanced on the stranger with an outraged look and right away Darlene knew he had made a mistake. The stranger studied Wendel for a moment, then reached between the man's legs and grabbed. Wendel, with his pants still at his ankles, screamed in agony. The stranger ignored the howls and pushed Wendel facedown into the couch. The lawyer struggled for breath, choking and screaming silently into the coarse fabric. Darlene inched away, convinced the stranger would strangle Wendel before her eyes. Suddenly the man placed the barrel of the gun against Wendel's anus. He pushed and Wendel stiffened. The man laughed quietly.

Wendel lay on his stomach gulping for air. His voice was weak. "Please . . . please."

"I'll do anything you say," Darlene said quickly. "Anything. Just don't hurt me."

The man gave a half smile in acknowledgment and then turned his attention back to Wendel. The lawyer by this time was furiously pulling up his pants with one hand and trying to regain some dignity. He was doing only a half-ass job at either task.

"Do you want money?" Wendel choked. "There's jewelry in the safe. What do you want?"

Vincent sat in a chair and leveled the gun at Wendel's belly. "I want to know where Kwoh stores the stuff from Sylmar."

Wendel's eyes shot up. Darlene was not surprised. This guy had not just dropped in from the sky.

"Who?" Wendel said. Even later, Darlene was amazed at the speed with which Vincent struck Wendel. The gun butt landed heavily on Wendel's nose and the lawyer crumpled. He began bleeding freely.

"Once more. Where does he hide the stuff?"

"I'll tell you," Darlene said quickly.

Vincent turned to her. "You know?"

Wendel panicked. "Shut up," he screamed.

This time the stranger's hand moved even faster than before. Darlene shut her eyes as a blade flashed across Wendel's face. It cut a deep furrow from his eye to his lips. The bleeding erupted anew.

"Please, not me," Darlene said softly.

Vincent turned to her and raised his eyebrows.

She pointed. "It's all in the safe. Every deal we did for

Kwoh, everything we're working with. I can give you everything—warehouse receipts, account numbers, everything you want."

"Show me."

Wendel no longer offered even token resistance. Darlene ran to the safe and pulled out check registers, correspondence files, articles of incorporation, board minutes, telex traffic, and anything else she could find within the two minutes of life she felt the stranger might give her. She dumped everything on the floor next to him.

"That it?"

"Most of it," she said. "There's some more stuff in his desk I can get you."

Vincent gestured toward the prone Wendel, who was now crumpled up in a ball, groaning with each breath. Vincent had to go slow. He remembered the problem with Martinez. All of a sudden the hemorrhaging would start and then the pale look. He had to be careful.

"Is there anything you *don't* know? Does this guy know *anything* you can't tell me?"

Darlene shook her head rapidly. "Absolutely not. I know everything *including* where Kwoh's warehouse is." She looked at Wendel with faint contempt. "I do all the work around here."

Vincent made a decision. If she knew everything, there was no use for the old fuck. He grabbed a box and threw it at Darlene. She caught it like a shortstop and began jamming all the documents into it. Vincent placed the gun gently underneath her chin. She stiffened, came to attention, and thought of her daughter. She would do anything he asked.

"Last chance. You tellin' me the truth? Is that everything?"

"It's everything, I swear."

"Good."

She slumped with relaxation as the stranger lugged the box toward the exit. Then she watched in utter shock as Vincent came back to Wendel, yanked his hair so that his mouth opened, put the .38 inside Wendel's bleeding mouth, and squeezed the trigger twice. Wendel's head exploded and Darlene bent at the waist against the vomit

which erupted in her throat. The stranger had his gun
back in his jacket and was lugging the heavy box out the
door. He turned to her with irritation. "What are you
waiting for?"

She looked up with confusion. "What?"

He sighed with exasperation. "You want to look like
him?"

"No," she said quickly. "Absolutely not."

"Then let's go."

Darlene ran to the door. "Yes, sir."

Darlene was led blindfolded in front of Vincent into a
room deep underneath the Green Palace. When she got
there Vincent pushed hard and she fell to her knees. The
blindfold was removed and she saw three young men
dressed in black kneeling next to her before a flat table.
There was a speakerphone on the table. Behind them two
other Chinese stood with drawn guns. The kneeling men
had their hands tied behind their backs and the men in
back of them grasped them by the hair. The kneeling
men were jabbering excitedly in Chinese. Occasionally a
solemn voice from the speakerphone would respond.
After ten minutes the room quieted.

There was an older white man behind the table and he
smiled when he approached her. He was about fifty years
old, short and squat, overweight although with a powerful wrestler's build. His complexion was oily and the
sweat formed on his face in dirty rivulets. He took the
arm of the Hispanic stranger who had killed Wendel and
conferred with him briefly. After he was done he came to
her. He helped her to her feet with a hand cool and dry
to the touch.

"Good evening. My name is Robert. I believe your
name is Darlene?"

"That's right."

"I don't want you to be afraid. Can you understand
that?"

No, she thought. "I guess so."

Another smile. "Good. Let me explain what we're
doing here. The gentleman on the speakerphone wishes
to hear what you have to say about Mr. Stewart Kwoh-

Fang and his relationship with Mr. Wendel. He needs details. Specifically details about where Kwoh hid the . . . well, furniture he stole from Sylmar. Also, how much he's sold it for so far. Can you do that?''

She stole a quick glance at Vincent. She would do anything the man wanted. ''Of course.''

''Excellent. And I assure you,'' he said sincerely, ''when you're finished with this, you'll be taken wherever you want to go unharmed. Do we have an agreement?''

His smile was warm and trustworthy. She shook his hand. ''Absolutely.''

She talked into the speakerphone for thirty minutes. The voice on the other end asked a few questions but otherwise listened quietly. She told everything, names, dates, places and amounts. When she was done, the room was quiet.

Eventually Chang lost patience. ''Mr. Lee?''

''Yes,'' the disembodied voice said.

''We would like to begin tonight, if possible. Do we have your permission?''

There was a long sigh on the other end of the line. ''Betrayal is such an ugly thing.'' There was more silence. ''All right,'' the voice said finally. ''Do what is necessary.''

''Thank you, Mr. Lee,'' Chang said.

Chang turned to Vargo with a broad grin. They shook hands excitedly.

Darlene was happy that everybody else was happy. She looked at Chang with expectation.

That brought Chang back to earth. ''We need to solve these issues,'' he said to Vargo, gesturing with his hand.

''I agree.''

''My people or yours?''

''Yours, I think, but not here.''

Chang laughed. ''Of course not. This is my office. Do you realize the value of that rug?''

Vargo recognized the irony of it all. ''I do indeed. I once had the same problem.''

Chang barked some orders in Chinese and the Chang operatives moved close to the kneeling Chinese. They pulled them to their feet and dragged them away, the captives wailing in protest. Then Vincent reached for Darlene. She suddenly got it and began her own screams. The death pleas of the four reverberated helplessly off the walls of Chang's office. Soon they were down in the soundproof basement kneeling again. Darlene thought of her daughter one last time. Vincent later said they were still screaming when the bullets entered their heads.

37

WHEN SHE ESCAPED CHEROKEE INTO THE SOFT L.A. night, Angela Moore thought she was finally safe. She had swept quietly past Baker and Romano and was certain the two men had not seen her. Now, out on Sunset in front of the restaurant, the actor expertly hustled her into his convertible and into the traffic flow heading west. The luxurious dark of Beverly Hills soon engulfed them. Neither of them saw or cared about the dark blue Mercedes that exited a nearby parking lot and was also traveling on Sunset a quarter mile behind.

The actor turned right off Sunset into the elegant, verdant hills and the night got black and secret around them. He was driving an expensive late-model foreign convertible, used and leased, an accessory endemic among actors, working or otherwise. The open car was a blessing because it allowed Angela to turn around and see who was following them. The quick look relaxed her even more. When they made the turn into the hills, no one followed. Even when they were a half mile further up the windy road she could just make out a single set of lights far behind. In the faint glow of the rare streetlights, she saw it only as a dark sedan with the distinctive tripronged emblem on the hood. In this neighborhood, such a symbol was as common as swimming pools and foreclosure notices. She leaned back and took a deep, relaxed breath.

The actor saw the gesture and misinterpreted it. He reached for her, groping gently. She opened her eyes and smiled at him. "Soon," she said.

At the crest of the hill, the actor pulled into a turnout, a little make-out spot for the few local teenagers whose parents didn't let them just do it on the couch during family dinners. The lights of the city sparkled far below them, falsely suggesting the dream city that never was. Angela was relieved. This would be easy.

Ten minutes later it was over. The actor was stunned, his eyes surprised and bulging. Angela buttoned up, then flipped down the visor to check her makeup. The actor had been vigorous but hadn't messed her up too bad. He was actually cute in a soft way. She could have taken him over the top in about three minutes with her mouth and fingers but a mixture of compassion and self-interest caused her to play with him a while longer, a cat with a mouse, bringing him to the edge of the abyss four times before she allowed him a release, smiling gently as he moaned curses at her. Such language, she was shocked. At the end she whispered in his ear what she would do to him for such behavior and that was it for him. He wailed and spurted and then looked drunk, drowned, and unhappy even though he was none of those things.

She was staring at the visor mirror fixing her eye makeup when the gleam of a headlight reflected sharply. The car parked and the headlights turned off quickly. In the dim light she could make out a large, dark blue Mercedes.

Angela had no belief in coincidences. "Let's go," she said abruptly.

The actor stared at her without understanding and Angela had to say it again. Then the guy got it and pulled out of the small cutout and back on to the main road. The dark Mercedes didn't follow. They made their way back to Sunset. She breathed easier.

"Where to now?"

She sighed. "Take me to work."

The strip bars along the dirt roads near El Segundo are the saddest commentary on the demise of the southern

California defense and aerospace industry. There was once a time the town was crowded with gleaming high-tech facilities and the buzz of production of heart-stopping fighter aircraft. Now the only aircraft sounds are the lumbering roar of chunk-laden 747s lifting inches off the runway at LAX, skimming over the brown waves en route to Sydney and Singapore, leaving precious little behind except the noise and smoke hovering over El Segundo.

The Odyssey Club was neither the worst nor best of the airport strip joints. It was jammed under a freeway overpass in what was formerly a sheet-metal holding warehouse for Hughes Aircraft. Now it had a broken concrete parking lot and signage that said SPORTS BAR— TOTALLY NUDE in English, Chinese, Japanese, and Tagalog. The 50-percent owner, an amiable gringo named Ferrante, would have had a Korean translation up too if there had been more room on the sign. The Asian trade was worth big bucks to the Odyssey.

Inside the club was a hodgepodge of competing attractions. There was a dirt pit in the center of the dance floor where in the evening, for a fee, wealthy patrons, inevitably Asian, could wrestle in the mud with a girl dressed in a bikini. Then there was a steady stream of strippers, trying not to look bored or hungover while grinding naked against a shiny metal pole. In between acts all the girls would come out bare-breasted and mingle to the blaring sounds of heavy metal music. For a price, minimum five dollars, they would sit on the customer's lap and permit the man to bury his face in a pair of breasts. Thirty seconds later a waiter would come over and blow a loud whistle in the customer's ear. The waiters were dressed as basketball referees.

Ferrante could never understand why anyone would pay five dollars to bury his face in a pair of bare breasts for thirty seconds, but he now completely understood the economics of it all. "I'll tell you what my partner told me," he told his accountant, a motherly woman of sixty who also didn't get it. "The guy pays five, the girl gets two, the ref gets one, and the house gets two. I got fifteen girls per shift and they're averaging forty-four minutes of dancing an hour." He shrugged. "We're not sadists, we gotta let 'em pee or whatever. Figure it out? For that kinda bread I'll bury my face in your tits."

His accountant ignored the compliment and figured it out. "That's two dollars profit per thirty seconds averaging forty-four minutes an hour times fifteen hours a day." Her eyebrows went up. "That's almost forty thousand dollars a day."

"You got it," Ferrante said, puffing out his chest. "And that's before I get my cut of the mud and the booze."

The accountant was stunned. "You got six clubs!"

Ferrante shrugged. "That don't mean nothin'. I got only one club makes money."

"I don't believe it."

"I'm telling you the truth."

"I've seen the numbers, Ottavio. Just multiply the Odyssey Club profit by six."

Ferrante shook his head. "You don't know what you're talking about. The Odyssey is special. Some of these other clubs you're lucky you got two drunk pilots on a good night."

"Special? Why special?"

"Let's just say in the Odyssey I got a partner. And that's made all the difference."

"Who?"

He sat back. "What are you doin' for the next hour?"

"Nothing."

"Great. Stick around to meet her."

It was nearly two in the morning and the Odyssey was still mobbed. The accountant, Mrs. Luella Robinson, sat with Ferrante in the front row. She was flanked by four Japanese in dark business suits, smoking obsessively, plane tickets jammed in the outside pocket of their suits.

At precisely 2 A.M. the lights dimmed and the room quieted. There was an electronic drumroll and even the guys on the pool tables stopped to watch. When she came out the jukebox began blaring some ultra-loud Chili Peppers. She ignored the driving beat and strolled across the stage like she was walking across a Milan runway. She wore a silver sequined gown and hooker heels. When she got in front of the Japanese men she stopped and put her hands on her hips.

They stared openmouthed. She stood on a stage three feet above the floor. She was six foot two in flats and the hooker heels added three inches more. Her legs were bare, tan, and muscular, and her breasts were full, pushing against the material of the low-cut dress. Her red hair fell in waves down her back.

When she was sure she had their attention she smiled and gestured to a curtain. It lifted and a nineteen-year-old blonde dressed as a UCLA cheerleader emerged. She waved her pom-poms then lifted the letter sweater to her neck. One of the Japanese screamed as his ignored cigarette ash burned a hole in his leg. His buddy turned to the nearest referee-costumed waiter.

"Thousand dollars."

"Pardon, sir?"

The man pointed furiously at the mud pit. The referee wrote it down and shrugged. A thousand might not be enough.

Luella Robinson watched the exchange in amazement. She turned to Ferrante. "Did that man just bid one thousand dollars to wrestle that cheerleader in the mud?"

"So far," Ferrante said. He sat back to light a Cuban, puffing with satisfaction.

The redhead on stage was an expert at getting her price and soon the young blonde's skirt was gone. That got the bidding up in a hurry and in five minutes the guy with the burnt hole in his pants had the price up to twenty-five hundred dollars.

"Hell of a thing, the fuckin' yen," Ferrante observed, a recent student of foreign exchange. "That's like seventy-five cents to these clowns. The U.S. of A. is going to the dogs."

Maybe so but until then there was money to be made. To the driving beat of the Chili Peps a succession of girls walked onto the stage under the watchful eye of the tall redhead. When a customer got abusive she cut him off with a gesture, the ever-present referees swinging into action to sweep the drunk away and replace him with another, more pliant, inebriate. After an hour there were twenty thousand dollars' worth of mud bids and the refs were collecting. The tall redhead left the stage and joined Ferrante.

"Great job, babe," he told her as she sat down.

"Thanks." Angela fixed her hair and ordered a Coke. "We got to talk."

"Anytime."

"Okay, now. Incidentally, I'm Monica Davis." She held out her hand to the accountant.

"Luella Robinson, Mr. Ferrante's accountant."

"Perfect. He needs an accountant." She turned back to Ferrante. "How're the receipts?"

"I can't bullshit you. We're making a fortune."

She nodded as though it didn't matter to her. "We'll work it out in the morning. Tell the girls to come in for their cut."

"Where the hell you goin'?"

Her head swiveled. "I got a problem. I need to change apartments in a hurry."

"Yeah? Who's chasin' you?"

Who indeed. "Let's just say an old flame. Anyway, I need to get to my car and *quietly* get to my apartment."

"No problem. You want one of the refs to go with you?"

She thought about that, then decided against it. "No thanks, just take care of things here. I may be gone, I don't know, a few days."

"Don't worry about it. I'll take care of everything."

Luella Robinson laughed at that. "My dear, before you came on the scene, Mr. Ferrante was in the process of filing his fourth bankruptcy petition. Now he appears to be a very rich man. Try not to stay away too long."

"Half of it's mine, Mrs. Robinson."

"My dear, I will make sure you get it."

"Thanks."

38

IT WAS CLOSE TO 4 A.M. WHEN SHE FINALLY GOT OUT. The streets under the freeway overpass were empty. She had three blocks to walk to her too carefully hidden car and immediately wondered whether she should have brought one of the refs along after all.

As she walked, her heels sounded like clattering pots and pans. She knew that sound would draw the attention of anyone awake in the neighborhood. And like any jungle, whoever or whatever was awake and prowling at this time of night was trouble.

A few of the wigged derelicts jammed under the freeway gave her a quick, "Hey, baby," as she hurried past. That unnerved her enough to try a shortcut across a darkened parking lot. The lot was crowned with once effective and now shot-out arc lights. The darkness gripped her in a hug and for a moment reassured her. It was a false reassurance.

In retrospect she never remembered the three of them rising at her out of the gloom like predator fish silently slinking from an undersea cavern. All of a sudden they were just there, broken surfers with beer-battered bellies and faces. They lived on the street and had been sleeping it off on filth-encrusted bags between two vans. She looked up and there they were, watching her with hatred in their eyes. The only exit was through them.

The fear rose within her. One of them had a broken wrench which he tapped against the side of his leg. Their faces were soiled and matted with dirt. One grinned with a mouth only half-filled with teeth.

The leader was tall and fat. His hair hung in dirty yellow ringlets. An unlit cigarette dangled from the corner of his mouth, held in place by two blackened teeth. The two others stared at her with sullen faces. She had no idea why she made them so angry.

There was nothing much she could do in high heels. And when one of them nonchalantly walked behind her, there was nothing at all she could do.

The fat one talked to the others. "Where you want to do her?"

"Please," Angela said.

They ignored her.

"How 'bout there?" One of them pointed to an oily pile of rags heaped between two cars.

"No, please," Angela said again.

"What about after?" one of them said.

"What do you mean, after?" the fat one said. And then he laughed with a grinding, choking sound. The others, after a moment's hesitation, joined him, and soon the night quiet burst with the sharp, taunting noise.

Angela stood frozen, alone, paralyzed with fear. A young woman raped and beaten to death under a freeway overpass, especially one with her past, wouldn't merit a line in the *L.A. Times* or a whisper of interest from the overburdened homicide forces of the LAPD. This war zone city had more shootings in a day than Sarajevo, and quite simply nobody would give a shit.

She had to run, not because she had any hope but only for something to do. Before she could do that the fat man grabbed her purse and ripped it off her shoulder, upending the contents onto the oil-soaked concrete. The two others stared at the scattered bills and for an instant ignored her. She turned and ran.

She didn't get far. The leader threw the wrench and she felt the metal hit hard in the small of her back. She spun with the pain, tripped, and fell heavily to the ground, her cries echoing helplessly. The fat man with the yellow-ringed hair walked up and kicked her hard in the stomach. She groaned and doubled up. The two others laughed with tinny, manic bursts of sound.

She looked up and saw the leader readying to kick her again, saw the foot go back and begin to come forward. It all seemed to be happening at half-speed and she closed her eyes against the agony to come. Then she heard three soft pops which were undoubtedly her ribs breaking and she braced for the sharp aftershock. When it didn't come she opened her eyes, blinking with confusion. The fat man was leaning against the hood of an abandoned, painted van, now ignoring her, his face white as death. He was clutching his bare stomach where it protruded six inches below his dirty T-shirt. His hands turned red with blood as the flow ran between his fingers to form a pool between his legs. Then he screamed once and pitched face first onto the gravel of the parking lot. His two friends backed up, staring at something approaching them out of the mist. The offshore fog hid him at first, then as he came closer she saw him clearly. He was tall, heavy-set, and wearing a dark suit. His shirt, too small, pinched his beefy neck. His face was round, olive, and flawless, what they call a baby face. His mouth was full and cruel.

He held out his hand to her. She took it and got up, her eyes wide with fright.

"You okay?"

She nodded wordlessly. She couldn't take her eyes off his beautiful face.

He turned to the others and raised the gun. His movements were slow, lazy even.

"Please don't," she said quickly. Her voice was hoarse.

He looked back at her. "They would have killed you. Maybe if you were lucky they'd have done it fast. But I don't think you would have been lucky."

She put her hand on his arm. "Please don't."

He didn't understand and shook his head to say so. He walked over to them. His gun was level. The two men backed up against the painted van with their arms held high, babbling incoherently. They begged with increased hysteria as he drew near. He seemed to savor the moment before firing. The four gunshots were silenced and again she heard the same small pops. The two men screamed. The bullets had blasted their kneecaps into oblivion and they fell to the ground trying unsuccessfully to stop the flowing blood.

He turned his back on his victims and held out his hand for Angela. "My car is over there. I'll take you where you need to go."

"What about them?"

"What about them?"

"They'll die here. They'll bleed to death."

"No they won't, they'll just complain for a while. Anyway, I ain't got time for them. Let's go."

He grabbed her arm forcefully, scooped up her purse, and marched her through the parking lot to his car, a late model, dark blue Mercedes 560. She recognized the car immediately.

"You were following me," she said, turning to confront him. "Ever since I left Cherokee."

"Just get in. You can sit in the back."

She did as she was told, although she didn't like it. She directed him to her apartment.

"Go ahead. I'll watch you walk up."

Angela sat back and crossed her arms. "I'm not getting out until you tell me why you were following me."

He shook his head. "Forget that shit. Get your ass into that house. No tricks, no questions. Got it?"

She stared at him. "Anything else?"

"Yeah, there is. You never saw me, understand? You never saw this car, never saw me. Got it?"

"Yes," she said. "Except the answer's no."

He held his hands to his temples as though experiencing a great pain. "Why, sweetheart, why are you bustin' my balls? Can you tell me that?"

"You saved my life."

"So you bust my balls for saving your life? I do that every day. I'm sort of like Robin Hood."

"Will I see you again?"

"What?"

"What part of that don't you understand. Will I see you again?"

"Sweetheart, once again. Get in the fuckin' house."

"I'm not moving."

"What?"

"I'm not moving until you answer me."

Lazy Sal smashed his head twice against the steering wheel. Romano would kill him for this. "Look, baby, I'm not gonna tell you again. Get your ass in the fuckin' house or I'm gonna beat it till it's black and blue."

"No." She folded her arms over her chest.

He leaned back in panic and exasperation. "Ain't this a son of a bitch."

"Will I see you again?"

"What's your phone number?"

"Will you use it?"

"Yeah, I'll use it," he promised. His voice was weak.

"You're lying. I'm not moving."

He began cursing in a language Angela couldn't understand. She thought it might be Spanish.

"Is that Spanish?"

"Look, I'm not gonna tell you again. Get your little buns in the house. I got a job to do."

"When will I hear from you?"

He gave up. "Tomorrow. Tomorrow you'll hear from me."

"What time?"

"Six o'clock. Six o'clock you'll hear from me."

"And what're we gonna do?"

"What do you mean, what're we gonna fuckin' do?"

She handed him a slip of paper. "I mean, you'll call this number at six and then we'll spend the evening together. I'll get to know you and have all my questions answered. Now what will we do?"

"We're gonna go eat," Sal said. "And before you ask me any more questions, we'll go eat Italian. And that's it. No more questions. Tomorrow night at six. You got it?"

"What's your name?"

"Sal," he said with irritation. "That's it. Next question, I smack you." He raised his hand.

Angela leaned over, put her thumb under his chin to raise it slightly, and kissed him on the lips. "Till tomorrow, Salvador."

"Sal. Nobody calls me Salvador."

Angela smiled. "I do."

39

WHATEVER THEIR DIFFERENCES, CHANG AND VARGO
had one goal in common, a need for speed. Within hours
of the mysterious Mr. Lee's enigmatic approval, Chang's
black-clad gunmen had moved. Like all good generals he
sought surprise and a crippling of his enemy's ability to
fight back. Just before dawn Chang achieved both.

The location of Kwoh's warehouse was the last coherent sentence Darlene spoke before she died. At 5 A.M. a
pair of white vans drove up to it and parked outside. A
skinny, weirdly grinning twenty-year-old named Jimmy
Sun approached the double doors and punched three
numbers into an outside digital lock. One of the four
lights above the lock changed from red to green. He
pressed the asterisk key, inputted three more numbers,
and the second light changed color. He repeated the exercise twice more until all four lights were green. Then
he pushed the button marked simply "open" in Chinese
characters.

The great double doors slid back, grinding rust against
rust. As they opened, a nineteen-year-old with pimpled
skin emerged, bathed in the insistent headlights from the
vans. He held a handgun in one hand and tried to shield
his eyes from the glare with the other.

"Good evening," Jimmy Sun said pleasantly in perfectly accented Mandarin.

The kid squinted and Jimmy Sun opened fire with the
MAC-10. At over one thousand rounds a minute, it took
no more than a three-second burst to splatter the young-
ster across the white wall behind him.

The gunfire and death screams attracted two other
guards who ran brazenly into the glare of the van's headlights. Each was cut in half by a fusillade from a half-
dozen MAC-10s. Then Jimmy Sun gestured and the vans
rolled over the dead remains and into the warehouse.

Inside the warehouse the van doors opened and ten Chang gunmen poured out. They sprinted around the warehouse strategically placing timed incendiary devices. Jimmy Sun swaggered, ignoring the stored guns and hunting for the cocaine stash he knew was there. He knew he found it when he saw the nondescript packing crates piled high on wooden pallets in a dark corner of the warehouse. He broke open one crate to find finely crafted Chinese dolls. He smashed a young ivory princess against the concrete floor. Inside was a tightly woven brown bag.

He yelled in Chinese and the rest of the gang howled in reply. They gathered around their leader and the small mountain of white powder on the soiled concrete floor of the warehouse. Jimmy Sun fell to his knees and grabbed a handful, bypassing his long ago exploded nasal passages and jamming the pure product into the membranes at the roof of his mouth. The others did the same and soon their dark jogging suits were splattered with pale powder. Satisfied, the leader rose and shouted. "Load up and let's go."

They only had an hour and had to use forklifts to drag the wooden pallets filled with tons of packing crates out to the waiting trucks. They then had only five minutes to screech away before the place blew—a gorgeous incandescent explosion of light and color that could be seen clearly for thirty miles in every direction. The roof of the warehouse blew straight up and went careening down the side of a hill, coming to rest in the middle of early rush-hour traffic on the San Bernardino Freeway. The fires escaping from the exploding building lit the dried brush on the brown hillside and ignited a series of residential fires that took twelve hours to bring under control. By dawn there were as many reporters and TV crews in Monterey Park as police, and the Bamboo war had begun.

Julie Beck woke at five and took thirty minutes to admire the dawn rising above the gilt-laden hills. She put on a robe and walked to the driveway to collect the four newspapers she read each morning. Her neck was stiff from another night of sleepless twisting. She returned to her room and put on some coffee, then turned on the news.

The TV screen was filled with images of the developing war. A helicopter high above Monterey Park was reporting live the chaos below: fire engines screaming, flames leaping from a dozen structures, and a freeway of early morning commuters clogged with debris from the fallen roof.

The picture darkened and the action shifted to a pair of talking heads in the studio. Julie strained to listen.

"So just to recap, Joe," the blond anchorwoman said, "we have now confirmed four dead in the latest breakout of violence in the small Chinese community of Monterey Park."

"That's right, Andrea," the man agreed. "And for you commuters it looks like slow going on the old San Berdoo. Between the lookie-lous and the emergency equipment using the roads, we'd suggest alternative routes to downtown."

"Now, Joe," the woman continued, "do we have any new information on the cause of this senseless violence?"

"Well, the best answer to that, Andrea, is to check in with our on-site reporter, Hector Rodriquez, in Air Copter Channel Four. Hector, can you hear me?"

"Loud and clear, Joe."

"Tell us, Hector, any new information from your end on the cause of the violence?"

"Great question, Joe. You know it's a little hard to answer those questions from a thousand feet up here in Air Copter Channel Four."

The anchorpersons agreed and roared with shared laughter. Julie wanted to break through the television and strangle all three of them, even the guy in the helicopter.

"But we do have a little more information now than we had an hour ago," Hector said. "The local police chief has requested FBI assistance in his investigation."

"The feds! That certainly is important, Hector."

"That's what I think, Andrea. It's the chief's view that this is a gang vendetta of some kind. There were apparently a lot of weapons at the warehouse that was bombed. Maybe some drugs, too."

"Well, that certainly does complicate things, Hector. Tell us, any more word on the identity of the victims?"

"Not really, Joe. There were three bodies at the warehouse but they were too charred to make an ID. Then we've got one dead in a freeway crash when the debris hit the San Bernardino."

"That's four all right," Andrea agreed.

Julie turned off the set.

The phone rang insistently near Medina's ear for a full minute before he answered. Baker was asleep on the couch. Medina finally picked up the receiver. His voice was clogged. "Hullo."

"Medina, this is Julie."

He looked at his watch. He could barely read the numbers. "Julie, it's like . . . what, four in the morning?"

"It's almost six. Listen, I want Baker in."

Medina cursed silently. He tried his best to sound upbeat. "Again? Okay, what time?"

"Six-thirty."

He instantly came awake. "Six-thirty? Julie, we're in Venice. You're in God-knows-where. Even if we . . ."

"You got till seven, Medina. If you're not here, I'm assigning someone else to Baker."

"Julie, give me a break. Julie? Julie?" He was talking to a dead line. He began screaming a string of incredibly abusive Spanish curses before falling back on the bed and grabbing his pain-engorged temples with both hands.

She walked into the windowless room at seven sharp and threw a paper on the conference table. Through the miracle of computers the *L.A. Times* had managed to slap color aerial photos of the carnage onto a quick extra morning edition. The paper seemed almost warm to the touch.

"I don't suppose you've seen this yet."

Medina stared at the paper through bleary eyes. Baker didn't even bother.

"Have you got any coffee?" he asked.

"Over there. Be quick about it." She pushed the paper toward Medina. "Read this and then let him read it. When I get back we'll talk." Then she left the room.

Medina and Baker drank bad government coffee and read the paper. The front page had a full-color picture of the exploded warehouse. The headline, with slight excess, blared "CRACK HOUSE EXPLODES IN CHINESE DRUG WARS." There was a quickie one-paragraph story on the jump-page obliquely referring to a long-standing battle between unnamed drug lords for control of the lucrative cocaine trade.

"What are we supposed to do, go stop this?"

"I think so. I'll ask Her Majesty to get you a gun."

Julie came in ten minutes later. Baker was leaning back reading the sports section. "I see the dog-ass Dodgers are still in last. Ah, well, at least Wimbledon's coming up. Who you like, Becker?"

She ignored him and tapped the front page. "Have you read this?"

"Yeah," Baker told her. "So what?"

"It was you who told me about the Chinese banks."

"I don't think the bankers are doing this."

"Very funny. This is a big-time drug war and it's occurring in the same city you told me to look out for. I don't believe in coincidences, Baker. Now what's this all about?"

Bobby Lee looked at Medina. "You know what this is all about?"

Medina was not about to bite the hand that fed him. He studied the paper intently. "It says here it's a drug war," he told Julie.

Julie Beck rolled her eyes. "Medina, I read the fucking paper."

Baker interceded. "Two questions. First, what does this have to do with me? Second, what does this have to do with Vargo?"

"Two answers. If all this is happening in Monterey Park, then maybe Vargo's in the middle of it. As for you, you're the one who told me about this place. So when I go there today, you'll be with me."

"What?" Medina shrieked. "That's suicide in there."

"Don't worry about it," Julie told him. "You're off this."

"But why . . ."

"Why? Because you two are a little too chummy for me. Medina, this man is a convicted felon, not some goddamn hero."

"Julie, you've got no right to . . ."

"Jesus, that is bullshit . . ."

Neither of them got to finish his sentence. She was gone.

40

SHE WAITED FOR EVENING BEFORE SETTING SAIL. IN THE meantime she jammed him into a cell in the marshal's lockup, just to give him a taste of what his future might be. At dusk an agent he'd never seen before, Robert something or other, came and got him. He was young and stern and uninterested in conversation of any sort. He cuffed Bobby Lee's hands and feet for the ride on the elevator to the twelfth floor. Even Julie had to roll her eyes at that one.

At dusk they pulled out of the FBI parking lot beneath the federal building in a nondescript government car. Robert drove. Julie sat in the front with him. They put Bobby Lee alone in the back, like a prisoner, which he was.

It should have taken no more than ten minutes to get there. Now, driving through a war zone, it took over an hour. All the surface streets were blocked by police barricades and emergency equipment. There were CHP cars at every freeway entrance and local police at all the major intersections. Newly burning fires still brightly lit the night sky.

The disorienting screech of competing sirens deepened the sense of panic and chaos. Robert's government car had a siren as well and he decided to use it. As he reached the outskirts of the city with his screaming siren the road clogged. He made a quick U-turn away from the crush and found he was facing a river of oncoming traffic, also at a standstill. He wound up sitting foolishly, his red light and siren competing unsuccessfully with the horns of the drivers whose lane he had just clogged.

The combined noise was deafening.

"Nice move, Robert," Julie shouted over the din. She did not suffer fools gladly.

"No problem, Julie," Robert said quickly. "I'll have us out of here in a jiffy."

That proved a bit optimistic. Robert did manage a courageous move onto a sidewalk but once there he still had nowhere to go. Passersby stared into the car with curiosity. Julie was squeezing the bridge of her nose to cut off the pain. Bobby Lee wondered how he and Max ever managed to lose to these mopes.

"As long as we're stuck here, can I run in and get a little takeout?"

"You're not helping, Baker."

"Sorry." He sat back, content to let Robert bleed slowly. There was a lot to look at. The night sky was once again lit with new fires. The moon-filled night let the smoke mingle with passing clouds to create eerie, interesting patterns.

"Don't worry," Robert said. "I'll just go up that alley."

Baker looked at the narrow alley. This ought to be rich. Robert inched the car through the pedestrians and made a quick right turn down the alley. The alley was wide enough, barely, for the car to fit through.

Robert was a new man. "I'll just pop out the back side," he announced confidently.

Baker saw a gorgeous disaster sailing nicely down the canal. He had been in this sort of alley before. He sat back and smiled.

"Are you sure this goes through?" Julie asked nervously.

Not a chance, thought Bobby Lee.

"Absolutely," said Robert.

Robert was wrong, the alley was blind as well as narrow. The back end had a high stucco wall, a small fully enclosed concrete patio, and that was that.

"How about we just shoot through the wall?" Bobby Lee suggested amiably.

"Baker, shut up," she barked. She turned to her agent. "Well?"

Robert was panicking. "I was sure this went through." His head swiveled. "Don't worry, I'll just back out and start again."

Right. Robert slipped it into reverse and turned to look out the back window. Baker saw the sweat on the man's upper lip.

"Just a second here," he said, then squarely hit the left-hand wall. Everyone's head snapped backward.

"Sorry."

He tried again, this time with the battered tail of the car more or less centered. He inched backward. Now, the right side of the car scraped against the right wall. There was a sickening tearing of metal. Robert held up his hand to show he was in control and quickly put it in drive. That got him off the right wall and right back onto the left wall.

"Jesus," Julie said to herself.

"It's good you're praying."

"Why's that, Baker?"

"Because with three inches of clearance on either side, you're going to be praying a lot more once he wedges us in."

It was true. Once wedged in, they'd starve to death in this car. The radio would be useless between two concrete buildings. They'd sit and wait for someone to come along who would recognize their plight, who could speak English, who would give a shit.

Julie got it. "Jesus, Robert, you're going to get us killed. I'm going to starve to death in a fucking car with Bobby Lee Baker."

"Not necessarily," Robert said. Not for nothing had he starred at FBI school in Quantico. "We could kick out the windshield."

"There you go," Baker told her. This was more fun than the dancers at Cherokee.

Julie was breathing hard, trying to control herself. "Robert, I want you to listen carefully and do exactly as I say. Drive straight ahead, right into that little patio. It's only five feet so try not to get stuck. Then I'm getting out. So's he." She jerked her thumb at Baker. "Then you can try to back the car out. If you get stuck in the alley . . ." She left the rest unsaid.

It didn't take Robert long. Baker and Julie stood safely in the open air watching Robert grind the car first against the left wall and then the right. About a third of the way down the alley, the grinding stopped. All four wheels were now off the ground. The engine roared uselessly.

Julie walked to the front of the car and held up her hand like a traffic cop. The roaring of the engine stopped. Julie gestured to Baker and the two of them climbed over the hood, the windshield, the roof, the tail. It was now clear to the street. The dusk had long since turned to harsh darkness. Baker could now make out red flames inside the dense smoke. Julie rapped on the rear of the car and Robert rolled down his window. His eyes were large and panicked in the dim light.

"Robert, we'll call and get somebody back here for you. Do me a favor and don't try to kick out the windshield. You'll only hurt yourself."

"Julie, I'm sorry, I don't understand how—"

She held up her hand, the traffic cop again. He stopped talking.

She turned back to the street, lost in thought. Bobby Lee spoke for both of them. "Kind of weird, huh."

She spoke to the street. "Yeah, I'd say that. Hey, Baker?"

"Yeah?"

"I've got an idea."

"Yeah?"

"You wanted to show me something, right?"

"Right."

She gestured toward the waiting street. "Show me."

They left the alley and headed west, by no means arm in arm but at least side by side. The night sky reflected the glow of newly torched buildings and the air was dense. The scream of fire sirens drowned the traffic noise. They had to speak loudly to be heard.

"Well," she said after they had sidestepped through a block-long string of fire watchers.

"Well, what?"

"Where are we going?"

"So demanding. Why can't you enjoy this more? This is like a date. Me and you, the night, beautiful fireworks, the wonders of Monterey Park."

"Baker, I really don't have time for this."

"No date?"

"Right."

They walked further, maneuvering around barricades and small crowds of people with their necks craned. Baker figured they were about six blocks from the Golden Dragon. They turned onto Brooklyn, the main drag, and the foot traffic increased. They passed four burned-out convenience stores in the next three blocks.

"Julie, let me ask you something. Did you ever think maybe, just maybe, you could be wrong?"

She barely heard him. "About what?"

"About anything, really. But I was thinking about me."

"Baker, let's keep the conversation on Vargo, okay?"

"Why, are you embarrassed?"

"No, Baker, I'm not embarrassed."

"Then what?"

She stopped. "Bobby, I have no regrets, okay? Everything I did I'd do all over and love it. And, no, it never occurred to me I was wrong, not even once. Now if that answers your questions, can we get down to business?"

"Sure, but why don't you want to—"

"Bobby, stop it!" she screamed. Her face was flushed.

"Okay, okay."

She took a deep breath. "Now answer my question. Where are we going?"

"To a restaurant."

"A restaurant." She sighed. "I'm going to get an FBI car to pick us up."

He grabbed her shoulders. "Julie—"

"Let me go."

"I just want—"

"Let me go or I promise your worthless ass will be back in Boron tomorrow morning."

Baker immediately dropped his hands. "Sorry."

She shook her head in exasperation. "Why the hell don't you just come clean, Bobby? Tell me where Vargo is and I'll try to help you."

"I don't know where he is."

She shook her head again like it sure was a waste.

"But I can help you," he said quickly.

"How?"

"I can show you where he's been."

Her eyebrows raised. This was progress. "Really?"

"Really. It's about six blocks from here. Just listen to me while we walk."

"Does this place have a phone?"

"I'm sure it does."

"Then let's go."

They turned down Alcorn bending toward the south. As they walked, Baker talked as precisely and coherently as he ever had to a jury. He knew he only had one shot at her, lasting six blocks, less than twenty minutes. He talked about Vargo and banks, about Faldo and his obsessively prepared Green Bible, and about Monterey Park. As they walked, he pointed out the banks they passed, five to a block, nondescript bunkers with barred slits for windows. He talked about his suspicions, about the ongoing federal investigations into these banks, which always went nowhere, about what he suspected went down behind the bland concrete walls. Her attitude changed from irritation to concentration. She examined each bank they passed with growing interest.

"I've heard about these banks," she said finally. "They were set up for the Hong Kong and Taiwan money coming in."

"And that's the type of place that can keep secrets, right?"

"Sure. They engage in kind of reverse money laundering. They don't smuggle money out, they smuggle money in." She thought about that. "That's why nobody cares about them. Plus they're solvent. Who would ever indict a solvent bank?"

"Maybe someone should. If these banks can launder inbound currency, they can do the same thing with—"

"Outbound," she said. "You're right, Baker."

Progress. "So, let's walk some more," he said.

They arrived at the Golden Dragon at about 9 P.M. The restaurant was much more desolate than Baker remembered, a commercial victim of the carnage and desolation around them. He stood with Julie across the street and surveyed the entrance. Julie looked at him quizzically.

"So?" she said finally.

"I know you'll find this hard to believe, but I'm sure Vargo's been in there."

"Why?"

Bobby Lee pointed to the small gold-plated sign for the Asian Interbank Trust. "That was Vargo's bank. When he escaped that was the bank that wired his money out of the country. We came here the other day—me, Faldo, and Medina."

"And what happened?"

He told her everything, from his trip to the roof, with his aerial acrobatics, to his confrontation with the Chinese. Julie looked faintly amused.

"Medina was supposed to be paying more attention to you than that."

"He was, I just sort of went out on my own for a while."

"You're lucky you didn't get killed."

"Would you have cared?"

"No."

"Anyway," Baker said, "let's go check it out."

"Are you sure it's got a phone?"

"I'm sure."

"Let's go," she said.

41

A LITTLE MORE THAN TWELVE HOURS INTO HIS WAR with Kwoh, Chang was in control. The first six hours had been a blitzkrieg of incendiary bombings and drive-by shootings. With the advantage of surprise, Chang's gang eliminated the Kwoh forces with almost military effectiveness.

As soon as Jimmy Sun left the Kwoh warehouse he took his ten gunmen to a small house on a residential street that Kwoh's second in command, an accountant named Harold Chen, used as a combination office and *pied-à-terre*. Three Asian teenagers burst into the house, their MAC-10s sputtering. Chen's bodyguard was immediately cut down along with Chen's consort for the evening, a twelve-year-old Filipino. Chen was in the bathroom and died on the throne when a stream of bullets shattered the door and took Chen with it. Thirty minutes later, a second Kwoh warehouse erupted in flames, leaving in its wake a block-long fire storm and four more dead bodies. Two of the bodies were children. The media went berserk.

Chen's murder demoralized Kwoh and left him without his right hand and best friend. Two hours later Kwoh desperately tried to forge an alliance with two rival gangs. He had to promise a lot but a meeting was finally set up at the Golden Dragon between a senior Kwoh ambassador and twelve emissaries from the two gangs.

The staff at the Golden Dragon spent hours preparing for the meeting. The men came in soberly one by one, trying to meld into the vastly diminished dinner crowd and eventually settling in at two large white tables near the back of the restaurant. The manager came out, snapped his fingers twice, and mounds of dim sum appeared on the shoulders of waiters. The conversation became hot and heavy in Chinese.

* * *

243

Julie Beck and Baker walked into the Golden Dragon fifteen minutes later. They had been arguing across the street for thirty minutes and never noticed anything unusual. When they tired of arguing they both gave up and went in.

They sat at a table twelve feet from the group being lavishly attended to by the manager. They paid no attention, thinking separate thoughts, oblivious to the thirteen loudly jabbering Chinese.

"What now?" Julie asked finally.

Baker grabbed the menu. "The Szechuan duck, I think, that's what they're having. Then I would go with the vegetables, maybe some broccoli and chicken. The pea pods look fresh. Look at the service in this place. It's really special."

"Is there a phone here?" Julie looked around. "I'm going to get a car to pick us up. This is a waste of time."

"Don't forget Robert."

"Right." She got up and left.

Baker went ahead and ordered anyway. The waitress was slim and pale with gray eyes. He ordered for two and topped off the meal with a couple of Tsing Tao beers. He didn't know if the government would pay for any of it, but maybe by the time she went nuts he'd at least have one of the beers down. As expected, she was not amused.

"What's all this?"

"Sit down and relax for a minute. I'm tellin' you, Vargo's been here, trust me on that. How about we split this beer?"

Julie ignored him. "I called but it'll take forever for an agent to get here with this traffic. Where's the bathroom?"

"No splitting the beer?"

"Right."

He started to gesture toward the kitchen before his fingers changed course, scratching his head briefly then pointing to the dark stairway leading to the paneled offices downstairs. She got up and flounced away.

He watched her go, hoping for the best. The thirteen men at the next table never saw her walk down the dark stairs. Their voices rose and fell in some alien argument known only to themselves. They jabbed the air with lit cigarettes. Four waiters hovered solicitously, clearing plates and serving food with an efficiency only an owner can expect.

He saw her emerge from the stairway five minutes later. Her face was drawn. A young Chinese in a dark suit had her firmly by the arm. He pushed her roughly into the room and pointed, speaking sharply in Chinese. Julie walked in a trance over to Baker's table.

"Did you find the bathroom?" he asked innocently.

"What?"

"The bathroom? You know, tinkle, tinkle."

"I don't believe it."

"What, my baby talk?"

"It's like an army camp down there. They've got men —boys actually—sleeping in the hall next to their rifles or machine guns or whatever. I stepped on one in the dark."

"No wonder he looked angry."

"I was frightened and ran from him. I opened a door and . . . you wouldn't believe it."

"Kind of high-tech?"

"Exactly. It's a command center. Paneled offices, computers, communications equipment. They've got stuff in there we don't have at Main Justice."

"Maybe they need it for the duck."

Her look back at him now had more interest than irritation. "Tell me again," she said.

He took it from the top, telling her again the tale of Vargo and Monterey Park and the Green Bible and his leap across the void and his battle at the bottom of the dark steps. He left out Cherokee; no need to get her confused by Angela and Romano and Lazy Sal. At the end he was sure he had her.

"So that's it," he said finally. "Now do you believe me?"

Early begging always leads no place. She shook her head. "Your knowledge of Vargo is exactly what I thought. You must have been in it up to your ass."

"Eyeballs," Bobby Lee suggested softly. "A more elegant way of saying that. Up to my eyeballs."

She actually began picking at her food. "Anyway, we'll get picked up in a few minutes. Jesus, what's that racket?"

The thirteen men at the next table were close to blows. Two of them were banging the table, causing plates with food to turn lazily in the air before dumping their contents on the hard tile floor. The waiters efficiently descended to clean up the mess. The men paid no attention, their voices now rising to even greater hills of anger. There was much finger-pointing and fist slamming and puffs of eerie, purple smoke.

"This doesn't look like a bowling league," Bobby Lee observed. "You know any Mandarin?"

She pointed to the door. "I can't believe it. There's my agent. Let's get out of here."

Baker turned and saw a man in a blue suit fill the doorway. He looked stiffly right and left before spotting her. He signaled with his hand in a generous, optimistic way and picked his way through the tables. It was the last gesture he ever made.

Later on, when he thought about it, Bobby Lee sort of remembered the three waiters standing shoulder to shoulder behind the agent. He clearly remembered an unfocused, unformed sensation of fear that caused him to stiffen. He scanned the room and reached involuntarily for her arm. She tried to pull away. He squeezed tighter until it hurt her. "Let go," she ordered.

"Shut up," he said.

She opened her mouth but this time didn't argue. The agent was three-quarters of the way across the room. The thirteen men at the table twelve feet away continued their loud argument. Then Bobby Lee saw him clearly, the waiter on the far right. Jimmy Sun grinned and pulled a MAC-10 out of a paper bag.

"Down," Baker screamed to the agent, who was dead but didn't know it.

His voice was lost in the din of clattering plates and loud arguments. The agent heard it only as a greeting. He moved into the line of fire just as Jimmy Sun opened up. The agent took the first volley dead in the back and the high-powered slugs cut him down as efficiently as they had the guard at the Kwoh warehouse. He fell open-mouthed and wide-eyed. He was dead long before his head hit the floor and bounced.

Baker grabbed Julie by her short white hair and yanked her under the table, then turned the table over in the direction of Jimmy Sun. The table formed a barrier of sorts. The food toppled around them.

The firing then started in earnest, a muffled sound, like a deck of cards being shuffled. The thirteen men at the table stood and screamed, providing better targets for Jimmy Sun's gunmen. The outraged howls of the dying competed with the ping of bullets ricocheting off walls and the shattering of glass and plates. Baker pushed Julie facedown into the tile floor, then lay heavily on top of her. A dead Chinese fell next to them, his sightless eyes staring, blood streaming from his mouth.

Julie could hardly breathe. When she struggled, Bobby Lee put more weight on her, shouting "Don't move, you hear me, don't move." Suddenly a new burst of gunfire shattered their table. Baker felt a searing burn in his legs and shoulders, followed by a warm, sticky feeling. His blood mingled with that of the dead Chinese on top of Julie. Still the firing continued.

Finally, there was silence. Baker could hear the clicking of ordnance as guns were reloaded. Then more of the quiet sputtering. He looked up to see Jimmy Sun finishing the job. He walked only to the thirteen men and kicked each one, ignoring waiters, customers, and whites. One groaned when he was kicked. Jimmy's MAC-10 spit and the groaning stopped.

The three gunmen then backed out the door, firing a final burst into the ceiling. After thirty seconds, Baker opened his eyes. The room was dark and smoke-filled. A lone streetlight cast a pale glow over the lonely sounds of the dead and dying.

He fought against the waves of nausea rising in his throat. The moans of the survivors penetrated deep inside his skull. Julie remained facedown on the floor, now no longer struggling. He took her hand and helped her up.

Her face was impassive, drained of blood and emotion.

She raised a hand and he flinched involuntarily to ward off the blow. Her hand lightly brushed his cheek. "You're hurt," she said.

He felt the blood drip along his hairline. The crashing of the broken cutlery had cut deep into his scalp. She inspected him closer and found the bleeding in his shoulder and his hip.

"You've been shot?"

He could feel the blood seep and flow. "I don't know . . . I think so." He began to feel faint.

She inspected him coldly. "It looks like superficial bleeding in the head and the shoulder, maybe a little deeper in the . . . hip."

The first bullet had torn through the back of his leg and exited through the right buttock. The second flew through the fleshy part of his shoulder. Only his head seemed to have taken a direct hit from the broken plates.

He felt nausea and light-headedness flow over him. "I feel like shit."

"I know," she said. "Listen . . . rest for a moment. Let me take care of . . . of this."

"Okay."

She coughed and struggled with a new notion. "And, uh . . . thanks."

Where were the bells? "You're welcome."

She didn't say any more, just sat Bobby Lee against the wall and crawled across the floor to the phone. She called in her report and then crawled back to him. He was now writhing with pain.

She tore a tablecloth into sheets for his bleeding head. To examine it, she grabbed his hair and yanked backward. She ignored his howl of protest and peered intently at the cut.

"It looks superficial," she said finally. "You're not losing much blood from there."

He groaned and twisted on the floor. She held him firmly and turned her attention to his shoulder. "This is a little deeper. Let me wrap it." She took off his jacket and ripped his shirt so that the shoulder was exposed. She fashioned a crude tourniquet that extended around his shoulder and across his bare chest. That done she turned him unceremoniously facedown to inspect the bleeding gash in his leg and hip. His pants were soaked with blood. "Take these off," she said abruptly.

"What?"

"Right now," she ordered. "I don't have time for games."

Bobby Lee shook his head. "No way."

She grabbed his belt and tugged at it.

"Hey, cut it out!"

She paid no attention and within seconds his trousers and underwear had been yanked to his knees. He felt an embarrassing breeze where he shouldn't have.

"Goddamn it."

"Don't be a baby." She examined the wound. "Can you move your leg?"

"Not with my pants down."

"Fine. I'll take them off."

"No, honest, I can move the leg."

"Good." She grabbed more strips of cloth and wrapped them tightly around the wound. The bandage had to come up between his legs and his genitals had to be tucked in. She did both. His attitude changed.

"Would you do that again?"

That did it. Her eyes flashed and she pulled his hair back, suddenly unconcerned with what she was doing to her carefully placed head bandage. Her face was two inches from his. "You lousy bastard. Tell me the truth."

"I didn't do it," he said simply.

"Liar."

"I promise you I didn't do it."

She leaned over, dropped the torn white tablecloth, and kissed him full on the mouth. She kept the kiss hard and firm until the wails of the arriving ambulances cut through the night around them.

"Liar," she said again, and didn't know what she thought.

42

THEY SCRAPED BAKER OFF THE FLOOR AND STUFFED him in a crowded ambulance for the run to USC, one of the few remaining emergency rooms willing to operate in a city of five kills a day. Bobby Lee wondered absently if they might have some old pictures of his glory days as a Trojan on the walls but then the pain washed that thought away. Julie watched him writhe on the stretcher until the ambulance doors were about to close. Once settled he reached for her. She pulled away.

"Not now."

She got an FBI agent to drive her back downtown to her office. Once there, she immediately called Barrows.

He sensed there was something wrong. "What's the matter? You sound upset."

"Have you heard the news?"

"You mean about the agent being killed?"

"Yes."

"Of course. It's been on all the news channels. I've also received three faxes from Washington."

"Well, I was there."

"What!"

"That's right. Can you come over here right away?"

"Of course."

He rode over with rising concern and fear. The ante had now been raised considerably. The local press was already obsessed with the developing drug wars. The machine-gunning of an FBI agent would now dominate the national media as well, and every politician from Sacramento to Maine would be demanding an investigation. And it was all her fault. Without her presence there, no agent would have been sent to pick her up. No agent, no dead agent. *What the fuck was she doing there to begin with?*

He got off at the twelfth floor blind with rage.

The receptionist locked in her wire cage knew who he was. "You here to see Julie?" she said.

"That's right, Julie Beck."

"You working on the Vargo case?"

"That's right."

"From Washington, right?"

His impatience was now palpable. "Right again."

"You're after Bobby Lee, right?"

After Bobby Lee, how quaint. Territory folks must stick together. "I'm after the truth."

"You heard what happened to him, didn't you?"

"No, what happened to Mr. Baker?"

"He was shot in that restaurant."

Barrows stiffened. So *that's* why she was there.

"Is he dead?"

"Not yet."

Pity. "Miss, I'm a very busy man. Tell me where he is."

The receptionist snorted. She was civil service. "Go fuck yourself," she said amiably.

He was eventually led into Julie's office by a first-year agent fresh from Quantico. He found her sitting stone-faced. Her clothes were rumpled and stained with brown, dried blood.

"You look like you had a rough night."

She didn't answer.

"Julie, tell me about it." His tone was solicitous.

"An agent was murdered before my eyes."

"I know. But what were *you* doing there?"

"Baker brought me there."

"Baker!" He stood up and advanced toward her. "Julie, what in the world were you doing there with Baker?"

She waved the question away. "It's a long story. Suffice it to say I'm starting to change my mind about some things. He can help us and we ought to let him."

"Julie, that is a very dangerous remark."

"Why?"

"Baker is a . . . criminal. You above all people should know exactly what he is."

She above all people. "That's right," she said enigmatically.

"So I don't understand what you would be doing alone with this man without an escort. Can you explain that to me?"

"We had an agent. What happened was . . . it doesn't matter. The important thing is I think we're closing in on him."

"Who?"

"Vargo, of course."

That's exactly what he was afraid of. He struggled to keep his voice calm. "What makes you think that?"

"Strangely enough because Baker's prediction turned out to be true. He told me that restaurant was tied in with Vargo. The bank next door too. You see . . ."

Now Barrows was close to panic. The woman knew everything. He shut the door softly behind him and stood against it affecting a grave expression.

"I was afraid of this."

"What?"

"This Baker fellow. How many people know of your relationship with him?"

There it was. Twice in her life she had opened up to a man and twice in her life it had blown up in her face. There was a definite lesson here.

"What does that have to do with anything?"

"I don't think you would have been assigned this case if Jim Price had been made aware that you had a personal stake in the matter."

Jim Price. Her boss. The man Barrows had once so gallantly offered to help her with.

"I don't have a personal stake in the case."

"I disagree. I'd like to ask you to gracefully resign."

She laughed. All of a sudden he didn't look so good in his pretty suit. "Over my dead body."

"I understand. There are political considerations. You must not be seen to be fired."

"That's not it at all. I won't resign."

"Think about it. I will take over operational control for the next several days. You can even remain in place, at least for cosmetic purposes."

"Forget it."

"Julie, you're making a mistake. Don't turn this into a public battle of wills."

"I don't mind battles. I usually win them."

"You wouldn't this time." He crossed the room and looked out the grimy window. "Julie, you're an Assistant U.S. Attorney in a field office, that's all. James Price and I were at Princeton together. Arthur Manion became Attorney General in part because of support from my family. Am I making myself clear?"

Julie was a very political animal. She did get it. "You can have me forcibly replaced."

"At the drop of a hat. Julie, don't confuse responsibility with influence. Or power. You have the first. You don't yet have the others."

She knew he was right. He could get her removed with a few phone calls to people who wouldn't even take her calls. For Julie to fight him she'd have to go through channels, to the head of major frauds in L.A., to the chief of the criminal division, to Price, and maybe after all that, *they* would get to make a call to Washington. If they wanted.

Barrows was the sort of guy who didn't have channels, just back channels. And he probably wouldn't even have to play his ace in the hole, the Baker-Beck relationship, that she had so stupidly told him about.

Her mind shifted into sharp professional focus. It was time for damage control. "All right," she said. "I agree. What do you want me to do?"

He felt immediate relief and his smile was magnanimous. "Excellent. You've made a wise choice." He thought for a moment. "On the surface, let's just keep everything as it is. Only now, I want you dealing only with the airports. I'll clean up this Monterey Park business."

"All right."

"Now Baker is another story. I'll deal with him as well. Where is he now?"

"MDC," she lied easily. "They took him to the hospital there."

"Good," he said. Then he was gone.

When the door slammed, she picked up the phone.

"Medina, hi, Julie. Listen, you're back on the case. . . . Don't thank me, just answer a question. Where's Bobby now? . . . USC? Good, keep him there. . . . Hey, Medina, are you a friend of his? . . . I thought so. . . . Meet me at the hospital. Thirty minutes? . . . Good."

43

BY TEN THAT EVENING BAKER WAS LOUNGING UNDER an assumed name in a semiprivate room at the trauma ward of St. John's Hospital in Santa Monica, a few blocks from the beach. Medina had personally hauled him out of a roomful of moaning gang-shooting victims at USC Medical and driven him across town to the relative quiet and peace of St. John's. There he had flashed his badge to a stern no-nonsense nun and promised that the U.S. Government stood behind the bills. That got Baker his semiprivate with a Guatemalan nurse named Imelda. "Like Marcos," she told him. "Except without all the shoes."

Imelda and a Pakistani doctor who spoke no English took off the tablecloth from the Golden Dragon and put on some decent bandages. The doctor was appalled. He pointed to the widespread dark coloration on the make-shift bandages.

"Blood?" he asked Imelda.

"Plum sauce, I think," Baker told him.

Imelda got it. "From the duck, of course." She had watched all the coverage about the shootings and was eager to hear more. Baker proposed a bargain: he would answer all her questions if only she would slide out and bring back a little Black Bush, plus ice.

"I can do much better than that," she said coyly.

"Yeah, what?"

"You'll see."

The better than that turned out to be much better than

that, a monster prescription that Imelda wrote up and the Pakistani signed without looking at. It required a hypodermic needle stuck deep into Bobby Lee's right buttock, the one without the bullet hole. Baker hadn't had this many women pulling down his pants in years.

Imelda's drug was the Babe Ruth of painkillers and quickly did the job. He had a crooked smile when Julie arrived with Medina.

"He needs to go to sleep now," Imelda said.

"No way," Baker said. "Bring me some black coffee. I don't want to miss a minute of this."

Julie relaxed. "If he's giving you trouble, he can't be that badly hurt."

Imelda snorted and gave a quick swivel of the back end on the way out. "He don't cause me no trouble at all. Maybe you just don't know how to handle him."

"You tell her, Imelda," Baker crowed. "Hey, Julie, you want to see my wounds again?"

"Show them to Medina."

"She's playing hard to get," Baker told Medina. "But she can't fool me. I'm gonna get a medal for saving her life."

Julie found herself smiling. For once he had not succeeded in annoying her. "How are you really, Bobby?"

He made a big show of reaching under the front of his hospital gown. "They're still there!" he howled inanely.

"Jesus," Julie said.

"I don't think he's gonna be dancin' at Cherokee for a while," Medina said.

"Will too!"

Medina shrugged. Julie was panicking. As Barrows said, time was short.

"Listen, Bobby, can you be serious for a minute?"

"Absofuckinlutely."

"Okay, try to listen to me. I think you're right about the Chinese."

"Good thinking. They almost killed us."

"I know. What do we do now?"

He gestured with a blurred hand. "Send in the Marines. Put about five thousand guys in there. Bomb the shit out of them. Go house-to-house and worry about legalities later."

"Let's assume I can't do that."

"No Marines? You don't need them." His voice was now seriously slurred. "Give Medina ten guys. He'll get Vargo. Won't you do that for me, buddy?"

"Let's assume that's no good either."

"Why? You're the goddamn government, for Christ's sake. You get to screw whoever you want. Like me." Then he thought about that remark and found it so funny he was soon pointing and choking with silent mirth.

"Very funny. There are . . . let's say limitations to what I can do."

"Oh, God." He had to wipe his eyes. "How many guys can you put on the ground?"

Julie bit her lip. "Very few."

"Yeah? How many is 'few'?"

Julie took a deep breath. "Maybe like us?"

That led to another minute of howls and finger pointing. "You're joking, right?"

"I wish I was."

"You're goddamn nuts." He turned to Medina. "She's nuts. You know how many people they got. Like billions, they're the fuckin' Chinese."

Medina shrugged.

"Bobby, try to focus for a moment. Let's just say I'm really stretched thin. I've got people all over the city and they won't give me anybody for Monterey Park."

"But didn't you tell them . . ."

She held up her hand. "Yeah, Bobby, I told them."

Baker leaned back against the pillow. "It doesn't matter. I've got these drugs in me and I'm laying in bed and I don't give a shit about Vargo."

"Bobby Lee Baker, you listen to me and pay attention! Wake up!"

His eyes had been slowly closing. He snapped them open. "Sorry."

"Listen to me and concentrate. What can we do to smoke out Vargo?"

"The three of us? In Monterey Park? Didn't you see what it was like in there?"

Medina agreed. "He's right, Julie. You saw what happened tonight. They've got two armies fighting each other in there."

"The only army we've got is at Cherokee," Baker said. He was smiling and drifting off to sleep again.

"That's the second time I've heard that," she said. "What's he talking about?"

"Girls . . . dancing girls . . . little girls in black . . . pull up the pretty skirts and see what's . . ." Then he closed his eyes and fell asleep.

"It's just as well. He needs it and he's not making any sense." She turned to Medina. "So tell me, what's he talking about?"

"Julie, it's nothing, just something we kind of turned up when we were looking into this."

"You mean by yourselves?"

"That's right. Sorry."

"Don't worry about it." She looked at Baker sleeping and felt a sudden stab of tenderness. She rearranged his pillow. She resisted the urge to actually tuck him in.

"You do that well."

"Yeah." She turned back to him. "So go ahead, tell me."

He told her everything. A lot of it Baker had already alluded to during their walk through Monterey Park, but this time Julie was paying a lot more attention. She heard in detail again about Faldo, the hunt for Angela, the meeting with Romano, and the hatred Romano had toward Vargo. When he was through, Julie was thoughtful.

"Romano's a criminal, a hoodlum."

"That he is."

"But he's a hoodlum that hates Vargo."

"That, too."

"And there's a chance he's tracked down Angela Moore. She's very important in this."

"Yeah, he sent one of his people after her. Kind of a sleepy sort of guy. I don't know what happened."

She jumped to her feet, the information energizing her. "Medina, it's time to meet Mr. Romano."

Medina wasn't sure. He checked her out up and down. "You got anything with sequins?"

44

THREE MILES SOUTH, NEAR THE BORDER OF VENICE AND Santa Monica, Salvador Del Corso, also known as Lazy Sal to his boss, waited in a parking lot near the beach for Angela Moore to meet him for their date. He could not remember being this nervous since his first kiss in the back of a stolen car in a drive-in when he was twelve.

Lazy Sal had been thinking of nothing else but Angela all day long. Romano finally had to tell him if he didn't start paying attention, he'd have to slap him a little to wake him up. Lazy Sal just smiled at Romano, not even hearing him, so Romano had to give him one in the back of the head.

"Hey," Lazy Sal had said. "What's that for?"

"Christ, it's like I'm on another planet. Who the fuck you think I am?"

"Sorry, Mr. Romano. I got something on my mind."

"What do you got on your mind? Pussy? Is that it?"

"No, Mr. Romano, I promise that ain't it. It's just that I followed this girl like you told me to."

"Christ, I knew it. Pussy! That's always the fuckin' problem with you, Sal. I'm tellin' you, stop thinking about pussy and listen to me."

"No, Mr. Romano, that ain't it," Sal said imploringly. "She's not like that at all. She's beautiful."

Romano rolled his eyes. This was worse than he thought. "So she's beautiful pussy. That's still pussy. Now you can either think about pussy and at the same time think about getting a new job, or you can listen to me when I talk to you. Which is it going to be?"

"Don't worry, Mr. Romano, I'll pay attention."

But he didn't, or couldn't, which got him a few more smacks from Romano. Eventually, the whole story came out. Romano was incredulous.

"You did what! You were supposed to tail her, don't get made. Was I talking to myself?"

"She was in trouble. What was I gonna do, let her go down? Then you'd be mad at me for that."

"Jesus, I don't believe this. What next, flowers?"

"Yeah, I thought so."

Romano almost strangled him. Lazy Sal tried to defend himself.

"I figured that was what you wanted."

"Why would I want that?"

" 'Cause now we can pay attention to her, know where she goes. I can even bring her in here, you want."

"You are a fucking idiot." He wandered around the bar talking to himself, trying to figure it out. All he wanted to do was get Vargo, and these guys had just dropped into his lap. The girl was a link to Vargo, he was sure about that. He turned back to Sal, his voice now more conciliatory. "You can bring her in here?"

"Sure."

"And why's that? You got a date or something?"

"Yeah, tonight."

Romano covered his face.

"It's not like you think, Mr. Romano," Sal said quickly. "I was just doing it in case you wanted to see her."

It was like his father had always said, sometimes you got to make the best out of a bad situation. He patted Lazy Sal on both cheeks. "I'll tell you what I want you to do, Sal." He took out some crumpled hundred-dollar bills and jammed them in Sal's shirt pocket. "You go buy her some nice flowers, like you said. Then you buy her some pasta at Amalfi's and wash it down with some Brunello di Montelcino. The Riserva, not the cheap shit. Then, when she's all relaxed, bring her down to see me."

"You got it, Mr. Romano."

Angela walked down the steps of her apartment and Sal almost choked when he saw her. He hopped out of the blue Mercedes and held the door open.

"Thank you, Salvador," she said.

When he got in, she leaned over and gave him a kiss. He gave her the flowers. "Salvador, they're beautiful." She kissed him again. "Where are you going to take me?"

"I thought we'd get something to eat, some pasta. Then maybe we'd go dancing. You know, over at Cherokee."

She didn't like that idea at all but decided to keep her mouth shut. After all, what were the odds of Baker being in there again? As for Romano, she'd never even met the guy, and was sure he couldn't distinguish her from the hundreds of young women who worked for him all over town.

"Great," she said finally.

He drove to Amalfi's, a Romano-owned restaurant in West Hollywood. To Sal, Amalfi's was too fancy and a little light on the red sauce. But the Brunello was good and it was free so he could hardly bitch. Sal was careful with the wine. Romano would slap him all over the bar if he ever showed up drunk.

"Listen," he said finally, when the check and coffee had come and gone. "We got to split soon."

"Why? I'm having fun."

"Don't you want to dance with me?" He puffed out his chest and pointed to it with both hands.

She grinned. "I'd *love* to dance with you. You want to go now?"

"Sure."

Lazy Sal felt sick all the way to Cherokee. He wished he could tell her about Romano, about how he was a good guy once you got to know him. He also wished he could warn her but he knew that was out of the question, more like suicide actually. Maybe Romano would let him hang around after he brought her in, making sure she was all right. Romano didn't seem mad or anything; it wasn't like she had ripped him off. Nevertheless, he felt sick. He stopped the Mercedes a block from the bar.

"What's wrong?"

"Nothing. It's just that . . . aw, nothing. Let's go." He drove on. Angela stared at him quizzically.

* * *

260

Romano was sitting alone at his standard table. Lazy Sal had a hangdog look. Romano stood up and Angela stiffened. This was too weird.

"Hey, Sal, you look like you're gonna die. Sit down and have a drink. Who's the pretty lady?"

"Mr. Romano, this is Angela."

Romano made room for Angela to sit next to him. His manner was its most charming, which made Angela a little more relaxed and Sal a lot more nervous. "Come in here, sit down," he said heartily. He waved to a passing waitress. "Hey, sweetheart, take the lady's drink. So, tell me, you a friend of Sal's here? You know any friend of Sal's is a queen in Cherokee."

Angela decided to make believe she had never set foot in the place before. Then, at the first opportunity, she'd grab Sal and get the hell out of there. She'd worry about the job later.

She smiled at him and even Romano was a little taken aback by her sheer beauty. "Salvador is wonderful. I owe my life to him."

"I heard. Sal's real good with his hands. Sometimes not so good with his head, but real good with his hands."

Angela reached for Sal's hand. "He's good all over as far as I'm concerned."

"How sweet," Romano said. Sal looked like he wanted to slide under the table.

"Anyway," Romano continued, "I'm glad you could stop by tonight. I want to ask you something, a personal question if that's okay."

"Yes," she said.

"Now, I don't want you to be nervous."

"I'm not."

" 'Cause there's nothing to be afraid of, right? I understand you work here sometimes, so you know the place, and you know Sal here, right?"

She shifted slightly, trying to figure it out. "Right."

"So, I need to know some things, just the answers to a couple questions, you know? You see, a few years ago, three, four years ago, I got a call from a guy in L.A. See?"

Angela nodded.

"And this guy had an idea to make some money. You see, there was a few hundred acres of land sitting there vacant, someplace down south next to the freeway. And the oil companies used to dump some shit on the land. So nobody wanted to use it. Understand?"

"Hazardous waste?"

"Jesus, smart and beautiful both, I can't believe your luck, Sal. That's exactly what they call it, darling. Hazardous waste. And this land was on the market for about five million bucks 'cause the guy who owned it had to get out. So this guy's idea was we could go in there, pick up this land for two million, three million, who knows. We'd go to the politicians, clean it up using my company to do the cleanup. We'd get the city to pay us maybe ten, fifteen million for the cleanup. Got it?"

Angela's brow was furrowed. There was something oddly familiar about this deal and she nodded slowly.

"So the guy says we make a killing because when it's cleaned up, the property's worth like two hundred million, three hundred million. Sort of the chance of a lifetime, understand?"

Angela didn't say anything. She kept the smile fixed on her face to hide the cold fear creeping through her.

"And all I had to do was raise the money. What could be easier? So I call around to my friends back in New York, Jewish guys, you know? Guys in the garment industry. Upstanding people. Good guys, you know what I mean? Friends of mine, for Christ's sake. Guys who are always there for me and who trust me. So these guys get hopping and go to their friends and we put together this package. We come up with four million dollars. Understand?"

She picked up her glass of wine and knew right away that was a mistake. Her hand trembled slightly and Romano saw it. "I don't really under—"

"Yeah, you understand." He patted her on the back. "You understand just fine. You know what we eventually got for our money?"

She licked her lips. "Mr. Romano. Please let me expl—"

"Please, Mr. Romano!" His face was flushed. "How

about please, Mr. Rosen, Mr. Grossman, Mr. Glickfeld? Those are the people you should be saying please to."

She switched gears. "Mr. Romano, I was just an employee. Most of his deals were far too complicated for—"

"Now, darling, I know that ain't true. We done some checkin' on you. You are one smart cookie. Your friend Baker says you're smarter than Vargo."

Baker. That meant Romano had a lot of information. She glanced toward Sal and saw a sad, unsmiling face. No help there. She decided to try one last-ditch lie.

"It's true," she said. "Sometimes I did know. On this deal though I just never knew—"

"Never knew? Never knew?" Romano stood up and was shouting. "Don't lie to me. You knew enough to fuck Mr. Rosen, didn't you? And then when you got done fucking Mr. Rosen, you fucked Mr. Grossman. And then you fucked Mr. Glickfeld. And then when you got done fuckin' my friends, Vargo fucked me big time."

She gave up and stared him straight in the eyes. "I had to, Mr. Romano. That was my job."

Sal tried to intervene. "Mr. Romano, I don't think she knew anything. Maybe she was just working for him."

Romano turned furiously to his subordinate. "Sal, when I want you to talk, you know how you're gonna be able to tell? I'm gonna say, 'Sal, why don't you talk?' But when I don't want you to talk, I'm probably not going to say anything. Got it?"

Sal slumped backward in his chair, defeated.

He turned back to Angela, who was now sitting rock still, impassive, waiting to see how it would all come out. Romano was impressed. He patted her arm, now the charming Italian again. "Hey, darlin', relax. It's not the end of the world. This ain't the movies, you ain't gonna get dipped in the river, for Christ's sake." Angela took a sip of her wine, then a bigger gulp. Her eyes stayed glued on Romano.

"That's it, drink up," Romano said approvingly. "You know, you and I could do business together. Brains, guts, and looks. That's not something you run into every day."

"What do you have in mind, Mr. Romano?"

"Well, first you got to help me out with Vargo, make up for the past."

"No problem."

"That's great." He turned to Sal. "Sal, you know that lawyer we use?"

"You mean Mickey?"

"Yeah, Mickey. The skinny guy." He turned to Angela. "You'll like him."

Back to Sal. "Sal, Mickey's gonna be in tonight. Tell him to stop drooling at the puss for a while because I want him to do some work. Then you take him and your girlfriend here downstairs. Got it?"

That made Sal real nervous. "Yeah? Then what?"

"Then what?" He leaned over and kissed Angela lightly on the cheek. Sal shifted in his chair. "Then, Angela's gonna sing Mickey a song, and then Mickey's gonna know it all. And then Mickey's gonna tell me. And when I figure out what I'm gonna do, I'm gonna have a job for you, Sal. Something you're good at. Not tailing little girls and getting confused. Got it?"

"Yes, sir," Angela and Lazy Sal said together.

45

WITH IMELDA'S BEAUTIFUL DRUGS, BAKER SLEPT LIKE a baby for almost twenty-four hours. He was asleep when Julie arranged for him to be moved by private ambulance from St. John's and asleep when the attendants put him almost naked under a thin white sheet in Julie's guest room. He was asleep when Medina, Julie, and Patsy ate dinner near the pool with some take-out Mexican as the light died over West Los Angeles. He was asleep when Medina and Patsy left at nine, promising to come back if the need arose. He didn't awake until 4 A.M., when the birds sensed the arrival of day and heralded it. He opened his eyes groggily, the sadly diminishing drugs clouding his memory. The pain was dull, persistent, and oddly reassuring. He found himself lying sweat-soaked in a strange bed in a strange house, naked, except for a pair of Boron-issued white boxer shorts. He had kicked the sheet off the bed. He had no idea what was going on.

He rubbed the insistent clouds from his eyes. He remembered the nuns and Imelda and the hospital and sedatives, the faces of Medina and Julie, and a small argument, and that was pretty much it. Now his room was dark except for the healthy shine of a full moon that slid effortlessly through the blinds. It cast a reflective glow through the room as though he were in a black-and-white movie, sending patterns of horizontal lines across the blank wall.

He got out of the bed and fell, cursing at the sudden sharp pain. A set of crutches leaned against the wall and he grabbed one and limped to the window. The enthusiastic moon lit the golf course with a cold glow. The blank Spanish clubhouse sat on the faraway hill like a haunted mansion, isolated and unmoving. The green expanse of lawn below it was like a friendly lake, ghostly and peaceful, lacking only clouds of mist from British moors.

But L.A. is a desert and there are no mists in deserts. Not real ones anyway.

He heard a splash. The sound was as jarring as clattering plates, interrupting his reverie. He saw her slim body slice through the water, effortlessly, fishlike. She came to the end of the pool and rose out of it, turning and swimming in the opposite direction. He saw her clothes piled carelessly on a beat-up lawn chair near the far end of the pool.

There was a time that sight would have moved him to walk through a wall to her. Now it did very much less and he was surprised by that. The drugs, the pain, the icy stillness of the moonlit course below left him in a trance, uninterested in moving, even for her.

He stood in the window and watched her swim strongly through the water for twenty minutes. When she was finished, she pulled herself out of the far end of the pool, lifting her face to the moon, arching her back. Her breasts pressed upward. She shook her hair to clear the water.

Baker limped out with one crutch and stood near her. She watched him approach but didn't move. She made no attempt to hide her nakedness.

"Did you just wake up?" she said finally.

"A while ago. I was watching you swim."

"How do you feel?"

"Confused."

"And your injuries?"

"Better living through chemistry."

"Those drugs will wear off soon. You'll be in a lot of pain."

He shrugged.

She patted the ground next to her. "Bobby, sit down. It's time we talked."

"Do you want to put something on?"

"Sure. Hand me that shirt if you would."

He sat beside her and gave her an oversized flannel shirt. She put it on but didn't button it. He didn't object.

"Where's Medina?" he asked.

She gestured toward the road. "Patsy dragged him off. He'll be back tomorrow."

"So it's just me and you?"

She smiled weakly. "Just like old times."

They used to swim a lot in this pool. And on nights like this, with the moon bright as the sun and the course lit far below them, they would sit for hours, swimming and talking. Once they stayed there till dawn. He couldn't take the all-night session and slept most of the next day. She was at work promptly at nine and put a drug dealer away for twenty-five years in the afternoon without breathing hard. But Julie was Julie and if you could handle a woman like that you had to get used to it, and like it.

But they both knew it wasn't really like the old days.

"Bobby," she began.

"Yeah?"

"There's nobody in the house now."

He knew. "Yeah."

She struggled to make the suggestion. "I've been thinking about it. If you'd like to go in, I wouldn't mind."

"I don't think so."

A sudden chill came up. She pulled the shirt around her. "Why?"

"Why? Because you put me in prison. Because you hated me. Because you didn't trust me."

"And that's something you can never forgive, is that it? You can't understand what I was thinking. I'll never make it up to you?"

"As far as I know, you still believe it all. Maybe you're a little confused now that I was a hero and all, but down where you live you still believe I did it."

She thought about that. "You may be right," she said.

Goddamn right he was right. He leaned over and scooped up some water, then splashed it over his face. It woke him. She stood up and came closer to him, straddling the diving board facing him. He was naked except for the white Boron-issued briefs. She was naked except for the man's shirt which had never been other than fully opened. "Let's talk," she said.

They talked until dawn. By the time they were done, they had covered everything, her hatred, her feelings of betrayal, her absolute conviction that he had taken the information given to him in confidence and passed it on to Vargo. He got to talk about lack of trust, how she had never even asked him whether he had done it, instead assuming his betrayal. When they were done, the sun had crested the hills behind the club. They had reached the point where there was nothing left to say.

"So what now?" he asked. "Do you believe me?"

The answer was still no, she realized. There were layers of defenses built up inside her that only time could scrape away. Yet that didn't mean she had to act rationally.

"Yes," she lied. "I do. Now will you take those off? They make me sick." She gestured to the Boron shorts.

"Are you sure you believe me?"

"Absolutely."

"Okay." He began struggling with the one hand that worked.

"Here, let me." She gently pulled off the shorts, avoiding the bandages. He reacted normally.

"Is it cold out here or are you just happy to see me?"

"You've always had a one-track mind."

"I assume your injuries will not prevent, well . . ."

"Normal function?"

"Yes."

"The parts that you're interested in were not hit."

"That seems true. And you're well rested?"

"Fully."

She held out her hand. "Then come with me."

He sighed. "I'll do my best."

46

THEY SLEPT UNTIL THE SUN WAS HIGH AND THE GREEN course below them was baked. They were battered from the lack of sleep but energized from their night together. When he woke, she was sitting next to him, still wearing the oversized, open shirt. She had two steaming cups of coffee and the paper.

He kissed her and took the paper. The front page of the *Times* had another lurid color photograph of the fires in Monterey Park. Underneath was the banner headline: "CHINESE DRUG WARS CONTINUE TO ERUPT IN EAST LOS ANGELES." The photo on page one was of a Chinese restaurant two blocks east of the Golden Dragon. At 3 A.M., mercifully after the patrons left, incendiary bombs were thrown in through the plate-glass window. The building had exploded in a fireball and took half the block with it.

The *Times* was really getting good at riot photos. "At least they didn't do that to us," Baker observed.

"It's just like you said. This is no coincidence. Vargo's involved and we've got to get somebody's attention today."

"Like who?"

"I've got somebody in mind. He . . . he's very influential. Right now he's going down the wrong path but I think he can be turned."

"By 'wrong path' do you by chance mean 'out to fuck me'?"

"I'll be honest with you. He definitely wants you back in Boron."

"If a guy like that finds out you're hiding me . . . not to mention the other, that's not going to be real good for your career."

"I don't care about me. I care about having agents on the ground in Monterey Park." She consulted her calendar. Bobby Lee ignored the irony of him and her and a calendar naked in this room.

"Bobby, Vargo's just about run out of time. We've got to get somebody's attention right away. Barrows is . . . well, he's DEA and he's influential. If we can convince him then we'll get what we want."

"And if we don't you can visit me on weekends. They have this trailer in back of the tennis court. I've always wanted to use it."

"Bobby, I won't lie to you, there's a risk."

"So why take it?"

"Because we're living on borrowed time. You're supposed to be at MDC. When they find out you're not all hell's gonna break loose."

"Which is not good for Julie."

Her eyes flattened. "Baker, if I was concerned about that you wouldn't be here."

Fair enough. "We got no choice is what you're saying."

"They're going to start at MDC, then to USC, then St. John's, and then here. And that's as sure as the sun popping up in the east."

"But if we get to him first maybe it makes a difference?"

"Maybe."

She was right. He couldn't stay there forever waiting for them to kick in the door.

"All right. Go ahead."

She grabbed the phone before he could change his mind. Baker heard one side of the conversation.

"Covington, this is Julie. . . . I'm fine, thanks. . . . I'm sorry, too. . . . No, there's no hard feelings. . . . Listen, let me tell you why I called. I'm here with Robert Baker. . . . No, I'm not calling from MDC. . . . No, I'm

not going to tell you that and it doesn't matter where.
. . . Yes, I'm quite safe. . . . I'd like to see you and bring
Baker with me. . . . Yes, I do think it's a good idea. I
think he has a lot to tell us and I'd like you to hear it.
After all, if he's the criminal you think, he should have a
lot of information. . . . Well, about lots of things but
mostly about Vargo. I think when you hear what Baker
has to say we'll be able to pick up Vargo in a matter of
hours. . . . Yes, I know the problems this creates. . . .
Okay, that's fine. . . . Yes, about one hour.''

She hung up the phone and stared at it, now slightly
unnerved. There was something weird in the man's
voice, a combination of anxiety and anticipation. The
voice was not a wholesome voice.

He reached for her and brought her near. Her skin was
warm under the oversized shirt. ''However this comes
out, I just wanted to tell you . . .''

She held a finger to his lips. ''Not yet.''

They entered the lobby of Checkers just before the
noon hour. Baker was nervous and had a sudden urge
for a quick pop in the bar before the confrontation. The
bartender was filling bins with ice. He limped over.

''Black Bush, rocks, twist, please.''

Julie stared in disbelief. ''What do you think you're
doing?''

''Forget the rocks, just in a glass.''

''Bobby Lee Baker, stop fooling around this minute!''

The bartender watched the exchange and the look on
Baker's face, then poured a large one into a glass.

''Here, buddy, this is on me.''

Julie helped him limp across the lobby, scolding the
whole way, and pressed the button for the eighth floor.
When they exited the elevator the hallway was still.
''He's in a suite,'' Julie said quietly. ''Right at the end of
this hall.''

Barrows' room had a double walnut door with gleaming hardware. Julie knocked quietly. At first, there was
no response and Baker shifted painfully from foot to foot.
Julie raised her hand to knock again. She never got the
chance. The door swung open and a man stood there

impassively staring at them. Only slowly did they realize he was holding a gun, which he quickly placed under Baker's chin.

"Very slowly. Both hands on top of your head. Now!"

Baker did as he was told; the drill was very familiar. He followed the drawn gun into the room. A man in an elegant gray suit with a pale blue tie stood watching the confrontation. Good-looking suit, Baker thought. Julie, her face flushed with anger, walked resolutely up to him.

"What the hell do you think you're doing?"

Barrows' voice was patronizing. "Arranging for the arrest of a criminal, I believe."

"You son of a bitch. We had an agreement."

Barrows' eyebrows rose. "We? I had no agreement with this man." He gestured to the man with the gun. "Take him away."

Julie stepped in front of the gun. Her hand darted into her bag and came out with an ID shield. "Stop right there. I'm Assistant United States Attorney Julie Beck. I'm in charge of this investigation and this man has been released to my custody. You have no right to interfere." She stared at the man, a young, smooth Hispanic agent. He wasn't familiar and she knew all the Hispanic agents because there were so few of them. "Who are you, anyway?"

The agent remained silent. Barrows interceded. "He's from Washington. Main Justice. He hasn't worked out here before, which is just as well."

Baker chuckled softly. "Yeah, he's from the FBI. Me, too."

"Shut up," Barrows barked.

"Julie, I'd look at some credentials if I were you. Maybe make some phone calls."

"Let me see some ID," Julie ordered.

The agent with the gun didn't move. "That won't be necessary," Barrows said. "You don't have to take orders from a criminal."

Julie shrieked, "A what!"

"Or those harboring criminals," Barrows added, smoothly correcting the record. He gestured to the agent. "You know what to do."

The agent marched Baker to a wall and kicked his good leg so that he was more or less spread-eagled. This really is like old home week, Baker thought. The agent rapidly patted him down. "Nothing," he said.

"Barrows, I demand an—"

"You'll demand and receive nothing," Barrows said imperiously. "Get him out of my sight."

Julie stepped to the door in front of the agent.

"You can't take him away without listening to him."

"Watch me."

"You're making a mistake. He knows about Vargo, knows what he's doing in Monterey Park, knows the cause of all these bombings, and a lot more. You'd be a fool not to listen to him."

The agent grabbed Baker by the collar and marched him around Julie toward the door. "Wait," Barrows said. She was right. It would be a lot better if he knew what Baker knew.

Barrows walked close to Baker. "Where is Vargo now?"

"About five minutes from here as the crow flies."

"She said something about Monterey Park. I assume that means Chinese banks. What do you know about Robert Vargo and Chinese banks?"

"Everything."

"Fine, this is your chance. Tell me your suspicions."

"I don't have suspicions, I know what he's doing." There was a newspaper on the couch and Baker gestured to it. "Look at the front page."

Barrows glanced at the paper. "Vargo's blowing up restaurants? Is that what you're here to tell me?"

"In a manner of speaking, yes."

Barrows snorted. "What a waste of time. Take him."

"Okay," Baker said. He held out his hands for the cuffs. He smelled a bluff.

Barrows hesitated. "You seem rather sure of yourself."

"On some things."

"Like what?"

"Well, for one thing, he's no agent." He jerked a thumb at the Hispanic.

272

Barrows ignored that. "What else do you think you know?"

Baker caught the tenseness in the man's voice and decided to toss a grenade. "I know all about the Firenze Corporation accounts maintained at the Asian Interbank Trust in Monterey Park."

Barrows' set smile stiffened. "Yes?" he said. His voice was bland as cream. "What about them?"

Baker was on the top of his game now. The Hispanic was a phony agent and the man from Washington was nervous. He threw another bomb.

"Well, there's a restaurant next door, the Golden Dragon. Ever eaten there?"

More stiffness. "No."

"No? Too bad, it's got great food. It's too late now. That's where the agent was killed."

"And?"

"There's a connection between the two, the bank and the restaurant."

"What makes you say that?"

"Lots of wires going between the two, for one thing. Also the rooms downstairs. By now you've probably got a report on what goes on downstairs."

Barrows spoke before thinking. "No one's been downstairs. We've sealed it off."

Julie reacted with shock. "What! That's where the nerve center is. Who ordered that?"

Baker got it. The phony agent. The beads of sweat on Barrows' upper lip. The hustle to get him to tell what he knew. Just like the old days, whoever talked lost.

Barrows got it too. He couldn't risk trading quips with this guy anymore. And he could no longer risk having Julie Beck wandering the streets. He caught the Hispanic's eye and looked quickly at Julie. He gave a quick, imperceptible nod in return.

"Take them both," Barrows ordered.

"Not a chance," Julie said. She left the door and headed for the phone. Barrows stepped in front of her, smiling.

"I don't think so."

"No?" Julie walked close to him and smiled back.

"Think again," she said, and she brought a very sharp, very sturdy heel down on the middle of Barrows' instep with all the force her very athletic right leg could manage. The blood left Barrows' face and he fell, howling. She walked easily to the phone.

"We'll get Medina over here and straighten this out."

She was reaching for the receiver when it exploded, the plastic of the receiver flying in shards to the near wall. She turned to see the agent pointing the gun at her.

"Next time it's you."

Barrows rose, his face contorted with pain and rage. "Take him," he ordered. Then he walked to Julie. "Take the bitch, too."

She spit squarely in his face.

Vincent cuffed Baker and marched him out first. Julie was next, her neck squeezed by Vincent's hand and a cold gun pressed to her back. Vincent walked them both to a set of metal, interior fire stairs near the elevator and herded them down seven deserted floors. At the bottom the exit door was open. A black Lincoln with smoky windows sat idling.

When they exited Checkers into the light the driver emerged. He was a young, pockmarked Asian with an odd and seemingly perpetual grin. His real name was Jimmy Sun. He reached under his dark coat and extracted a squat handgun. He pointed with it to the backseat of the car.

It was a short ride to Monterey Park. Julie tried to work them the whole way.

"You people are crazy to think you can get away with this. I am a federal officer and this is a kidnapping. That's a life term."

She didn't even mention him, and Baker wondered whether there was even a penalty for kidnapping a felon. They probably gave you a reward.

When nobody answered her she tried again.

"Why go down for Vargo and Barrows? It makes no sense. Vargo will be out of the country in a day or two with nothing but money. You guys will be holding the bag. Be smart for once. I have the authority to make a deal right here. Give us Vargo and you guys walk. No questions asked.''

Baker had to marvel at her. She just never gave up. He looked at her quizzically, wondering how a guy was supposed to live with a woman like this for thirty or forty years. Oh yeah, the legs.

Vincent was driving now and didn't need to wait thirty years. He'd heard enough.

''Do me a favor,'' he said without turning. ''Shut her up.''

Jimmy Sun was sitting next to Julie with his fixed, happy grin. He swung easily, openhanded. Her head whipped sideways from the blow. Baker moved instinctually but wisely stopped when Jimmy snapped open a knife and held it to Julie's white, bare throat.

''Any time she mouths off, do it again,'' Vincent ordered from the driver's seat.

They drove in silence after that. After an hour of weaving through stalled traffic the Lincoln stopped in front of a structure that was once a highly regarded Chinese restaurant. Now it was blackened and charred, like a steak left overnight on a grill. Vincent pulled into the rear parking lot over cement still wet from the firemen's hoses. He turned to Jimmy Sun. ''Did you see a car tailing us?''

Jimmy twisted, his scarred face peering out the back window. ''No, I didn't see nothing.''

''I swear it was in back of us coming out of downtown. It stayed with us on the freeway. I think it left us a couple of blocks ago.''

Jimmy twisted again, scanning the driveway. ''There ain't nothing back there,'' he said. ''Stop fuckin' around and let's go.'' He smiled at Julie.

Vincent was deathly afraid of Jimmy Sun. ''All right, get them out of here.''

THEY WERE LOCKED IN THE DARK IN THE WINDOWLESS basement of a bank building, essentially a cellar, what might once have been a coal bin. The only difference between their prison and a coal bin was the fortified metal door leading to the outside air.

It was pitch black in the room except for a thin line of light which valiantly fought through a three-foot air grating sitting astride the door. The brazen light gave the cellar a ghostly look. There was no furniture in the room. Julie, the side of her face discolored by Jimmy Sun's openhanded blow, sat against the wall. Baker sat down near her.

"You all right?"

She didn't answer. Baker could see her shoulders shake with rage. He tried to hold her but she resisted. He had to pry her arms away from her body to hold her close.

She quickly quieted. Right now she was using him as an anchor in a black, formless sea, but he had no doubts about her strength. When she was ready, she broke the hold and sat back on her heels, breathing deeply. The pale light from the insistent night sky played across the swelling around her cheekbones. "Let's get to work," she said abruptly.

She walked to the black, locked door.

"Guess what, it's locked," she said. She scanned the darkened room. It was airless except for the single grate high above the door. There was nothing in the room except Julie Beck and Bobby Lee Baker and a whole lot of problems. "They could leave us in here forever," she said. "They wouldn't find us till the stench started bothering the neighbors."

"Are you always this cheerful?"

She tried the door some more. There was no give to it.

"It's brand-new," she said. "The metal is welded flush into the door socket. There's no hinges on this side."

She looked up at the grating that was the only link to the outside. It was about three feet wide and eighteen inches high. "How about that?"

"You think you can squeeze through an air grating?"

"Just lift me up."

"Whatever you say." He made a stepladder with his hands and she climbed up. He winced with pain. Once hoisted to the top she stood on his one good shoulder. Baker, feeling like an acrobat, tottered beneath her. "What now, a back flip?"

"Move closer to the wall," she ordered. "And a little less lip would be appreciated." Good old Julie, every man's dream. He eased her toward the wall. She reached up and ran her hand over the opening in the grate. "Not bad. The screws are on this side. If I can unscrew this thing I think I could squeeze through."

Baker's last good shoulder was aching and he was getting a little grumpy. "I don't have a screwdriver."

"Let me down."

"Gladly." He moved back and she jumped easily to the floor, a regular jock. "Give me your shoe."

"My what?"

"Baker, I don't have time for this." She reached down and pulled off his loafer. She inspected it. "This will work."

"You're going to bang down the door with my shoe?"

"Very funny. You ever walk into federal court with these shoes?"

"All the time."

"What happens?"

He shrugged. "The beeper goes off?"

"Exactly. Then what happens?"

He looked at her. "I take off my shoes?"

"Right. Why?"

He shook his head, empty of thoughts. He felt like he was back in the second grade.

She turned over the shoe she had pulled off his foot and pointed at the sole. "There's a hard metal strip that runs down the center of the sole. It sets off the metal detector."

Baker scratched his head like Stan Laurel. "So what?"

She smashed Baker's beautiful loafer hard against the coarse cinder-block wall. Baker's howled protests were ignored. After twenty minutes she had the top layer stripped off and was breathing heavily.

"Okay, your turn. Rip at the sole until we can expose the metal. I only need about a quarter inch."

Baker wondered if these few moments might be a precursor of their life together, particularly the ordering around part. Nevertheless he did as he was told. It was excruciating. His fingers ached and he had to frequently stop to stretch them. Each time he did, she stared at him reproachfully. After almost thirty minutes of tearing, stretching, and staring, the tips of his fingers were bleeding and he had lost the top half of a fingernail. Yet amazingly, he felt something hard beneath the sole. "I think I'm getting it."

"Scratch harder."

Heartless bitch. He scratched away for another half hour. At the end, he had torn the sole in half and exposed a small, hard metallic point. The rest of the sole was still encased in leather.

"I've got to stop," he said, leaning back against the dark wall and sucking on the ends of his bleeding fingers.

She inspected the torn shoe.

"I think you've done it. Lift me up again."

Apparently no smoke breaks for the Nubians. He rose and sagged toward her like a reluctant pack mule. She again climbed onto his good shoulder and stood under the grating. She worked on the screws with his shoe. "It works," she shouted. "It's moving."

The first screw took six minutes to get out. His shoulder was numb. He wisely decided against remarks about the unwieldy weight. When she got it out she hopped once and held the screw triumphantly above her. "That's one!"

"Ouch! Jesus, are you nuts? Don't jump up and down."

"Be quiet, only four more to go."

"No way!"

"Stop whining," she said, and otherwise ignored him.

He was starting to remember some of the doubts he had back in the old days, even before it all came crashing down. He was also panicking, calculating quickly that at six minutes per screw, it would take her almost a half hour to finish the job, not counting hops. He figured anybody who could hold a woman on one shoulder for that long, regardless of the relationship, should join a circus.

He only lasted through two screws. By that time, his shoulder was screaming at him and he was screaming at her. She continued to ignore him and held up a second screw. At least this time she didn't jump. "That's two," she exulted.

She never got any farther. Just as the second screw hit the ground, they heard the lock turning. He furiously tried to get her down but the most he could accomplish was some sort of ridiculous parody of a trained seal. She shouted at him as he left the safety of the wall with her square above his shoulders. He got a little pissed and started to answer back when the door sprang open and hit him flush in the face. They fell down together. Baker's nose started bleeding.

It was too dark for Vincent to tell what had gone on. "Get the fuck away from the door," he shouted. "You hear me."

"You got it," Julie said quickly.

"Jesus, this sucks," Bobby Lee said, trying to put on his shoe and figure out which part of his body hurt the most.

Julie moved toward him. "Let me look at that nose."

"Please." He held up his face hoping for a little attention.

"Forget that shit," Vincent said and pulled her away. "Both of you get moving."

They had to put their hands above their heads and walk single file to the car. Jimmy Sun stood waiting for them with the rear door open. He had a boyish friendly grin.

Julie stopped. "Where are we going?"

"For a ride," Vincent told her, trying out his own unsuccessful effort at a grin. "Just get in and shut up."

Julie felt a sudden chill. "Bobby, I . . ." she began.

Baker's nose was bleeding profusely. "God, this hurts."

Jimmy Sun had a drawn gun, which somewhat diminished the friendliness of his grin. He forced them into the rear seat of the Lincoln. Vincent again drove, now with a Chinese teenager holding a knife in the front seat. The kid kept his head turned and his eyes on Baker and Julie, just in case Jimmy Sun should get bored.

Vincent was in a tense mood and glared at them in anger as he pulled into traffic. "You assholes been causin' people a lot of problems. Those problems are gonna end real soon."

"What people?" Baker asked quickly.

"People, I said 'people.' You got shit in your ears?"

Julie leaned forward. "Is Vargo back there?"

"Who?"

"You know who. Is he back there?"

Vincent shook his head. "Never heard of him."

"Come on," Baker said. "What does it matter now?"

"I told you to shut up. You're starting to piss me off."

That was the point. "Man, you're way too nervous for this. You ought to look into different work, trust me."

Vincent shook his head and Baker figured maybe he'd gone too far. "You know, you got a real mouth on you. I think I'll do you first, let her watch, and then she can, you know, talk me out of it."

"That'd be okay," Julie said quickly. "Whatever it takes. Barrows won't get mad at you, I promise."

Vincent snorted. "I don't take orders from that asshole."

"Yeah, right," Baker said, trying to prod some more. "Who then, your mother?"

"Fuck you," Vincent said. "Hey, Jimmy, shut that fucker up."

Jimmy Sun sighed at Vincent's stupidity. "Don't use my name, moron." Nevertheless he turned to Julie and tickled her throat with the knife. "Do me a favor. Shut up. Okay? Your friend, too."

Julie nodded obediently.

They drove for thirty minutes through the crusted urban decay surrounding downtown Los Angeles. They stayed off the freeways and wound their way through warehouse districts littered with men with shopping carts sleeping briefly after a day of baking in the dusty sun. The only lights were half-working streetlights, blinking pointless warnings at the sleeping drunks. There were no residences, no retail establishments, no hint of humanity that might rise and help them. Vincent pulled into the driveway of a corrugated tin warehouse crested by a rusted sign heralding a long gone owner.

Baker felt his adrenaline surge. He had no real choice. When they opened the door he'd make a run for it and drag her along with him. The chances were one in a thousand they'd make it ten feet before they were cut down by a stream of metal biting down the back of their legs and back, leaving two twitching corpses on the soiled concrete. Nice thoughts, great imagination, he realized. Yet what choice did he have? Once they were inside the warehouse it would be all over fast.

Baker got out of the car slowly, scanning the street.

Vincent nudged him with the gun. "Let's go."

Jimmy Sun dragged Julie from the car by the hair, laughing as she twisted against him. Vincent ignored them and scanned the empty street. "I swear I been followed," he said to himself. "I've had that feeling all day." He shrugged. "Who the fuck knows."

Baker decided this was it, do or die, probably do *and* die. He'd hit that vicious-looking Chinese, drag her away, and break. He took a deep breath and was about to charge when they all heard it, low and scratchy, the sound of a car moving slowly over gravel. The noise got louder and closer. Then the darkness was broken by a bright pair of beams twisting into the driveway between the gap in the link fence. A dark blue Mercedes settled aggressively on the edge of the oiled concrete, its high beams trained impudently on them. Vincent held up his hand to shield his eyes. "I fuckin' knew it!"

Julie strained against Jimmy Sun's embrace to see who was inside the car. Her fear, although palpable, was now diluted by hope. She knew, like Baker, that once inside the warehouse, they wouldn't come out, and she also knew in her bones that the dark Mercedes was a surprise, something brand-new, even for the Chinese gangster who still held her by her short, white hair.

A man in a dark suit got out on the driver's side. A striking, tall young woman with red hair got out on the passenger's side. She stood protected by the metal door. The man was tall and beefy, in his mid-forties, and held his hands close to his sides. Jimmy Sun let Julie go and moved forward.

"How ya doin'," the stranger said pleasantly.

"This is private property," Vincent shouted. "Get that car out of here."

Julie screamed, "Don't listen to them, help us!" Jimmy Sun turned quickly and swung backhandedly. The crack was audible and her head snapped. She was furious at the tears that welled in her eyes.

The stranger laughed cruelly. "You sure know how to shut 'em up." The young woman stepped into the light. She was fashionably dressed, balanced on heels which made her even taller. "Maybe you could help the little lady and me here with a problem we got," he said.

"Yeah?" Vincent said. He was now thoroughly confused. "What's that?"

The man gestured and the woman walked forward again, squinting at the glare of the high beams slicing through the dark. She pointed at Baker and Julie. The man nodded in understanding.

"So what's your problem?" Vincent demanded again, his voice rising as his nervousness increased. "And what the fuck's she doing?"

"Nothing much," the stranger said. He pointed to Baker and Julie. "We've had a little breakdown and . . . well, we'd like those two to come with us, sort of help us."

Vincent stiffened. He had never believed this guy had just dropped in out of the rain. Jimmy Sun had been staring like a tethered cat watching a mouse, waiting for just a touch of encouragement. He turned to the young Chinese who had ridden shotgun and gestured imperceptibly. The youth nodded, moved easily, showing a knife identical to that which had so recently been nestled against Julie's soft, white throat.

The stranger saw the knife and shook his head. "Not a good idea," he said sadly.

The Chinese youth didn't get it. He was a hunter and only knew how to strike. He slithered forward soundlessly and when he was close enough, he lunged. The man moved with ghostlike speed from a position of almost total repose. He grabbed the knife hand and twisted. There was an audible crack as the kid's right wrist broke in two. Then the stranger brought his knee up hard into the kid's groin and the boy screamed in agony as his testicles shattered. The man took the now broken and helpless wrist and drove it flush into the youth's exposed midsection, the sharpened knife slicing deep under the breastbone. The boy coughed once, blood spurted, escaping from his lips, and he dropped dying to his knees. He bled to death on the soiled concrete, taking twelve minutes to do it, howling and clutching the knife with his broken wrist.

Vincent got it right away. He looked at Julie, his only hope. The distance was about fifteen feet. The man smiled and now his hand had a gun in it. "Don't even think about it. I suggest you just get in your car and drive away."

Jimmy Sun didn't move. Vincent stared at the visitor with fear and hatred mixed in some strange and unfamiliar stew.

"Who are you? Who sent you?"

"It don't matter," the man said, smiling even more in an unhurried, lazy way. "But you can call me Sal."

48

SAL PUT THEM IN THE BACKSEAT OF THE DARK BLUE Mercedes and drove them quickly back to Cherokee. He wondered aloud whether he should have finished Vincent and Jimmy Sun, which completely infuriated Angela.

"Salvador, you've got to be reasonable. That one man

was trying to kill you but the other two weren't! They were just standing there! You can't go around just killing people because they're standing there!''

Baker didn't agree with that at all, nor did Sal.

"Angel, I don't know. Those guys looked bad, I can tell. That Chinese guy wasn't grinning 'cause he was happy.''

Julie leaned forward. Her face was as puffy as Baker's. "Did he say 'Angel'? Like in Angela?"

"Absolutely,'' she said twisting around. "Bobby Lee, long time. You look great! Except maybe your face.''

"Thanks.''

"Angela?'' Julie asked again. "Like in Angela Moore?''

"Yeah, the hair's different but I'm the same girl. Except now, I've met Sal.'' She snuggled closer on the front seat.

"How sweet,'' Baker said. He dabbed at his nose, which was starting to bleed again.

Sal brought them in and soon it was a full table at Cherokee—Romano, Lazy Sal, Angela, Bobby Lee, and Julie. Julie was cautious. As much as she was consumed by the chase for Vargo, she was equally wary of Romano and his henchmen. She decided she would sit quietly, poker-faced, and try to gauge how if at all she could use these people.

Romano had the black-skirted waitresses humming. They came in waves, bringing antipasto, excellent Chianti, three different types of pasta ("take a little of each, it's good for you''), a veal with roasted potatoes and fried spinach, and tiramesu to lay on top of all the rest. When Julie ignored her food, Romano was merciless.

"Would somebody tell that broad to eat? Here, sweetheart, you're insulting me, let me put some food on your plate. Come on, eat up.'' He threatened, maybe only half in jest, that he would get Lazy Sal to feed her if she didn't shape up.

After the tiramesu came the espresso and grappa. Romano sat back and opened his belt. His enormous stomach expanded and he let out a gigantic belch. He held up his grappa. "Here's to the chef.'' Julie stared at him with disgust. Baker ate and drank anything they put near him.

"First of all," Romano said once the toasts were done, "let me tell you, you two look like shit."

That was true. Baker had been fighting various blood clots for forty-eight hours now. Julie's face was spotted with angry red blotches. There were black-and-blue marks under her right eye.

"Anyway," Romano said. "I guess you got questions."

"Could I have more wine?" Baker asked.

Julie had different questions. "I want to know everything. Who you are, how you got hold of Angela, what's your interest in Vargo."

"Fair enough. I been after Vargo for years after that prick stole money from me and my friends. My friends are from New York and when I tell 'em a deal's good they don't ask questions, they just send their money. Mr. Rosen—he's the main guy—he's been patient. But he wants his money back and he wants his interest too. And soon."

"Are you afraid of this Mr. Rosen?"

"Let's just say our relationship's not the best these days."

"And Angela?"

He gestured toward Baker. "We got your friend to thank for that. Sal's *real* grateful, too grateful, you ask me."

"So why were you following us?"

"Good question. I'll tell you what I figured. I got your friend here walking in my club with this Patsy broad that we all know is OCID. I listen to his story but I still smell a rat. So I tell Sal, 'follow this asshole around.' Maybe he's straight, maybe he's OCID, maybe he's tied into Vargo, who knows. Anyway let's find out."

"And then Sal saved us. Why?"

Romano was insulted. "Nice talk. You want us to give you back? I can arrange that."

"Don't misunderstand," Julie said quickly. "I'm very grateful. But I need to know. Why?"

Romano pointed to Angela. "My guess, you owe her. She always said Baker was a good guy. And Lazy Sal, well, he listens to her a little too much. Maybe this time

she was right." And that was that. Angela told Lazy Sal
to save them and he did. Otherwise, the two of them
would be sleeping in a box in a warehouse tonight. Julie
nodded her thanks and Angela smiled weakly in return.

"So what now?" Julie asked.

Romano pointed his cigar at her. "Good question.
Great question! What do *you* think?"

"I'm an Assistant United States Attorney. There are
procedures I have to follow. What I should do is call the
office, tell them about Barrows. Once they understand
we'll be able to get some help."

Romano laughed heartily. "Sweetheart, you crack me
up. I don't want to rain on your parade but we already
checked that out. This guy Barrows is a hero over there
and you're what they call persona non gratis. Matter of
fact, they're looking for you a lot harder than they're
looking for Vargo."

Baker bit his tongue hard, deciding wisely to pass up
the opportunity for ironic comment.

Julie got it without Baker's sarcasm. "They're looking
for *me!* Are you kidding? For *me!*"

"That's right. You and your pal there. And they ain't
gonna give you no medal when they find you."

"Oh my God." She held her head to blunt the
throbbing in her temples.

"Hey, don't worry about it," Romano said. "Once we
nail that slimy fuck you two will be heroes."

"How?"

"Leave that to me and Sal. Incidentally, does he got to
be alive?"

"Yes," Julie said.

"No," Baker said.

At midnight Sal put them back in the Mercedes and
drove where Julie told him. They wound their way up
Sunset watching the sidewalks disappear and the elbow-
to-elbow sleaze shops change to green grass and high
hedges. Beverly Hills changed to Bel Air and Bel Air
became the Palisades. Through it all Julie sat frozen, staring out the window as it all came clear to her. She was a
hunted woman. She could deny it till hell froze over and

it wouldn't matter. She was now a blip on an FBI radar screen, as juicy a target as Bobby Lee Baker, her once and present lover. She turned to the great man as she thought of him and found him sleeping the sleep of the just, an innocent man hunted long enough to long since lose the thrill.

The Mercedes turned onto Via Veneto and she saw it right away, a blue van parked inconspicuously under a Canary Islands pine. Sal saw it too and looked in the rearview mirror. "That's them, miss," he said.

"I know." She didn't have to guess. They used the same vans on her cases. "Just keep driving and we'll get out of here."

"And then where, miss?"

She was too tired to think. "Wherever Romano wants," she said.

Sal drove them to the Bel Air Hotel, where they spent the night in a nice room prepaid by Romano. Once there, Julie sat awake and made notes, trying to let work eliminate the danger and dread. That effort was effectively squelched by Baker's snores, spewed from a beached form lying on his back on the luxurious bed. A regular Valentino, she thought, poking him rudely in the back until he turned over. Lazy Sal and Angela, for protection it was said, had the room next door. Julie suspected it was really the way bonuses were given in Mobville.

The next day she rose at dawn, hunting for Romano. He didn't show up till noon. He shrugged at her furious protests. "Relax," he said. "We move at night. That's when the animals get active."

Julie was apoplectic. "How can you be so casual about this? He'll be gone in two days."

"How the hell you know that?"

"Trust me. We've had this information from the beginning."

Romano laughed. "Who's we, Tonto? Anyway it don't matter. All I need's one day to get him. Go take a nap and we'll talk tonight." There was no arguing with him. Julie resigned herself to a day of nervous pacing around the hotel pool. Baker, spread on a towel like a caught trout, never moved from nine in the morning until three in the afternoon except to eye an occasional bikini-clad patron taking a dip.

Okay, she thought, when she couldn't think of anything better, I'll just call.

The secretary to James P. Price, the U.S. Attorney for the Central District of California, was a woman named Madelaine who had been a government employee for twenty-five years. She recognized Julie's voice at once.

"Julie, is that really you?"

"Hi, Madelaine. Is Jim in?"

"Just a second, let me see if he's on the phone. Julie, it's great to hear your voice."

"Thanks."

It took a while for Madelaine to get back and when she did, her voice had changed. It sent a chill through her. "Julie, I can't seem to find him. It shouldn't take me too long though, maybe five minutes. Where are you calling from?"

Julie got it right away and the sadness clutched at her. She cleared her throat. "Madelaine, I need to talk to him right now."

"Oh, sure. I know." Madelaine's voice was nervous, high-pitched, like she had an audience listening to her. "But can't we call you back? Just tell me where you are."

"Madelaine, you're not very good at this. Tell Jim I need to talk to him right now. Otherwise, I hang up before the trace catches."

Now Madelaine's voice was officious, government-honed. "Just one moment."

He came on the line almost immediately. "Julie, is that really you?"

"Yes, sir, it is. I need to talk to you right away."

"No problem. Where are you, anyway?"

"That's not important."

"Okay, no problem. Can you come in? We'll be waiting here for you."

That they would. "No, sir. I can't do that right now. I just want to tell you what I know."

"Sure. Go ahead." His voice had the false heartiness of the locker room.

"First, you need to know about Covington Barrows. I know this will be hard to believe, but he's tied in with Vargo. Anything we tell him goes right to Vargo. He's been working to get Vargo's job done and get him out of the country."

She could actually hear the click of the tape machine. Typical government equipment. "Barrows, huh. Now that's interesting. I'm going to make a note of that right now."

Now the rage threatened to affect her. She fought against the anger in her voice. "Jim, listen to me. We made a mistake about Baker."

"We did, huh? What mistake did we make, Julie?"

Patronizing fuck. "Baker and Vargo are enemies. There are a lot of questions I have now. We may . . . well, I'll say it. We may have had an innocent man in Boron for the last three years."

"Innocent, huh? That's a very serious matter. Are you with Baker now by chance?"

"What does that have to do with it?"

"You are, aren't you?"

"Yes, I mean . . ."

"What do you mean, Julie?"

"I mean I know where he is."

"And is that because you're with him?"

She was quiet for a moment and then realized she could think of nothing clever. "More or less."

"I see." There was a long pause. When he spoke again, he had given up all attempts at deception and his voice was grave. "Julie, I'm sorry to see this happen to you."

"What the hell does that mean?"

"Just answer me one question. Actually two."

"Yes?"

"First, Barrows tells me you were sleeping with Baker before he tipped Vargo off. Is that true? Second, Barrows tells me you're sleeping with him now. Is that true?"

Be calm, be calm, she said to herself, don't give the fucker the satisfaction. She coughed to clear her throat and held the phone away from her face so he would not hear. She could hear him talking from a distance.

"Julie, it doesn't have to be hard for you. Barrows
an old classmate of mine. I've talked to him and he as
sures me this is just a case of . . . well . . . a woman be
coming emotionally involved. I'm a man. I *understan*
that a woman can't always control her emotions.
doesn't mean you *knew* Baker was working with Vargc
After all, you prosecuted the case and that stands fc
something."

Julie screamed into the phone. Her voice was com
pletely wrecked. "Don't you fucking understand wha
I'm saying! Barrows is a traitor! He's working wit
Vargo. If you're so fucking stupid you're taking order
from Barrows, you're as good as taking orders fron
Vargo!"

James P. Price clicked his tongue gently. "Julie, com
in. Leave all those people now. Tell us where they are
and we'll have agents out there immediately. Julie
there's still time. Don't let this destroy you."

She held the phone away from her and looked at it. The
voice of her boss was still coming through the receiver
garbled, tinny from the tiny speaker. She hung up.

49

AT DUSK, EVERYONE ASSEMBLED FOR THE ASSAULT. THE
bar was closed and empty except for a few trusted wait
resses and Romano's troops, eleven of them, dressed i
dark windbreakers, high-necked sweaters, and running
shoes. They were all inspecting and loading handgun:
while Lazy Sal loaded a half-dozen shotguns on the bar
Baker knew right away this was war.

Romano laid down the rules. Lazy Sal would ride with
him in the lead car together with Angela, Julie, an
Baker. They would make their way into Monterey Park
around 9 P.M. Baker and Julie would direct them to the
Golden Dragon. Once there, Romano's troops would
take over. "We'll find something in there, no matter how

much yellow tape they got up," Romano said confidently.

Julie was ready for action, too, just not with Romano. Every instinct told her to get out of there and back where she belonged. Yet she knew exactly what that choice would bring. She looked to Baker for advice. He was eating pasta and drinking red wine, watching the men load the guns with interest.

"Bobby," she said, "we have to talk."

"Sure." He went back to his pasta and wine.

"Now, Bobby!" Her voice was exasperated. It would not be easy to live with this man.

"Sure," he said easily. He wiped his mouth and gestured for her to sit down. "Mind if I continue eating?"

She did but decided to bite her tongue for now. "Bobby, we're in big trouble," she said, sitting close to him. "These people"—she gestured around the room—"they're hoodlums. And here we are getting ready to . . . to I don't know what. What the hell are they planning to do anyway?"

Good question. "Would it frighten you if I said I'm not sure?"

"You bet your ass it would."

"Well," he said, "I'm afraid that's kind of the situation." He had the good manners to stop eating and put his hand on her arm. "Look, we've got no friends in this thing. That also means we've got no choice." He patted her arm considerately and eyed his rigatoni out of the corner of his eye. It was covered with smoked salmon and a fresh pesto sauce. The Chianti had washed it down with a lovely melded flavor. He hoped this conversation wouldn't take too long.

"I don't buy it, Bobby," she said and pushed his plate away. He watched it depart with keen disappointment. "If we team up with these people we're as bad as they are."

"What the hell does that mean? These people, as you call them, saved your life! These people are the only thing between me and Boron. You do remember that part, don't you, the Boron part?"

"Of course I do. But Bobby, think about this for a

moment. Do you really think you'll be happy if the price of your freedom is secret deals with mobsters?''

He looked at her like she just dropped down from Mars.

"Okay," she said quickly, "maybe that wasn't a good argument." He nodded vigorously in agreement. "Let' try another. Maybe there's a better way?"

"Like what?"

"Like trying to get somebody to listen to us. Maybe Medina can help."

He laughed heartily at that and abandoned all pretense. He took a long pull of his wine. "Go ahead and try, see how it turns out. Maybe they'll let us time our parole dates so we get out together."

"Not so fast. I still think if we can get to the right person we can do this the right way."

"Yeah, me too," Bobby Lee said. Now he did go back to his rigatoni.

She got the irony as soon as she heard her own words. Who was she kidding? The government was now out to get her as much or more than Baker. All she was doing was looking for sympathy and he was much too hardened by now for that. She had only been living this nightmare for a couple of days. She had made him live it for three years.

She dropped her head against his shoulder, hoping to gather strength from her nearness to him. He responded, stroking her hair and turning to kiss her eyes. "Don't worry, baby. This time tomorrow it'll all be over."

She resisted the urge to pull away. "You sure?"

"Absolutely. We'll go in and get him, and that will be that."

She laughed and the pain eased. "And that's all there is to it?"

"That's all there is."

Well, almost all. It took her no more than thirty seconds to take her head off Bobby Lee's shoulder and start pacing again. When she couldn't stand pacing anymore she confronted Romano.

"I want to know what your plan is," she demanded.

Romano shrugged. "Easy. Go in and look around, ask questions, grab his ass. What the fuck else?"

"In twenty-four hours he'll be gone."

"No shit. You got any better ideas?"

She thought about that question for a moment and then it hit her. *Jesus, Julie, you're a goddamn idiot.*

Romano was a chivalrous man. "Don't be so hard on yourself. You're a good-looking broad."

She grabbed him by the lapels. "You got a beeper or something? Some way to get hold of you?"

"Sure, I got everything."

"Listen to me. You go ahead and take your people into Monterey Park. Ask anybody whatever you want, I don't care." She knew he wouldn't find anything but if he happened to get lucky and trip over Vargo in the street, all the better. "I'll take Bobby Lee with me."

"Be my guest," Romano said, pulling back and straightening his lapels. He winked at one of the black-clad waitresses and she went for his drink, a little Crown Royal, rocks, no twist.

"We're going to surprise you, Mr. Romano," Julie said intently. "We'll find him before you do. And then we'll tell you where to go."

Romano was already bored with the conversation. He had his eye on the waitress who brought him the drink. "Yeah, baby, you give me a call."

50

SHE GRABBED BOBBY LEE AND A ROMANO CAR AND POR-table phone and was on the road in thirteen minutes, her left hand dialing Romano's beeper number into the memory of the car phone and her right hand taking notes on a pad spread across her bare legs. Baker complained the whole time. He was still complaining as he turned onto Sunset.

"This is a stupid idea," he told her. "More to the point

it's gonna get my cracker ass right back in Boron, not to mention your own little butt, cute as it may be, wherever they decide to display that."

"Bobby, I promise I'll be careful. Just try this for me, okay?"

He grumbled some more out of habit but knew there was no hope of changing her mind. Maybe lots had changed between them, but not that.

He drove east on Sunset until they crossed Alvarado. All the glitz of West L.A. was now far behind them. At Alvarado, on the cusp of downtown, the corner restaurants were not celebrity havens but taco stands, the patrons not actors but hardworking gardeners sprinkled with gang members, their Raiders caps worn backward and their eyes sweeping the streets for business or danger. Of the five L.A. kills a day a good three are teenage Hispanics in turned-around Raiders caps and baggy shorts.

She pointed to the curb and he pulled over. The heat was stifling and the visibility about a block and a half. The smog hung in brown gauze sheets, increasing in thickness as you looked through the gunk.

She dialed a number on the portable phone and he locked the door, his head swiveling like the gang-bangers watching for the next drive-by. Her voice took on a formal, almost clerical tone.

"Hello, hi, is this Checkers? . . . Great, is Covington Barrows in? Not till six? Okay, will you connect me with the front desk? Thanks."

Then she began humming and drumming her fingers on the dash.

"Hi, front desk? This is Alice Cooper, I'm Mr. Barrows' secretary. How are you? I'm doing Mr. Barrows' expense report and I need to see his room bill. . . . I'd like to come by and get a copy in about five minutes, if that's okay. . . . Great, thanks."

She pressed the button terminating the call and began scribbling furiously on her pad.

"You are really a piece of work," Bobby Lee observed.

"Drive, Jeeves," she said without looking up.

* * *

Thirty minutes later they sat parked in a construction zone back in gangland. Julie had a copy of Barrows' room bill in front of her. Bobby Lee was still swiveling his head looking for shooters.

"Can't you read faster?"

"Keep your shorts on." Her fingers flew down the page. "He actually hasn't made that many calls I can't identify. We can forget about the Washington calls and the calls to the U.S. Attorney's Office." She crossed those off. "Here's two to my house, we can cross those off too." Baker looked over quizzically but got ignored. "That leaves only . . ." she counted ". . . six numbers."

"So what?"

"So let's try them." She checked her list and dialed. "Hello, what hotel did you say this was? . . . Beverly Wilshire? . . . Do you have a Robert Vargo registered by chance? . . . Thanks anyway."

She scratched some more. "There were two to that number. That leaves four, three of which are to the same number."

She dialed. "Hello, who's this?" She covered the receiver and whispered "answering service" to Bobby Lee. "Whose office? . . . Thank you. My boss has a meeting there tomorrow, can you give me the address? . . . Thanks." She wrote it down and triumphantly tore the sheet off the pad.

"Charles Wendel. 555 South Flower. Suite 2700."

"I can't believe you."

She pointed. "Drive."

They found 555 South Flower to be a relatively standard fifty-story downtown L.A. bank building. It was surrounded on all sides by either urban decay or half-assed and half-finished efforts at urban renewal. The bums enjoyed the shade of the building in the heat of the day and ringed the structure like blanket-clad sentries. Broken streets and construction vehicles added to the general sense of bombed-out disintegration.

Julie had more on her mind than wondering whether *Blade Runner* days had finally arrived. They drove Romano's Chrysler into the bowels of the building and headed up the elevator to the twenty-seventh floor. The elevator doors opened and that's when they saw the yellow tape.

"Now what?" Baker asked.

"I'm not sure," Julie said slowly. Then she checked her notes. "Suite 2700, that's what they told me." Then she got it and her face drained of blood.

"What's wrong?"

She ignored him and walked inside. They turned a corner and confronted a uniformed policeman writing in a tiny spiral notebook. Beyond him police technicians in suits were laying out tape and snapping photos. A bored-looking suit glanced up at her from a spot on the edge of a desk.

"Can I help you, ma'am?"

Julie moved fast, rifling her ID from an inside pocket of her blue blazer.

"Assistant United States Attorney Beck," she announced. "This is Special Agent Baker, FBI."

Special Agent Baker puffed out his chest, as befits a special agent.

The detective came over and checked Julie's ID, then shook her hand. "Lieutenant Marks," he said in a kind of no-bullshit he-man way. Baker didn't shake his hand, just nodded briskly, one cop to another, two pros.

"So what do you got here, Lieutenant?" Julie asked. "And before you ask, we can't tell you yet why we're interested. Grand jury, you know."

The cop shrugged, he could give a shit. He consulted his notebook. "Charles Wendel. Some sort of businessman or lawyer in the past. Now a 'consultant,' whatever that means."

"And he's not here anymore?"

"Well, parts of him are, just not his head. Somebody stuck a gun in his mouth and just about took that off."

"I see," Julie said, trying to stay calm. "And the body's been . . ." She was hoping more than asking.

"Taken out of the room, yes ma'am. It's right over there on the gurney, under the white sheet."

"Excellent." She grabbed Baker's arm. "We'll just go in and look around."

* * *

It took her about half an hour to find Wendel's phone bills, and she soon had them spread out across the dead man's desk. She had Covington Barrows' phone records from the hotel next to them. Baker knew what she was doing, hunting for matches. Each of them tried to ignore the picketed brown stains splattered widely on the wall and couch.

"Anything?" he asked hopefully.

"Yes," she said slowly, examining the two lists. "The Beverly Wilshire." She looked up. "Both Barrows and Wendel called there. That means Vargo stayed there."

"But under a fake name."

"Exactly." She thought some more. "If we had time we could go out and show some pictures, maybe find out who's been there for two weeks. We could do it."

"I got news for you, babe. He's got maybe two days. This is like Dracula. He's left that crib."

She smiled and kissed him lightly. "All those people who said you weren't that smart. I always disagreed."

"Thank you."

She went back to her twin lists. "Well, one thing's certain."

"What?"

"Wendel made about three-fourths of his calls to one number. Let's try it."

They dialed the number from the speakerphone on the dead man's desk. After a series of weird clicks a tinny voice came on the line. The voice spoke in a high-pitched singsong foreign language.

"Chinese," Baker said. She nodded.

Soon the tinny voice changed to a man's voice speaking in heavily accented English.

"You have reached the Monterey Park branch of the Asian Interbank Trust. Our office hours are nine A.M. to five P.M., Monday through Saturday. Evening transactions can be arranged by consultation with your account representative. For wire transfer information, please press one. For overseas account information, please press two. For correspondent banking information in Hong Kong or Taiwan, please press three. For correspondent banking information in Singapore, please press . . ."

Baker hung up. She looked at him quizzically. "Is that the bank . . ."

"Next to the shootout. You got it."

"Yes, I do." Her head spun around the room. "Small operation," she said to herself. "Files should be right nearby."

The file drawer in back of the dead man's desk was locked. It took Baker no more than a minute to rifle the desk drawers, find a key, and get the files open. The sounds of the police muddling around in the adjoining room grew louder.

"I tell you," Julie said admiringly, "sometimes it's good to have a felon working with you."

He ignored that and started inspecting the files. "Bingo," he said quickly. He hauled out three linear feet of expandable maroon folders. Each was tagged with a plain white label: "Asian Interbank Trust."

"Did you just say 'bingo'?" Julie asked innocently.

Baker was flipping through the files. "You know, I like you better on your back, moaning," he said.

"Me, too," she agreed.

It took him less than five minutes to decide he couldn't make heads or tails of the files. "I'm confused," he said, throwing them down.

"Why?"

"It's just a bunch of corporate documents, filings with the secretary of state, articles of incorporation, offshore tax returns, a lot of nothing."

"So what do we do?"

"We need somebody who knows about this shit." He thought some more. "Bingo," he said.

"That's the second time you've said that. Did you learn that in Boron?"

"You know the next time I get you naked we're going to try some games. You'd look really cute tied up."

"You're right," she agreed.

"Give me that phone." She didn't move. "Please," he said.

Faldo was there in thirty minutes, wide-eyed from the cops and dried brown blood and yellow tape. He shook hands with Julie and his eyes got wider when he realized who she was. The pleasantries over, he sat at the dead man's desk and looked at the spread-out files marked "Asian Interbank Trust." The only thing missing was a jeweler's monocle.

"This is easy," he said after ten seconds of examination.

"What's easy?"

"These are the original documents for the companies in the Green Bible. All the backup we never had. Christ, there's the original articles for Firenze Corporation." He said it like an archeologist coming upon a rare vase.

Baker was disappointed. "And that's it? Just stuff from the old days?"

"Not really," Faldo said slowly. "Some of this stuff I've never seen before. Yes, look at this," he said, ripping a manila folder out. "This company was formed only three weeks ago. And this one, too," he said pulling out another folder. "Jesus, there's a lot of information here. Where did this guy get this stuff?"

Where indeed. Bobby Lee grabbed a dictating machine and popped in a microcassette. He looked to Julie and she nodded in agreement. "Faldo, listen closely. Go through everything here and dictate a gigantic memo on anything you find. We're particularly interested in bank accounts and cash movement."

"I *know* that. I know more about these companies than *anyone*."

"Great." Baker patted Faldo on the shoulder. "When you're done get it typed up at your office. We need it like yesterday."

"And what will *you* be doing while I'm working so hard?"

Good question. "We have an army to meet."

Julie was up and out the door before his sentence was done. The form under the white sheet on the gurney seemed to wish them well as they passed.

51

SHE WAS GETTING REALLY ADEPT AT USING THE PORTA-
ble phone and being a backseat driver at the same time.
Within minutes she had Romano rerouted and heading
over to the Golden Dragon. Simultaneously she was able
to put her hand over the mouthpiece and poke Baker in
the shoulder to make him turn. He finally got pissed off
at getting poked.

"You know, I don't need you to find this place. *I'm*
the one who brought *you* there, remember? As I recall,
that's when the FBI you love so much got stuck in an
alley and you wanted me back in Boron."

She was fixing her hair and eyes in the mirror on the
visor, frowning at the black-and-blue splotches. "Why
do men always bring up completely irrelevant ancient
history? It must be something in the testosterone."

"Ancient history! It's not even a week!"

Her eyes finished as best she could, she turned and
kissed him gently on the cheek. She was beautiful, he
realized, and could probably get away with this shit forever. It was a sobering thought.

"Not even a week," he said again, this time softly.

She patted him on the knee. "Ancient history, darling,
and I've promised I'll make it up to you. Incidentally"—
she poked—"shouldn't you turn here?"

Romano's eleven gunmen were immediately dis-
patched to the Golden Dragon after Julie's call. The restaurant was brooding, shot to death in the conflagration
that had ripped Julie Beck from her complacency. The
now familiar yellow tape was stretched across the entrance but there were no cops around. In a city of five a
day even a massacre doesn't get to hold on to the cops
for too long.

Romano paced along the sidewalk next to the yellow

tape. He was a little bantam rooster, strutting like Patton.
His eleven troops were sitting ready in two nearby cars.
Baker paced along with him and the two conversed intently. Julie had been excluded and stood quietly looking
at the dark restaurant. Next door the offices of the Asian
Interbank Trust were black as a crypt and every bit as
secure. Only a pale, ephemeral light from below the restaurant fought its way through the darkness to cast tiny
strands of illumination helplessly into the night.

Baker and Romano finished their conversation and
shook hands. Julie did not like this at all.

"Tell me right now what you're planning to do," she
told Baker when she got him alone. "Every step."

"Easy. We wait here for a while and see if anybody
shows up. If it's Vargo, I finger him to Lazy Sal. Then
they do whatever they do, put him in cement or whatever."

"How does that help us?"

"I don't know, maybe they give us the cement, which
we give to your boss."

"Be serious. I want Vargo alive."

"We get credit for the bust, or whatever's left of him.
I get out of Boron, and you get a man to come home to
you at night. Plus you get to brag to your girlfriends that
you're having sex with an ex-con."

"Okay. What if he doesn't show up?"

"Then I go down."

"Down where?"

He pointed to the interior of the restaurant.

"With Sal?"

"No. Sal stays with you and Romano and Angela over
there." He pointed to a nearby car where Sal had Angela
protectively placed.

"And I never see you again?"

"That's negative thinking."

She shook her head and the short, white hair flopped
from side to side. "No way, nohow, no offense."

"No offense taken but you're not going with me."

Julie gave a fake smile that said there was no room for
argument.

"I've got a better plan."

"What?"

"If we get caught down there we've got to have a story. So we tell him we're running from the government. That part's true enough. Then we tell him we've got information for him."

"About what? He doesn't need us, he's got Barrows to help him."

"Not the investigation."

"What then?"

"Barrows," she said softly.

Baker squinted and didn't get it. "He already knows everything about Barrows. They're partners."

"What if Barrows was out to screw Vargo? A paranoid guy like Vargo might believe that."

"Maybe. But how could you possibly know what Barrows' plans are?"

She didn't answer.

Then Baker got it and his eyes flattened. "You know, take you out of a courtroom and you're a regular little slut. How long did it take you to drop them for Barrows?"

Now it was Julie's turn to anger. "First of all I didn't, not what you think. Anyway it was your fault. If you hadn't been in Boron, it never would have happened."

"My fault!" Bobby Lee screamed. "You put me in Boron!"

She patted his cheek, now somewhat calmed. "I told you before, let's not dredge up that old chestnut. Anyway," she said with a finality he had come to know, "I'm going with you."

52

THEY STEPPED OVER THE YELLOW POLICE TAPE, through the shattered door, across the chalk drawings of bodies on the floor, past the turned-over tables with bullet holes still in them, and down the steps of the Golden Dragon. It was as he remembered it, bleak and dangerous. Julie walked at his side, touching his arm from time to time. She tried not to project past the dark doors in front of them.

At the bottom of the steps, Baker pushed against the double doors. They opened easily. The hallway in front of him was deeply carpeted. He listened for sounds of danger and heard nothing. After a few beats, he gestured to her and they walked down the hall.

The last time he was in this hall, Chinese gunmen had come leaping from the side to intercept him. Now, the doors on either side opened only onto empty sleeping quarters for the Kwoh forces who had once lived there. At the far end of the hall, there were more double doors, mahogany this time, emblazoned with Chinese characters. They walked forward.

Julie leaned her ear against the ornate doors and listened intently. Nothing. She imagined Vargo waiting patiently on the other side of this door, flanked by the gray-haired man and a dozen young Chinese gunmen. They would blindly walk through, just as they had at Barrows' suite at Checkers. The doors would then close behind them and they would never be heard from again.

She looked to Baker for support. He was idly standing in the corner, looking bored, practicing a golf swing.

"Goddamn it, stop that!" Her husky whisper bounced off the hallway walls.

"What?"

"Fooling around, that's what. We could get killed."

"Sorry." He stopped golfing, then gestured to the door. "Why don't we go in?"

The man was an insensitive lout. "I'm not sure. What do you think?"

"I think we should go in."

Then he walked past her and pushed open the double doors.

Vargo wasn't there at all but Stewart Kwoh-Fang was. He sat facing them behind a black walnut desk. The room was dark except for a dim desk lamp. Baker recognized this man as the dignified, elderly gentleman who had interceded on his behalf the last time he had ventured down to these quarters. He suspected then, and knew now, that this man was in charge of the Chinese gunmen who had threatened him. Back then he had felt primitive fear at the sight of this man. Now, he walked forward without concern. Stewart Kwoh-Fang would never again be a danger to anyone.

The man's naked body was riddled with bullets. He sat back in his chair with his head lolling against his shoulder, dried blood crusting against the corner of his mouth. Julie's lips tightened but otherwise she didn't flinch.

"You want to go back upstairs?" he asked.

"No." She moved closer.

"You ever see a dead body before? I mean one not under a sheet."

"I saw three of them once, Bobby. They looked about like he does. Even the girl."

He didn't say anything to that.

They heard some movement in the hall, and a moment later Lazy Sal came in. Angela walked in behind him. "Oh my God," she said.

"Sorry," Lazy Sal said, "Romano couldn't wait." He walked over to the body, inspecting it professionally. "It looks like two guys did him."

"Did you see anybody when you came down?"

Lazy Sal shook his head. "There's nobody down here except us. My guess is they're running for the hills."

"Then let's look around," Julie said abruptly. They did as she ordered, splitting up and inspecting each room in the basement of the Golden Dragon. Baker remembered the thick black wires snaking from the roof of the bank building into this basement. They found the wires and followed them to a sealed room. Lazy Sal shot his way in. The room was filled with high-tech computer and telecommunications equipment. The computer looked intact.

"Anybody know anything about computers?" Bobby Lee asked.

"I do," Julie said. She sat at the computer and started punching in commands. There was a loose-leaf pad next to the keyboard. "They left all the passwords here. What do we want to know?"

"How about where's Vargo?" Baker suggested.

Julie shrugged. "Why not?" She typed in Vargo's name and had the machine do a search. In an instant, the screen was filled with entries. There were twenty-three different categories involving Vargo, including corporate names, bank accounts, telephone numbers, and similar information. Julie studied the screen.

"I remember these companies. They're the same ones we saw at Wendel's office, the ones your friend's looking at."

It was all Greek to Baker. "What are those dots at the bottom?"

She ignored him. Angela looked over her shoulder at the screen. "I remember all this stuff. A lot of this is from the days when Kwoh and Vargo were working together." She realized they didn't know what the name meant. "Kwoh's the man in the other room. Stewart Kwoh-Fang."

"Ancient history," Julie said. She punched in more commands. "Let me scroll this. Tell me whether any of this is new."

The lines on the screen moved upward. Angela stared intently. "Wait, what's that at the bottom?"

Julie brought the entry back up onto the screen. "It says 'Havana Corporation.' "

"I never heard of that. What's it mean?"

"Let's find out."

She pushed some more buttons and the directory for "Havana Corporation" came up.

"It's dated last week. This is a new directory."

Lazy Sal and Baker crowded around to look. There were two names at the top of the directory: Hector Menendez and Manuel Menendez. Brothers perhaps. Underneath was information about flights and arrival dates. Whoever Hector and Manuel were, they arrived in Chicago on the twenty-fifth of June and were due to arrive in Los Angeles on the thirtieth. A local phone number was provided.

Underneath this information was a series of entries in Spanish.

"Anybody know Spanish?" Sal said.

"Me," said Baker. "*Uno mas cerveza, por favor.*"

"I do," Julie said. She translated for them. "This is the text of letters Stewart Kwoh-Fang was faxing to Havana. He's bad-mouthing Vargo."

Her fingers traced along the screen. "Then it looks like Havana responds to him. They tell him Hector and Manuel Menendez will arrive in Los Angeles on the thirtieth. If Vargo isn't out by the thirtieth, *'el sera asesinato.'*"

"Which means?"

"Hit, I think," Lazy Sal said.

"Right," Julie agreed.

"Does it say where Vargo is now?"

"Sort of," Julie said. "Kwoh says Vargo is working with somebody named Chang. They're expecting a delivery. Kwoh wants the Cubans to stop it."

"The thirtieth?" Baker checked his watch. "That's today, troops. I got news for you. Vargo's gone."

Nobody answered. Romano was standing by the door listening. He walked up to Angela. "Vargo ever do business with somebody named Chang, sweetheart?"

"Sure, both of them." She gestured in the direction of the bullet-ridden Kwoh. "Him most of the time, but Chang a lot. Kwoh and Chang hated each other."

"You wouldn't happen to know where this Chang guy hung out, would you, sweet stuff?"

She pointed to the screen. "Right there, where it says the delivery's going. That's Chang's warehouse."

"You know where it is?"

"I think I do now."

"Okay, baby, don't let me die of old age here."

"I think it's where Salvador helped these people." She gestured to Julie and Baker.

Romano moved fast. "Hey, Sal, you think you can find that warehouse again? The one where you saved little miss tight-ass here?"

"Sure, Mr. Romano."

"Let's go."

53

AT AROUND 9 P.M. ON THE THIRTIETH OF JUNE, 1991, the world as Baker knew it converged on an isolated warehouse in the city of Alhambra. From the west came Bobby Lee Baker, Julie Beck, Lazy Sal, Angela, Romano, and his eleven gunmen.

From the east came Vargo, sitting in the back of the Lincoln with Chang, Jimmy Sun sitting up front with Vincent. Vincent winced as he drove, his face swollen and blackened from the furious beating Vargo had ordered after Baker and Julie escaped. Jimmy Sun had orchestrated the beating and even now, hours later, Vincent's head listed hard to the right. He would never get full use of his left arm again.

Vargo's violent response was born completely of frustration. His precious time was now almost out. The Colombians had already advised him that Cuban assassins had left Havana, reached the U.S., and made contact on the ground in Los Angeles. The Cubans would be scrupulously fair. They could not attack until midnight of the thirtieth day without risking the ire of the Colombians. But Vargo knew there was no grace period.

Vargo had tried in vain to get a little help from Chang. Just send the money, he begged. That way we avoid slip-ups like the truck getting lost or rolling over a nail. Chang had smiled at Vargo, his face encircled with blue smoke.

"The payment will be made when we receive the goods. Fifty percent of wholesale value."

"But—" Vargo began. And Chang had laughed.

The Mexican furniture was scheduled to arrive in a big rig which at 9 P.M. was confirmed barreling north on the San Diego Freeway about an hour south of Los Angeles. When the truck arrived at the Chang warehouse, Jimmy Sun's henchmen would off-load the furniture and test the cocaine. If all was in order, the driver would be released with an empty truck and Vargo would depart with Chang to frantically arrange for the wire transfer that would save his life.

Baker and Julie knew none of this as they approached the Chang warehouse from the west in a long limo which acted as the lead car of the Romano motorcade. Romano, squeezed in the front with Lazy Sal and Angela, was in a jovial mood.

"You know, Sal, it's been a long time."

"Long time, Mr. Romano."

"And you know what, Sal? I was starting to think I was gettin' a little old, you know?"

"No, you're not old, Mr. Romano."

"What do you think, Sal? You think he'll be here?" He was like a kid at Christmas wondering about the bicycle.

"Yeah, Mr. Romano, he'll be there. Don't worry."

Romano slapped Sal on the back. "That's what I like to hear, Sal. We'll take care of him together, right?"

"Right, Mr. Romano."

Romano stopped the convoy a block from the warehouse. He ordered everybody out of the cars and began walking around giving pep talks to the troops. The guy does think he's Eisenhower, Julie thought.

Sal walked over to Baker and Julie holding a small bag. "You guys know how to use these?" He held up two handguns. "They're .38s," Sal explained. "Is that too heavy for you?"

Baker grabbed one of the guns and twirled it around his index finger like a cowboy. Julie held hers by the edge of the barrel, staring at it like it was a dead fish.

"I can't accept this," she said.

"If you want to stay around here, you gotta have one, Mr. Romano's orders."

"Here." She handed it back to Sal. "I'll stay with him, tell Mr. Romano it'll be okay."

Sal turned to Baker. "You know how to use this?"

"Sort of."

"Here." Sal grabbed the gun, loaded it in front of Baker, then broke open the magazine and emptied the bullets. "Now you try."

It took Baker three tries to get it right. After that, however, he was loading the gun with what he thought was professional speed.

Sal took the gun back. "Now, it's just point and shoot. Like a camera. Got it?"

Baker aimed and pulled the trigger. The gun clicked. He loaded it, like Sal had taught him. There was a dead tree fifty feet away. He held the gun extended from his body, pointed, and squeezed. The gun jerked in his hand and the report was abrupt. The bullet tore a football-sized hunk of bark from the side of the tree.

"That's all there is to it," Lazy Sal told him.

By the time Vargo and Chang arrived, Romano had the place pretty much surrounded. The lead car was the limo, with Lazy Sal and Angela in front, and Baker, Romano, and Julie in the back. The limo was parked like a guard dog in front of the warehouse, the engine idling and the lights on. There was no effort at secrecy. A second car held down the south side, also alive, illuminated, and purring. A third car secured the north. Romano was next to Julie, occasionally squeezing her on the bare leg for reassurance, ignoring her blistering looks, otherwise listening to a Verdi tape with his eyes closed.

"I love this shit," Romano said, referring to either music or anticipation or Julie's bare leg, Sal couldn't tell which.

Vargo and Chang were in the middle of a heated argument when their Lincoln turned into the warehouse driveway. Vargo was begging for early transfer of funds to Havana; Chang was again laughing at the idea. Their argument had gotten so intense that neither noticed the large car facing them from the warehouse driveway. Jimmy Sun saw it first; he got so excited he began jabbering in pidgin Chinese and pointing. Vincent stopped the car fifty feet from Romano.

Vargo stopped arguing. His jaw dropped lifelessly. Chang said the obvious.

"Who, may I ask, are they?"

"I got no fuckin' idea," he said weakly. "Vincent, get your ass out there."

Vincent hesitated no more than a heartbeat. He had already been beaten like a whipped dog. He got out and walked toward Romano's limo.

He didn't get halfway there before Lazy Sal stepped out of the limo, protected by the driver's-side door.

"Stop there!"

Vincent stopped. He remembered the voice and remembered Sal. He started to reach into his coat out of habit.

"Are you nuts?"

"No."

"Take your fuckin' hand out."

Vincent did as he was told. Lazy Sal cocked his head. "Mr. Romano?"

"I don't want to talk to this putz. Who's in the car?"

"Who's in there?" Lazy Sal barked.

"It don't matter," Vincent said quickly. "You want to live, get the fuck out of here now."

It was not an empty threat. Two carloads of Chang operatives had pulled next to the Lincoln, seasoned soldiers drunk with the blood taste of the recently decimated Kwoh troops. Young Chinese emerged and there was a loud clicking of ordnance. The sound galvanized Romano's men. They poured out of their support cars. There was an unmistakable sound of the pumping of shotguns. As they say, the battle lines were drawn.

"It's Vargo," Julie said excitedly. "It's got to be. He's in that car." She forgot Romano's intrusive pats and leaned forward, caught up in the chase.

"It sure as shit is," Romano agreed. He bellowed to Vincent. "Tell your boss I want to see him. Have him come over here to the car."

"Who are you?"

"Who am I?" Romano laughed heartily. "Tell your boss I am a friend of Mr. Rosen."

Vincent turned and left. He was inside the lead car for several minutes. When he finally emerged, he was accompanied by Jimmy Sun, black-clad and armed.

"My boss will see you now," Vincent said. "Right here." He drew a line in the dirt driveway with his heel.

Romano laughed again. He was having a great time. "Hey, Sal," he bellowed. "Let's dance."

54

THE GREAT MEETING TOOK PLACE ON EITHER SIDE OF A line in the dirt outside a corrugated tin warehouse in the city of Alhambra at 10 P.M. on June 30, 1991. The smog-clogged sky hid the moon, which was up there someplace although not adding much to the action. Romano stood with Lazy Sal next to him. Sal had a shotgun pointed to the purple, greased sky. Julie Beck and Bobby Lee Baker had left Romano's limo and stood quietly to his right.

Sal had Angela stashed back in the car, and told her not to move, in a tone Angela knew was serious. Vargo and Chang walked out of the Lincoln flanked by Vincent and Jimmy Sun. Both bodyguards were armed with MAC-10s. Behind both groups the foot soldiers were hidden behind hunks of steel and glass, armed to the teeth, pointing automatic weapons and shotguns into the black mist of the polluted night.

Vargo squinted when he came to the line drawn in the dirt. His head swiveled and he looked confused, then angry. Baker realized the source of his confusion: this was the most important meeting of his life and the only face he recognized was Baker's. Vargo had never met Julie Beck, even during the investigation, and Romano was a complete mystery to him, as was Sal.

"I got to ask one question right off. Who the fuck are you people?"

Romano was smoking a cigar and now began chewing furiously on it. "Who am I? Who the fuck am I? How 'bout I rip your fucking throat out and then you'll know who the fuck I am."

Sal interceded, trying to keep it cool. "This is Mr. Romano. He is Mr. Rosen's representative."

Vargo thought for a moment. "Mr. Rosen?" Then he remembered. "Ah, yes," he said finally. "And her?"

"She's my fucking wife," Romano said.

311

"My name is Julie Beck."

Vargo's eyes grew wide. "No shit?"

Julie smiled sweetly at him. "No shit."

Vargo waved his hand at Baker. "Him I know. He ain't shit."

"Am too," Baker argued.

Romano pointed to Chang. "Who's he?"

"This is Mr. Chang, my business partner."

Romano sniffed. It didn't matter to him. Vargo spread his hands. "Well, this is all very interesting, but would someone please tell me why you people are here?"

Romano took out his cigar. "I thought I told you. To rip out your fucking throat."

"I understand your problem," Vargo said quickly. "It's the Rosen problem. I promise you I intended to contact Mr. Rosen before I left. It's just that . . ."

Romano laughed so hard he choked on the cigar smoke. Vargo shut up. When Romano stopped laughing and choking, he flicked some of the ashes on Vargo's shoes. "Don't bust my balls, okay?"

Vargo bowed slightly, furiously trying to placate Romano. "Let me state it another way, then. What do you want?"

"Better, much better," Romano said. "Ain't that better, Sal?"

"Yes, Mr. Romano, much better."

Romano moved across the line, closer to Vargo. "We want money, Mr. Vargo. Lots of it. Matter of fact, we also want to know what you and Mr. . . . whatever . . ."

"Mr. Chang."

"Yeah, him, what you two are doing here. Then maybe I can tell how much money I want."

"You are a most impolite man," Chang said.

"Ain't that the truth," Romano agreed.

Vargo tried not to panic. The Mexican furniture was due to arrive at any moment. The last thing he needed was Romano and Chang insulting each other. He had to make a deal and he had to make it fast.

"I got an idea," he said to Romano. "Why don't you and I speak privately?"

"No," said Chang.

Romano smiled. "He don't trust us."

"Mr. Chang, I only wish to speak to him privately in order to resolve our differences," Vargo said, putting a hand on his partner's shoulder. "Then you and I may continue with our business arrangements."

Chang wasn't buying it. "Resolve your differences right here," he ordered, pointing to the line in the dirt.

Vargo felt the sweat bead on his upper lip. He hoped Romano wouldn't notice. "I understand Mr. Rosen's problem," he began. "Give me a number and I'll try to meet it."

"A billion dollars."

"Mr. Romano, I'm serious."

"Half your action, sight unseen, whatever you got goin' on here. Drugs, little girls, little boys, I don't give a shit."

"Mr. Rosen's claim was, I believe, four million dollars, is that correct?"

"Ten million, with interest."

"That's impossible."

Romano yawned.

"All right, ten million," Vargo said quickly. "What if I commit to having that in your hands by tomorrow morning?"

Romano turned to Sal. "See how easy that was, Sal? We take one little drive out here to the country, I ask a man for ten million dollars, and he tells me I'm gonna have it tomorrow morning. What do you think about that, Sal?"

"It sure was easy, Mr. Romano."

"The number's twenty million," Romano said.

"What!"

"I told you, interest. What do you think about twenty million?"

"I can't do that." Twenty million would not only eliminate his profit but would also cut into the money earmarked for the Cubans. Twenty million given to Romano would not save his life. "Besides, it's extortion." Even Julie laughed involuntarily at that one.

Romano didn't answer, and for a moment there was an eerie silence, each man thinking his separate thoughts, concentrating on his separate agenda. It took a woman to break the quiet.

"Can I ask him something while you're all thinking?"

Romano stepped back. "Sure, sweetheart, ask away."

"Mr. Vargo, how did you find out we were going to move in, that the grand jury was going to indict? How did you know enough to kill those three people?"

Vargo awoke as if from a trance. "What?"

"Please answer just that one question. Who told you?"

Vargo snorted. "I got no time for this shit."

Romano moved across the line in the dirt and grabbed Vargo by the throat. "You got no time? Is that what you said?"

Vargo squealed, "Wait, wait!" Romano let go and Vargo rubbed his throat. "Okay." He gestured to Baker. "He told us."

"What!" Bobby Lee shouted.

The blood drained from Julie's face. "Are you sure?"

"That's the truth."

"How can I believe you?"

"I'm telling you it's the truth. You were fucking him and that's how he found out you were ready to move in. Then he told us. Would I know you were fucking him unless he told me?"

Now she was as pale as the hidden moon. "No."

"So, there you go."

She only looked once at Baker. His jaw was slack and the light had gone from his eyes.

"Thank you," she said, retreating back toward Romano.

Romano cleared his throat. "Sorry about that, baby. You, too," he said to Baker. Then to Vargo, "Let's get back to our business."

55

LIKE ALL BUSINESS SETTLEMENTS, THIS ONE TOOK A LIT-
tle while to resolve, and in the end everybody was a bit
unhappy and a bit happy. They finally agreed on fifteen
million dollars. Vargo was apoplectic at the end.

"Fifteen million! That's four times what he lost."

"Then I'll get a bonus," Romano said agreeably.

The mechanics of payment took another ten minutes to
negotiate. Vargo suggested they reconvene at Chang's
bank the next morning and Romano would get paid there.
Romano almost had a heart attack laughing.

"That Vargo sure is a funny man, isn't he, Sal?"

"Sure is, Mr. Romano."

"Hey, Chang. Let me ask you something."

"Yes?"

"If you had to, could you wire fifteen million dollars
out tonight?"

"Of course." Chang had banks just like Kwoh did, just
not as many. There was a pride of technicians in the
bowels of his banks twenty-four hours a day. There was
always a need for transfers of cash in a hurry.

"Then let me take you over to my car here. Because
like Sal will tell you, we're living in a new age. These
limos got phones in them and bars and everything except
a john and free pussy. Why there's even a fax machine in
that limo. Ain't that right, Sal?"

Sal agreed and they took Chang over to the limo. Romano gave him a slip of paper with wire transfer instructions. "Chemical Bank, New York," Romano said.
"Should be easy as pie."

Chang took the car phone and dialed a number, barking
instructions in Chinese. He was angry and nervous that
he had agreed to release funds without receipt of product
and the nervousness showed in his voice. When he was
done he handed the phone back to Romano.

"It is completed. Chemical Bank will call this number back to confirm."

Romano smiled. "No shit," he said politely.

They sat there waiting for the confirmation. Vargo was ready to jump out of his skin. Twenty minutes later the confirmations came in the form of back-to-back phone calls from Chang's bank and Chemical Bank. Two minutes after that a fax clattered over Romano's machine from the mysterious Mr. Rosen. Romano grinned.

"It's a beautiful new world, Sal."

Vargo grabbed the fax and read it. " 'The arrangements have been made,' it says. 'Congratulations.' Now will you leave?"

"I guess s—" Romano began. And then he stopped.

They all heard it, the rumbling of a large tractor trailer bouncing through potholes in the Alhambra streets. All eyes turned in the direction of the sound. The big rig roared up the beaten street and turned into the driveway. Its headlights poured light onto the warehouse. The driver sat impassive, the motor rumbling with a low growl.

"You expecting somebody?" Romano asked innocently.

Vargo froze with fear. It was exactly what he had been trying to avoid. It was now almost eleven o'clock. He had one hour to do it all.

"It's none of your affair," he said quickly. "You've been paid."

Romano turned to Sal. "You hear that, Sal? It's none of our affair."

"I heard that, Mr. Romano."

"Let me tell you something," Romano said, turning back to Vargo, his voice soft as sleep. "When I ask you a question, it's always my affair. If it wasn't my affair, I wouldn't ask you the question. Make sense?"

"Mr. Romano, we had a deal."

"And maybe we still got a deal. I'm not sayin' we ain't got a deal. I'm just sayin' you got to answer my question."

Chang was watching the exchange impassively, puffing on a cigarette. Now that the truck was safely in his driveway he could give a shit how it turned out between Romano and Vargo. As a matter of fact he was starting to feel good: Kwoh dead and a truck laden with cocaine just sitting there for him. Besides, Vargo now owed him fifteen million dollars plus about ten points and a lot of interest. A great day.

He didn't even object when Vargo gestured to Romano and the two of them left the line in the dirt and walked toward the big rig. Eventually he followed only out of idle curiosity.

Vargo was out of options. He put his hands on Romano's shoulders. "Mr. Romano, I need your help. It's very important to me that we move quickly."

"Really? Why's that?"

"That's what I'm going to tell you."

It took Vargo less than five minutes to hit the high points. Romano did not ask him to repeat any of it. He got it all right away.

"So if Chang doesn't pay tonight, matter of fact in the next hour, you're a dead man?"

"That's correct."

"And these two guys. What're their names?"

"I know them only as Hector and Manuel."

"Yeah, those two. You know what this reminds me of, Sal?"

"What's that, Mr. Romano?"

"It's like that Disney movie. With the pirate?"

Vargo started shifting. Romano pointed to him. "You know which one I mean?"

"No, sorry."

"Sure you do. C'mon."

Vargo could feel a vein beating against the side of his head and a sudden icy pain like none he'd ever experienced. "*Snow White. Alice in Wonderland.*"

Romano shook his head. "Christ, *Alice in Wonderland* don't have no pirate. What's the one with the pirate?"

"*Peter Pan?*" Baker suggested, wandering over to watch.

"Now there's a guy knows his Disney. In *Peter Pan*, you see, there's this alligator. And wherever the pirate goes, the alligator goes, just waiting for the pirate to fuck up. And as soon as the pirate fucks up, the alligator is waiting to grind his bones into alligator oatmeal."

Vargo was so frustrated, he thought he might cry.

"Anyway," Romano concluded, "that's what this Hector and Manuel remind me of."

"So are we finally done?" Vargo asked hopefully.

"Yeah, I guess so. Incidentally, what's in that truck?"

"Mexican furniture."

"I love it when you bust my balls. It's probably drugs. That'd be my guess. What do you say, Sal?"

"That'd be my guess too, Mr. Romano."

"But it's none of our business, right?"

"Right," Vargo said.

"As long as this guy pays what he's supposed to in the next hour"—Romano pointed to Chang—"you don't got no alligators chewing on your ass, right?"

"Right."

"That's what I thought." Then Romano reached under his coat, pulled out a snub-nosed .38, and shot Chang in the forehead.

At first, everyone froze as the back of Chang's head exploded in an orgy of red and white. He fell, face first, dead on the concrete, bounced once, then lay still. Vargo stepped back in shock, staring wordlessly at the dead man. Julie found herself empty of emotion, her eyes flat and uncaring, unmoved by the sight in front of her. Jimmy Sun recovered first, screaming as he raised the MAC-10 toward Romano. Sal was there ahead of him, lowering the shotgun and firing twice. Jimmy Sun flew backward, hit in the chest with the full force of the blasts, dead before he hit the ground.

Vincent never even went for his gun and Lazy Sal ignored him. Vargo stood stunned, watching his world shatter around him.

The gunfire then started in earnest. The second carload of six Chinese was immediately pinned down by a dozen shotgun blasts from the Romano forces. One survivor staggered out bloody and disoriented with his MAC-10 spurting. He ran straight at Julie howling in Mandarin. Baker took out the gun Lazy Sal had given him and fired with both hands and his teeth clenched until the magazine was empty. The man fell to his knees, dying. The MAC-10, fully automatic, continued firing, now directing a hail of .45-calibre bullets at the delivery truck driver. The driver screamed and threw himself to the ground while bullets ripped through the cab and the underbelly of the van. There were two extra gas tanks welded to the quarterpanels to enable the truck to go long distances without refueling. Lazy Sal shouted "Hit the ground!" just before the bullets tore open the half-full gas tanks and the explosion shook the warehouse with a deep shaking growl. The back of the trailer was blown to the smog-draped heavens and flames leaped toward the sky. The big rig burned slowly.

Vargo howled and ran toward the back of the trailer. He ripped open the rear doors and began furiously pulling out pieces of burning furniture. He actually tried to climb in the back of the truck through the flames and was stopped only by the combustion of his jacket. He spun and pulled it off, beating the flames into the ground. He had only managed to get one ancient chair out the rear doors. Seconds later, the conflagration grew uncontrollable. The warehouse was brightly lit as if by arc lights by the flames from the burning truck.

The second carload of Chinese gunmen never joined the battle. Stung by the death of Chang and the massacre of their colleagues, they slunk away into the night, tearing off with squealing tires. Julie got up quickly, brushing herself off, ignoring Baker. She looked once at the carnage and then, when she realized it meant nothing to her, looked away. Her face was white and lined. She was beyond tears, beyond caring. Romano walked to the center of the driveway, exulting in his victory.

"Hey, Sal, you think that'll teach him he shouldn't fuck with Mr. Rosen?"

"I sure do, Mr. Romano."

"Me, too. Sal, let's get out of here."

"Okay, Mr. Romano."

"I don't . . . I don't want to go with you . . . with him," Julie said.

"Sal, just throw her in the car. We'll sort it out later."

"Right, Mr. Romano."

"Hey, Vargo," Romano yelled.

Vargo turned, stunned, hopeful.

"Watch out for that fuckin' gator."

56

To Julie the ride back to Cherokee was torture, a witch's brew of sounds that made her want to cover her ears and scream. In the front of the limo Romano and Sal were celebrating, replaying endlessly the look on Vargo's face when Chang died. Romano thought it was especially funny that a Chang gunman had blown up the tractor trailer. And when Sal did an imitation of Vargo pulling the burning furniture out of the back of the truck, Romano had to tell him to stop, his side was aching too much.

In the back of the limo there was nothing but cold silence. Julie sat tight-lipped and ashen. Baker stared out the window with quiet concentration. From the outside they heard the scream of sirens racing to the site of the explosion that turned the purple, misty sky blood red.

She didn't want to go into the bar with Romano but knew she didn't have much of a choice. Once inside she hated the idea even more. The bouncers had been ordered to empty the place in preparation for the celebration and the out-of-work actors had already been hustled to the exits. Bottles of Roederer Cristal Rosé champagne were chilling in ice buckets at every table, three hundred bucks a pop retail. A truckload of flowers had arrived from the grateful Mr. Rosen in New York. Julie ignored it all. She walked to a corner and sat sipping a glass of water, staring straight ahead. Baker sat at a nearby table sipping a tall Black Bush and smoking furiously. His brow was knitted in thought.

After a time, Romano went over to visit him. "What's the matter, you don't like my party?"

"I like it fine," Baker said. "I'd like it a lot better if I could figure something out."

"What?"

"Why Vargo fingered me."

Romano pounded his head with a finger. "I forgot about that. I agree, you got a problem." He thought about it. "How about I tell her to lighten up, let bygones be bygones?"

"I don't think that'll be enough."

"You're probably right. Incidentally, nice shooting back there. You saved her butt. Maybe that counts for something."

"I don't think so. Take a look."

Romano did. "Yeah, you're right, she's pissed. Well, maybe she's got a point. Did you do what Vargo said? Tell him what she was up to?"

"No."

"So who did?"

"I'm . . . not sure."

"Well, maybe you can figure it out. What's so hard?" He gestured to Julie. "Who knew what she was gonna do?"

Baker was stunned by the simple purity of that question. He thought hard and then he got it. It made him sick but he got it. He grabbed Romano by the arm. "I need a favor."

Romano expanded his chest. "Whatever you want, you got. I mean whatever. Understand?"

"I understand. I need Sal."

"That's too bad, he's having a good time."

Nevertheless, they got Sal off the dance floor and away from Angela. He sat at the small booth with Romano and Baker.

"So what do you need?"

Bobby Lee told them. They both listened intently. It took about ten minutes to say it all.

"That's quite a story," Romano said.

"No shit."

"You know what you gotta do?" Romano asked Sal.

"Sure, Mr. Romano. What's the address?"

Sal brought Faldo in an hour later. The little tax lawyer had pencils in his teeth and legal pads under his arms. Sal carried a bulky briefcase. Faldo got distracted a bit when he spied the black-clads twisting on the dance floor to recorded music that was all beat and no words. Sal let him watch for a moment and then nudged him none too gently toward Romano's table.

Baker got up when Faldo arrived and let him slide into the booth. Romano recognized him immediately. "Hey, this is that rock star without the wig." He shook his head in disapproval. "Believe me, you get more puss with the other outfit."

"He's not here for that," Bobby Lee said and Faldo seemed to agree. "Did you bring the memos?"

Faldo didn't answer right away, and Romano had to give him a tap like he sometimes had to do with Lazy Sal.

"Ouch, sorry. Sure, I've got the memos. They're in that briefcase." He hesitated. "There's something else in there you should look at."

Baker grabbed the case from Sal and spread the papers over the table, forcing Romano to move his Crown Royal. There were two memos in the pile, one a fourteen-page, single-spaced, dour description of all the documents in Wendel's files. The second was shorter, two pages, with a red stamp marked CONFIDENTIAL on the blank cover sheet. Finally there was the "something else" Faldo had mentioned, encased in a brown, untitled envelope.

Baker picked up the short memo. "This is the one I should read, right?"

Faldo nodded. Now his concentration was riveted on the table.

Baker read the two-page memo and turned as pale as Romano's white shirt. When he finished he dropped it on the table and turned to look at Julie. She was still sitting, drinking water, staring sightlessly at a kitchen door three feet from her nose. Baker grabbed Romano's Crown Royal and downed it, then brushed the hair out of his face with both hands.

Romano read the memo, then snapped his fingers for another Crown Royal.

"Just tell me what you want me to do," Romano said. "I owe you big time and I pay my debts. When I need to get even I get even, and when I need to pay my debts I—"

"Thanks, I get it," Baker said, before the entire Sicilian national anthem could be played. "I need Sal, and I need a car, and I need her in it." His head jerked in Julie's direction.

"You got it," Romano said.

"Mr. Romano, what if she don't want to come?"

Romano sighed. His Crown Royal had arrived and he accepted it, patting the waitress gently on the butt before she left.

"Sal," he said, with the patience of Job, "don't bust my balls."

57

IN MANY WAYS, IN ALL THE IMPORTANT WAYS, IT WAS all over. What now remained was the messy job of cleaning up after a very messy parade. But even during a cleanup people can get hurt.

They arrived an hour later, when the 3 A.M. moon had set under the Malibu mountains and the morning fog got sucked in over the beach, entranced by the interior heat. At daylight the beach would be covered with fog and departing planes at LAX would be delayed, forbidden the mystery of rocketing over the dank waves into the mist. On the ground, near the beach, it was Londontown, dark and shrouded, the blankets wrapped around the crack-dealing bums twisting as the onshore wind twisted the giant palms under which they slept.

He walked up the steps to the empty door and knocked. There was no response. He knocked again, harder now, and a dim light appeared deep inside the green bungalow. Soon a porch light came on and a moment later the door was opened a crack. The man was shirtless and stared at Baker with wide, flat eyes.

"Bobalee, is that you?" He said it in dialect, maybe out of shock, just like they were back in Carson together.

"The one and only."

"I can't believe it. I heard you were . . . you were . . ."

"What did you hear?"

"Nothing much. I mean I heard you were . . . you know, back in Boron."

"Really? Where did you hear that?"

"Around, you know how it is, nowhere special."

Baker smiled amiably and otherwise didn't push the point. "Well, aren't you going to invite me in?"

"Sure," Max said quickly. "You just come right on in."

"Who is it, Max?" a woman's voice cried, insistently and angrily over the black death of the ocean wind.

"Nobody, baby, just stay put."

"Like hell I will." She came out into the dim light of the parlor. She was tall and angular with a pouty, puffed face. She was also young and her satin robe was open, revealing thin breasts and a long neck.

"Who the hell are you?" she said.

Baker held out his hand. "I'm nobody, baby, just like Max said."

"This is my former partner," Max said quickly. "His name's Bobby Lee Baker."

"So what the hell's he doing here at three in the morning?" she whined. She sat on a nearby chair and lit a cigarette. She made no effort to close the robe. When she had the cigarette lit she leaned back and blew out the smoke, her knees wide and the open, thin robe flapping in the breeze off the ocean.

"Jesus, Claudia, can't you get dressed?"

"Fuck that," Claudia said. She looked to be more than a little drunk.

Baker was a taken man and didn't want to spend too much time checking out Claudia's show. After a decent interval he turned back to Max.

"So Max, how's it goin'? I didn't even know you had a girlfriend, show you what I know."

"Bobby, what are you doing here at this hour? Have you been drinking?"

"Not just yet, soon though, just not yet. I came to talk

about a little business, Max. And as for the time, I'm
sorry, it's an emergency."

Max thought he understood. "You've escaped, right?
I heard they were sending you back to Boron and you
couldn't handle it." He shook his head. "I'm sorry but
any help I give you is a crime. Harboring a felon. I hope
you understand."

"Fuck him," Claudia said helpfully. "Just throw his
ass in the street."

"Claudia, shut up," Max barked. Then back to Baker.
"Maybe I can scrounge up a few bucks but that's all."

Bobby Lee smiled. "I understand, Max, you got your
license to protect."

"Right."

"So don't worry about it. I just need to talk to you for
a few minutes about my case. Can we walk over to the
office, maybe talk in private?" He gestured in Claudia's
direction.

"Sure," Max said quickly. "Just let me get dressed."

They walked down the dark path together. Neither of
them spoke. Max used his key to unlock the office door
and Baker remembered how easy it had been back in the
old days—working by the beach, an office twenty steps
from where he lived, trying cases with a great partner and
having fun. It was all another person's life a thousand
years before.

He sat in Max's office and looked out at the view.
During the day there would be dank ocean and courageous sailboats filling that window. Now, nothing but
darkness and a foretaste of gloom. Appropriate.

Max lit a cigarette and stared at him. Then he went into
the drawer for the Black Bush. He poured two water
glasses half-full and pushed one in Baker's direction.
Then he sucked hard on the cigarette and drank half the
whiskey in one gulp.

"I see lots of changes, Max," Baker said softly, after
helping himself to a snort. "A new girlfriend, taken up
smoking, still love the Bush of course. Got to keep changing in this life, I suppose."

Max looked down at the burning end of his cigarette.
"What do you want me to say, Bobby? I drink too much,

I smoke like a chimney, I've gained twenty-five pounds of pure fat, and I'm sleeping with a woman who's a straight, cold bitch. That make you happy, Bobby?''

Baker shrugged. "A little, not much. How's business?''

More sucking on the cigarette and the whiskey. "We're strung out to the max on the line of credit, I haven't taken a draw in six months, and we're down to two secretaries and a receptionist. We're going in the toilet, Bobby, and it's just a matter of time.''

"That's a bitch. Want to change places?''

Max laughed a little and coughed as the smoke grabbed him. "You'd be surprised, Bobby, what I'd do.''

"Not anymore, Max," Baker said quietly.

Max looked at him with surprise and the room became silent and still, watchful, anticipating. They both sipped their whiskey and Max lit another cigarette.

"What is it you think you know?'' Max asked at last. Bobby Lee wasn't surprised. Even drunk and beaten Max was still shrewd, a smart guy and in his time a good lawyer. He wasn't about to jump off a cliff until he was convinced there was no other choice.

"Pretty much everything, buddy. I know you're the one who tipped Vargo about the grand jury, and I also know you told him about me and Julie. That's for starters.''

Max never flinched. He sipped his whiskey with studied casualness. "What makes you think that?''

"Does it matter?''

"Not really.'' He finished his drink and poured another just as large. "What else?''

"All of it, Max. I know you had a piece of Vargo's action from the start. I know about your Panama bank account, about your trips to the Caymans to collect your money, and your ownership in 1989 of Siena Corporation.'' He took Faldo's two-page memo and slid it across the table. Max picked it up as if in a trance and read it through. When he laid it down he was calm in an eerie deathlike way, not burying his face in his hands or anything like that. He sat erect and dignified, with the cigarette burning in his fingers and the whiskey burning in his throat. And he just stared.

Baker wasn't done. "There's more, Max."

"Bobby, you don't understand," his former friend and former partner said. "I got screwed. He promised me so much he never delivered."

"That explains it, I guess. Anyway, Max, I said there's more."

Max's face was now flushed. "What?"

Baker took the two photos that Faldo had discovered in Wendel's files and handed them over. Max picked them up and squinted as though he'd never seen them before. Then he got it and the blood left his face.

"Oh my God."

"You know, that's exactly what I said, Max."

Baker took the photos back and looked at them again. They were blurred, as they should be, considering they were shot from Vargo's surveillance camera. After all, no one had the chance to pose, or get focused, or anything like that. Nevertheless certain things could be made out with precision. There was Max, for example, standing against a pale wall, dressed in a dark suit, the tie loose and the white shirt unbuttoned, his hair matted and sweaty. Then there was Vargo, standing facing Max, his back to the camera, holding something in his right hand. They were odd photos, saved by Vargo and given to Wendel, even after everything else had been destroyed, maybe as a memento, maybe as a way of making sure Wendel never left the reservation.

And it was doubtful Wendel ever would, not once he saw the photos. Because Max and Vargo were not the only figures in the photos, although they were the only living figures in one of them. The first photo showed three humans on their knees facing Max, two women and a man, their vulnerable backs to Vargo. In the second photo the three kneeling figures were now facedown, their tightly bound hands still in back of them, large brown stains spreading from the back of their heads.

In the second photo Max was against the wall, his mouth open in shock. Vargo was inspecting the bodies, the gun hanging loosely in his right hand.

"Who could have figured it?" Bobby Lee said unnecessarily.

"Who indeed?" Max agreed after a long silence. He sighed and the color returned to his face. "Ah well." He opened a drawer and reached inside and his hand emerged. Now it had a gun in it. The revolver was blue-black and squat. He moved his thumb and there was a loud click.

"Not a good idea, Max," Bobby Lee suggested.

"Oh, I don't know," Max said. His voice was weary and cracked from the alcohol and the woman next door and the sight of the photos. "After all, you're a fugitive, you broke in, scared me and what's her name." He laughed at that one. "Who could blame me?"

"You never know," a lazy, disembodied voice said. Sal walked into the room, his own well-used gun framed on Max's forehead. Angela was on one side of him and Julie on the other. They had gained entrance with Faldo's key and had been sitting comfortably in the next room, listening to it all. Julie looked at Bobby Lee and let him know she had something to make up for.

Max gazed amiably at Sal, not at all frightened. "Who, may I ask, are you?"

"You don't ever want to know."

"Why's that, 'cause you're about to shoot me? Go ahead." He laughed maniacally, his voice defeated and cracked.

Angela stepped forward. "Max, put it down, please."

Julie's head went back and forth. "You two know each other?"

"Oh yeah," Max said, his voice now crushed as the Black Bush hit home. "We're old friends, right, Angela?"

"Old friends," she agreed. She picked up the photos. "I guess I was standing off to the side. Throwing up, as I remember."

Nobody moved or said anything after that. Max looked sleepy, like he wanted to just curl up and let it die. However, the gun was still in his hand and it was still pointed at Baker. That made Sal nervous.

"I think it's time to end this," Lazy Sal said. He moved in front of Bobby Lee, his gun still pointed at Max.

"You're probably right," Max said, waking up a little. "No matter how long a trial drags on, there has to be finality sometime. Isn't that what the judges always tell us, Bobby?"

"Yes," Baker said, and for the first time got scared.

"Bobby Lee, let me ask you something," Max said, his voice now fighting to make sentences, slurred almost beyond recognition.

"Okay."

"You remember back in the old days, when you, me, and Montel used to hang out, and De'Andre was the quarterback, and I got everybody the towels, and we were all sixteen years old?"

"Sure."

Max's head lolled. "Me too. You think that was the best time of our lives, Smoke?"

Nobody had called him that in a long time. "Maybe. A hell of a lot better than the last three years, wouldn't you say?"

"Yeah, Smoke, I sure would." And then he started scratching his chin with the barrel of the gun, like he was thinking about those old times, and Bobby really got scared.

"Hey, Max, don't do anything stupid." As much as he wanted to hate the man he still didn't want it to end this way. "Goddamn it, Max, that doesn't help anybody."

Max's eyes opened and he grinned. He was still scratching the underside of his chin with the gun, seeking to erase an itch that just would not go away. He was not debating internally as much as savoring the moment: no more guilt, no more Claudia, no more waking up at 3 A.M. to wait for the dawn. No more hangovers or raspy throats from cigarettes or the business going to shit. And most important, no more memories of the events in those photos, of three innocent people shot before his eyes, of Vargo kicking them to see if they were still alive, of the third one begging, of the second one begging, of Max himself falling to his knees and gasping for air with the sound of Vargo laughing derisively in the background. And no more envy of their death, an innocent death, a death he could never hope for.

Yet if not an innocent death, at least a redemptive one, a death that might make things, well, not *exactly* right, just *more* right.

"Sorry, Smoke, I can't help you out."

And then he fired.

58

THE FLACKS AND HACKS SPURRED THE STORY WITH CATtle prods, foamed into a frenzy by the charred remains of Chang and his gunmen, lit to glowing by the long burning big rig. When that grisly fuel was consumed the talking heads moved seamlessly to the "tragic suicide of Max Rafferty, prominent Westside attorney, and, it is now learned, associate of fugitive financier Robert Vargo." Max's demise was a solemn affair, reported in hushed tones, always accompanied by fine film of dawn over the Pacific, and a sheet-covered gurney being pulled from a green bungalow into a yellow coroner's van.

Barrows immediately fled Los Angeles and disappeared, his Washington home abandoned and his credit cards showing only a blizzard of travel in a twenty-four-hour period from L.A. to Houston to Cincinnati to Chicago to Barbados. The trail went cold in Barbados as did the government's ability and interest in hunting him further.

Vargo was not so lucky. He lasted two weeks on the run until his body and that of a companion were dumped out of a speeding car onto the side of the road on Spring Street in front of the federal courthouse. The bodies were naked and bound hand and foot with barbed wire. The throats were slashed and the tongues yanked through the grisly incision. Each tongue was nailed crudely to an unfortunate chest, creating a pair of grotesque crimson ties. Hector and Manuel Menendez had left a classic Cuban signature.

The second body was identified as one Vicente Morales, twenty-four years old, originally from Cali, Colombia, via Miami. DEA files had him down as a suspect in at least eleven unsolved murders, including the machine-gunning of seven people in a seedy motel in Hollywood in March of 1986. His fingerprints were also found at the site of the murder of Gilberto Martinez, a DEA informant who had orchestrated the bust of the Sylmar warehouse, and at the offices of Charles Wendel, a murdered associate of Bamboo Gang members from Taipei. A DEA spokesman announced that the elimination of Morales "was a major breakthrough in the war on drugs in the southern California market."

The deaths of Morales and Vargo were big news but paled in comparison to the saga of Bobby Lee Baker and his partner, Max Rafferty. The press loved the tale of betrayal, of Rafferty's cold-blooded representation of Baker during his trial, and of the jailing of an innocent man. Eventually the whole mess went back to O'Donnell, the alcoholic judge who had sentenced Baker in the first place. He barely remembered the Baker case but was still sober enough to read the papers every now and again. He made a long speech to the press from the bench about the integrity of the criminal justice system, then announced that the government had dropped all charges against Baker "in the interests of justice." Later that day a U.S. Attorney's Office press officer read a one-paragraph statement "apologizing to Mr. Baker for any inconvenience caused by these unfortunate events."

About a week after the classy government announcement Baker realized with sudden ice-cold clarity that the woman was going insane and in the process taking him with her. She had developed the habit of wandering around the guest house half-naked, which in itself was fine, except there was always a phone affixed to her ear and she was always shouting into it. Bobby Lee was into total relaxation these days and her screaming was interfering with his enjoyment of the afternoon truck-pull competition on ESPN. Things had really improved in the last three years on the old cable front.

On the ninth day he decided to put the potato on the fork, live in the nineties, be forthright and expressive about his feelings. She was walking around in bare legs, sheer panties, a white T-shirt, and nature's blessings, howling at some Washington bureaucrat named Abramson. Cellular phones were the devil's workshop, no doubt about it.

"I can't stand it anymore," he screamed.

She half-turned to him in surprise. "What?"

"Can you put that thing down, maybe talk to me for a moment?"

She stared. "Why would I want to do that?"

"Are you kidding?" he screeched.

She held up a hand. "Abramson, I'll get back to you, I got a problem here. No, nothing serious, the plumber has a question. Yeah, check with O'Neill, he follows every rumor in the building, tell you what high school the guy went to. Great. Thanks."

She hung up and turned to him. His attention had momentarily been diverted by the spectacular near levitation of an eight-wheeler over a mud pit. The driver pumped his fist in triumph; it was true what they said, there was no substitute for talent.

"Would you look at me, please?"

"Sure." He turned, got an eyeful, and turned off the TV. Trucks were trucks and all . . .

"Why were you bellowing?"

"I wasn't bellowing," he said quietly. "I was trying to get your attention."

"I was having a critical conversation with a deputy assistant secretary at Justice who has deep access to the Attorney General. We may be able to get this started again."

She had her hands on her hips. The phone was dangling in her right hand. Her mouth was pouting and he wanted to just rip her apart right there on the shag rug.

"I'll tell you what I want to get started again."

"Don't be a pig. We've got important business to take care of."

"My sentiments exactly."

"I see," she said, letting the phone dangle. "Do you feel neglected, maybe? What's it been, six hours?"

"That's a long time. Men have *needs*. I don't even *like* truck pulls."

"You could have fooled me. Anyway, if you have extra energy you can help with these Washington calls."

"I don't think it'll be the same." He leaned back on the couch, adjusting his boxers. "Besides it's a complete waste of time."

"What is?"

"All these calls about Barrows. Don't you get it, it's *over!* Vargo's toast, Max is dead, rest his scum-ball little soul, I'm out of Boron and goddamn grateful for it, and you're wandering around in your undies, which I'm also grateful for." He paused to gather the breath for the big scream. "So why the fuck are you on the phone all the time!"

She sighed. "You're so immature."

He complained to anyone who would listen, which turned out to be Romano mostly, his last remaining friend. Romano had the answer to the whole problem.

"Get her out of town, give her a few pops in some romantic place, you know what they like."

It was a crude offensive suggestion which demeaned her as a woman and a dedicated lawyer. "You think?" he asked hopefully.

They decided on Italy after Romano told him don't worry, Sal's making all the arrangements. She even balked at that, worried that for a week she might be unhinged from her precious phone. At the end Sal had to threaten her with kidnapping and Baker with ripping the phone off the wall before she agreed.

The four of them—Sal and Angela too—piled into a G-III leased by a grateful Romano for the event. ("It's a hundred grand, what do I care, you guys saved me millions! Besides, I owe Sal a treat.") If Julie was impressed she hid it well.

"Can I make calls from this thing?" she whined as they banked left over the glistening orange of the Pacific for the long journey east.

They landed in the heat of the Italian day. Sal had a car waiting and expertly took the wheel, cursing his way out of the Milanese traffic onto green-tangled country roads.

Two hours later signs for Lake Garda appeared and Sal pulled into the driveway of a magnificent three-story lakeside villa. A tuxedo-clad concierge appeared.

"Welcome to the Villa Scacciapensieri," the man said, bowing slightly. "As guests of Mr. Romano all arrangements have been made. Please follow me."

The man walked ahead of them to a room on the third floor. The whole way Julie elbowed Baker and silently mouthed: "Fax machines, ask him about fax machines." Baker had been pushing aside her pokes and mouthing back either "Stop that!" or "Shut up!" They were both in a spectacularly foul mood when they reached the third floor.

The man opened the door and handed Baker the key. "This is our finest room," he said, "Carlotta's Room. Do you know the story of Carlotta?"

"One of your many overseas operators?" Julie asked hopefully.

The man permitted himself a polite smile they must have taught him in concierge school.

"Mussolini's villa was two kilometers east of this spot," he said, gesturing toward the lake. "His mistress, Carlotta, lived in this room. It is as it was then, when Il Duce was . . . how you say in English . . ."

"Justly shot by his countrymen?" Baker ventured.

"Perhaps," the man said. "When that unfortunate event happened Carlotta fled. As shall I." Then he bowed and left.

Say what you will about Mussolini, he knew how to take care of the ladies. Wherever there was not red brocade there was marble, except for the tightly colored fresco on the ceiling. The bed was a deep four-poster out of a fairy tale, large enough for Benito, Carlotta, and at least a half-dozen brown-shirts. The open casement windows, three stories above the ground, let in warm, faint breezes filled with the smells of the lakeside dinner being prepared below. It was a magical room, perfect for a magical night, and marred by only one tiny defect.

He turned to her and saw her standing stiffly, at almost military attention. Her mouth was rigid, set in a manic smile. It took every muscle in her face to pull her lips away from her teeth. Her head wanted to turn to the left, where it was, sitting white and inviting, with gold numerals and a faux-1930s cradle, but she resisted and instead she twitched, slightly.

"Don't even think about it," he growled.

"I'm not," she said without separating her teeth.

"Good, I got it in writing." He held up the agreement he made her sign on the plane.

Her eyes became as wide as an addict in distress and she rushed at him, abandoning all pretense.

"Bobby, please, just one call, I promise. They met this morning in Washington to consider assigning more agents to the Barrows case. I *must* know how it came out."

"Goddamn it, we're supposed to be on vacation. This is *Italy*, you get that? *Romantic* Italy. You should be parading around here in something . . . I don't know, black or whatever, like what's her name wore for Mussolini."

"One call only, Bobby, I promise, and then I'll do anything you want." She reached for her sweater and pulled it over her head. "And naked, I'll make the call naked."

"God, you're pathetic, you've lost all judgment." She smiled and let her fingers play with the zipper of her skirt.

He had the self-control of a two-year-old.

"Okay, one call."

When she was done she stuck out her tongue at him, turned and shook her bottom, then disappeared into Carlotta's bathroom to dress for dinner. He half suspected her of stashing a cellular phone, like a drunk stashing a few mini-bottles, and had to stop himself from putting an ear up to the bathroom door. Then she emerged, bathed and dressed for dinner, and he gave up worrying about her phones.

Dinner at the lakeside table was the stuff of brochures and photographs. Julie and Angela had dressed for the event and had the waiters muttering to themselves and men at nearby tables stealing glances when their wives weren't looking, which eventually became simple stares, forget the consequences. He held her hand as they drank Brunello, ate light-as-air pasta and trout pulled straight from the lake, and watched a virile moon sit motionless on the far shore. At midnight her smile emboldened him, and, his judgment marred by the Brunello, he leaned over and whispered in her ear.

She sat back in shock. "My God," she howled, loud enough to wake Mussolini, "how do men even *think* of such things?"

Baker flushed deeply and Sal roared, slapping his leg. Julie smiled at his discomfort and held up four fingers.

"Forget it," Baker said. "I can't believe you're bargaining with me." Julie wiggled her fingers suggestively and Baker retreated right away.

"One, that's it," he said sullenly. "One call and no more."

"Suit yourself. *I* can live without it, no problem."

That was complete bullshit, but the last thing Baker needed was a war of wills on the point.

"We had an agreement," he said weakly. He held up the crumpled paper.

"I'd like for you to find that disgusting proposal on that piece of paper," Julie said. Sal roared some more and Angela leaned forward on her elbows, interested.

Baker coughed. "Two. I'll go two and that's it. I'm being goddamn fair."

"Well, two is half of four. That gets me half of what I want. That's okay as long as the second part's not important to you." She grinned widely. "Pervert."

It really was unfair.

59

IN THE MORNING, THE BARGAIN FAIRLY MET, THEY again convened for breakfast. Lazy Sal had a copy of that morning's *International Herald Tribune*.

"Looks like you're back in the papers."

Baker grabbed the paper and his eyes grew wide. "Oh, shit."

"Oh, shit? Did I hear you say oh, shit?" She grabbed the paper and Baker saw the blood creep up her cheeks. He knew she was looking at a grainy black-and-white photo of Covington Barrows on page one. The article identified Barrows as a former high-ranking DEA official, once responsible for Caribbean drug interdiction, now a fugitive as a result of the Vargo affair. The picture showing him smiling, the sun in his eyes and his arm around a young brown-skinned girl. They were leaning, laughing, against a seawall on the Malecón seafront. In Havana.

"Fuck, fuck, fuck, fuck," she shouted in ever louder curses.

"Hey," Lazy Sal said, protective of Angela's virgin ears, "you eat with that mouth?"

"I do all kinds of things with this mouth," she snapped. Baker decided this would be a good time to hold his glass up to the light, check for impurities.

"This is what I was afraid of," she screamed. Then she rolled the *Trib* into a tight ball and threw it far into the pristine lake.

"Nice arm," Sal had to admit.

The waiter came over, bowing, solicitous. "The *señora* is all right?" he asked. What he wanted to ask was, "The *señora* is crazy? Throwing papers in our lake and cursing like a fishmonger?"

Baker decided to take action. He sprang to his feet and grabbed her arm. "Come with me."

"No."

He yanked and she flew from her chair. "That's the ticket," Sal said appreciatively.

He pulled her away from the villa and down the gravel steps to the shore. When they were alone he put his hands on her shoulders and turned her to face him.

"Now, what's the matter?"

"Nothing, goddamn it."

"So how come you're acting like this? You're practically crying, for Christ's sake."

What a man. They must have given out sensitivity pills at Boron.

"I'm not crying. Anyway, you wouldn't understand."

"Why, because I'm a man?"

"That's a pretty good start."

"That makes no sense at all." He took her hand and led her down the rocky beach. The light from the early morning sun glanced off the lake and lit their faces. A hovercraft buzzed slowly offshore, preparing to take tourists to the ancient Medici castle of Sermione on the opposite side of the large, lazy lake.

"Now let me try that again. What's wrong?"

She breathed deeply. "I just feel so . . . so . . ." She couldn't finish.

"So what?"

"Pissed off," she spit out. "I don't know. Something else. Like he's won and we can't do anything about it. You know what I mean?"

"No, I don't. I only know there's you and me and beautiful Italy and we're supposed to be here to have a good time and forget all this nonsense. So to answer your question, no, I don't have the foggiest idea why you're upset."

She stopped and turned to him. "Bobby, don't you get it? I'm upset because they did this to you. And to us and to me and to three victims and even to Max in a way. And now they've won."

"Vargo hasn't won anything," he said and meant it. Vargo was now feeding the worms and Baker couldn't care less whether they ever caught Barrows, he barely knew the guy. He was out of Boron and in Italy with a beautiful woman. Max he was sorry about, that would never end, but Max brought it on himself. Beyond that he could give a shit.

He let her go, picked up a rock and skipped it across the water, a small gesture of freedom. The shiny rock sliced through the green waves and rose to hit the bow of the hovercraft. They heard faint curses in Italian across the lake.

"Jesus, Baker."

"Sorry," he shouted to the boatman. He turned to her. "Anyway, I've got an idea."

"Believe me, Baker, now's not the time."

"I'm not talking about that. Look down there."

She followed his gesture down the rocky beach. There

were a series of docks, then a fortress of rusticated stone, one hundred feet high, bleak against the dark blue of the lake. A lone fisherman cast a pale line between the moored boats.

"Nice," she said.

"That's D'Annunzio's."

"What?"

"Not what, who. D'Annunzio. One of the great early twentieth-century Italian romantic poets. He made a fortune doing something or other, then built a mansion up the road. At the end of his life, he had so much money left over he built that castle as a boathouse."

She looked at him blankly.

"There was a brochure at the desk. I wouldn't make that up."

She sat down weakly on the rocks. Baker paced in front of her, explaining about the poet's castle boathouse, gesturing toward the sunlit lake. As he talked she felt like she often did when he was around, a little better, her rage and anxiety fading in the cadence of his voice. She put her chin in her hands, watching him, wondering what perverse spirit had put this man in her life. When he was done orating, he took her hand again, snapping her to her feet and marching her down the beach to D'Annunzio's fortress, then up the hundred stone steps to the parapet. By the time she was at the top, she knew one thing anyway.

"I love you," she said simply.

"What?" He was again pointing at the horizon, declaiming about D'Annunzio.

"I said I love you." She laughed at his stare and felt the release surge within her. Her lover had brought her to a strange place, the top of an aging castle, a monument from a rich, dead man. And he was right to do so. Up here no one had heard of Covington Barrows, of Robert Vargo, of dead hoodlums named Jimmy Sun, Vincent, and Chang. Up here the ghost of D'Annunzio could mate quietly, poetically, with the ghost of her frustrated dreams, and she could leave both ghosts behind. Once she had dreamt of monuments; now she was in one, a dead man's monument, just like Carlotta's room. Baker, say what you will about his multiple faults, was as real as toast.

"Bobby," she said.

"Yeah?"

"You've got two choices. Here on the stone floor or back in Carlotta's room."

He had never been a man to defer gratification. The sun came in through the parapet slits, thin and insistent. The dappled shards of light played across her skin. Their noises were shuttered by the buzz of the hovercraft on the lake below. At the end, when she screamed, when his rough face scraped up the front of her tender skin, irresistible and demanding, her voice bounced off the ancient walls, slithering through the gun turret and sliding into the bright Italian day.

Afterward Baker walked naked to the stone window opening onto the lake below. The air was freshening, plumes of clouds gathering for an assault on the fortress. Julie sat against the stone wall, enjoying the view of his strong bare back and wide shoulders silhouetted against the dark stone. She also looked at his muscled legs and thin, bare hips and thought of things to come.

She would never let him go, even if she had to tie him down, a wicked thought which made her smile.

"There's a storm coming in," he said. He turned to her. She liked that view even more. "We've got to talk, don't you think?"

"Yes."

He walked to her and knelt on the stone floor, sitting back on his heels. "Let's see if I get this. Are you hunting Barrows for me or for you?"

What an *interesting* question. She really should not underestimate him. "Partly for you, I guess."

"Okay, so let's eliminate that part. I don't want to spend three good years trying to get even for three bad years. If I see Barrows lying in the road someday, I'll run him over. But if I have to drive around the block to do it, it's not worth it to me."

She shifted slightly. "I understand," she said, and sort of did. "It's your injury and you should be able to deal with it as you want."

"That's right. And that also includes you."

"Why?"

"Because if you're out of my life, or pissed off all the time, or on the phone all the time, then they've *really* won."

She put her face in her hands. "God, this is complicated."

"And why's that?"

She spread her hands. "Because you want me to do something I don't want to do and so far it seems you're right." She thought hard for a moment. "There's only one thing to do. We'll compromise."

"Compromise! When I'm right we compromise? What do we do when you're right?"

Her laugh was joyful. "What a silly question. Then there's no dispute of course."

He was choking on that one when they heard footsteps on the stone spiral staircase. They immediately abandoned the battlefield and began a frenzied search for clothes. They were about halfway to decency when a uniformed guard appeared carrying a bag. His pants were ripped.

"Ah, lovers in D'Annunzio's boathouse," he said, sizing up the situation pretty well. "He would have approved. Do you speak Italian?"

"*Si,*" Julie said. She translated for Baker.

"Tell him we're old lovers arguing about the past. And what happened to his pants?"

More Italian. "He said that's too bad and we should forget the past. He also told me to forgive you, that 'men have needs,' whatever that means. As for the pants, he was walking along the beach. A beautiful red-haired woman was eating breakfast near the lake at Carlotta's villa. He tripped over a boat line and fell on the gravel."

Angela again. "Sorry about that," Baker said. "Tell him trust me, it could be a lot worse."

"So how shall we compromise this?" she asked, turning away from the guard.

Her tone had changed and he had to smile when he heard it. This was how they started together so long ago, cutting a deal on Vargo, and she had unconsciously slipped back into her negotiator's mindset. Well, two could play at that.

"What are you offering?"

"A year. One year. And you work with me the whole time."

"A year! You're nuts. I'd rather be in Boron."

"No, you wouldn't. Anyway, what are *you* offering?"

"Thirty days," he said. "And the work starts *after* this vacation."

Her laugh was gay and genuine. She knew she had him on a slippery slope. "Oh no, no, thirty days will never do." She made believe she was thinking. "Nine months."

"Forget it."

"And your counter?"

"Five weeks and that's as far as I go. And I better not have to sign up with Justice again to do this."

"Don't worry about that, darling, they'd never have you, felon and all you understand, even if you did get out on some technicality."

"Technicality! I was innocent!"

Her hand fluttered. "Whatever. Anyway I can go six months and we're getting down to bedrock."

"We're way past bedrock." He crossed his arms over his chest. "Six weeks. Take it or leave it, there's nothing you can say to change my mind."

"Okay, bedrock," she said. "I need four months, that's what I've always needed. There's a lot to do."

"Forget it. Six weeks and not an hour more."

"Four months," she said and held up four fingers. The gesture looked familiar to him and he couldn't remember why. Then she wiggled the four fingers and he remembered.

"You have no morals. None. Zero."

Her fingers were still moving and her eyes were bright. "Whenever you want, day or night, plus I'll throw in whatever else your perverted brain can come up with. Within reason and along the same lines, of course."

"Of course." He tried to focus on the negotiations but his imagination escaped out the back door and began playing on its own.

"Day or night?"

She could afford to be magnanimous. "Afternoon, twilight, dusk, you name it."

"I see." He coughed. "I'll have to think about it."

"Absolutely," she said, standing and brushing herself off. There was no need to rub it in. "You'll let me know?"

"Of course."

The guard was watching the whole thing with eager eyes, thinking he was following the exchange. As Julie stood he talked to her rapidly in Italian. *"Si,"* she answered.

"What did he say?"

"He said, 'At night all cats are black.' "

"What does that have to do with anything?"

"I'm not sure."

"Jesus," he said. "D'Annunzio lives."

She turned to leave. Baker grabbed her by the arm. He spoke hurriedly and it was as good a speech as he had ever given outside a courtroom. He knew this fool's quest would lead nowhere. Did she really want to give Barrows that ultimate satisfaction? She listened politely until he had said it all. The squall now hovered over the lake, sending shafts of wind through the open window. When he stopped talking following a beautiful rhetorical finish she stood on her tiptoes and kissed him hard.

"Hey, Smoke, I've got some news for you."

The kiss and the reference threw him off balance. "What?"

"Number one, he won't win. Number two, you'll never regret it."

Then she reached behind him and patted him hard, to give him something else to think about, and was gone.

"Bravo," said the guard.

Why the guard was rooting for her was a mystery to him. The Italians were supposed to be macho, stick up for the guys once in a while.

"What's in the bag?" he asked the guard, pointing.

The guard held it up. There was a pear, a block of cheese, and a bottle of rough Chianti.

"May I?"

"Si," the man said.

They walked to the open battlement together, trading the Chianti bottle. The lake was now black with the incoming squall. He saw her far below, walking away from the protective fortress, a small creature with white-gold hair, huddled against the wind, fighting upstream as her footsteps became thickened by the storm. She turned her back to the force of it, struggling against the accelerating wind. He waved in spite of himself; even the guard held up the bottle in salute, and he didn't know anything. She probably couldn't make out the small figures hidden in the top of the stone monument to a dead poet. In any event she turned away from them, marching with struggling steps without them, into the developing storm.

He sighed. "This will be way too hard," he said quietly, thinking nothing about Barrows and everything about her.

"Si," the guard said, understanding enough about either English or human nature to get it.

He turned and ran down the steps after her.